OPEN SEASON

BLACK MAGIC OUTLAW
BOOK EIGHT

Domino Finn

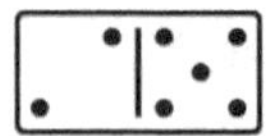

Copyright © 2021 by Domino Finn. All rights reserved.

Published by Blood & Treasure, Los Angeles
First Edition

Cover by James T. Egan of Bookfly Design LLC.

Print ISBN: 978-1-946-00808-4

DominoFinn.com

Magic is Real

Not only that, it's all around you. Energies, events, encounters. Dark places filled with mythic creatures every bit as dangerous as their legends.

Opening your eyes to this reality isn't easy. Silvans are tricky. Vampires operate in the shadows. Even wizards greedily hoard their secrets.

What you need is an outlaw. Someone with nothing left to lose. A tour guide to the supernatural underground who packs enough grit and spellcraft to handle anything in your way.

What you need is Cisco Suarez, a hard-talking, hard-fighting, hard-luck hero.

Welcome to the exciting world of *Black Magic Outlaw*. It isn't always easy, but it's always a blast.

Previously in
Black Magic Outlaw

The name's Cisco Suarez, and I'm a necromancer. It's all fun and games till you wake up dead in a dumpster, but I broke out of my zombie curse, got revenge on the people who did this to me, and took my life back.

Trouble returned when a serial killer named Manifesto introduced the city to animists. I put him down but landed a spot on prime-time news as the anonymous Shadow Man, a distinction that made me the FBI's latest person of interest.

Notoriety is bad for business. As I hunted the Stygian witches behind Manifesto, they laid a trap for me. Besides forcing the ruling class of silvans into compliance, they infected Milena with a blood curse that forever changed her in ways we still don't understand.

Which brings us to now…

BLACK MAGIC OUTLAW

Chapter 1

Taut strips of yellow tape caught the wind like kites. Cars crammed the swale of the narrow residential road. What had every right to be a lazy Saturday was spoiled by a burgeoning crime scene.

I parked the Firebird a block out and weaved past City of Miami Interceptors, unmarked Fusions, news crews, and a Fire Rescue truck. I wasn't sure how paramedics contributed to a murder case, but that was bureaucracy for you.

The tumultuous activity was jarring against the azure sky, as was the sun fighting off the stiff breeze. Without a cloud in sight, the dense roadside vegetation seemed to frame a masterpiece whodunit.

Clearly, the police were intruding on the serenity of San Marco Island. The small land mass was one of several connecting bridges between the mainland and Miami Beach. Respectable houses cozied up to vibrant ocean backdrops, though most showed signs of age and had a population to match.

Under towering palms, I approached the white iron gate. A uniform eyed my ratty tank top and opened his mouth to object to my presence.

"Got an extra windbreaker?" I asked to head him off.

It wasn't jacket weather in the classical sense, but when you live in a tropical paradise where even the water is warm, mornings aren't supposed to come with a chill.

The officer frowned at my request for free police-issued gear, and I cut him off again before he could speak. "Carry on." I attempted to skirt around and continue to the house.

"Wait a minute," he finally mustered.

I pressed my lips tight. "They're expecting me inside."

"Credentials first."

I checked my clothes in case I had accidentally put on a uniform or anything remotely official. Nope. White tank top, scuffed jeans, and red alligator boots. Not even a plastic badge from the dollar store.

"Do you want a note from my doctor or something? I don't have credentials. I don't even have a doctor."

"Okay, smart-ass..."

"Look, I'm Cisco Suarez. You called me. Not *you*, specifically, but *you*, the cops. The collective you."

The officer crossed his arms over his chest. "I know what you're doing. That thing in the movies, where you act like you belong and talk fast and nobody messes with you, right? It's not gonna work, bro, and if you don't leave my crime scene I'm gonna put you in cuffs."

"Yo," called Booker from the front door.

He was a bald black dude and a gym rat. The kind of guy

with his sleeves tailored to his biceps, who happily volunteered for SWAT, and who wore black BDUs even though there wasn't any action in sight. I wasn't sure which Booker oozed more: being a cop or being a badass. So it was a good thing he belonged to my friend's special unit.

"This guy's okay," he explained as he converged on us. "A consultant for DROP."

The other cop sighed and grabbed a clipboard and pen resting on the gate post. "Keep this up and the guys are gonna start talking," he grumbled. Despite effectively having the duties of a security guard, he turned to me, unimpressed. "Cisco...?"

"Suarez, no accent." I started up the driveway. "How you doin', Book? You try that *lechon* I told you about?"

"I did and it was legit. Part of my regular lunch rotation now. I'll hit you back with the lobster mac and cheese from House of Mac. Believe me, you're in for a treat."

"Sounds like it."

He stopped halfway to the house. "And Cisco? You gotta stop messing with the rookies, man."

I glanced at the gate officer. "Hey, I just play the hand I'm dealt."

"Mm-hmm. Go on ahead. *El jefe's* inside."

I snickered. He pronounced "the boss" with an English J. The man knew his food but Spanish was beyond him.

Book headed back to the gate as I pushed ahead. An artsy-but-browned wreath of hemlock hung on the open front door. I followed the voices into the living room.

Detective Mullen saw me first. He was an older guy in

his fifties I'd worked with on several occasions, solid and practical but unaware of the truth beyond that I was called out when there was weird.

If you asked me, though, the scene in the living room didn't scream weird.

Last night's dinner sat half-eaten on a stout coffee table. The black pleather sofa rested on its backside, the only occupant of the house dead behind it. He was currently attended to by a crime scene tech.

"He was ambushed from behind," noted Mullen as he adjusted his blue nitrile gloves. "TV was on when we got to it. By the channel and rough time of death, I'm gonna conclude he was a Vikings fan."

I exhaled sharply. "You sure it wasn't the fourth quarter that killed him?"

Evan appeared through the back archway. "You made it." He pocketed his phone, stomped over, and locked his hand with mine. Unlike Mullen, he wasn't wearing gloves.

"Just here for your looks?" I jabbed.

"Hey, it was either me or this guy." He hooked his thumb over his shoulder at Mullen.

"Screw you," muttered the veteran. His back was already to us.

I followed Mullen's gaze to the crime scene while Evan waited behind me. I guess he wanted to see what I thought.

Officially, I was an occult consultant for the Miami Police Department. If there was a serious crime involving an eyewitness to the unusual, or evidence of mysticism like a bloody pentagram or decapitated chicken, I got a call. It didn't happen a lot and that was fine by me. The side gig afforded me a sliver of access, a few friends on the right side of the law, and, best of all, legitimacy.

This particular scene, however, didn't have the stink of spellcraft on it. If anything it smelled kinda musty. Maybe an animal lived here, or maybe some of last night's rain leaked in. Aside from the house being a little larger than average and sitting fifty feet off the water, this living room could've been anywhere in Miami. There was a modest flat screen, mixed furniture, and a Douglas Fir with blinking rainbow lights in the corner. Everything was exceedingly... normal.

Which wasn't to say spellcraft was always obvious. With the morning light streaming through the blinds, it wasn't nearly dark enough for me to perform an investigative spell.

"Killed on Christmas," I said. "Bummer."

"Screw Christmas," groused Mullen. "It was Friday night. If someone offs me, I would hope they'd have the decency to do it at the end of the weekend."

Evan snorted sardonically. "Yeah, because this is a Monday-through-Friday gig." He eyed me another moment. "You don't see it yet, do you, Cisco?"

"I was hoping you would end the suspense," I replied.

"It's our vic. Recognize him?"

I stepped closer to the body. He lay on his back, as if he'd been yanked backward while sitting, consistent with Mullen's ambush-from-behind theory. His height and weight were average, if a little mushy around the edges. He wore the casual attire of a bachelor spending a holiday alone. Socks, no shoes, dirty from traipsing across the tile floor.

The man's face had a stiffness to it. His skin was pocked and greasy and his comb-over lay askew, revealing a powdery white scalp. There was no sign of blood but the man's eyes were red, indicating asphyxiation. Nothing about the scene triggered my alarm bells, and it seemed entirely plausible the dead guy had a violent reaction to a chicken bone.

"It's Quentin Capshaw," revealed Evan. "The hypnotist."

I tensed. Not too long ago, Quentin had been a potential target of the Manifesto Killer.

Looking closer, I barely believed it was him. I'd personally chatted with Quentin not four months ago. The guy looked a lot worse corpsified and without his stage makeup. As with the interior of the island home, the reality didn't live up to the idea.

"Quentin doesn't live in Miami," I pointed out. "I thought he was holed up in an airport hotel."

"He's a snowbird from Jersey," explained Mullen, somewhat derisively. "The house is a rental. We spoke with the owner and have a follow-up with her this afternoon."

Jensen, the crime scene tech, swatted my alligator boot away so he could snap some photos. I pulled my eyes away from Quentin. "You think there's another serial killer? Finishing what Manifesto started?"

The two detectives shared a covert glance. They would have already considered the possibility, of course. Perhaps they weren't convinced. Or there was something else.

"That's one take," said a man walking into the room from the front of the house. He was Mullen's age but walked with upright shoulders as if he were twenty years younger. A white guy with a buzz cut of sandy hair, he was dressed in full blues.

Evan straightened. "Major. What brings you here?"

The man's expression sagged ever so slightly. "Same as you, I suspect. How did I know the DROP team would show up to my scene?"

"It's just to provide support, sir. We've crossed paths with the vic in a possibly related matter."

"Ah, yes, your serial killer theory." He turned to Mullen. "Have you found anything suggesting a repeat offender or the beginning of a spree?"

The veteran cleared his throat. "No, major."

"I didn't think so. We shouldn't rule anything out, but there's another possibility here and everyone knows what it is. Revenge."

I didn't say anything because the last thing I wanted to do was wade into departmental politics, but I didn't like the fact that everyone seemed to know what he was talking about except me. Evan was my friend but he was only a lieutenant, and the metaphorical bar on his collar was worth much less than the golden leaf on the major's.

"A word outside, Detective." The ranking officer motioned Mullen toward the door and they exited the room. Evan gritted his teeth.

"Who is this guy?" I asked under my breath.

"Major Bruce Petty is the head of the Criminal Investigations Section. That includes Mullen in Homicide."

"That include you?"

"Not technically. The DROP team reports directly to the mayor, but Petty could make my life hell."

Jensen snickered. "Understatement of the year. The major grew into exactly the man his authoritarian father wanted him to be."

I frowned. "Is he gonna be a problem?" I asked.

"Not if we don't give him a reason to be," said Evan.

"Meaning?"

"He's strict. He likes things by the book. Petty oversees all detectives in the city and asks them to run clean, no-nonsense investigations. It's a commendable ideal." My friend's body language didn't mirror the assurance.

"Okay. What's this he's talking about revenge?"

Evan blanched. "It's the other likely motive for killing Quentin."

"Which is?"

"...There's a very public figure who has a bone to pick with Quentin."

I nodded. "Manifesto. But he's dead."

"Not Manifesto, Cisco. Someone alive. Someone with a secret identity that Quentin Capshaw publicly claimed to know. An identity he threatened to reveal on several occasions."

My face deflated. "You don't mean..."

"It's already making headlines. The going speculation is that the Shadow Man killed Capshaw to protect his identity."

I grimaced, but not outwardly. Jensen was in the room, after all, and the secret identity of the Shadow Man was none other than yours truly, Cisco Suarez.

Chapter 2

"LMAO," chortled Jensen. "Give me a break. The Shadow Man's the new scapegoat of Miami."

Evan cast the tech a sidelong glance. "I take it you're not a true believer?"

"In conspiracy theories? Nah, man. That video was obviously manipulated." Jensen circled Quentin's body in a squatting position, finding an alternate camera angle. "The Shadow Man's just a convenient excuse for what ails you, a reason for online fringe groups to take up pitchforks. He's a call to action."

"The action is what scares me," I grumbled. "Either way, I think we can rule out the Shadow Man for this one. Quentin's claim of knowing his identity was a giant publicity stunt. Every time he was supposed to make the big reveal, he came up with a new excuse to delay."

I didn't voice the evidence backing up my claim. Quentin never knew the truth. His pronouncements were made at the behest of the FBI in an attempt to entrap the Shadow

Man.

Of course, there was the additional fact that I, as the eponymous Shadow Man, simply hadn't killed Quentin. That was about as definitive as it got, but it was information I couldn't readily volunteer.

"Regardless," said Evan soberly, "the public believes Capshaw was in the know, that he was pressured into backing down and keeping mum, and that he was finally silenced for good."

Jensen shook his head. "Conspiracy theories, man. You can't rationalize with these people."

"Well, we know better," I said firmly. "Any idea who really did this?"

"That's what you're here for," returned Evan. "How about a run through of the scene? Watch your step."

He waved me to the back of the house. Evidence markers called out small piles of dirt. They almost looked like footprints, but they were intermittent and not well defined. To be honest the place wasn't the epitome of a Mr. Clean ad. Ample dirt and grit sullied the tile.

Evan stopped at the French doors leading to a rear patio of stamped concrete. "These were unlocked. Easy in, easy out."

I examined the backyard and frowned. "That's a lot of dirt to track in coming from a patio." Beyond the pool was a dock to the Bay, though there was no boat.

"From the dock to the door, there's no opportunity to step in dirt. We're thinking the killer entered from the front yard, came up one of two sides of the house. Both have heavy tree coverage and plenty of soil."

"Or he could've come by boat and scoped out the sides before entering."

One thing was sure: these French doors were definitely the entry point. A patio table with a metal frame and clear plastic surface lay on its side, bent and smashed. The small shards resulting from the destruction were still present, which meant the damage was recent.

"Did you find any tracks outside?"

"Negative. It rained in the early AM, and you know how the wind is out here. It's like a pressure washer. We're still looking but so far the outside is clean. Except for several shallow holes in the ground." He watched me expectantly as he delivered that last bit of info.

I nodded at a pair of food bowls outside, filled to the brim with dark water. "Sounds like a dog to me."

"Could be, but we haven't found one. There's no stash of dog food inside. Jensen suggested it was the dog that tracked dirt into the house. Quentin put it outside before he was killed, so maybe the dog was stuck outside in the rain and ran off."

It sounded plausible but it was hard to say. Dog hair can stick around for a long time, and those old bowls outside were so neglected it was difficult to tell if they were there a day or a year. The rain really hampered any guesswork.

I turned back to the tile and the footprints we did have. The coverage was uneven, with clumps of dirt loose in some areas but stamped down by a foot in others. It meant not all the soil came from the bottom of a shoe. Or...

I crouched beside one of the larger clumps. "Are those toe imprints?"

Evan dipped his head. "It definitely looks like it. I'm still trying to decide what kind of killer breaks into someone's house barefoot."

"Any chance this was a random crackhead?"

"When are we ever that lucky?"

"Point."

We followed the evidence markers back to Quentin's body, presumably tracing the killer's steps leading up to the deed. Sunbeams from the window highlighted scratches in the white tile.

"What are these?" I asked.

Evan pointed to a marker representing the grouping. "Not sure yet, but the scratches are fresh. This one cuts through a clump of dirt. The killer brushed across the soil on his way out." Evan turned to the crime scene tech. "Jensen, do you mind?"

The man shrugged. "I have nothing else to do. The ME is taking his sweet time." Jensen set down his camera and waved me over. "So this is our corpse."

I leaned close as Jensen pointed a gloved hand to the back of Quentin's left forearm, which he had to lift slightly to display. "An incidental wound, possibly defensive, except it's the only one of its kind."

So there was blood. A good sized gash curved along Quentin's forearm. The cut was shallow but had drawn enough blood to scab over a section of flesh. It was obvious when you looked at it but easy to miss, as I initially had.

"Small blade, probably," continued the tech. "It's fresh, made when the deceased was still alive, but it couldn't have killed him. Cause of death is the second wound.

Jensen flicked on a pocket-sized flashlight and pointed it at dirty bruising on Quentin Capshaw's neck. "See this pattern of imprints? It's consistent with some kind of linked cord. The spacing indicates a heavy metal chain maybe."

"Could've been what caused the scratches on the floor."

Evan watched silently from a distance, hands crossed. He would've already come to the same conclusion.

"It's too early to definitively say," relayed Jensen, "but I think we're looking at an open-and-shut strangulation."

I blinked, surprised I had missed the marks on the neck too. "Isn't the bruising a little light?"

"You might be surprised. Most manual strangulation doesn't leave a mark."

"Even with a chain?"

Jensen hedged. "The bruising isn't as overt as I would expect, but it only takes four pounds of pressure to occlude the jugular. And it's always possible Quentin had a blood condition. The ME will test morbidity and look for other signs of strangulation, like damage to the hyoid."

His flashlight beam pivoted to the floor by Quentin's hand. "Here we have an eight-inch length of brown hair that could've dropped during the struggle. We don't know whose it is or when it fell here, but it's safe to say it doesn't match our vic's comb-over." Jensen moved the flashlight close to the body's fingers. They were coated with dirt. "It looks like we might have some DNA under his nails too."

I frowned. "There's no way he was eating fried chicken with so much dirt on his hands, right?"

Jensen pulled away to face me. "You get attacked from behind, what do you do?" He raised his hands behind his head. "You strike backward and grab a hold of whatever you can."

I nodded in understanding. "Maybe pull some hair out or scratch someone's face."

The tech smiled. "Now you're talking. I believe our vic even turned his head and got a bite out of an arm or hand." He shone the light on Quentin's face. His cheek was smeared with dirt, and some of it blackened his teeth. So it wasn't Quentin with the hygiene problem, or a possible dog... it was the killer.

Bruce Petty stomped back into the room with Mullen in tow. "Is this really necessary?" he carped.

Evan sprang to my defense. "He's a consultant, major. He's not touching the body."

"You realize what a good defense lawyer can do with an amateur stomping around our scene in cowboy boots?"

"He's just a set of eyes. I promise."

The major brusquely nodded. "And what does this set of eyes see?"

Everyone turned to me. Which wasn't exactly fair. I'd been here all of ten minutes and was still catching up. That didn't abate Evan's pleading stare. He wanted me to pull magic out of my ass at a moment's notice. Something to impress the major and justify my involvement here.

And I could do that, no problem at all, with regular-old

shadow magic. But everyday, honest-to-God intuition? That was a different kind of spellwork entirely.

I sighed and contemplated the body. In an ideal world I'd kick everybody out, close the shades, and do my thing. That kind of intimacy was impossible with this scene. I checked Quentin's socks. While he could've possibly left some toe impressions wearing them, there were no signs of fresh soil in the cotton.

His outward injuries were minor, though I did find the marks of dirt on his neck curious. The dirt was the key. It was out of place here, and too abundant to have been tracked in.

Major Petty raised his chin in an open invitation for me to speak. Mullen remained quiet in the background. Evan swallowed, gaze dropping to the floor. I pouted at the loose soil nearby.

Jensen cleared his throat. "Sir, there's not a lot more we can deduce from a preliminary investigation."

Petty's lips jutted in disappointment, but the expression was almost triumphant.

"He brought dirt with him," I blurted out.

All eyes fixed on me, Petty's with an expectant brow. I did my best not to shrivel under his glare.

"The killer tracked in dirt, but there's more here than came in on his clothes. His weapon, a chain, was kept somewhere outside. It left dirt on Quentin's neck. And the soil clumping suggests a mass of it, possibly as the metal unfurled." I studied Quentin's soiled mouth again, and then matched it against his hands. "I don't think this muddy mess came from clawing and biting. I think Quentin was doing everything he could to get the dirt *out* of his mouth."

Jensen's eyes narrowed. He leaned down and shone the flashlight into the dead man's mouth. "How can you see that? Rigor's essentially locked the jaw shut."

"Can you open it?" asked Evan.

"I can, but the ME won't like it."

"Do it," ordered Petty.

The tech went to a kit and produced a set of specialized tongs. With some work, he forced the stiff jaws apart. Quentin's mouth was dirty, but not full of the stuff. Petty grunted.

"He would've been desperately shoveling it out," I explained, miming a puking motion that explained the dirt on Quentin's fingers and lips.

Jensen carefully positioned the flashlight deeper inside the mouth cavity. "I think he's onto something here."

The tech went to his bag and grabbed a long instrument with a mirror on the end, something a dentist might use, and used it to scoop a mass of dirt from deep down Quentin's throat.

"It explains the light bruising," concluded Jensen. "The chain around the neck was for compliance, but it didn't kill him. Cause of death was asphyxiation, not strangulation. Our vic choked to death on a mouthful of dirt."

Chapter 3

Major Petty, after extended deliberation, conceded a begrudging nod. "Fine," he announced. "I'll be a good sport and cooperate with the mayor, even if I don't see an occult angle. But Mullen's lead on this thing, copy?"

"One hundred percent," assured Evan.

"Dirt," said the ranking officer, shaking his head. "What do you make of it?" he asked Mullen.

"It's... uh... too early to say," hedged the detective.

"It's to dispel zombies," I said plainly.

Petty and Mullen looked at me like I was crazy. "Are you saying our vic was a zombie?" asked the major.

"He's an expert in occult lore," explained Evan. "He's stating what our killer may believe, not what he believes himself."

"Yeah," I added with a snort. "Zombies? Next you'll tell me magic is real."

My friend glared in warning. "Let's do without the commentary, Cisco. What's significant about choking on dirt?"

I shrugged. "Call it a hunch, but I'm assuming it's not the sandy stuff from around here. Some practitioners believe a handful of cemetery dirt down the throat, along with a healthy dose of blood magic,"—I indicated the cut on Quentin's arm—"can permanently dispel the walking dead."

Petty humored me with a dubious nod. "It sounds like a theory, not proof. You have a familiarity with these rituals?"

"Let's just say, after my disappearance, I spent an unhealthy amount of time in underground circles in South America and the Caribbean."

"The islands." He frowned. "You're talking voodoo. You think this is the work of one of the Haitian outfits?"

"They're one of many who share the belief." I chewed my lip rather than continue. I'd done enough damage to the local voodoo community already. I wasn't about to throw them under the bus to this jerk, especially since there wasn't a shred of evidence implicating anyone specific.

My gaze darted to Quentin's wound and I suddenly saw the scab in a new light. Something bothered me about the cut. My blood magic theory was plausible, but it had holes in it, point of evidence the first that Quentin wasn't an actual zombie.

"Is it possible to clean the wound?" I asked Jensen.

"They'll do that at the morgue."

"Have you examined the shape of the cut?"

Jensen looked up to find Mullen, Evan, and the major waiting for his answer. "I, uh, already took pictures, so it won't hurt to do a wipe."

The tech grabbed a wipe from his kit, moistened it with a solution, and dabbed the dried wound, careful to put any scrapings into a bag. As Quentin's skin was washed and the cut was exposed, everyone leaned forward.

The knife had cut some kind of symbol on his arm. I couldn't read it, but it resembled a magic rune.

"What the hell?" grumbled Mullen.

I turned to Major Petty with a grin. "There's your proof of occult activity."

Jensen added the wipe to the evidence bag and hurried back to his camera. The flash went off as we morbidly scrutinized the ominous blood scrawl.

"Come clean with me," said Jensen. "This is all BS, right? Some fancy scam like fortune tellers use?"

Evan grunted. "Ask Quentin if it's BS."

The silence that followed didn't linger long. This was a team of professionals with a lot of experience. I doubted there was an indecisive person in the bunch.

Detective Mullen piped up. "I checked the grounds outside. It's possible our killer was a digger. We found holes, although no chains. We'll do another sweep now that we know what to look for, but if what Cisco says is true about the dirt not being local, I'm betting we won't find anything."

"So your next steps?" asked Petty.

"Recheck the perimeter, finish searching the house, and wait for the drag-ass ME to show. Jensen?"

The tech ran with the ball. "Several DNA samples are ready for the lab. Soil composition is testable as well."

The major nodded. "I'll put a rush on your requests. A minor celebrity with a possible Manifesto link makes this one high profile. Capshaw's been notorious in Miami ever since his close encounter, and every mouth breather in the city has an opinion. Capshaw was either a witch or a hero. They'll want details. So we keep a lid on it, which means keeping the circle small. Lieutenant, I'd like you to minimize your team's contact on this."

"Yes, major."

"Keep things close to your chest, Mullen. And no reporters."

"Of course."

"I'll work on a statement to the press. In the meantime, you have my personal line. Keep me updated."

Mullen and Evan agreed even as the major was on his way out, off to tackle the next crisis. I could only imagine the political plates someone like him had to spin.

I expected Petty's exit to spur everyone into action, but we all stood around twiddling our thumbs, expecting someone else to take charge. Normally that was my thing, but I couldn't proceed with my brand of investigation until the room was cleared.

"So this Petty guy," I starting with a grimace.

"The major," corrected Evan.

"Yeah. So he's some kind of straight shooter, but does he know what he's doing?"

"He's not just a suit," he answered. "He used to be a detective."

"A good one?"

"Good enough. People don't whisper in awe about his natural instinct or anything, but he handles procedure in a way that pleases the higher-ups. He's the hard-ass we don't deserve but the hard-ass we need."

I rolled my eyes. "You just say that 'cause you're exempt from his oversight."

My friend flashed a smug smile.

Detective Mullen grunted. "I don't want to stand here and listen to you snip about my boss. I'm gonna search the perimeter for some plausible deniability." He went for the edge of the room but paused and turned to Evan. "Wanted to ask, how's Junior doing? He's seemed... distracted lately."

Evan's smile was warm. "He's not a rookie anymore, and he takes his job seriously. Following in the footsteps of his old man."

Mullen seemed to redden at the sentiment. "Okay, okay, just a question." He waved his hand my way. "Just do your thing already." He marched for the back door.

Huh. If I didn't know any better, the portly detective might know a little more than he let on. I strolled to the window to make sure he went outside. I pointed to the vertical blinds. "Mind if I close these?"

"You better not," said Jensen. "I took pictures, but the angle of the blinds determines visibility. It might be important if the killer staked his victim out through the window."

I hooked my hands in my pockets. "Fine, I won't touch anything."

Evan mirrored my posture before swiveling to the crime

tech. "Jensen, you mind stepping outside and giving the ME's office another call? I'd like a word with my consultant."

The tech couldn't bring himself to muster a heartfelt sigh. "Sure, whatever." He returned his camera and tools to his bag, but left it in the room and headed out.

Alone at last.

I had a feeling this respite wouldn't last long, so I hurried into a crouch beside the body.

"Can you like..." Evan shrugged. "I don't know... talk to him?"

"Quentin?" I shook my head firmly. "His spirit's long gone. At least if it wants to be. But I might be able to relive his final moments of life..." My teeth involuntarily clenched. I didn't get out of bed this morning hoping to experience being violently choked to death.

"You seem hesitant."

"Yeah, I just... Quentin was grabbed from behind, clearly overpowered, and died still facing the TV. I'm not sure he saw anything except the box score."

Turning my examination to Quentin's mouth and the smears of dirt, I unzipped my belt pouch, produced a small pill bottle, and used the plastic lid to scoop some dry dirt from the floor. The cops wouldn't miss the tiny amount. Even as Evan pretended not to notice, I screwed the lid closed and made the bottle disappear into my bag before I could be arrested for interfering with evidence.

Evan paced back toward me. "You really think the cut's for blood magic? Seems more like torture to me. Or a message."

I shrugged. "I'm not saying the killer didn't enjoy inflicting pain, but the signs are there. The confirmation will be the lab finding blood on the dirt in the mouth. The real question is, what kind of animist uses someone else's blood for a simple spell?"

"An animist who doesn't want to leave behind DNA evidence. Gone are the days of anonymous witch's brews and poisons. Academics like Jensen have revolutionized the job."

"People like us are a dying breed," I muttered sympathetically.

He laughed. "Jeez, we're in the prime of our lives, man. You make it sound like we're as old as Mullen." As if on cue, the detective strolled by in the grass outside the window.

I lowered my voice out of an abundance of caution. "What was that he mentioned about Junior?"

"Oh, nothing. His son's in my squad. They don't spend as much time together as they should so they use me as their go between to check in on each other."

I snickered. "There's a Mullen on the DROP team too?"

"Yeah. You've seen him before. I'm sure of it."

I guess it wasn't surprising. Policing tended to run in the family. I often wondered if Evan planned to train up little John McClane to follow in his footsteps. I supposed Fran was in that conversation as well, but I wanted something different for her. Nothing specific, just...

Was it set in stone that a father had to pass on his life's troubles to his children?

Unable to touch the blinds, I looked around for something that could serve as a tarp to shield the sunlight. I considered a sofa cushion, but figured that would be more intrusive than messing with the windows. The moment of mulling it over turned out somewhat productive as I spotted a bit of dog hair on the pillow, though I wasn't sure what to do with that info just yet. In the end, I craned over Quentin closely and hoped my body provided enough shade.

A tickle ran along my dog-collar bracelet. Quentin wasn't really in shadow, per se, but what small amount of dim sunshine was present seemed to fade further.

Using spellcraft to darken the room in order to use my shadow sight was a bit like burning the candle at both ends. The result was much less effective, and the strain to get there was twice as intense. Still, it wasn't like I was in the midst of a life-or-death struggle here. I could afford to be inefficient.

After Quentin's body significantly darkened, I blinked and my green irises cracked open. The black from my pupils flooded them. From my awkward vantage above the body, I made out the faintest trace of the Intrinsics glowing in the back of Quentin's throat.

That was confirmation of spellcraft. This was genuine blood magic and not just for show. Which was strange because I knew zombies, and Quentin was no zombie. Not before, and definitely not now.

Heels clacked harshly against the tile floor. As I pulled away, I caught more traces of magical energy on the wound. But the room was too bright. My eyes already burned. And

Rita Bell was marching straight at me.

I blinked the spell away.

"Cisco Suarez," she enunciated with daggerlike precision.

"What is this, a beach party?" I grumbled.

Special Agent Rita Bell was an FBI agent with an ax to grind. She'd come to Miami during the Manifesto spree, and while she was a sharp tack she tended to find joy in poking the wrong people. Case in point: she had incorrectly suspected me of being the serial killer.

On the other hand, she'd been convinced I was the Shadow Man even before the moniker existed, so let's call it a draw.

"Special Agent," muttered Evan through pressed teeth.

"I've been meaning to talk to you," she said, ignoring Evan completely. Her narrow lips curled in anticipation of a fight, and her heels (and the fact that I was on the floor) made her seem seven feet tall if she was an inch. "You were supposed to contact my office. Instead you skipped town for over a month."

I winced. "Milena needed drier weather to recover."

She paused for a stiff moment. "How is she?"

"She's okay."

Agent Bell nodded. "Well, you're here now."

Evan stepped forward. "He's an acting consultant for the City of Miami. I don't want you interfering with our investigation. Trust me, we're taking this homicide as seriously as you."

"I didn't accuse you of otherwise. Not yet." She crossed

her arms. "So let's see it. Consult away."

I grunted and pushed to my feet. "Sorry, you missed the show. I'm done."

Evan was disappointed but tried to hide it in the spirit of a unified front.

"That's too bad," remarked Agent Bell. "I suppose the FBI will need to hire our own occult expert. But here's a freebie for the City of Miami. There's an additional motive on the table. Namely that Quentin Capshaw was an informant for the FBI."

I put on my shocked face. "An informant? That hack?"

Evan chortled. "The feds will take anybody these days."

"Regardless, it means Quentin could've been killed for his association with me. If that's the case, anybody who knew he was working with the FBI is added to the suspect pool."

I stared darkly at Evan before pinching the bridge of my nose. As if I needed yet another motive pointing my direction. Rita had previously tried setting a trap for me using Quentin as bait. As a consequence, I'd almost found myself in federal lockdown. But just because I'd gotten away didn't mean Rita was backing down. I think it just made her even more eager.

"I'm out of here," I said, more for Evan's benefit than Rita's.

The special agent snapped a business card from her pocket and handed it to me. "Come in soon then. Since we'll be working together, we need to clear the air."

I took the card but grumbled extra loud for her benefit.

It was the strongest objection I could come up with considering she could take me into custody right here and now if she wanted. Luckily, with Quentin cold and stiff on the floor, she had bigger fish to fry.

And so did I.

Chapter 4

I stepped into the sun, muttering angrily. Who would've thought a crime scene would be so flooded with... investigators? I mean, sure, yes, it was obvious in retrospect. That didn't make the inability to work any less aggravating.

Still, don't let it be said that ol' Cisco Suarez didn't have a couple of wild theories. The trouble was getting from point A to point Z.

The cop at the gate regarded me with a wry smile. Between the major and the FBI, he must've known I was in a jam. Booker was MIA, so I approached Mullen on the right side of the house.

"Anything?" I asked.

He shook his head with unsurprised boredom, like he was just going through the motions. "Dirt's sandy, like you said. If there was any evidence out here, it washed into the Bay with the rain. For what it's worth, I think your theory's dead on, as crazy as it sounds."

"So why're you trampling through the bushes then?"

"Half this job is confirming what you already know. If you don't do it right, no one else will."

That had a sort of cold sense to it. "And the other half?"

Mullen shared a rare smile. "Getting lucky. And I don't mean the time I met my third wife."

The grizzled veteran continued to methodically work the yard. His detachment didn't signify apathy or carelessness. He was serious about crossing the t's and dotting the i's, even if they were useless adornments.

I wandered back toward the gate. An orange dumbbell in overgrown grass caught my eye. Upon closer inspection, it wasn't a real weight. It was a chew toy.

I eyed the yard again. There were too many signs to ignore. As Mullen said, if I didn't do this right, it wouldn't get done. And it wasn't that I couldn't depend on the cops, but this was what they were paying me for.

I skirted around the side of the house opposite Mullen and the crime scene. The bushes and grass covered most of the real estate between the building and the weathered panel fence, with the exception of a few holes dug into the ground. The rain had smoothed their edges, making it impossible to tell how fresh they were.

Instead of focusing on the holes, I checked the side of the house for entrances into the crawl space. It was sealed pretty well. As my boots hit the concrete patio, I confirmed the absence of sheds or other structures on the property. A doghouse would've been too easy.

I stopped at the water's edge and stared out at glittering Biscayne Bay. My tongue clicked sharply. The boat theory had one thing going for it: the killer might have been barefoot. Still, I wasn't a fan. It wasn't the stealthiest of ways to approach, though I supposed it depended on the boat.

I sighed and backtracked through the patio when I noticed dirty splotches of black. Muddy cat prints. How had I missed those? This animal, at least, wasn't much of a mystery. There were no cat bowls or litter boxes around the house. It was probably a wandering stray.

I resumed walking, keeping my gaze on the cat tracks until they ran right to the fence where the bottom half of a wood plank was missing. I crouched and peeked into the neighbor's backyard. It was lush, no cement patio, with more trees and grass cover than this one. Also notable was the ten-inch divot in the dirt.

Another dog hole. Which suggested Quentin's dog regularly escaped to the neighbor's yard.

I considered the broken table on Quentin's patio. What if the hypnotist wasn't a slob? I mean, except for the dog fur. But he hadn't left dirt tracked in the house. The damage to the patio table was likely new or it would've been set aside. It was a possible sign of a struggle. Except Quentin was ambushed inside...

What would a dog do, injured, locked outside in the rain, without shelter?

I squeezed through the hole in the fence, which wasn't an easy thing. My first concern was other dogs or residents, but so far I was in the clear. My eyes settled on a greenhouse in the rear of the yard. It had a shaded glass roof with propped-up windows and a nudged-open door.

Keeping low, I entered the structure and found myself surrounded by plant life. Beneath a table of potted orchids lay a dog that resembled a beefy German shepherd, but larger. His long-haired coat was made up of browns and blacks with highlights of gray. Between his size and coloring, he looked like a wolf.

The dog growled softly at my approach. It wasn't a harsh sound, more like a warning, and an exhausted one at that. He repeated the rumble between breaths, each time he exhaled, and he did it without moving. He was hurt.

"Easy boy." I raised my hands carefully. "I'm not gonna hurt you."

I scooted closer on my knees. The dog objected but only halfheartedly, which was a bad sign. I put my hand to his nose and he blinked warily. Though he was still growling, I grabbed a hunk of fur at his neck and rubbed it. It was matted and wet from a long night in the cold.

The animal was tense but, after a few seconds, his growling subsided. His expression relaxed. His face was brown and black but his jowls were white. I gave his neck a scratch with my other hand. He whined and his large tail thumped the ground.

"That's right. I'm a friend. Let me see what you got yourself into..."

My hand ran along his coat and caught the large piece of plastic embedded in his chest. Pulling his fur away revealed the pool of blood he was lying in.

I groaned. It was a lot of blood. So much I was sure there'd been a trail of it from the patio before the rain washed it away. Frankly, I was surprised the tough bugger was still alive.

He whined again. His tail stopped moving but he put his paw on my hand. He was in pain. I dug through my belt pouch for a numbing powder. The white stuff was potent. I only needed half a teaspoon or so in my palm. I put it to his nose and let him sniff it up.

In seconds, his body went slack. His muscles relaxed and he stopped whining. His tail thumped twice.

"You like that, huh?"

I scrubbed his neck and his paw pushed my hand.

"You did a good job protecting your owner, didn't you?"

His large brown eyes blinked at me, and he sighed a long breath.

"We're gonna find him. Don't worry."

The dog didn't last much longer. It wasn't anything I did. I just numbed the pain and gave him some company in his final moments. But I could tell it meant a lot to him. I could also tell he had done his best.

Maybe, with my help, he could do better.

I pulled the jagged scrap of plastic from his body and a wash of fresh blood spilled to the ground. "You wanna catch who did this to you?" I asked. "And to Quentin?" I worked my jaw and checked the yard to make sure I had sufficient privacy. With a nod, I said, "Of course you do."

I pulled the black twine at my neck and put the silver whistle hanging on it to my lips. It was, ironically, a dog whistle, except this one was special. It was a fetish audible only to the dead.

As I blew, the dog's large ears perked. The reaction was quick, no doubt driven by determination on his part. The rest was up to me. I produced a few vials of much more potent voodoo powders and went to work.

Chapter 5

I got the dog on its feet and back to my car. I did it in short order and without being seen. That said, my job was just beginning.

Deathwork was a varied process with layers upon layers of enchantments, depending what you wanted to accomplish. The call of my whistle could produce an ally in a pinch, but it was far from a complete ritual and lacked all accompanying benefits.

What I had on my hands was more than your average automaton. This was a dog who had intimately known the murder victim. He'd directly tangled with the killer. And, though he came up on the losing end, he potentially remembered the experience enough to assist my investigation.

Which wasn't to say the original doggo was still in residence. Whatever essence was at his core probably hadn't lingered. What remained was a collection of muscle memory and electrical impulses that needed only be decoded.

I headed to my condo, driving with the T-top on and the windows up as it was still too chilly for my liking. The corpse stayed in the back seat while I went up to the penthouse. Celine Dion blared from the speakers. An oversized pink unicorn floaty in my balcony pool squeezed against the window. It was one of those novelty inner tubes that was bigger than a person and about half the size of my standing water. Coconut filled my nose and an open blender sat atop my bar. Milena's wide-brimmed sun hat popped out from above the megafloaty.

I rushed out the glass door to say hi and froze when I was greeted by Kasper wearing Milena's hat and holding a piña colada with a paper umbrella in it.

"What's up, broham?" he asked, red-lensed John Lennon sunglasses shading his eyes. Steam from the heated water surrounded him.

I scrunched my nose. "Just expecting someone else for some bizarre reason. I thought you'd be minding the shop downstairs."

"Darcy's on it."

The pair took shifts at the coffee shop I owned. It was on the street level of my condo building, and I usually stopped in to check on things. Overall, I didn't spend a lot of time there. The business was mostly a front to legitimize ourselves. Since Kasper reveled in his illegitimacy, he rarely bothered with his shifts.

"Don't worry about it," he said. "She really likes running things. She's good at it."

"I'm not worried." I casually scratched the back of my head. "Anyone come by?"

He shook his head and slurped the frozen drink through a straw. "No. Expecting someone?"

I shook my head back. "No. I got a thing so I might be a while."

He nodded while he watched the skyline. It had been years since Kasper was a beach guy, so to speak. Probably before I did my time as a hit man. A recent brush with silvan poison had reintroduced the scribe to the healing powers of the sun, and now he was enjoying Miami to the fullest. Which I guess included lounging in my balcony pool with a girly drink and accoutrements.

Whatever. There were worse things to get up to.

I headed inside and waited till I was out of sight to check my phone. No messages, no news. I texted Milena, "What are you up to?" A minute passed before I shoved it back into my pocket and headed out the front door.

Unlike my biker pal, my girlfriend hadn't been so quick to recover from our time in the Nether. She'd been the victim of a much worse poison, one that nearly killed her, and it had been a rough couple of months since. She had good days and bad. There were times I thought I wouldn't have my Milena back, and other days I felt foolish for worrying. We'd kinda skated by without incident for a while, but now that we were back in Miami, I suspected the expectation of normalcy was amplifying any problems she experienced, however minor.

In other words, it was easy to ride things out on vacation,

but there was no room for avoidance once playtime was over.

I made it back to my car with half a mind to drive to her condo in Midtown to check on her. But then, Milena was a big girl and I really did have a thing. Instead of fretting over it, I drove to my Everglades hideaway off Tamiami Trail and pulled up next to an old pickup truck from the seventies. Unlike the Firebird, it wasn't officially mine in name. That made it useful for covert business, though I rarely used it because it was haunted. A large pentagram periodically spray-painted on the hood kept the ghost mostly in check, but it remained one of the nagging problems in my life.

"Come on, boy," I said, double-tapping my shin as I held the car door open. The giant shepherd obediently hopped out.

As far as zombies went, he was a solid job. My connection was strong and he was about as new as he could be. Ninety percent of necromancers in the world would stop where he was, but I wanted to do him better so I strolled him into the corrugated metal structure that was my cookhouse and busted out the big guns.

Voodoo is powerful, enigmatic, and frightening, but it's especially messy. There's blood and gross body parts and ground-up powders that stink to high heaven. The cookhouse is the place to do the type of work that wouldn't go unnoticed in a high-society condominium in Brickell.

I performed purification blessings to bolster the doggo to his undead potential. Blood magic strengthened his connection to me, and various enchantments forged his body and bones into armor. A mix of powders and pastes ensured the big boy wouldn't rot or lose clumps of fur, but I went beyond the amateur stuff to a whole new level of quality control. This dog's coat would feel vibrant, his eyes would sparkle with life. I was gonna make him look like he just came from the spa.

That took a good several hours, half of which waiting for the spells to completely permeate the subject. Like rising dough, you could often skip the step but got better results if you didn't. When all was said and done, I had a bulletproof minion that weighed over a hundred pounds yet appeared completely normal.

Then it was time for field work.

Necromancers quickly become intimate with the cemeteries in their city. The very nature of magic is secretive, but working with the dead is another level. There's knowledge people aren't privy to, and knowledge they would never care to learn.

Miami has a broader underground than most realize. The tourism commercials neglect to mention the city tops the nation in grave robberies. As the largest domestic hub for practices like voodoo, Santería, and all their numerous offshoots, it shouldn't come as a surprise.

And let's speak plainly here: grave robbing is frowned upon. It's part of what gives necromancers a bad name. As one myself, I won't deny I'd ever attended a body heist or two. (I used to run in sketchy circles.) But I'd never robbed a grave myself.

People bury their dead as a measure of respect and

closure. Eternal slumber and all that. The truth is it doesn't matter what happens to a body once the spirit moves on, but the loved ones of the deceased often believe it does, and that's enough for me to respect their wishes.

As for all the necromancers quite literally involved in bad juju? The last thing on their minds is human decency and respect.

I'd be lying if I denied doing things your average citizen would be horrified at. Quentin Capshaw, for example. Given the opportunity, I would've performed blood magic to witness his dying moments. While many would frown at the practice, excuse me for using unconventional methods to solve a murder or two. When it came down to it, it's what Quentin would've wanted.

The first stop on my boneyard ramble was Miami Memorial Park. The suspension of the rusty pickup bounced as I drove under the towering archway at the entrance. The well-known South Miami cemetery was large, and that's why I'd chosen it.

My plan was to hit the big sites first. My search was a random one that required a stroke of luck akin to hitting the lottery. With larger grounds and a larger resident population, this was my version of buying a handful of tickets at once. The odds were still long but a lot better.

The grounds were wide and even, neatly crisscrossed with paved roads. Flat tomb stones that you could drive a riding mower over were the predominant style in Miami, although many had popup flower pots filled with colorful well wishes. It was the middle of an unremarkable day and the crowds surprised me. Two funerals at opposite ends of the park and a large gathering near the center. My truck with the black pentagram attracted some eyes so I did my best to park in an unattended section.

I shut off the engine and debarked, leaving the door open and skirting to the back so I could open the tailgate. The large-framed dog lying in the bed stood at attention. He was over a hundred pounds but still managed to look rangy, like a wild predator who hunted across a huge territory but never had his fill.

"Okay buddy," I beckoned. "You're up."

He advanced and sank his nose into my palm. I scrubbed his neck in rough greeting and jostled the dog collar that I'd left on out of respect. I'd been so focused on the enchantments that I'd overlooked the actual tag. It listed a phone number that probably linked to Quentin, as well as his given name.

"Snickers, huh? I'm sorry, boy, but we need to leave your past in the past. So people don't ask questions." I removed the collar and patted him. "But you do need a name. How about Wolf?"

He cocked his head and whined.

Okay, maybe originality wasn't my strong suit. "A little obvious, huh?" The oversized shepherd did look well enough like a wolf, and it was a good name for inspiring fear in my enemies, but maybe I could do better. "How about Scout?"

He barked and wagged his whole butt. Scout it was.

I opened the container of soil taken from the crime scene

and held it to his nose. He sniffed it carefully, taking in the faint magical signature, and pulled away with a sharp bark.

"Good boy. Now go find a match."

Scout leapt to the grass and got started.

Chapter 6

You're not supposed to bring dogs to cemeteries, not even zombie ones. I directed Scout to the far side of my truck in relation to the office building. He darted from headstone to headstone, sniffing away. Not that we were looking for a specific body. That would've been a tall order. This was as simple as looking for a match in graveyard soil. And I could already tell, through the ghostly tethers that connected my minion to me, we didn't hit the Mega Millions.

It was only a minute before a couple from the large gathering diverted my way, probably to complain about the dog. They wore loose-flowing clothes, especially the woman's colorful dress, and didn't lack for jewelry. The whole lot of them were Roma, otherwise known as gypsies.

This was why I hated going to graveyards these days. The Miami necromancer community didn't like me much and gave me a hard time whenever they could. That reputation often extended to other animists, even the Roma who tended to keep to themselves.

"Hello friend!" the man called. "Paying your respects?"

I cleared my throat and shook his hand. And then shifted a step to block the woman from scrutinizing my dog. "Something like that."

"All are welcome," he said with a wide smile. "No one should be alone in a place like this."

The woman leaned in. "Especially not the dead."

I snickered but the two were serious. It was like I said. If they didn't know who I was, they at least knew *what* I was. There was a pentagram on my hood and one to match on my belt buckle... behind the skull. With the dog running around in broad daylight, magic was literally in the air.

And I knew what they were too, and not just because Miami Memorial housed more buried gypsies than any other cemetery in the city. They were animists, at least some of them, but not necromancers. The Roma were also a very insular group, distrusting of others just as they were distrusted. But you couldn't claim they weren't sociable.

"Join the party," said the man. "We can talk to the dead together."

"Thanks. I kind of have a long day."

"All the more reason to stop by," urged the woman. "Eat roasted pig and lobster with us."

I froze in the middle of shaking my head. "Roasted pig?"

I wasn't a big people person in general, but I had skipped breakfast and it was past lunchtime. A strong start to my hunt wouldn't hurt.

Besides, the gypsies were harmless. They often held cookouts and celebrated their dead. From the looks of it, half of them were already drunk.

So I joined them for a bite. We chatted about the cooler-than-usual winter and the afterlife. No one mentioned the Shadow Man, my past, or the undead canine sniffing around. And I got a belly full of pork.

It was a decent time that I wished lasted longer, but it was better to do my cemetery work in the daylight. I waved goodbye feeling a little better about my standing in the community. Maybe not *everyone* hated me. That was something to build on, right?

Scout trotted over and nuzzled my leg. Miami Memorial had been a welcome surprise, but it was still a bust. We loaded back into the truck and drove off.

Pinewood Cemetery was next. It was small but it was nearby, and worth considering as it had the distinction of being one of the oldest in the city. The rural yard looked more like an overgrown park, and I wasn't bothered. Unfortunately, it wasn't a match.

In this fashion, the dog and I slowly canvassed Miami. Graceland Memorial, Woodlawn, Flagler Memorial Park. Miami City Cemetery's a small historic park near the water notable for housing some of the founders of the city. No dice there either.

I avoided Lincoln Park and Evergreen Memorial for as long as I could. Both are historic black graveyards featuring above-ground crypts in the style of the Caribbean. They're also big hubs for voodoo and Santería, frequented by necromancers and worse: it was where I'd first tangled with the vampires of the Obsidian March.

On any given night the pair of cemeteries had a high incidence of funny business. They were smart places to look into, and even smarter to go while I had sunlight on my side, so I bit the bullet and got it over with. I received a few hardened looks, but the locals left me and my dog well enough alone. And, once again, we were disappointed by the lack of results.

This was how my day—and soon enough, my night—went. Splurging on roast pork turned out to be a good decision as I never had a chance to eat again. Once I hit the northern bounds of the county, I doubled back and visited the smaller yards. The worst part was, I had no certainty the grave we were looking for was in the area at all. It was just a hunch based on the local community.

They don't call it the Magic City for nothing.

It was a little after 3 a.m. when I wearily strode along a leaf-covered hiking trail in Kendall Indian Hammocks Park and butted up against the chain-link at its west end. A wooden sign read, "Medical Examiner Department—Dade County Cemetery." It still had the old Metro-Dade logo, before the county name was simplified to Miami-Dade. Ironically, I was close to the Turnpike, fifteen minutes from where this day had started.

The fence was double high and the gate was locked, so I crouched at the base and hugged Scout. With the area predictably empty at this time, I sunk into the shadow, pulled us between the links, and appeared safely on the other side.

The grounds were nondescript. A loop of broken asphalt

cut through a field of grass. A few bushes and trees stood out in the otherwise open space. Given the far border abutted a police department, I was counting on the cover of darkness.

Exemplifying the sparse appearance of this cemetery was the lack of headstones. This was a closed property for city use. A place to bury the lost and forgotten. It was a potter's field. Nowadays the only thing buried here were ashes, but that hadn't always been the way.

Scout perked and darted ahead. I lowered to the ground, afraid we'd been spotted. My senses attuned to the dog's. It wasn't a person he'd found, it was a scent. We'd hit pay dirt.

Or cemetery dirt, at least.

The dog raced to a mound in the ground and furiously dug at it. I hurried forward and was blindsided by a horrific smell that almost knocked me to my feet.

Pinching my nose, I slowed my advance and eyed my surroundings. A dead bird lay upturned on its back, stiff feet in the air, ants trailing from empty eye cavities. My first suspicion was a ritual but it hadn't been sacrificed. It also wasn't the source of the smell. Not by a long shot.

I pushed forward and dragged Scout away from his digging. Oddly, he gave the slightest bit of resistance to my command. It was an impressive and unexpected show of will for a zombie. But no matter how excited he was, I couldn't have him screwing up the site of... whatever this was.

But the damage had been done and it was a little late for preservation. The mutt had made incredible progress during his short exertion. And whatever had occurred here was days old. Fortunately, the rains in the Bay may not have reached these grounds.

The soil was soft. Freshly dug. By the looks of it, the dog was digging at a newly covered grave. Scout sniffed the area until finally plopping his snout into the dirt with a low growl.

Bingo was his name-o.

I considered the grave, having a hard time imagining what could possibly make a scent so pungent my eyes watered. Me, a voodoo practitioner. My trade was in pungent scents. This wasn't bodily fluids or rot, it wasn't chemicals or powders, but it *was* nearly too much to handle.

I pulled the burlap mask from my belt and tied it over my nose and mouth like a Wild West outlaw. The enchanted fabric filtered the air of anything toxic and neutralized the foul odor. As for Scout, while his sense of smell was more acute than mine, he was dead and didn't seem to have an opinion.

Magic crackled in my eyes as I studied the scene. Sparkles of crimson and gold weakly highlighted protrusions on the ground. At first the curved lines appeared random, haphazard disturbances in the soil, but the semicircle of sigils around the grave was impossible to ignore.

They were symbols and words, traced into the dirt. Runes, different from the usual Viking fare, with letters somehow familiar yet foreign. Larger glyphs were more artistic and just as strange. They were a direct connection to the wound on Quentin's forearm.

Half the ring was destroyed or covered over, either by Scout's digging or other activity between the ritual and now. I tried to play paleontologist and gently brush the offending soil away, but the Intrinsics had already been dispersed. There was no way to recover those signatures.

The runes that remained were fading and windblown, but my shadow sight picked up the details. At the head of the grave, marking the top of the ring like a clock, was a bastardized version of the number twelve.

A cold breeze prickled my skin. Here it was, officially Miami sweater weather, and I was still in my tank top. But I could hardly be bothered by a slight chill now. My long search was at an end and this was the payoff.

I examined the other glyphs. The clock comparison held up. At equal points in a circle around the grave were new symbols and words. There could've been about twelve of them too, had I been around to see them all, though their alignment didn't exactly match a Timex.

The camera on my cell phone was awful at nighttime shots, so I held it low to the ground and risked several quick snaps with the flash. The light would make my trespass visible from a distance if anyone cared to look, but it couldn't be helped. I would have to study these runes elsewhere.

I checked over the scene, making sure I hadn't missed anything. Nothing screamed for attention. Scout still stood with his nose in the dirt, so I scooched over to him and grabbed a clump. Loose soil fell through my fingers. A tiny glint tumbled somewhere within. What I first thought was a visual artifact turned out to be a physical object. I leaned close and picked it out from among the grains of black.

Three small links of steel connected in a chain.

My teeth clicked. The presence of a chain did somewhat match the scene of the crime, but whatever had subdued Quentin Capshaw was a lot larger than this. The links in my hand were almost toylike.

I sighed at Scout. "Okay, boy. Do your thing."

He pounced on the hole with scraping paws, flinging dirt behind as he worked in rabid excitement. I smiled and remembered he'd been an excellent digger of holes in life. It was handy to have him around doing my dirty work, so to speak.

I stepped back as he excavated. Scout darted from this side to that, changing angles and completely destroying any leftover evidence of spellcraft. It was probably for the best. After a few minutes he hit a wooden box.

I didn't know if the smell of plague was worse now, but I didn't dare pull off my mask to find out. I stepped into the ditch and wiped the lid of the old coffin. It had already collapsed into the dirt-filled box. These cheap coffins didn't always hold up.

The panel of wood wobbled as I moved it aside, rusty nails broken from the base. I had a sinking feeling as I dug into the box, revealing nothing but spilled cemetery dirt.

Now it was my turn to growl. Whatever this was, it wasn't your average case of the walking dead. The runes and the risk of doing this in proximity to a police station testified to that. Dark spellcraft was afoot.

Nothing like a little Christmastime necromancy to get you in the festive mood.

Voices called out in the distance. Beyond the fence, in the police parking lot, flashlight beams zeroed in on me.

"That's my cue," I muttered. "Come on, Scout."

We sprinted to the fence, shifted outside, and disappeared into the night.

Chapter 7

"For once, you didn't make the prime-time news," joked Evan. "Not a peep about grave robbing or vandalism."

"Hardly a surprise since I didn't do any of those things," I returned.

"Nope. Just the trespass."

"Just the trespass." Evan and I liked to give each other shit even when it wasn't called for.

It was late morning, the sunshine was hard to beat, and I was on a walk in a park with the people I considered my family. Evan, his wife and white witch Emily, four-and-a-half-year-old John, and our mutual daughter Fran, who happened to be the biggest bundle of joy ever since opening my Christmas gift.

We strolled along the concrete walkway of Bayfront Holiday Village, a pop-up marketplace among a backdrop of skyscrapers and ocean. Festive decorations dressed the palms and were joined by a new centerpiece, a towering string of lights in the shape of a pine tree. I'm sure the place was magical when all lit up at night, but this was the Sunshine State.

It was late days for the weeks-long Christmas festival. In fact, we'd barely made it together for its last weekend. Already past Christmas, even though the season technically continued into January, our commercial overlords deemed it best to move on to the Next Big Thing. Bayfront Park had to prep for the New Year's Eve ball drop.

So, while we could, we enjoyed what was basically a primped-up farmer's market with food trucks and tents of artisan wares. Parkgoers in rental roller skates weaved around those shopping and people-watching, all under the backdrop of the giant Christmas tree beside the famous waterfront fountain.

"Can't you boys discuss something besides work?" chided Emily.

"Hey," I protested, "work is the coffee shop. This is leisure."

She rolled her eyes. It was the most sophisticated, elegant eye roll in the history of human civilization, but it was an eye roll all the same. "I'm just hard up for a little sophisticated adult conversation," she said with a pout. "And you've been gone so long."

"You know I'm right here," reminded Evan.

She sighed. "I'd just like something resembling a social circle. Instead of..." Emily waved her hands in our general direction. Evan and I shrugged, and John ran circles around us with cotton-candy energy.

She left a lingering eye on her daughter. Fran walked

alongside us rather than *with* us, eyes soundly glued to her phone. It was the latest-and-greatest Samsung, the one with a super-premium zoom lens, but instead of practicing her photography Fran appeared to be having a conversation with an entirely different social circle.

"At least she's getting some use out of it," I said.

"It was entirely too expensive," rebuffed my ex-girlfriend.

I ignored the comment. It was true the phone was exclusive and a stunted supply made it hard to get, but I had connections. With as many burners as I went through, my local phone shop hooked me up. They received less than ten of these bad boys and customers had to wait in line overnight to get them. But not me, and not my little girl. It was the perfect gift.

Of course, that perfection was a double-edged sword. Because her attention was divided, I'd hardly gotten a smile from her all morning.

"Look, honey," announced Emily. "An olive oil booth. You love olive oil."

The screen lowered from Fran's eyes. "What an expert strategy to engage me, Mom."

Transparent as it was, it worked. Fran glued herself to the table of multicolored bottles of hipster gold.

"I see how it is," griped Evan. "It's too early for a churro but olive oil's fair game."

Emily clicked her tongue and joined Fran while the boys hung back in the middle of the wide walkway.

The last weekend of the festival had scrounged up a

sizable crowd. The ebb and flow of foot traffic battled off a breezy chill that rarely reached the city during the day. I couldn't remember a Christmas night with thicker jackets. Not that I personally owned one. I hadn't even layered up, leaving the house in a hurry this morning with my trademark tank.

Still, the weather was strangely quaint. It was nice to actually have seasons in Miami besides monsoon and gridlock.

Evan folded his arms and admired the girls. "They're glad you're back in town."

"We were away too long."

He flapped his lips. "Only a couple months. It was for the best. Things have been wild around here. And you saw the blood in Agent Bell's eyes."

I dipped my head. My absence couldn't be helped. I was just eager to get things back to normal as soon as possible.

"So I gotta head in in a couple of hours," he said. "It would be nice if my consultant had some new information for me."

"I'm afraid I don't have anything you can put in a report."

He groaned. John kneeled over a trail of ants at our feet.

"I found a grave in a potter's field. The soil was a match and there were signs of spellcraft. What there wasn't any sign of was a corpse."

"Ah, so your specialty then."

"It was old magic, unlike anything I've seen. And the choice of grave was strange."

"How so? A county cemetery like that is full of the poor and forgotten."

I recalled the toe impressions of the footprints. Corpses are often buried with shoes, but not always. Footwear was a luxury that most destitute dead men would forego.

"Usually santeros tap these old graves for bonework," I explained. "They need a skull for a ritual centerpiece, or a solid femur to carve a fetish. Even ground bone dust can—"

Evan's face was pale and full of disgust.

"Anyway, there was a box but the entire corpse was gone. That's in line with some sort of automaton, but the age of the coffin is concerning. There wouldn't be a lot of raw material to work with."

"So is it a zombie or not?"

"Not one I'm familiar with. Voodoo tends to focus on the living and freshly dead."

"Look what I got, Dad!"

Fran presented him with a skinny bottle of green oil. "What is it?" he asked.

"Avocado-chili."

"Yeah, but what's it for?"

"Eggs, tater tots, bacon." She shrugged. "Use your imagination, Dad."

Emily slipped her wallet into her bag as she rejoined us. "Your father has plenty of imagination, Fran. Just not when it comes to the kitchen."

They giggled as Evan muttered something about nothing being wrong with meat and potatoes. Emily took the bottle of olive oil, returned it to its fancy bag, and we resumed our pleasant stroll.

Fran was immediately on her phone again.

"That's it?" said Emily. "That's all the conversation this bottle of oil bought me?"

Evan snickered. "It beats talking about dead people."

"That reminds me," chimed Fran. "A new app called Everchat launched. Supposedly, people upload their consciousness to the cloud and stick around forever."

"I'm surrounded by enough dead things as it is, dear," I bemoaned. I was beginning to think the phone was a mistake.

Fran shrugged and moved on to the next distraction while our faces darkened.

"Elephant in the room," said Evan. "Is this situation another Manifesto? Are your Stygian witches behind this?"

I bit down. "They're gonna be *everyone's* Stygian witches soon enough. I have it on good authority they're looking into Miami real estate."

Emily's eyes widened. "Is that what you discovered on your wedding romp?"

"More like the after-party," I grumbled. "The stiges are hellions. Looking for a way in. After my encounter in the bowels of the Nether, I made a stop on the West Coast to visit a summoner I know."

"And?"

"And it's worse than I thought. The stiges are coercing silvan royalty, dealing with angels and jinns, and usurping devil kings. There are whole worlds out there I barely know about, and it's starting to spill over into our corner of the universe."

Fran lowered her phone. "Wait. Hell is real?"

Emily pressed her lips tight.

"It's a place I guess," I answered, not very convincingly. "It's pretty far away if that helps."

Her phone chimed and she immediately resumed her virtual conversation.

"So the witches send the Manifesto Killer," reasoned Evan, "put down a few magic types. Make dark deals with the Obsidian March. Make power plays in the underworld. And then what? You think this is more of the same?"

I gritted my teeth. "I wish I knew."

We paused as Fran perused a jewelry booth, phone momentarily at her side in testament to her ability to multitask. It just went to show, she was paying attention to her surroundings even when it didn't look like she was. She had a lot of the carefree eleven-year-old in her, but she was more than that. I just worried she would grow up too fast.

"Speaking of weddings," prefaced Emily in an encouraging tone, "what happened to your proposal? And don't tell me you canceled it because you lost the ring."

I sighed at the inevitable introduction of so-called sophisticated adult conversation. "It was more about losing the moment."

Sympathetic baby-blue eyes flashed my way. "What happened?"

"Life happened. I don't know. I'm gonna go ahead with the proposal. I just need a new plan."

Evan obliviously appraised me. "Where is Milena,

anyway? I'm surprised she isn't here."

I winced. "Under the weather. She didn't recover as fast as Kasper did."

"That's understandable," afforded Emily with a nod and a steadying hand on her husband's shoulder.

"Lemonade!" cried John.

"You already had juice," admonished Evan. "Drink your water."

Emily checked her bag with a start, and then looked from me to Evan. "Drat. I left it in the car. Why don't you take him to get it?" she asked. "You can pick up that churro you wanted," she quickly added.

"Score," he said. "I get cinnamon sugar while avoiding an awkward conversation. Sorry, Cisco." He grabbed John's hand and left me to the sharks.

I suddenly didn't know what to do with my hands or my lips. They twitched while I checked on Fran, seemingly bored with the jewelry offerings.

"Milena went through a lot," started Emily. "It might change things for a while."

"It might change things forever."

"Don't say that. She's a fighter."

"I'm not sure what's happening to her." I swallowed and almost left it at that, but then I admitted, "I don't want to add to her burden."

"Forget about the ceremony. Forget about the logistics." Emily grabbed my hands and smiled tenderly. "Think about each other."

I shook my head. "Sometimes, when we're just focused

on each other, it's like we're unstoppable. Nothing else matters, you know?" I chewed my lip. It wasn't easy coming clean to Em like this. After all, in our younger days we might've had a similar conversation.

"Build on those feelings," she suggested.

"Our feelings aren't the issue. There are very real—physical—complications happening with her. It's a big weight on her."

"Burdens are an inherent part of life and relationships. Have you considered that your proposal might lighten her load?"

I wasn't sure how to answer. The sentiment was nice, but this wasn't a fairy tale. Engagements are more than symbolic. They're real commitments that come with actual concerns. The truth was, I was afraid Milena was no longer sure she could make that commitment.

Fran bounced over and I was all too happy at her return. I disengaged Emily's hand and grabbed my daughter's.

"Where are we going?" she asked.

"Check this out."

I led her two booths down. A weathered Panamanian man sat between two tables piled high with leaves and roots. His eyes widened in recognition of me and I returned a nod. I had to be careful here. I didn't want anyone to know that Fran was my daughter or that would put her in danger. That part was easy, since even she didn't know. For the same reason, I also didn't want anyone to know she was an animist. So I trod lightly.

"How's my favorite root witch?" I joked with the man.

"Same shit, different day," he chortled.

Fran gazed peculiarly at the chopped lengths of plants stacked higher than her head. "What are these?"

"Nigel sells ingredients for restoratives, salves, you name it." I sidled up and grabbed a hunk of willow bark. "This is poisonous in the wrong doses, but can treat pain and inflammation when used correctly." I tracked my finger across the selection. "Aloe leaves for soothing balms. Mandrake roots for charms and hexes. Burdock for warding. If there's a Wiccan or santero in need, Nigel has them covered. Am I right?"

I turned to the root witch, who was suddenly decidedly less jovial. "You must get out of here, Cisco."

"What are you—"

"These are dangerous times. There's a price on your head."

I chuckled. "Tell me something I don't know. It's..." My eyes narrowed. "Did you drop a dime on me, Nigel?"

"How could you think that of me? I did no such thing." His eyes searched the distance until he pointed out his target. "She did."

The woman at the olive oil stand nervously averted her eyes. My chest rumbled in anger. "What did she do?"

Several bystanders beside our tent were rudely shoved away. "Cisco Suarez!" shouted one santero out of five. "You're coming with us."

The rest of the crowd took the hint and quickly evacuated.

Chapter 8

I bit down and put a solid step between the bad guys and Fran.

Johnny Red, despite utterly unoriginal branding, was a no-name santero crew leader. His people wore chicken-bone charms and staked their place on the magical ladder somewhere between hucksters and dabblers. Which didn't mean the freckled Cuban and his merry men could be completely ignored.

My eyes scanned the crowd. Many had fled during the initial panic, but others watched in rapt attention from a modest distance. I locked eyes with Emily behind a young couple.

The santeros eyed me hungrily, trading chuckles and boasts. They'd come after me before, and they must've been stubborn 'cause they were trying again. Knuckleheads, every one of them.

Johnny's work boots marched boisterously across the concrete. "I read the shells this morning," he declared, to the crowd as much as to me. "Today's a momentous day for Johnny Red."

Ugh. Did I sound like that when I referred to myself in the third person?

The crew leader faced his cohorts with raised arms. "Before long, this whole city will know my name."

The santeros cheered, too stupid to realize they were in over their heads.

Johnny rounded back to me, holding a length of bone as a teacher might point a pencil. "Tell me, isn't a day full of blessings the best time to finally take down Cisco Suarez?"

I winced as he announced my name before a slew of witnesses. This was out in the open. My face was plain as day. I suppose it was lucky he stopped short of calling me Shadow Man, if he was even smart enough to suspect it.

But so far, no harm, no foul. There were no weapons publicly visible. No accusations that couldn't be taken back. This could've been drama between a couple of quarreling alternative medicine booths, for all anyone knew. If I could just calm things down, this encounter would be a blip in everyone's day.

My daughter shoved ahead with hardened brows. "You can't hurt us, you losers."

I forced her behind me as Emily pushed ahead. I welled with pride at Fran's bravery, but it scared the shit out of me too. She was becoming a teenager too fast. "Think about what you're doing, Johnny," I warned. "This isn't smart."

He spat a loogie on the cement. "Don't get cocky because of before. The orishas are with us this time. You haven't seen their power."

"You know you're only supposed to invoke the orishas for good, right?"

"Getting rid of you *is* good. Now unless you want people to get hurt, I suggest you come with us with your tail between your legs."

I eagerly drew nearer in order to space myself from Fran. My movement was too quick, too thoughtless, and a few of the santeros flinched. They hadn't expected me to be so accommodating. Although none held what spectators would consider traditional weapons, they were all armed. Wands, feathers, bracelets.

I had to hand it to Johnny. He wasn't a complete idiot. He had come after me in public. In the middle of the day, sunlight bearing down and weakening my connection to the shadow. But he still had to know he was outmatched. After all, I had nontraditional weapons of my own.

"Why don't we take a walk to my truck?" insisted Johnny.

"Let's talk about it first," I countered.

"Ain't happening. Come with us or we let the orishas loose."

The sun brightened like it does when a large cloud moves on. I considered my options. Pulling my shotgun would be reckless in this crowd. In fact, any overt actions would be pinned to me if any of the witnesses were halfway reliable. Wouldn't Rita Bell just love pegging an unlicensed firearm on me?

But I could play with the shadows. The booth canopies

cast wide havens from the sun. The two santeros in the rear stood at the edge of one such shadow. The other three were in the sun, but a little reach with a dark tendril wasn't a problem. People might think they saw something weird, but if I kept the spellcraft subtle, it might slip by as a trick of the light.

Speaking of the light...

"What's this?" griped Johnny. The crew squinted against the brightening sun that seemed to focus on their faces. Emily, at their backs, held spread fingers in the air.

"Spellcraft!" barked one of his men. He threw a colorful parrot feather to his forehead and mumbled in a strange tongue.

The other santeros followed suit, including Johnny Red. They jerked and twitched and shook in a hypnotic display, casting spells in complete disregard of onlookers.

I flicked my wrist and the shadow tightened around the ankles of the two men in the rear. The spell was a simple one. The execution? Not so much. I had to really push things to get a firm grip. Emily's light display was fading my shadows past tangible levels.

It was just like my ex to work against my plans.

Johnny lurched awkwardly to the side and stood still, if stiff, mastering his orisha before the rest of his crew. It was talent like that that put him in charge. His eyes opened, now blood red, and he held his little bone up to his neck and pantomimed slitting his throat with a playful chuckle.

Instead of managing multiple tendrils of shadow, I pooled the Intrinsics into a single large kraken tentacle behind me. It coiled beneath the root witch's table, ready to strike.

"Human," said Johnny in a now higher-pitched voice, "you're in for it now." He took a menacing step forward.

A burst of gunfire opened his head like a watermelon. I dove to Fran and shoved her to the ground. The crowd screamed and scattered. The santero with the feather spun and identified the new threat between panicking parkgoers, only to be raked in the back by another stream of bullets.

Two men wearing gray camouflage and wielding AR-15s descended on the possessed santeros. As they approached from different vectors, it confused santero and onlooker alike. Panicked bystanders screamed and retreated in all directions, many charging right into the lines of fire. The animists had difficulty focusing on a target amid the chaos. The coordinated ambush was stunningly expeditious. It picked the santeros apart before they could regroup.

"Fran!" yelled Emily, nearly bowling me over to get to her daughter.

I stepped around them and out, carefully, into the fray. The light display had dispersed. The gunfire had abruptly stopped. Shadows tingled at my presence. Retreating screams could still be heard but they faded with distance. Very little activity remained in the immediate area. Five dead santeros lay ripped apart on the walkway.

I jerked my palms to the air as the men neared, guns pointed. Despite the paramilitary uniforms and gear, they wore no official badges or name tags. They weren't armed forces or civilian police. But their arms did sport a single patch: a red shield against a field of gray.

Which had me consider whether I was just rescued or kidnapped.

The men converged on the bodies. One swept the area, including me, for additional threats. The other one, a young white guy with a crew cut, jostled the santeros with his boot to make sure they were dead.

"Holy shit," he said. "We got 'em."

"Sure did," said the other, a black man with a fade. "But not all of them."

I kept my palms out to defuse the situation. "Wait a minute, guys. Thanks for the assist, but there aren't any more threats. Let the police take things from here."

"The Vanguard steps in when the police fail," recited the black man.

"The police," muttered the other. "We should bail."

"We still need to take out the witch."

He raised his gun.

There wasn't time to think, there wasn't time to reason, there wasn't time to analyze. All we could do was react.

Paint hissed from a can as Emily traced a protective circle around her huddle with Fran. I didn't even need to look to know they were safe.

As for me, I no longer had a choice. My skin was enchanted, not bulletproof but bullet resistant. I couldn't take on a pair of modified ARs in spitting range. The Helm of Awe tattoo on my palm blinked to life, turquoise light budding out into a rounded shield.

A single round exited the rifle, flying by me and

punching through the root witch's collarbone. He pitched to the ground.

The paramilitary men were caught between the dual reactions of satisfaction at a job well done and utter surprise at the bright flash of visible magic reflecting off their faces. My shield was more overt than the santero possession spells. Doubtless, based on their morphing expressions, more eye-opening than anything they'd ever seen in their entire lives.

It was the Shadow Man, prime-time news, in the flesh.

"He's one of them!" snarled the black man.

Both rifles twirled my way.

"Police!" shouted Evan. "Put down your—"

The white guy spun toward my friend. The kraken tentacle lunged, narrowly missing the nearer militia member but nailing the target. Crew cut slammed to the ground and nearly lost his rifle.

The other guy didn't waste a second. He opened fire on me and the bullets splashed against my shield. At the same time, Evan steadily advanced. Colt Diamondback rounds cut into my attacker's side, and he crumpled to the ground.

"Traitor!"

The guy wrapped in the shadow tentacle was down but not out. He swung his weapon around but Evan was faster. Two more gunshots ended the violence.

The two of us stood there, the bark of the Diamondback seeming to linger in the air. Slowly, Evan lowered his weapon. He'd been steadying his revolver with both hands, one of which now wielded a crushed half-eaten churro. John was parked five booths down, crying.

"Everyone okay?" asked Evan, relieved at the site of his unharmed wife and daughter. Emily broke the circle and sprinted for John.

I checked the root witch. "Nigel's dead." I surveyed the distance with a sneer. All the vendors had fled, including the olive oil lady who'd spurred on this violence. On the plus side, there were no paramilitary reinforcements, and not an eyewitness in sight.

"Look at that," said Evan sardonically. "A shitstorm you *didn't* cause."

My face sagged. "Ha, ha."

The cop in my friend took over. He assessed the scene and shook his head. "Eight dead. This is a mess."

"The santeros usually aren't this bold," I said.

"It's not them I'm worried about." He nodded toward the military men. "Guys like this, they don't congregate in twos. These are the radicals we've been seeing online. The militia that's been hoarding weapons for a coming war."

My throat constricted. "He said they fight when the police fail."

Emily returned to Evan with John, and Fran went in for a communal hug. Did it make me sentimental that I wanted to glom in with the lot of them too?

"You know what I think?" asked Evan dourly. "I think you should get out of here."

I tensed at the suggestion. And then, like clockwork, the sirens started in the distance.

Evan produced his phone. "This is a police matter," he asserted. "Nothing good can come from you being in the news again. Better to be one of hundreds who fled from the gunfire, and that's if they track you down at all."

I snorted. It didn't sound like me to run from a fight, but I got his point. Besides, if I knew how things worked, and I generally did, Special Agent Rita Bell wouldn't be far behind the caravan of officers.

Without explaining the sudden show of affection, I grabbed Fran in a big bear hug, relieved she was okay. Then I spun on my alligator boots and left them to it.

Chapter 9

"Get up."

I flung open the curtains, forcing the sunlight to fall over Milena's bed. Her hair was matted with sweat, and the blanket was on the floor. She wore an Outlaw Coffee T-shirt over her underwear, and it was impossible not to soften at the view. Baby got back.

The sweat was new. Normally I'd be concerned for her health, but the likely culprit was the thermostat. I found the heat set to a balmy seventy-five and shut it off. It was the afternoon and the condo was a sauna.

This is what happens when Miami dips into the sixties.

I put my hand on Milena's backside. "Get up."

She moaned, and I'd be lying if the noise didn't turn me on. "What are you doing here? You should've called."

"I did. Five times."

Milena had been using the under-the-weather excuse. I'd been using it for her too. Maybe there was something to that mentally, but physically she was fine. We'd checked her out with the doctor, we'd checked her out with spellcraft. She even passed a WebMD quiz with flying colors. Milena was the specimen of perfect health...

Only she wasn't. She'd been sitting out events, self isolating. I might even go so far as to say she was depressed. But hey, I'd agreed to support her any way she wanted, and, for now, this was it. Give her encouragement. Give her space. And be confident she still loved me.

She rolled to her back and beckoned with her hand before pointing to her cheek. See that? Eyes still closed but she needed me. I sat beside her, kissed her cheek, and we smiled at each other.

"What's so important you gotta disturb my beauty sleep?"

"If you get any more beautiful I'm gonna shrivel under your gaze."

A single eye opened and lasered onto me. Luckily it was just a warning shot.

"Ouch," I said, pulling out my phone to explain it with video. A picture's worth a thousand words, but I could give her thirty frames per second.

The news report started with a wide angle shot of the Holiday Village aftermath. The area was cordoned off, police went about their work, and multiple bodies were covered. None of those facts had prevented the press from gathering the relevant juicy details:

A troupe of santeros incited the carnage by offering a ceremonial blessing. Two militants in camouflage took offense and gunned them down in the middle of the performance. Possibly race or gang related. The incident carried undertones of the Manifesto slayings, as the militants also killed a vendor of fringe medicinal herbs. Luckily, an off-duty police officer and hometown hero witnessed the attack and took swift, decisive action.

Evan was gonna rub that moniker in my face. But credit where it was due.

The race and gang angles were bunk. That would be evident when the media uncovered the identities of the shooters. The root witch observation, though, was a bull's-eye. In the coming days, the whole city would know those people were killed because they were practitioners.

The summary shots transitioned to closeups of individuals describing what they saw. The press had already scrounged up witnesses. I tensed when one mentioned the involvement of a well-known local trickster. Luckily, it wasn't me but the victim, Johnny Red. Or rather, they reported his real name as Jonathan Perv.

Suddenly the need for a nickname made sense.

And, in retrospect, ol' Johnny Red turned out to be a good hand at reading his cowries. He'd been absolutely right: today the whole city learned his name.

Somehow, Cisco Suarez escaped mention. At least so far. I could only hope no one with more information would step forward.

I returned the phone to my pocket. "The santeros were after me. You might not be safe."

Her blink was weighed down by fatigue and disinterest. "They're dead."

"The riflemen saw my magic."

"They're dead too."

I pulled away from her and the bed. "Can we not pick at technicalities right now? My name could still turn up. Other animists or militia members might've seen me. I'm not saying we're under attack this very minute, but we need to take sensible precautions."

Her skepticism vanished and she sat up, taking my concern seriously. "Fine," she relented. "Hunker down at your penthouse fortress?"

"You got it."

She puffed up her pillow and collapsed back onto it. "Here's my deal. You let me sleep for another hour or two. When I get up, I'll pack some things and see you before the sun goes down. Take it or leave it."

I sighed. It was exactly what I wanted but on a more relaxed timeline. Probably the best I was gonna get. I narrowed my eyes, offered my pinkie, and locked it with hers.

There was no reneging now.

Chapter 10

Darcy worked the counter of Outlaw Coffee & Colada wearing skinny jeans and a non-company shirt. She hustled between serving a surprise afternoon rush and training the new employee. I didn't know Clarence well. He was a thin kid with glasses, quiet but studious. They were so busy, Kasper and I skipped the counter and grabbed a table in the back.

"Let's make this quick," he said. "I still have a load of bullets to etch."

I bit down. Kasper was a talented scribe. He'd inked my tattoos, he'd outfitted my penthouse with protective wards, and now he'd marked up a batch of ammunition for the Haitians.

"I can't believe you agreed to cross that line," I said. "You were always so adamant about only selling defense."

He gave me a knowing nod. "You ink wards and everybody loves you. Sure, you might help protect some enemies, but you protect everyone. I've sold shields, armor, the whole nine yards. And I've never had a complaint."

I shook my head glumly. "You sure there's no getting out of this? Once you go into selling offense, there won't be so many smiles. One of your products is bound to get turned on you."

The tattoo artist scoffed. "This wasn't a measured business decision, Cisco. It was the price for Chevalier's help with Milena. She was in a bad way when we brought her to him. Without the Bone Saints, Milena never would've made it to the silvans in time for proper healing."

"I know," I grumbled. "It just... You're a tank selling anti-tank artillery, man."

"Which is why this is a one-time deal. I ain't no weapons dealer, but I'll do what I need to protect my friends."

I smiled weakly at him. The old biker was an artist with ink. Apparently he was an artist with laying down guilt trips too.

"Speaking of which," he said, "how is our girl? I haven't seen her in a while."

"She's fine. After that business today, she's gonna be staying over. So maybe, you know, don't wear her hats."

He shrugged. "Done deal. I should probably hurry and tidy up the place. Is she coming now?"

"Nah, she wants to catch up on sleep before she swings by. You have time."

"Hmm. I suppose she keeps strange hours with her work."

There was more to it than that but I was desperate to change the subject. Luckily I had plenty on my mind.

"What say we get straight to business?"

I slid my phone across the table and he took a minute to scroll through the picture gallery.

"These symbols," he said with some concern. "They look like spellcraft but I've never seen them before."

"Not even their style?" I was hoping the scribe could give the investigation a frame of reference, somewhere that I could start. He'd come through with similar requests before.

"I'm sorry, broham. I see the twelve, but the adornment is wrong." His eyes strained at the zoomed-in pixels. Unlike my shadow sight, the runes weren't nicely highlighted in the photographs. "These others don't look like numbers at all. Are these all of them?"

"Unfortunately. Most were already disturbed beyond recognition." I didn't mention the overeager zombie dog.

Kasper grimaced. "Tough break."

He spent more time studying the limited collection, especially focusing on the photo Jensen had sent me of the glyph at the crime scene. It was the only clear image of the set, taken with proper lighting and a real camera. But even that was imperfect as it had been carved into the flesh of a squirming victim.

"About the best I can say is these runes belong to the same family," he concluded. "They're written with different instruments on different mediums, so it's impossible to determine if they're by the same hand, but the script is similar enough. They're related."

That much confirmed my hunch, which was entirely expected. Kasper didn't have anything new to contribute so far, but it was only a matter of time. Sometimes stuff came easy, and sometimes it took hours of careful study. Kasper knew the drill.

"It'll take some time," he said. "Something this foreign, and that other thing needs doing today. I'm meeting Jean-Louis tomorrow."

I winced because my next request was a big ask. "Is it possible to wrap them both up today?"

His eyes hardened.

"Look who the cat dragged in," Darcy remarked as she approached the table.

Kasper and I blinked at her before turning to each other. He pointed to me, then himself. I just shrugged.

"I'm talking to you, old timer," she clarified, making Kasper's white beard twist into a frown. "Your shift starts soon. Does your presence mean you're actually gonna work today?"

A chuckle escaped my lips and the biker took an indignant tone. "I wish I could, but it appears, on top of being whored out to Little Haiti, I'm needed elsewhere."

I watched his tantrum with amusement. Darcy was at a loss for words so I explained. "Kasper's working on a special project."

"Two," he corrected.

"Two special projects. I don't think he's gonna make it today."

"That works," appeased Darcy. "Clarence asked about picking up extra shifts."

"You see?" I decided. "Everyone's happy."

Kasper grumbled at his failure to find appropriate sympathy. He sent the images to his phone, abruptly excused himself, and stoically marched through the door leading into the building's lobby.

Darcy conspiratorially leaned onto the table, whisked her bangs out of her eyes, and asked, "What's his problem?"

"Drama queen," I answered. "But he's not the problem. We've got a Code Red."

"Is that bad?"

I scrunched my eyes at her. "Of course it's bad. It's red."

"I mean, is it grading-on-a-Cisco-scale bad or just normal-everyday bad?"

I sighed. "When is it ever normal with us?"

"Point."

She pushed away and hit the espresso machine, and I transferred to a spot at the bar. The familiar sounds of the grinder, pressure pump, and steam wand made my mouth water. Darcy whipped the sugar like a pro, and within a minute I had a warm frothy *cafe con leche* in front of me.

The young woman dropped her elbows on the counter. "So no yellow, no orange—we're going straight to Code Red now?"

"You know what? I'll scale it back to an orange if you'll drop it."

She grinned. "Code Orange dropped. What's up?"

I told her about the zombie, the santeros, and the militia. "So I don't know where you're staying these days," I continued, "but it might be best to close ranks and take a bed upstairs."

As I sipped my coffee, the gears were turning. "You think animists are in danger. This is another serial killer situation."

I beamed at her proudly. "Look at you with the baseless speculation. You're all growed up."

"It's not that baseless. I knew something was up. Simon's in town."

That... put a damper on things. It shouldn't have, but it did. Part of it was Darcy's sullen tone. She hadn't left the Society on bad terms, but leaving at all was a break.

"How do you feel about that?" I asked.

She hiked a shoulder. "It's not like Simon and I were besties. He was my boss, but he barely knew me. He wasn't even my recruiter."

My lips pressed tight. That distinction was reserved for Shen. He was her friend too, or he had been. He'd tucked tail and left town, leaving his protégé on her own. I still had a bone to pick with him about that.

Not sure what to say, I attempted to casually check my phone. Only it wasn't so casual.

"Expecting someone?"

I shook my head. "Not really. I'm just surprised Simon didn't give me a heads up. He was my lawyer, you know."

"You fired him."

"Still, it's professional courtesy."

"Maybe you're not that important to him."

"I'm important to everybody. I thought you knew that."

She peeped in laughter. "Oh, yeah? Why, because you think I have a high school crush on you?"

I picked up my coffee mug and spun around to rest my back on the bar. "Nah. I'm practically married."

"You're not even engaged."

"I'm practically engaged."

My phone buzzed.

"Ah, you see that?" I took a gulp of Heaven and triumphantly set down my mug. "Your ex-boss wants to keep me in the loop after all."

Only when I checked, it was Fran calling from her new cell phone. It was nice to see the person who gifted it to her was finally worthy of receiving a call.

"Hey there," I answered.

"Cisco," she said in relief. "My dad's not answering the phone, and my mom says not to worry, but..."

I tensed and stepped away from the bar. "What is it?"

"There's been a strange car outside our house all afternoon. Mom says it's nothing, but I can tell when she's lying."

"Get in your best hiding spot. I'll be there in five." I hung up. "It's Fran. I have to go."

"Hold up," said Darcy. "She in trouble?" Despite the age difference, the two had become fast friends and sparring partners.

I shook my head and went for the door.

"I'm coming," she said. Darcy leapt over the counter. "Clarence," she called. "You're in charge of the store."

The new guy stiffened. He'd been my employee for all of two weeks and preferred to melt into the background. "Alone? But what do I do if someone wants to talk to the manager?"

"You're the manager-on-duty, doofus. Do whatever you want."

Clarence blinked in trepidation and looked at me.

"Hey," I said, "I just own the place."

We pushed outside and joined Scout in the Firebird.

Chapter 11

The silver sports car veered through the side streets of Brickell, Darcy and I determined but grim. There might even have been a little rage in there. The thought of anyone messing with Fran and Emily was a total body takeover.

Which was a completely expected reaction from a father. Truth be told, Darcy's laser focus surprised me a little. Not that I'd call the teenager unreliable, but she could be aloof at times. Darcy was a loner, not out of selfishness but survival instinct. She'd been on her own much of her life. To see her care about someone, be protective over her, was almost familial.

Darcy calmly clenched and unclenched her fists between deep breaths. Her Society combat training was kicking in, and she was ready. People were always most dangerous when they had something worth fighting for.

The wide tires screeched through the final turn, painting lines across the asphalt. Emily stood across the street from her house with her hands raised. A slight reflective quality marred her person, like a glare on a mirror. She was running her mirage-like defenses, shifting the light and, therefore, shifting her visible position.

Which meant danger was near.

The Firebird fishtailed and our doors were open before we skidded to a stop. The back wheel bumped the curb and my open door shoved back into me. By comparison, Darcy practically flew out the opposite side. As I pushed the door open again, Scout excitedly trampled over me on his way out.

I sighed. We were gonna need to work on that exit.

Emily had marched toward a shaded area of tree cover, but the commotion of our arrival spun her around. As I finally made it out of the car, I spotted the parked Lincoln with limo tints.

Instead of pacifying Emily, my presence emboldened her. She turned to the bushes separating two properties and, in broad daylight, lit her fist with a glowing beam of light.

Scout and I charged forward. Darcy, ahead of us, paused warily. The dog rushed past Emily and barked at the bushes. A figure stirred within. The white witch readied her spell.

"Gotcha!" cried Darcy, facing the entirely wrong way.

I spun around. In my haste to stop Emily, someone had attempted to attack from behind. Darcy brandished her wooden fetish of Hecate at a heavily muscled man, pinning him in place with a quiver of her wrist.

"Everybody stop," I ordered.

Scout obediently ceased barking, but the others were a tougher crowd. Emily just barely held back her spear. Darcy kept the pressure on, unmoving yet concentrating on holding her opponent tight.

"Nobody..." I said slowly, "do... anything."

The beam of pure light in Emily's hand danced and sparked, but it didn't fly. Which was a start.

"Come on out, Trinh," I called out. "You should know better."

The vampire sidestepped from behind the bush. Slowly. With her hands in the air. "She means to strike, Cisco."

"She won't."

Emily blinked back frustrated exasperation. "You know them?"

"I know them." I gulped, dreading the earful I'd get later. Behind me, Lago strained against the telekinetic witch's magic. It wouldn't do him much good. "Darcy, you can release him. They're... friends."

Trinh snorted. "You make the word sound painful."

"They're vampires," warned Darcy.

"They are," I agreed.

We stood in mixed sunlight so they couldn't shift to their monstrous forms, but they had no need to. They meant no harm.

Darcy pursed her lips, shrugged, and lowered the statue to her side. Lago's weight returned to the ground, and everyone stood still for a tense moment.

"Emily," I prodded.

She jerked her head at the crackling magic in her hand. Then she eyed the vibrant neighborhood she called home. The brilliant magic extinguished before anyone nearby took notice.

Lago grunted. "We weren't going to hurt anyone."

The immediate danger was averted, but I was still afraid of attracting eyeballs. We weren't the most inconspicuous crew around. Trinh and Lago wore black tactical gear, except...

"Lago," I scolded, "would it kill you to put a shirt on, just once?"

His pecs momentarily flexed. "Then no one would see my tattoo." The traditional Samoan sleeve ran down his full arm and would've been hard to miss, shirt or no.

"What is this?" demanded Emily, whirling her anger toward me. "Why are they here?"

Trinh's sharp expression was only outdone by her tone. "We're helping."

"How?!?"

I took a breath and guessed. "After what happened at Bayfront Park, they're watching your house."

"In case anyone seeks reprisal against your hero cop," Trinh confirmed.

Emily glared at just about everybody involved except the dog. "How was I supposed to know that?"

"You know now," I pacified. I wanted to bring everyone a step closer, to make this less of a scene, but they weren't there yet.

The white witch shook her head. "Do I need to remind you what a vampire did to me and my sister? To you?"

"Upirs aren't asanbosams."

"Okay, upirs then. The ones who kidnapped my

daughter."

"That was the Obsidian March," said Lago with a defensive grunt.

Darcy chuckled to lighten the mood and strolled closer. "Come on, it's not like they could hurt Fran anyway."

"Darcy..." I warned. She was trying to help but was doing the opposite. It wouldn't do to go around mentioning my daughter's spellcraft ability. Trinh watched the exchange with attentive eyes.

"They're not welcome here," asserted Emily. "I don't trust them."

"Do you trust *me*, Em?" I asked, moving in and placing a calming hand on her arm. "Because they're not a danger to you."

She scowled in our general direction, which was better than an outright rejection.

"Do me a favor," I said in a lowered voice. "Get back to the house. Fran's worried."

Emily's gaze darted to the top-floor window where the girl was avidly watching the confrontation. Her daughter's presence seemed to surprise her.

"Fine," she decided, "but you haven't heard the last of this."

I sighed. I knew. Still, it was a huge relief when Emily headed back across the street to her house.

"You two are very... familiar," jabbed Trinh, watching the dog as she approached. "Don't tell me you're hot for hero cop's wife."

I snorted. "You know I'm engaged, right?"

"You're not engaged."

"I'm *practically* engaged. Jeez, what's with the wedding police today?"

Darcy laughed. "Us ladies like to point out when a hot guy is still available."

"Please," scoffed Lago. "As if a human could please Trinh." The vampires chuckled and Lago laid a kiss on her cheek.

I shook my head, refusing to play in any of their vampire games. "Look, guys, I appreciate the sentiment, but you're not needed here."

"It wasn't a favor," pointed out the femme fatale.

Which I knew. They were soldiers, doing as they were told. Taking things out on them would miss the point.

"All the same, you think you could back off the animist who specializes in light magic, something you might recall is anathema to your kind?"

Lago shook his head. "No can do." He blinked at the dog avidly watching them.

"At least don't be such stooges about it. Who watches a house from across the street? Can you be any more obvious?"

"The intention is to be seen," explained Trinh.

"Just give the house some space. Park on the corner of the street, all right?" I backed away to the street and Darcy fell in line. "All right?"

Lago frowned. "Your dog's not following you."

"That's 'cause you didn't agree to my terms yet."

"He's not breathing either."

I snorted. It was disconcerting the vampire could so easily see past my charms, but I didn't show my surprise. "Scout's long past breathing," I warned.

Lago sneered at the animal, likely assessing how best to dismantle it if necessary. Trinh's playful fingers tickled his shoulder. "We'll watch the house from the corner. With any luck, it will instill any troublemakers with a false sense of confidence." She grinned at the thought of dealing with them.

I turned and crossed the street.

"Your dog," called Lago.

I put the silver whistle to my lips and blew. Scout sprinted over before I was fully across, wagging his tail like he hadn't been seconds away from tearing the flesh of his enemies. Trinh and Lago were friends, but they were battle-worn vampires who respected strength.

I was half surprised Emily had left the front door unlocked, but then how would she bitch me out if she didn't let me in first? Darcy innately sensed the impending dressing down and waited outside with the dog. I found Emily upstairs with Fran. She was still visibly upset so I started by giving my daughter a hug.

"You did a great job by calling me and staying inside like I asked."

She accepted the compliment with a shrug. "Yeah, well, that's because I got reamed by my parents for sticking up for you at the Holiday Village. They don't understand the point of our training."

I eyed her sternly. "Neither do you, apparently, so I'm

gonna pile on. You can't ever do what you did in front of that crowd, standing tough and openly announcing your power."

She drew away and crossed her arms. "You're ganging up on me too?"

"I am."

"I can nullify powerful spellcraft now. Why can't I stick up for you?"

"Because these people aren't coming at us with spells. They were armed with rifles. Your magic is no good against bullets."

The harsh reality angered her. I switched my tone from admonishment to supportive.

"Fran, every single animist in the world worries about their defenses first. History is full of practitioners being burned or drowned or buried alive. Knowledge is the first barrier, because people can't act on what they don't know. And if they knew what you could do, it would scare them. Your power would scare a lot of animists too. Your spellcraft would only make you a target."

Fran pouted instead of going with a snappy rejoinder. She was a bright kid who learned fast.

"He's right," joined Emily in a solemn voice. "This Vanguard, they're zealots. After the presence they've built on social media, it was only a matter of time before something like this happened. I know you're not a baby, Francesca, but you'll always be *my* baby, and you're grounded until this is resolved."

Her eyes crinkled. "Really?"

Emily hugged her daughter. "And I am too. With your dad swamped at work, I'll be right here beside you. We don't need a vampire protection detail. We'll look out for each other."

I was pleased with them taking things in stride. Plus, Em and I being in agreement about Fran softened her anger over the upir fiasco. Sometimes parents need to band together and ignore small trifles in pursuit of the greater good.

"Any word on Evan?" I asked, trying not to interrupt the moment but capitalizing on the mention of him.

"He's stretched thin," Emily answered, still clutching her daughter. "His team has been so focused on the Obsidian March, they hadn't yet gotten a handle on the militia situation. And apparently it's worse than everyone thought."

Oops. The DROP team was meant to assess high level risks to Miami's five political districts. The only thing today's bloodbath proved was that the DROP team had *dropped* the ball.

Man, that joke will never get old. Where was Evan when I wanted to give him a hard time?

But laughs aside, I had a big part in this. Ironically, it had been my urging that pushed Evan onto the Obsidian March, and here I was defending a pair of vampires outside their house. This was turning into a complicated stew, and the only thing for it was to take it one ingredient at a time and set it to a simmer. Anything faster was liable to burn down the kitchen.

Chapter 12

Every hearty stew headlines meat and potatoes. For this particular Christmastime blend, the meat is the necromancer in Miami and whatever he brought with him. They're the main act, what everyone's really here for. That said, the potatoes are a just-as-vital counterbalance. More numerous but relegated to a supporting role, the spuds will be placeholders for our militia members.

Then you've got the usual suspects. The cops serve as the dependable onions. You can't ignore their contribution to a dish. Though in Rita Bell's case, she might be an especially bitter garlic. Let's call the santeros and other street gangs the carrots, celeries, and so on. You get the picture.

Where a stew gets interesting, though, is once it gets going. You no longer need to subscribe to any hard-and-fast recipe. You're free to mix and match as you like. Heck, half the time you might not know the next ingredient until you run across it deep in your pantry. And each is integral to the whole.

The broth, of course, is what makes the stew a stew. It's the part that ties the whole shebang together. With broth you tweak it, season it, try to guide it in a general direction, but you never really know how it'll turn out with a new recipe. The broth is the essence of everything combined, surpassing the sum of its parts. Sometimes the ingredients and portions work out and... sometimes they don't. Even the best chef can only make educated guesses when using a new set of ingredients. Beyond that it's just a matter of cooking and tasting.

Hungry yet?

It would be presumptuous to assume there was any single chef in charge of this meal, especially so if I presumed it was me. Maybe the chef is God, or maybe the world is just a bunch of random stews constantly boiling over and intermixing, with no one in control. Things certainly seem that way sometimes.

That said, I wouldn't be Cisco Suarez if I didn't allow myself *some* measure of conceit. So when it comes to me, I'll do my damnedest to be the ladle, the tool that's going to dip into every ounce of this stew, stirring, scooping—and, yes, seasoning and tasting like a chef—until everything's cooked exactly to my liking.

Which meant it was time to address a few more seasonings. I dropped Darcy back at the coffee shop and drove on a few blocks to the chic headquarters of Clan Beaumont: the contemporary jazz steakhouse, Carbon.

Scout growled at the entrance and I was beginning to

suspect he didn't like vampires much. Although the restaurant wasn't yet open for dinner, I was couth enough to resist towing a grumbling dog into a fine-dining establishment. I left him on the sidewalk and pushed through the unlocked door, surprised to find Beaumont's back table empty. I supposed even upir crime bosses needed to stretch their bloodless legs every now and then.

The hair on my neck prickled as I experienced a momentary feeling of displacement. Or rather, I felt out of place more than usual in the Beaumont den. Maybe it was seeing the restaurant, for all intents and purposes, empty. Sure, a few employees busily prepared the dining room, but they ignored me and I ignored them. The restaurant was both unsettling and unsettled because it missed its host.

Beaumont was an attentive businessman and was never far away. I strolled into the kitchen, alligator boots carefully stepping on freshly washed rubber mats. A man stacked boxes from a walk-in freezer while another checked a window of dry-aged beef. They were taught well, focusing only on the food and never giving strange visitors like me a second glance. Between the sounds of their labor, from somewhere out of sight, I caught the muffled basso of someone speaking.

My eyes fixed on the steps descending into the wine cellar. I knew Beaumont, and the man liked his wine. As I took a step toward my new destination, a light hand tickled my bare shoulder.

I spun around and shoved the person away, but she was quicker than I was. Tutti recoiled, swatted my blow aside, and pressed into me, shoving my back against the sous station and lightly panting cold air on my cheek.

"As I live and breathe," she drawled, exaggerating her southern accent with an also-exaggerated swell of her chest. She was a waif of a thing but knew how to flaunt what she had.

She was also a deadly upir, daggerlike obsidian claws only a thought away. One hasty move and she could cut me up good. Which was the crux of what made vamps so deadly. Give me a dozen of them with guns and out in the open any day of the week over a single one in close quarters. And these quarters were provocatively close. Let's just say, with her chest pressed against mine, I now knew she was a fan of risque piercings.

Tutti cocked her head as her twin pigtails wagged. They were dyed pink today, and she was inexplicably dressed in a schoolgirl outfit with a red plaid skirt barely large enough to serve as an effective napkin.

"How ya doin', mister?" she asked with a hungry wink, and I wasn't sure if she was fixing to seduce me or eat me.

"I'd be better if you got off me," I said flatly.

"Would you settle for getting you off?" she giggled mischievously.

"I didn't say that. I don't want any part of you."

Her lashes fluttered. "Ah, but there is a *part* of you that wants me, isn't there?"

She squeezed her hips to mine, and I was thankful upir mental compulsions were too weak to work on me. I was having enough trouble with the physical part.

"What's the matter?" she asked with a melodramatic pout. "Your sad girlfriend not putting out anymore?"

I grabbed her wrists to keep her black fingernails at bay and twisted her to the side. She gasped playfully. Instead of fighting my push she went with it, twirling around. The frills of her skirt fanned into the air and revealed the soft flesh underneath. She bent over, stretched her hands and ear onto the stainless steel kitchen island, and planted her ass into my crotch.

"Oh, but we could have so much fun!" she moaned.

Despite my best efforts (and my personal animosity towards Tutti in particular), I couldn't help but wonder what vampires were like in the sack. But I'd flirted with danger, quite literally, in the past. Mermaids, dragons... The whole lot were more trouble than they were worth.

The thought was fully formed before I realized the dismissal quite possibly applied to Milena now. I grew angry. At Tutti's games, at the fact her dry humping was actually a turn on, but mostly at myself.

I vanished into a puff of black shadow, traversed to the opposite side of the kitchen island, and materialized resting a shotgun against the crown of Tutti's head.

"You mention Milena again," I growled, "and I ruin your dye job." The headshot wouldn't kill an upir, but it sure would sting.

The vampire's prurient expression tightened into a scowl, and she pushed up from the counter. Carefully.

"And I thought you could be a little fun..." She harrumphed and went with pouty eyes, though her pupils were glued to the barrel of my shotty.

"I'm having fun," I innocently remarked.

She huffed and leaned on the same sous station she'd ambushed me at. "Whatever. He's downstairs if you want him so bad."

"And you?" I prodded.

Her scowl deepened. "Were just leaving."

She marched to the door without a twirl of a pigtail. The kitchen staff had disappeared into the back and, despite my apprehensions, I lowered the shotgun and returned it to the shadows.

By now Beaumont knew I was here. It wouldn't do to approach him armed so I took my attitude instead and stomped loudly into the basement. Leverett Beaumont waited amid his bottles with pocketed hands riding up his white dinner jacket.

"The wine cellar is for private business," he said flatly.

"Good," I said, trying to ignore the shaky vibes I'd been feeling since I walked into the place. "We have business."

"Oh?" The restaurateur's expression was neither interested nor apathetic. "Usually those I do important business with dress the part."

I glanced at my ripped tank and scuffed jeans. "That entirely depends on their area of expertise, I'd imagine."

"Touché. I apologize for my paramour."

"Tutti? I can deal with her. But I have to say, I don't know why you keep her around."

His thin lips pressed into a smile. "She's a mass of hot air that needs a release valve every now and then. It's a matter of control."

"It's a vain power play that's gonna bite you in the ass, maybe literally. Assuming you're not into that sort of thing."

"Power is what she responds to, Cisco. A life in the Obsidian March has instilled the simplest of desires into her: that of survival."

"Whatever."

I had to remind myself that, while Clan Beaumont didn't prey on humans and participate in the countless horrors of the larger Obsidian March, they were still a bunch of monsters from the underworld. The man wore a suit and hair gel and a plastic smile, but civilized society had an entirely different meaning to him.

And maybe it had nothing to do with biology or upbringing and everything to do with his current position in life. I didn't know too many crime bosses who succeeded without a domineering personality.

Leverett Beaumont pulled his hands from his pockets and crossed them. "You're here about the militia incident."

I shrugged my head. "Nah, they're the potatoes. I'm here about the meat."

The vampire eyed me strangely.

"There's a necromancer in town. I'm hunting the thing that killed Quentin Capshaw."

A curious eyebrow twitched ever so slightly as he processed the new information. But Beaumont caught on quick. "Ah, I wasn't aware you were working with the DROP team on his case."

"You don't have connections in the department?"

"Not the ones I need, apparently. But I have my eye on a rising star. You could say he's a friend of a friend."

My face darkened and I took a step toward him. "Evan Cross is off-limits. You approach him and you cross the line. Besides, he's not dirty, and him and his family aren't partial to vamps."

Beaumont didn't like threats, but he also strove to be the coolest head in the room at all times. He didn't go red-faced at name-calling and shows of disrespect, though you could bet he'd get even later.

For my part, I didn't throw around insults to prop up my manhood, I did it to protect me and mine. Beaumont knew this and even respected it.

"Your worries are unfounded," he assured me. "I only meant that our mutual cooperation can benefit from your friend's insights. Your association with him is all the interaction I need. I would never, as you say, approach him."

"Yet a couple of your most elite soldiers are sitting on their house."

He shrugged. "Protection comes with hidden costs. I don't need to remind you that, unlike the santeros, mafias, and Nether marches, the militias are not proper criminal organizations. They're unlikely to abide by my protective umbrella over Brickell, hence the necessity for boots on the ground."

"Mysterious cars ghosting them is bound to end with trouble. It almost did. Not to mention they have little kids. You're creeping them out. Can't you give them notice next time?"

He snickered. "You would have vampires, who they hate, knock on their front door? Wouldn't that increase the chances of violence?"

I glowered. He was right. Emily would kill me if I invited vamps to her stoop. "So give me a heads up then. That's how this works, right? You and I share relevant information?"

He looked around the empty cellar and grinned at my turning his point back on him. "Cisco, you're protective of them. They're the family you no longer have."

I shifted uncomfortably under his astute observation.

"It's commendable," he continued, "but I'm watching out for them too. That said, your request is a fair one." His hands spread open. "I agree. From now on, you'll get a call before I take overt action regarding their protection."

I didn't immediately respond. His acceptance came too easily. It wasn't that Beaumont didn't respect our working relationship, but I'd expected him to lecture me over the logistics of defending Brickell. In his eyes, there was only one boss here. One that was used to doing things his way.

Still, Beaumont had made concessions in the past that signified my value to his organization. This could've been more of the same. I nodded and offered a grunt in thanks, much to his amusement, and decided it best to move on.

"So about Quentin," I pivoted.

He dipped his head. "Your enemies have a habit of dying, don't they?"

"Quentin wasn't my enemy. He didn't know anything." While Leverett listened to my words, he stared intently.

"Wait a minute. You don't think I had anything to do with that."

"It just seems peculiarly coincidental, is all. But it's not necessary to convince *me* otherwise."

His emphasis implied that others would be less reasonable about their assumptions. My hopes for this conversation began to dwindle, but for another reason entirely. "You don't know any more than I do about what happened."

"Correct. The destiny of a minor celebrity concerns me little. Especially since prominent members of my organization had nothing to do with it." He nodded my way.

Beaumont was referring to me, as in, before our conversation, he'd believed it a distinct possibility that I was Quentin's killer. Just like the rumors on the street: the Shadow Man did it. What did it say about me that I associated with a person who thought I might be a murderer yet only seemed to care for the repercussions?

Then again, ours was often the business of killing. Maybe Beaumont's outlook wasn't as cold-blooded as it appeared. Maybe he simply trusted that if I *had* killed Quentin, there was a reason.

"I don't imagine you have any connections in the matter that I don't have?" I idly asked.

He grinned. "When it comes to matters of spellcraft, you *are* my connection."

Just as I'd thought. "What about neighboring criminal enterprises? You have to coordinate with them from time to time."

"You could call it a network," he allowed, "but please don't call it coordination. Yes, I communicate with various members of Miami's underworld, but the various factions don't ask many questions so as to mask their blind spots. If they ask, they admit to being in the dark, to having a gap in knowledge. In a world of showing strength, asking for information is akin to trading a favor at best, and admitting weakness at worst."

"I got it," I said. "Just FYI then, I'll be kicking over some headstones in the city. Seeing what else I can dig up."

I gave him a brief rundown of my leads, and while I didn't want to indebt myself to him by asking for said favors, he assured me that he'd convey any related information he came across.

As far as stews went, it wasn't a lot of exotic seasoning—more along the lines of your basic salt and pepper—but hey, there's a reason those are the staples. Ninety percent of the time, they're the basics that get the job done.

Chapter 13

I spent the evening at the cookhouse, trying to get a fix on the thrall loose in my city, knowing the whole while it was a long shot. Locator spells are a finicky business. On a small enough scale, almost any animist can pull one off. It simply takes an intimacy with the Intrinsics. The stronger the magic you want to find, the more of it that's left behind, and the easier it is to follow.

But that concept doesn't scale across the urban sprawl of the Miami metro.

Things like dowsing rods or snatching a hair from someone's head and forever after having a fix on their location—as far as I knew, these were fairy tales.

So I examined the links of the tiny toy chain every way I could think of. Shadow sight didn't reveal any enchantments, at least none that lingered. The metal wasn't useful as an anchor in a summoning ritual. Even the local ghosts had nothing to say.

The cemetery dirt was likewise useless, a side effect of

the magic rather than anything driving it. Something had come out of the ground, and the dirt had come with it.

The last tactic was both the most promising yet the least feasible. Promising because, at some point, I would almost definitely find it. When a necromancer raises a minion from the dead, an inextricable link is created from master to servant. This tether is magic itself. It can be detected, subverted, and extinguished. A common way for practicing necromancers to hone their craft is to simultaneously fight over a single zombie, stealing it back and forth until one dominates all others enough to seize unrivaled control.

Outright theft of a minion from someone who knows what they're doing is next to impossible, but I was focused merely on detection. While it's a surmountable challenge, plenty of obstacles remain. Minions can go a long time without an active link. On top of that, if you're not within throwing distance, you're not getting a whiff of walking dead. And since this thing wasn't tarrying around my Everglades boathouse, it was invisible to me.

For now.

Scout's hackles rose and a grim silence fell over the night. Hordes of crickets quieted all at once, and I was blanketed with a familiar yet unsettling presence.

"Been a while," I grated, idly digging through the cemetery soil with an ornamental knife.

The Spaniard drifted in the air behind me, worn leather scraping the wind, desiccated fingers peeking through holes in weathered gloves. His heavy helmet and breastplate were dull with age and marked by use, and his dirty skull had long shed its fleshy matter. Simmering coals of fire marked his eyes, but there was no malice in what expression I could make out.

"Look who decided to grace me with his presence," I added.

The old conquistador ignored my snide remark. He didn't do sarcasm. Scout remained acutely alert, but as my thrall he understood the Spaniard was an ally. Or at least he wasn't a threat to me. He was a wraith, but he was also my great great greatcetera grandpa.

"I could've used you yesterday," I said more artlessly. "The dog and I sniffed around a lot of graveyards."

"I avoid places of the dead," remarked the hollow skull unironically.

I canted my head. On top of having been bound to a powder horn for centuries, he'd been buried in my casket for the last decade. I supposed that was a good enough reason as any.

I caught the Spaniard up on the latest developments and the Capshaw case, half expecting him to already be apprised of things. Turns out he hadn't been silently following me around and had no idea. Which made me wonder what the wraith got up to when he wasn't around.

More disappointingly, the old ghost didn't have any special knowledge of what I was dealing with.

"That's right," I recalled aloud, "thralls aren't really your thing, are they?"

His glowing orbs watched me curiously. "And when have I said that?"

"You didn't. It's just something I've picked up on over time. Tell me, what kind of necromancer doesn't raise the dead?"

"One that thought he was above the others," he returned.

It was as vague an answer as he intended it to be. I'd hoped my glib remark would get him to share, but no such luck, which is why I was playing dumb. Personally, I knew of several types of death magic that didn't involve zombies. Divination, personal power over death, and power drawn from the deaths of others. That last one was especially evil since it turned lust and greed into genocide. The Spaniard's personal part in history was something I often pondered.

Whatever his past, the wraith seemed to desire redemption. He was eager to fight the stiges and keep the underworld from encroaching on humanity. And, ironically enough, he did have a helpful contribution to the problem. It just had nothing to do with his vast knowledge of forbidden spellcraft.

A withered finger pointed at the tiny links of chain. "Those belonged to a set of mail."

I blinked at the rusted metal loops I'd found. They were linked into a single strand, like a chain, but I hadn't realized they'd been woven into a greater net. I held them close to the Spaniard's own undercoat and realized the similarities.

"You're saying our zombie's wearing armor?" I frowned. The utter ridiculousness of it withered beside the conquistador's own gear. "So we're dealing with something old."

The skull shook. "Yes and no. The trappings do not make the man."

I followed his line of thought. "The body could've been dressed in ceremonial chain mail. Which fits with the elaborate ritual." I nudged the Spaniard's arm with my elbow. "Definitely makes more sense than a knight in Miami, am I right?"

The old one stared at me like I had affronted him. Humor was lost on him.

My phone buzzed and I checked the text. It was Milena. "So I'm in your condo after you begged me to come but you're nowhere to be seen."

I replied, "I don't know that I begged..."

"You totally did. I distinctly remember you on your knees."

"How long have you been having these hallucinations? We'll need to get you on a regimen of antipsychotics."

I snorted in laughter and turned to my friends for moral support. I was greeted by a ghostly skull and a dead dog that had his tongue hanging out but had forgotten to breathe for at least the last two minutes.

"Pant!" I rebuked. "You're supposed to pant when you're tongue's out." I turned to the Spaniard. "And would it kill you to blink once in a while?"

"It might," he answered sincerely.

I stared at them in bafflement, shook my head, and typed the rest of my text to Milena without a lick of humor. "Don't worry. On my way."

I sighed and made a mental note to find more time with

the living.

Scout jumped excitedly and followed at my heels, but I gave him a pat and made him a bed in the corner.

My condo may be a sweet top-floor luxury vacation home on the water, but it's still a condo, which means it has an HOA. After some early misunderstandings I managed to work myself onto the HOA board, but really... who has time for these things? I'd succeeded in my goal of not being nagged for minor violations, but I hadn't been able to effect real change yet.

Which is a long way of saying dogs weren't allowed. Scout may no longer be among the living, but he's still a big furry boi who can't come in the building. I figured he was used to being outside. He wouldn't mind some time in the cookhouse.

"Are you gonna be around?" I asked the Spaniard as I collected my various trinkets into a roll of cloth.

"If you require my service."

"I believe I'm going to."

I headed outside and trekked home, looking forward to a night with my favorite person. Even if Milena was in a glum mood, we'd be in a glum mood together. It sounded loads better than the day I'd had.

At least I'd scrounged up one lead. A set of chain mail wasn't much, but being subsequently attacked by santeros and then a militia had a way of derailing things. Today had been about preparation, closing ranks, and locking down family. In the end, without them, what else is there?

Chapter 14

"I still don't like this," I said. "You getting into the bullet-making business."

The Firebird hummed, Kasper rode shotgun, and we'd resumed discussing the finer points of breaking the law.

The old man grumbled. "I notice, for all your reservations, you jumped at the chance to mediate this meeting."

"I'm not mediating. I'm giving you a ride."

"To the Everglades."

"I have to pick up a dog. I told you that."

Kasper crossed his arms in protest. While the ride was convenient, taking him half an hour out of his way wasn't.

"What're you gonna do, Kasper? Ride your bike balancing a stack of ammo boxes? We're in this together."

"I said it was fine, didn't I? Just don't pretend you don't have an ulterior motive for coming with."

I sighed. "That's different. You don't know Jean-Louis like I do. Having something he wants is the best way to get him to listen."

"Doesn't sound special in that regard." He picked up the business card in the center console. "I wonder what Special Agent Rita Bell thinks of our business with the Bone Saints."

I snatched the card and added it back to the stack of fast food receipts, straw wrappers, and a stray parking ticket. I did my best to ignore the stack.

We pulled up to the boathouse and found Scout ready and waiting. I folded my seat forward and let him hop in the back.

Kasper's eyes widened. "Wait a minute. When you said you had to pick up a dog, you meant you had to pick up a dog?"

I looked at him funny.

"I just thought it was code for something, all right?"

The car transitioned from bumpy gravel back to the street, and we were on our way. The old man offered Scout his hand and scratched his head. "He's a big guy, isn't he? *Yes you are. You are a big guy.*" Kasper's eyes lit up as he pet the dog.

"He belonged to Quentin," I explained. "I guess I kind of inherited him."

"That's nice of you. He's a good mix. German shepherd with Alaskan malamute, if I'm not mistaken."

I scrunched my eyes. "Does that make him an Alaskan shepherd or a German malamute?"

"Alaskan shepherd."

Hmm. Didn't know Kasper was a dog guy.

Scout excitedly paced from one window to the other, disappointed to find both closed. That didn't stop him from checking again and again, just to make sure. It was still early in the day and surprisingly cold so I couldn't oblige him. The big dog happily did his rounds all the same and, it being a small back seat, constantly bumped our backs.

"He's excited to come along," noted Kasper, grabbing Scout's neck and giving him a rough pat. Then his eyebrows pushed together. "You just left him in the Everglades overnight? What did he eat?"

"He doesn't need to eat," I answered. "He's dead."

The old man recoiled with a scowl on his face and I broke into a fit of laughter. For an artist, Kasper sometimes lacked imagination.

I turned north on Biscayne Boulevard and we made our way to the north end of the city. We arrived at the apartment-block compound of the Bone Saints, the largest unified group of necromancers in the city. That didn't mean they made up the majority. Necromancing tends to attract loners. Plenty of practitioners within the same discipline branch out to separate paths. But the Haitians, for the most part, stick together. And after the recent gang wars and reshuffling of power, Jean-Louis Chevalier had made himself a notable leader of the city.

But for all he had going for him, he remained small-time. He lacked the political connections of Connor Hatch, the business savvy of Leverett Beaumont, and the institutionalism of the Society. Chevalier and his people worked the street, which meant drugs and scams and whatever else they could wiggle their fingers into. There were times I enjoyed leaning into my disreputable image, but compared to the Bone Saints, well, I was a saint.

I pulled the Firebird right up to the front gate and laid on the horn. Two bangers glared as they swiveled the chain link open. I parked just inside and unloaded. They knew me well enough and had expected Kasper, but the dog appeared to unsettle them. Though it wasn't like they didn't know the score. Just from where I was standing I spotted two undead pit bulls patrolling the grounds. Dogs were a smart precaution, both in the supernatural realm and out. It made me consider offering mine a permanent place in my crew.

A kid with a gun hanging from his belt nodded us ahead. Given it was the middle of the day and our business was illicit, I'd expected a sit-down in a musty studio apartment. But I suppose owning the whole block as well as the entire neighborhood of Little Haiti had its benefits. The boy led us to a cookout in the middle of the vast yard. Jean-Louis Chevalier manned the grill. His people parted respectfully so we could get to him, but when they closed off our exit, it felt more like we'd been outmaneuvered.

"It is not a good sign," Chevalier announced, "when the Shadow Man shows up uninvited. Tell me you are not reneging on my deal, Suarez."

The smell of lime and white wine was overpowering. "It's not my deal, and it's not my business."

Kasper stood beside me. I didn't have visual contact with Scout but I could sense him, just beyond the edge of the crowd, keeping an eye on things from a distance. Good dog.

"*Fout tonè!*" Jean-Louis passed the tongs to his co-griller and faced us. His face wasn't painted with bone makeup today. "Aggravating as it may be, I was hoping you were here to renegotiate. If you're not interested in talking bullets, your business must be even worse. Perhaps something I want no part of."

A tight smile played across my face. Damn did he have me pegged.

"Scotch bonnet octopus?" He offered me a paper plate with a grilled tentacle that must've been marinated overnight. There were buckets of it.

I wasn't feeling especially adventurous and shook my head. "I'm good."

The necromancer turned the plate to my companion. "Will you try, my friend?"

The old man smiled. "Can't say I had this before, but I'm game for anything."

He snatched the hunk of tentacle from the plate and chomped half of it off. Kasper's eyebrows rose as he enjoyed the spicy morsel, and he offered a grunt in return. With food, sometimes the absence of words was the best compliment.

Chevalier's lips opened to a wide smile of white teeth. "Have as much as you like. But my business before yours. Please tell me you have the ammunition."

Kasper held his lunch with one hand and reached into his pocket with his other. He withdrew a single round and tossed it to the gang leader. Chevalier caught it and held it to his eye. The .22 caliber full metal jacket was microetched with Nordic strengthening runes.

"It looks pretty," he commented, "but does it work?"

Scout gave a growl of warning. I pushed some people aside to get eyes on him. The dog's hackles were raised in a standoff against a large shirtless man with a round body.

Except it wasn't a man. Not anymore. His black skin was yellowed and putrid with decay. An old member of the neighborhood, perhaps, gone but not forgotten. He was an automaton like my dog, and just as protective of his master.

Chevalier called for a gun and someone placed a revolver in his hand. He loaded the weapon with the enchanted round and pointed it at Scout. "If you wish to bring a thrall to my block, you must seek permission first."

I bit down. I was a good hand at voodoo, but that bullet, with Kasper's scrawl on it, could puncture Scout's skin with ease. It didn't escape me that it would also penetrate mine.

"I trust you weren't dumb enough to also bring the wraith into my home?" admonished the gang leader.

I shook my head. "I don't control the Spaniard, but the dog's fine. He's with me."

"His very problem. I recall you putting down a dog of mine once. Perhaps I owe you the favor."

"That was different," I asserted. "We weren't friends at the time."

"Are we friends now?"

"Shoot that dog and we won't be."

Chevalier held firm for a protracted moment, though I spotted his playful grin. It was an odd concession for such a solemn guy. Just when I thought this whole thing was a bit of theater, the bastard sighed and pulled the trigger.

The enchanted round punched into the shirtless man's forehead and exited the back of his skull, taking chunks of brain with it. The expressionless guard silently folded to the ground.

I spun on Chevalier, angered by his ruse. Angered, maybe, about already being sentimental about a dog I'd raised two days before.

"That one was past its prime," announced the gang leader, "but still a tough one to put down. Your ammunition is impressive. Assuming you delivered an entire brick, our bargain is fulfilled."

I worked my jaw and eyed Kasper. He'd finished his octopus and had his fists ready in case of trouble. It made me wonder if the bullets were strong enough to get past his warded flesh. He nodded my way, moving ahead with the deal.

"Trunk's open," I said. "Take the bullets, leave the beer."

Chevalier grinned. "Don't be so sour. Pop one open. Eat something."

"Not in the mood."

He signaled his men. A couple made for my car while it took four of them to move the body of the large zombie.

"Use them wisely," cautioned Kasper. "Those are all you're gonna get from me."

"That remains to be seen."

Scout loped up and I patted his neck.

Jean-Louis frowned. "That one has an unusually strong

connection."

"You noticed that, huh? Let's just say he's motivated. I need this dog."

"Ah, so we've reached your business then." He led us away from the grill. The dog's eyes didn't leave him for a second. We followed a short distance from his men. "I assume this has something to do with the late Quentin Capshaw?"

"Something murdered him," I relayed. "A zombie wielding chains, wearing armor, and tracking cemetery dirt. I found an excavated grave at a potter's field in Kendall. There were runes around it. The spellcraft was outside my wheelhouse."

"Your magic and mine are in the same house," he noted.

Which was true in the broader sense. While Jean-Louis was a bokor specializing in pestilence, his patron was Babalu Ayé, and mine was Baron Samedi. Both were Haitian loas sourcing voodoo. I didn't know how to do what Chevalier could do, but I grasped the fundamentals behind it. This latest killer was new to me. And to him too, I suspected.

"Unlike that octopus," said Kasper, "these runes don't have any Caribbean flavor to them. I spent the whole day studying the script, and best I can tell, the language is Indo-Iranian. I'm no language expert, but that would explain why some of it's legible. The writing around the grave seems to be its own dialect, unrelated to anything I know, and features archaic letters and symbols."

Chevalier frowned. "What can you read?"

Kasper scrolled through the pictures on his phone. "This

one here says Solemnity. And this one says Massacre, which is never good." The runes were difficult to read on the small image, only so many pixels on a screen. "The only one I've identified in full is this one. This big guy at the top. It says Twelvetide."

Chevalier's eyes narrowed. "That can't mean..."

"The Twelve Days of Christmas," I said. "Capshaw was killed on day one, Christmas night. And today's Childermas, also known as the feast day of the Massacre of the Holy Innocents." Chevalier's features went stern. I pointed to the wide shot of the grave and the ring of mostly destroyed runes. "If we're right, this is part calendar, part to-do list."

The bokor frowned. "For a killer whose work is not yet finished."

I nodded grimly. "We need to rein this in."

"Who's we? You believe this has something to do with us?"

"It's a threat either way. Either a local is making headlines by killing innocents, or an unwelcome outsider's moving in. The necromancer community needs to band together on this."

"Bygones are difficult to come by after what you did."

"Which is why I'm coming to you. Your influence on the street is well-known. I can't approach the Igbos and some others without a fight. Even if they play nice, they'll turn on me the second they have the chance. And if they had anything to do with this and I was onto them, there'd be blood in their eyes."

Jean-Louis chuckled. "The blood is already there,

Suarez. You haven't heard how Ozo Ebu tried to stick it to you while you were away."

I swallowed uncomfortably. The Nigerian gang leader wasn't too happy with me after I'd blasted him and his men. In my defense, they ambushed me. Ozo Ebu had hoped to cash in the bounty on my head.

"What did that bastard do?" I asked.

"After your street fight, he approached Quentin Capshaw directly. The hypnotist's hotel was in Night Walker territory. He repeatedly boasted about possessing the identity of the Shadow Man, even though he didn't have it."

I ground my teeth. "Ebu tried to sell me out for real."

A nod. "He offered the name of the Shadow Man in exchange for a large sum of money."

"All the more reason I can't approach him," I said darkly. "He might get hurt."

"True enough. Though you might be amused by Quentin's response."

"Yeah?"

"The hypnotist wanted nothing to do with your real identity. He swore it would be nothing but trouble. For all his dramatics, unveiling the Shadow Man was the FBI's cause, not his."

I snickered in disbelief. The more I heard about Quentin behind the scenes, the more I respected the guy. So what if he was a showman? With Rita Bell handling him, he was between a rock and a hard place. It must've been all he could do to keep his nose clean. "Quentin was more sensible than I gave him credit for," I said.

"Not sensible enough to save his life."

"Yeah, well, no one gets to name their time. When death comes, that's it. Even for necromancers."

Chevalier's cheeks twitched. "Not all necromancers, Suarez. You of all people know that."

I bit down, refusing to get into it with him.

"I'll reach out to the Igbo," he agreed. "And the Yoruba. And the Palo Mayombe and other sects of santeros and brujos. I'll talk, but if I end up using my new bullets on your errand, you'll replace them free of charge."

Kasper scowled. I did too. "Don't use bullets then," I told him.

"Did you avoid a fight the last time you encountered the Igbo?" he returned.

"I'm not you. They won't fight you, and you won't start one."

We all stared at each other silently.

"Fine," grunted Kasper. "If you use them for this, I'll replace them. But only if I decide you had no other choice."

The bokor grinned ear to ear, and I wasn't sure if we were digging ourselves out or getting in deeper.

Chapter 15

I spent part of the day driving around the city with Scout, hoping I would luck out and get a fix on an out-of-place magical signature, but I was spinning my wheels and I knew it. It would take an incredible amount of luck to stumble onto Quentin's killer.

Scout enjoyed the drive though, and I ignored the cooling air so he could stick his head out the window like a real doggo. We were having so much fun together that I soured at the thought of leaving him in the Everglades again. I rationalized that the drive was too long, and that it was better to keep him close at hand just in case. So I left him in the car in the garage where he seemed just fine. It wasn't like he needed to stretch his legs.

It was the evening when I returned to the condo and found Kasper and Milena sitting cross-legged on the floor, a slew of tarot cards and paper printouts between them.

I gave Milena a peck on the cheek and regarded the deck of oversized cards arranged on the floor. They featured illustrations of modern characters wearing leather jackets and posing with guns and motorcycles. "I didn't know you were into tarot."

"I'm not," she said. "They're Kasper's. I just find them interesting."

I regarded the biker quizzically. I think it was more surprising to find out they were his.

"What?" he said defensively. "They would make killer tattoos."

Which made a heck of a lot more sense all of a sudden. Kasper wasn't into woo-woo stuff. The man was a lot of things. He was an artist with a drinking problem. Or maybe a drinker with an art problem. The order wasn't important.

What mattered was Kasper was more than all that. He was a friend. He gestured silently toward Milena, who seemed genuinely enraptured by the deck. It was good to see her engaged with something. She actually seemed to be enjoying herself.

The old man had his own stack of papers beside an open laptop. Not the tarot but pictures from the potter's field. Instead of attempting to divine the future, his focus was on translating the present.

"Clarence called a few hours ago," he reported as an aside. "Something about managing the shop."

My cell service on the drive must've been spotty. "An emergency?" I asked.

"Nah, he said he was on top of things."

I nodded. Despite my apprehensions, Clarence might actually work out as an employee. It had been Darcy's idea to hire him. I was worried he was a little too vanilla to hang around our crew, but she felt that was just what we needed. It wasn't like he'd be asked to do anything other than serve coffee anyway.

I looked over his papers with a frown. "Any hits so far?"

The biker rubbed the base of his long beard. "I've been running into a lot of conflicting information, but maybe some of it fits together." He fanned his papers into several rows, pointing out particular letters traced into the dirt. "See these here? They're Greek, or at least derived from Greek. But the rest of the language is most definitely not Greek."

"So we just need to look at all the modern languages with Greek roots," I said.

"Yeah... simple." His scowl stood in contrast with the statement. "Only I'm not sure how modern this is. I could be missing something, but this writing isn't documented anywhere online." He shuffled through more papers. "See the way this rune is drawn? And how it matches this letter? Those are Byzantine flairs." He rotated the laptop screen so it faced me. It showed a drawing of a scroll above a backdrop of an old church. I didn't recognize whatever similarity he was trying to show me, but I nodded along.

"You're thinking this is a traditional religious rite," I surmised, and I was rewarded with a nod.

It made sense. Twelvetide, Christmas, Childermas. So we were looking at some European-influenced holiday cheer.

Friggin' tourists.

"So it's still slow going," he admitted, "but that doesn't mean I came up empty. Armed with a bit more context, I noticed something familiar about the glyph on Quentin's arm."

The tattoo artist produced the printout of that photo and took a black sharpie to a blank paper.

"Here, this glyph, I thought it was bunk at first." He drew a simplified version of Quentin's wound on the paper. "But if you cut out this horizontal line, it looks like a mysticism symbol."

What Kasper had drawn and what had been cut into Quentin's arm did mostly match up, with the obvious strikethrough line missing. "What's the mysticism symbol mean?"

"Hypnotist, or hypnotism, or something along those lines. It's missing the context of a sentence."

"But that makes sense. Quentin was a famous hypnotist." I worked my jaw. "The strikethrough could represent a cancellation rune. Damn..."

Kasper arched his eyebrow at me. "What is it? I thought you'd be pleased?"

"I am, it's just that this is looking like Manifesto all over again. What if Quentin was targeted because hypnotism was his sin?"

He didn't answer. I shuffled some papers aside, hoping the thought would inspire other ideas, but it was useless. Kasper was the scribe. He may not be a language expert, but he was a Nobel laureate compared to me. The best thing I could do was tell Kasper what I was thinking and let him take it from there.

"Hey!" snapped Milena. "You're blocking my tarot cards."

She reached over to move a printout I'd carelessly layered over her project, only as she grabbed the paper her fingers tightened and crushed it.

"Relax," said Kasper. "I need that."

But Milena wasn't angry, or not entirely. Her teeth were bared, caught mid sneer, and her limbs were taut as if locked up by an electrical current. Her eyes rolled into the back of her head.

"Milena!"

I cradled her before she dropped and hit her head. Her legs straightened and she shook.

"Chains," she blurted out. "Stay away from the chains."

Kasper leaned in, worried. I watched with wide eyes. Quentin Capshaw had been attacked with a chain. Had Milena overhead that?

"Oh God," she bemoaned. "What is that smell?"

Her breathing grew frantic, and I couldn't tell if she was having an epileptic fit or hyperventilating.

"I have you," I assured. "Calm down."

Her shaking slowed, though I wasn't sure if she heard me. Her body was still wound up. Her pupils returned, filled with crazed panic as she stared off into the distance.

"The moon is full," she said. "The moon is full and at its peak."

Kasper's brow furrowed and he checked the ceiling where Milena was staring. "Woman, what are you..."

Her hand still clutched the paper with the graveyard glyph. With her other, she yanked the sharpie from Kasper and set it to the floor. Kasper had the presence of mind to slide a blank paper under the pen as Milena began to draw.

"She sees something," I said. "I don't know how it's possible but..." My eyes went to her death grip on the crushed paper.

"The moon is full and at its peak," she repeated. Without watching her hand, she scribbled a rough circle with some lines protruding from the center. She seized up again and almost inadvertently headbutted me. It took all my strength to contain her.

"Screw this," muttered Kasper. He grabbed the paper she was murdering, but Milena wouldn't let go. "Give me that," he growled.

Her brown eyes fixed on me. "You can't stop..." She choked up, breaths frantic. "It won't..." Her whole body convulsed. "Cisco, I'm cold."

The old man ripped the paper from her grip and Milena immediately fell unconscious. Her body went slack in my arms, and her breathing steadied. Kasper and I exchanged a concerned look that seemed to last minutes.

"What the fuck, broham?"

My head shook. "I don't know." I picked Milena up and set her on the couch. "Just... Keep those tarot cards away from her, all right?"

He nodded idly.

This was more than tarot cards. More than ailing health. The whole thing seemed like an elaborate hallucination or mental illness.

"She's okay," I asserted, hovering over her sleeping form. "She's okay."

Kasper swallowed behind me. "I'm sorry, Cisco. I thought she was in good spirits."

"What? No, you didn't do anything." I massaged my forehead. "There were things she mentioned, about the chains, and the horrible smell at the grave." I unballed the paper that had set her off. It was the printout of the Twelvetide rune.

Kasper frowned. "I shouldn't have been doing my research in front of her. I... I may have mentioned the smell. Just small talk, you know?"

"Okay, what about the full moon then?"

"I don't know."

"When's the next full moon?"

"I don't know."

I ground my teeth. Milena was resting so I quickly checked my phone. "It's tomorrow night," I said. "The December full moon is called the Cold Moon. That has to mean something, right?"

Kasper worked his lips without coming up with an answer, and I gazed at the hasty drawing Milena had made. Between drawing blind and all her shaking, it looked like a toddler had made it. I couldn't shake the circle being a drawing of the moon, but the lines exploding out of it didn't make sense.

Milena woke up shortly, and she was fine except for a headache and not remembering much. I gave her some water and aspirin, and she cradled the glass in the corner of the couch, opting not to talk about it. As much as I wanted to press her, Milena was in no condition to be a useful ingredient in tonight's stew.

Before I could decide what to do, there was a knock at the door. It was Darcy.

"Staying in tonight?" she asked.

"I don't know."

She peeked past me. "You guys okay?"

Must've been the expression on my face. I glanced back at Milena and sighed. "We're all still kicking. Come on in."

"Actually, I have plans."

For the first time, I noticed she was wearing a dress instead of jeans. It wasn't too formal, still a little edgy and cool, but unmistakably nicer than usual. Darcy was showing off some leg and wearing a bit of makeup.

I grinned. "Hot date?"

"Nothing like that," she said with a derisive snort. "I'm grabbing a drink with Shen."

"He called?"

Her smile crooked and she glanced at the floor. "I reached out, actually. He changed his number so I had to get it from Simon, who was all too happy to get us in touch because he figures if anyone can convince me to return to the fold, it's Shen."

I nodded along with a hint of concern. "Can he?" I asked. "Return you to the fold?"

"Not a chance." She punched my arm. "I'm into this legitimate outlaw thing we got going on."

I believed her, but that didn't mean the Society didn't worry me. They had taken her in some years ago. They were maybe the first stable family she'd had.

"Anyway," she said, eager to change the subject, "I just stopped by to help Clarence close up the shop. It's his first time. He mentioned someone in a suit walked in and handed him a letter for you."

She passed me the envelope. There was no address or postage, just my first name written by hand. "Simon?" I asked.

"Nope. That was my first thought too. This guy was older and more heavyset, but we don't have a solid description. I told you to install security cameras."

I nodded. It was always something. Darcy was right, again.

"Okay," she said, "I'm out."

I waved her off and frowned at the envelope as I opened it. The coffee business wasn't at the top of my list of concerns right now. Kasper was watching but Milena was checked out, staring off into space.

I sighed and checked the handwritten letter. There was a location with the statement, "Meet me tonight at nine." It was unsigned except for the symbol I recognized, the symbol that sent shivers through my spine.

Twelvetide.

Chapter 16

"I'm fine," swore Milena. "Go without me."

I winced. Kasper hadn't had any action since the Nether wedding and was itching to come, which would leave Milena home alone.

But wasn't that exactly what I wanted? The condo was a safe, warded location, under Beaumont's protection in Brickell. It was maybe the safest place in Miami. Milena didn't need a babysitter.

There wasn't much time to feel guilty because we were already gonna be half an hour late. Kasper and I hurried to the car. For a dog without a beating heart, Scout was unusually happy to see us.

"Can't say he doesn't creep me out," groaned Kasper.

Scout's tail beat against the back seat, and it was impossible not to smile. The silver Firebird peeled onto the street as we raced north.

Overtown lies at the north end of Downtown, and it's one of the most famously neglected neighborhoods in the city. Wynwood, just above, gets all the attention from the glitzy developers (as well as the Obsidian March). Not Overtown. It's just a ghetto in many people's eyes. Yet in any city as full of life as Miami, there's always a revival if you know where to look.

But Overtown?

The location in the letter directed me to a street corner, though I wasn't keen on announcing ourselves so directly. I parked two blocks away on the curb in front of a local pizza joint, Magic Pizza. The window had been bricked and then hastily boarded over with plywood. Graffiti on the neighboring wall read, "No more magic."

"Gang business?" suggested Kasper.

Scout sniffed around the storefront. "I don't know, but it looks like it happened today. There's still broken glass on the ground." The neighborhood itself appeared as deserted as ever. It wasn't the greatest place to find yourself late at night, but it seemed more quiet than it should've been.

"Strange times," muttered Kasper.

I nodded and headed into the adjoining alley. "Let's go."

We walked in a wide grouping, checking different angles, attempting to spot the other party before they spotted us. Since I wasn't given a specific address, I doubted we'd be going to an actual building. I figured there'd either be someone waiting on the street or, more likely, in a nearby car.

A block ahead and across the street was a storefront attached to a larger rundown office building. The lights were on and a car was in the lot. The place was anything but welcoming, however. The glass windows were covered over and there were no proper signs, though red letters painted on the wall read, "Liquor. Beer. Soda."

A man stood outside the store smoking. I looked at him and he looked at me. Then another guy walked outside holding a case of beer. The two laughed, headed to their car, and drove away, once again leaving us in eerie silence.

I sighed and pressed forward with the sinking feeling that I was late. This was a decrepit, no-name liquor store in the middle of nowhere, with no one around, and I was late.

An uneasy feeling welled in my chest. The hairs on my neck perked. The shadows seemed alive, as if trying to tell me something, and I wondered if I was supposed to go inside.

Scout's low growl filled the air. I paused, wary of some impending horror. I eyed the overgrown swale, the sagging chain-link fences, and the thoroughly empty streets.

The dog lunged. He jumped past me just before a loud bang erupted, followed by a whiz and a spatter against his zombified skin. Something struck and knocked him hard to the cracked sidewalk, and an echo like dissipating thunder crackled on the wind.

My gaze darted to the top of the office building. Someone perched on the other end of a long-barreled gun, readying a second shot.

"Sniper!" I yelled.

I sidestepped into the shadow as another crack pierced the night. Concrete exploded on the wall behind me.

I charged forward across the street, throwing my arm up

and flinging it aside. A manifestation of darkness massed beside a full dumpster and flung the large object like it was nothing, rocking it against the side of the old liquor store wall. The rifle above tracked me but quickly lost line of sight as I closed.

I hopped onto the dumpster and hopped again at the wall, using the shadows to give my boot a boost to the roof. I climbed over and immediately sank into darkness as a third round splattered through me.

"The rooftop!" I signaled to Kasper.

He was in the middle of the street. His powerful tattoo runework formed an impervious net that prevented even high-caliber rounds from penetrating his body. With ink like that, taking cover was an outmoded tactic. The biker charged past the liquor store to enter the interconnected-but-shuttered office building from the ground.

Scout barked up a racket. The direct hit would've immediately ended the life of any normal animal. As it was, the bullet was strong enough to pierce his enchanted skin, which was either an indictment of my skills or a testament to the sniper's. But that wasn't the whole story.

I might be called a dead man, but it wasn't a euphemism for the dog. He was literally dead. Whereas I bled and breathed and hurt, Scout didn't register pain. And while it would be a chore to patch him up later, the relatively small piece of metal inside him would have little effect on the Intrinsics that animated him.

I put the silver whistle to my lips to silence him, and then pointed ahead to Kasper. The dog followed. Above, the shooter backed away from the roof, realizing he was cornered.

I stood on top of a dilapidated liquor store that ran up against the office building. It was too high to climb. Two windows at my level were boarded over with wood. I charged ahead and slammed my shoulder into one. Spellcraft bathed me in protective force as I bashed through and landed inside.

The building was old and musty and hadn't been used for legitimate business in years, but that didn't mean it wasn't occupied. Old needles and beer cans dotted the hall. I made a beeline for a stairway and charged up three flights. Right before I threw open the door to the roof I froze, once again experiencing the strange itching of shadow I'd felt moments before, just preceding the sniper's first shot.

Was I sensing some kind of imminent danger? Were the shadows telling me something about the environment outside?

I didn't dare contemplate the questions while the sniper could've been getting away, but I wasn't dumb either. I stepped around the concrete wall and waved my hand. While I remained behind cover, a burst of shadow nearly blew the door off its hinges. The swinging door was met with the crack of the rifle, and I knew I had him.

Before my attacker could ready another shot, I spun around the corner and dashed ahead through the night. A man wearing black gear jerked up in disbelief as I charged straight for him. He attempted to pull back and shoot, but I kicked the rifle to the side. His left hand grabbed a knife strapped to his leg, but I twirled around and punched him in the gut, doubling him over. My elbow collapsed his exposed back and he slammed to the floor. Then, when the knife was finally drawn, the sole of my alligator boot crushed the small bones of his hand into the tar-gravel roof.

He bit down in muted pain as I kicked the blade aside. The man had taken three hard hits yet hardly yelped. That spoke to some level of training or experience, likely military.

"You part of the militia?" I demanded.

Disgust filled his face as he glared up at me. Then he spit on my boots. I kicked him in the jaw to soften him up some more.

"You just tried to kill me, buddy. Even worse, you shot my dog. Now's not the time to take a brave stand. Who are you?"

He still didn't say anything, but he didn't dirty my boots again so that was improvement. The man put his hands up in surrender and sat on his boots. When he lowered his arms, he slyly reached for one.

I sighed. This guy was really determined. My first thought was that he was a member of the Vanguard, but this guy looked to be of different stock. He wore no insignias. Instead of looking like a homegrown Floridian, I guessed European. Plus, he'd lured me here with a reference to Twelvetide, so he knew something of spellcraft.

"Apparently I'm not imposing enough," I reproved.

I put the silver whistle to my lips with a smile and pretended to momentarily lose interest in the prisoner. He predictably went for the sidearm in his boot. Scout barreled through the doorway and covered the ground between us before the man could fully raise his arm. Jagged teeth clamped his wrist and shredded clothes and skin alike.

The hardened man finally started screaming.

The gun hit the ground and I put it in a pile with the rifle and the knife. I let the dog play a bit; it was only fair after him getting shot. And the sniper took some convincing anyway. He managed to punch Scout three times in the skull.

This guy was no weekender militiaman. Those strikes were calculated and would've successfully put down a normal police dog. He was a tough soldier, all right. Even so, he was in over his head and, after multiple failures to gain the upper hand, was finally overtaken and reduced to a quivering schoolgirl.

I shook my head in amusement as an out-of-breath Kasper finally joined us on the rooftop. His fist was raised and glowing like a golden sun, but he pulled back with tentative restraint.

"Oh," he said, slightly miffed. "You seem to have a handle on things."

"Sorry to disappoint," I snickered. I thrust my hands in my pockets amid the whimpering in the background.

Kasper grimaced at the scene. "You, uh, you gonna call this off, broham?"

I shrugged. "What do you think, tough guy?"

More cries of pain.

I put the whistle to my mouth and blew. Scout released the captive, rounded my feet, and sat at my side, eyes on the target. The man released an exhausted and relieved groan. He was in a sorry state, all four limbs bloodied, clothes shredded, and one of his boots was somehow completely missing. I glanced around and, best I could tell, Scout had gobbled it up. The sniper tried not to move while keeping nervous eyes on all three of us, but especially the dog.

I waited a minute. Soon enough, all that adrenaline was going to wash away, his fight or fight reflex would wane, and he'd be in a lot more pain than he was now.

"You're not the Vanguard," I finally said, "but I will find out who you're with. So why don't you just make this easier on everybody, especially yourself, and tell me who wants me dead?"

The man forced himself to sit up, face hardening as he stared holes through me. "Everyone." His accent was thick. Eastern European.

He flinched, like he was about to make a last-ditch lunge at me, but his eyes snapped to the dog, already jumping to his feet. The man spun around, charged away from us, and leapt off the side of the building.

Scout barreled after him with overeager abandon, and I was so concerned with stopping him before he went over the edge that I didn't get a twine of shadow out in time to save the man. The sniper attempted to hit the ground with a controlled roll, but we were four stories up. His knees shattered against the asphalt of the parking lot, and he banged his head so hard he wouldn't be waking up.

My boots skidded at the edge of the roof. "Damn," I spat.

This sniper had been so afraid to out his employer that he took a one-in-a-hundred chance of escaping, even though the other ninety-nine eventualities ended with death or severe disability.

"That accent," remarked Kasper. "You think he's tied to the Twelvetide killer?"

I shook my head. "He knew spellcraft, wasn't surprised by mine, but he didn't use any himself. He wasn't an animist."

I scraped my boot over the roof's gravel. The accent was curious. Almost identifying enough that the sniper had opted not to talk or risk exposing his operation. But it was hardly enough to go on. "There goes our lead."

"It's not our only one," noted Kasper, retrieving a 7.62 millimeter rifle cartridge from the chamber of the sniper's rifle. "The man might not have been an animist, but he was using spellcraft." He held up the bullet to reveal the magical etching on its surface. Only it wasn't our bullet.

"You moonlighting on the side?"

He snorted. "This is pretty good, but it's not my handiwork. It's Cyrillic. You know of any elite weapon runners in Miami that use Cyrillic?"

My face twisted in anger. "The Russians are trying to kill me too?"

He hiked a shoulder. "Why not? You had a dustup with them a while back. They have more reason than most. This was a professional hit, but they took the care to lure you out of Brickell to do it. Who respects Beaumont's protection if not the mob?"

I couldn't argue with his logic, but I didn't get why the Russians of all people would come after me now, or what their link to Twelvetide was. But the time for study was over.

"The sniper probably checked in," I reasoned, "let his boss know we were late. That buys us time. Maybe the Russians won't realize their guy is dead for another hour or two. If we're gonna surprise them, we need to move fast."

"I'm with you, broham," he said, grimacing at the crumpled assassin in the parking lot. "Though I recommend taking the stairs."

Chapter 17

Kasper and I kicked down the back door of a Sunny Isles strip club named Pop Stars. Two Russians reached for guns, but they had less warning than the unconscious man in the parking lot, and they fared no better. They were disarmed and on the floor in seconds.

It was close to midnight and the music was going full blast, resounding far from the stage into the back hallway. Unfortunately, the dance beat wasn't enough to mask our entry. A man emerged from the curtain at the other end of the hall readying a shotgun.

"Weapon!" I called.

Kasper stood his ground to absorb the blow as I put my shoulder into the nearby office door, bursting inside as the shotgun barked. I crashed into a woman sitting on an older man's lap. She wore short shorts and knee-high boots but was completely topless. The man jerked his head up from sampling the goods.

Mid-fifties, gaunt face and pointed nose. It was Nikolai, a

small-time Russian boss. Just as I'd thought, he ordered a hit on me and was waiting it out in the public eye for deniability. It was how these guys operated.

The wall shook as Kasper undoubtedly slammed the man with the shotgun against it. Unsurprisingly, no more gunfire followed.

"Let's go, honey," I said, grabbing the girl's wrist and helping her off Nikolai.

She watched me warily, a mix of confusion and surprising modesty as she barred an arm over her fake breasts. Her eyes were red, as if she'd been crying.

"Wait," I said, the edge in my voice making her flinch. I realized my hand had overtightened on her wrist. I released her contritely, easing my features to calm her. "I bet you've always wanted to see someone do this."

I picked up my boot and pressed it between Nikolai's legs. He cried out in pain and shoved away, but ran out of room when the back of his office chair slammed against his desk. He pushed against my leg to lessen the pain, and I backed off just enough so he could breathe.

The girl's eyes flared as she watched, simultaneously scared and fascinated. She'd probably never seen anyone so much as talk back to this guy, and I had his balls in a vice. She exhaled long and slow as she took it in, and a hint of a smile cracked the edge of her lips.

"Okay," I said, nodding for the door.

She swallowed nervously and backed out of the office. Instead of returning to the club, she bolted into the rear parking lot.

"Just the person I wanted to see," I growled, leaning close to Nikolai, which just might have increased the weight on my boot.

"You're dead," he squeezed through clenched teeth.

"Apparently not. Does that surprise you?"

"I can try again."

"And until then, you can make good on your note and tell me what you know about Twelvetide."

He snorted, making it clear he had no intention of doing so. I pressed the alligator boot down and he squealed like a pig.

Then his eyes rolled back and he passed out.

"Nikolai." I removed the boot and slapped his face a few times. "Nikolai?" I clicked my teeth. "Maybe I came on too strong."

"Uh, broham," called Kasper outside the door. "We got company."

I stepped into the hall and peeked out the back, moving the door so it was mostly shut. Three Mercedes SUVs pulled into the parking lot. They were packed with men, but no one carried themselves with obvious urgency.

"Backup," said Kasper.

I nodded. "Nikolai must've gotten suspicious when his sniper didn't check in. They don't know we're here yet. They're just a precaution."

"They're a bunch of heavily armed precautions."

The first man unloaded. A gust of wind whipped his jacket up and revealed a strapped submachine gun.

"Is Nikolai cooperating?" he asked.

"He's unconscious."

Kasper bit down. "Then this just turned into an extraction."

I'd almost forgotten Kasper had served in 'Nam. It wasn't a perfect plan, but it was the best we had. Especially once the backup noticed the unconscious man outside. I nodded. "Front door."

I grabbed a drooling Nikolai and hefted him over my shoulder. Kasper and I pulled bandannas over our faces and hurried down the hall and through the curtain.

"Please give it up for the lovely Destiny," crooned a DJ who must've smoked five packs a day.

We found ourselves behind the bar with most of the crowd facing the stage on the far wall. Destiny collected dollar bills on the floor as she inched toward her discarded outfit. Kasper yanked the bar top open and we headed across the room.

The DJ sat in an elevated platform in the back corner and was the first to spot us. "Um... um... Destiny, give these fellas a little encore!" He frantically waved at security as he attempted to keep the crowd's attention on the stripper. Except Destiny saw me lugging her asshole boss. She screamed and fled backstage, leaving her clothes but not the money.

I pulled my shotgun on the first bouncer who approached, and two more pulled guns. Then I turned the sawed off on their boss.

That got us into a proper standoff. Difference was, Kasper and I kept moving for the door. We weren't fast, but we held the winning cards. One of the men got too close and Kasper shoved him out of the way. The threat to their boss proved too great for them to risk making a move.

We skipped feet outside before the heavy guns in the back made it to the front. A few men followed us but kept their distance. I tossed Kasper the keys and he took the driver's seat of my pickup. I chucked Nikolai into the bed and hopped in with him. By now we were a block out; the bouncers were too far to jump into their cars.

We were out of town before they could get a handle on what happened.

Chapter 18

Back at my secluded Everglades cookhouse, Nikolai was strapped to a chair with a paper bag over his head. I had offered to drop Kasper off, get him out of play before Nikolai ever saw him, but the biker was determined to see things through.

No one had followed us so time was on our side. I let the mob boss stew while I opened a jar of gator blood and painted a pentagram on the floor, leaving him at the center. It didn't do anything, but I had a reputation and wanted to leverage it. When I suddenly tore the bag away and nodded downward, his eyes widened in terror at the possibility of being sacrificed to some forgotten dark god.

Mission accomplished.

"Nikolai, Nikolai, Nikolai," I said as if chiding a ten-year-old who just stole a pack of gum and experienced his first ride in the back of a squad car. "I would've been fine never seeing or hearing from you again the rest of your natural life. And then you go and do this."

I expected him to spit at me like the sniper. After all, these guys thus far hadn't displayed any particular originality or grace. But Nikolai impressed me by one, keeping his cool, and two, sticking to civil discourse.

"I have done nothing you didn't already bring on yourself," he said with his flat, raspy voice. He didn't have much of an accent, indicating he'd lived most of his fifty-something years in the States.

"That may be true, but I already died once or twice. Or three times... I lost count. The point is, forgive and forget."

"The Bratva doesn't forgive, and Russians don't forget."

I simpered at him. "Clever."

"Neither do the Serbians, for that matter. Those animals fled our service after you killed their leader."

"I barely remember that."

"We remember. The Vucari give us trouble from time to time, as they believe we share some of the blame."

I snorted. "It was your dealings with a drug kingpin that put them in the crosshairs in the first place. But it's not like you care. You got sweet submarine money out of the whole thing."

"Yes," he said, momentarily losing his cool, "and my men arrested and half my warehouses seized."

I smiled and patted his shoulder in encouragement. "All the cost of doing business. And look at you—you bounced back. The model of resilience. So why go after me now?"

He turned his head to study Kasper, somehow managing to appear threatening while tied up, but the old man tiredly leaned against the wall with crossed arms. Kasper wasn't into politics. He just wanted to lend his gruff visage to the interrogation.

"Everyone is going after you," answered Nikolai. "The blacks, the South Americans. The shamans in the street hate you."

"Don't forget the militia," I added.

"Your carelessness is why this militia exists in the first place. You broadcast yourself on TV and make yourself a target. Magic is now a target, and they hate you for it."

I swallowed at the image of Magic Pizza in my mind. "It's not me, it's them. Manifesto, the Obsidian March, the hellions. They're pushing past natural limits, and they're not just coming for me."

Nikolai drew his head back and studied me. "Don't concern me with your war. You are the animist. You are the one they fear. And it's not just them. Your own people turned on you. The street gangs, the necromancers, even this new beast. There's an ever-increasing price on your head. Do you understand that?"

He cleared his throat and leaned forward hungrily. "You ask me why try to kill you now. It's simple. It's because your time has come. Everyone wants your head. The only question is who gets to have the honor."

I ground my jaw as he spoke. The Russians had always wanted me dead, I could see that now. Only now I was exposed by Manifesto, the feds were on my tail, the santeros and militia were gunning for me... Nikolai had finally seen the writing on the wall. It was now or never. If the Russians took out Cisco Suarez, they would get the payoff but, more importantly, they would garner a measure of respect and authority from the victory. A place in the new order of things.

But nearly lost in Nikolai's speech was mention of the new beast. It was the reason I'd taken his bait and gone to Overtown to begin with.

"What do you know of Twelvetide?" I demanded.

He paused dramatically and cocked his head. "I do not know these things, but there are people in my employ who do."

"Bull. Even if you didn't know before, you were apprised of the situation as soon as you heard about it."

Nikolai grinned. "Fair enough. But then, it sounds to me like you're negotiating for information. You would've been better served by setting an appointment and making me a business offer."

I pulled my bronze knife to his neck and leaned close. "You listen to me. *You* would've been better served by not taking a shot at me, and *this is not a negotiation.*"

Scout hopped up from his blanket in the corner where I'd taken a brief look at him. He bared his teeth and growled at the door nearest the street. That one was reinforced metal and double barricaded, permanently closed, effectively making it part of the wall. Which didn't stop it from flying off its hinges as a troop of armed figures with mixed firearms charged inside.

The dog's warning had been enough. Kasper had flanked the door holding a metal pipe, and my shotgun was already trained on the next person strolling through the door.

Following a stream of black paramilitary gear, a single formal white suit followed. Leverett Beaumont released a long sigh like *I* was the ten-year-old in the back of a squad car. "Cisco. Kasper." His voice was calm but convicted as he assessed the room, his features tense and authoritative. "I really must insist you cease this undertaking at once."

Chapter 19

For a few drawn-out moments, I coolly regarded the uniformed vampires. Although I didn't particularly recognize any of the gunmen, it was apparent they didn't mean me and Kasper immediate harm. They were here as muscle, to protect the leader of their clan as well as to enforce his directives. I wasn't technically under Beaumont's umbrella, but I was close enough to keep the rain away.

"What are you doing here?" I asked in stern warning. "And how do you even know where *here* is?"

Beaumont arched an eyebrow at the apparently odd question. "It's my business to know such things, and the answer to the first question is obvious."

I glared at a relieved Nikolai and worked my jaw. "You have an agreement with the Russians."

"Of course I do. Deals make the world go round. They also keep open war at bay. I detest having to mention it, but the Russian mob is larger than my clan, and they have a much wider reach."

I scowled. "Being outnumbered never stopped me before."

The vampire boss showed a hint of a smile. "Dialog, Cisco, is more important than ever. The alternative is a fight. If I allow you to do this, the Russians will turn on Clan Beaumont, a development the Obsidian March would be all too eager for. The Russians would leverage vampires and animists as their enemy. In these times of tension, the public would quickly side with the mob, and Miami would be lost."

I growled to myself. Beaumont's intrusion into my private sanctuary rankled me, but it was perhaps even more aggravating that he was making perfect sense.

I was a vigilante. An outlaw. Maybe not as much of a loner as I once was, but in some ways that made my position more tenuous. I'd taken on a drug cartel before, and what did the city get for it? A war in Little Haiti. Shootouts in the streets over drugs. A power vacuum all too happily filled by the encroaching Obsidian March.

For a time I'd been operating as a hit man for these shadowy organizations. The experience honed my instincts into a force to be reckoned with, into acting quickly and decisively when needed. Case in point was the Russian boss strapped to my chair.

That said, I wasn't that lone outlaw anymore. I had roots, an identity, and even, much to my dissatisfaction, ties to an underworld empire. I had to include that bigger picture into my worldview.

And yet...

"You can't let him off after this..." I stressed.

"And how do you imagine avoiding that? Are you the sort who executes someone?" Instead of showing the slightest hint of sympathy, Beaumont fired back with cold logic. "If you had come straight to me in the beginning, we could've made him pay for his infraction."

"I wasn't thinking about the business. Is that what you're telling me?"

"You need to learn to rely on your network and outsource some tasks. Are you not dealing with enough right now? Running around town like a mobile punching bag doesn't do anyone any good."

Kasper, leaning against the wall again, arms crossed holding a length of rusty pipe, cleared his throat. He did it long and loud and not so politely. "Speaking of business, what good is your so-called protection if it allows the mob to go after us?"

Beaumont's eye twitched. The two didn't like each other, and the criticism was a direct hit. No matter how I'd reacted to the situation, the point stood that the assassination attempt was a failure on Beaumont's part. A failure of his organization and of our deal.

"I'm exercising that protection at this very moment," returned the vampire boss. "If you kill Nikolai, I have no more say in the matter. Every connected Russian, contract Ukrainian, and mercenary outfit in their employ will go after you." His voice flattened into a grim warning. "You continue like this, and the only way you'll discover you made one-too-many enemies is because one will finally kill you."

I was admittedly spread a little thin, but I hadn't asked to be in this position. "Nikolai wanted me dead before," I said. "What's gonna stop him from doubling his effort now?"

"Nikolai is far from the top of the Russian food chain." He looked to the sub boss with a smile. "Excuse the poor choice of words."

By now, the Russian had recollected his full confidence and managed a chuckle.

Beaumont focused on Kasper before meeting my eyes. "I have assurances that this business is behind us. Nikolai is barred from retaliation. He'll be reprimanded in-house. Though, seeing as you've already struck back, and in order to avoid punishment on your end, I've agreed to afford Nikolai some leniency."

I let out a disgusted scoff. I could never tell if politics were above me or beneath me, but I was fine right where I was.

This was how the sophisticated criminals of the underworld dealt with their problems. An affront for an affront. Like two hurt kids on a playground, they were supposed to shake hands and declare evensies.

But I wasn't gonna drop this one so easily. Especially not with that smug strip club owner beaming at me as if he'd won.

"Put down your guns," I told the vamps. "You're not going to shoot anyone, not even if I do this."

I stepped behind Nikolai's chair and pressed the bronze blade to his throat. The guns were all trained on me except for one on Kasper. He appeared entirely unconcerned, and so was I. They all might as well have been loaded with Nerf rounds.

Scout growled and took measured steps forward, but I stopped him with a hand signal. One of the vamps swiveled his rifle toward him.

"You know what happened to the last guy who shot my dog?" I warned.

The gunman withered under the sheer conviction in my voice. He pulled his aim away and settled it somewhere between the both of us.

"Back to business." I tightened the knife on Nikolai's flesh. "You won't risk shooting the guy you're trying to save, so cut out the pretense already."

Leverett Beaumont clenched his jaw and then nodded. The men lowered their weapons.

"Good. I'll agree to your terms, Beaumont, because I believe your word. But everyone here isn't as trustworthy. I need proof that our Russian friend is willing to abide by the terms."

"He'll do as his boss tells him to do."

"I need to hear it from him." I jerked the knife slightly.

"I will," rasped Nikolai, a smidge less confident than a minute ago.

"Then I need a token of goodwill. I'll let you go, but only after you tell me everything you know about Twelvetide."

"That's not the deal," he returned, "and I don't need to tell you anything."

"You owe me."

"Not after you killed my guy."

"He jumped off the roof all by himself, which means I haven't extracted my pound of flesh yet." I pressed the knife deep enough to draw blood this time. Nikolai turned to the vampires for help.

Beaumont deliberated a moment and canted his head. "We need to ensure all parties leave here happy, Nikolai. Otherwise we're just kicking this can down the road, to revisit at a later date. My associate hasn't received reparations yet. His request sounds exceedingly appropriate to me."

Nikolai flushed with defiance. The Russian hated giving away information for free, but then, this wasn't exactly a fire-sale. How much was a life worth, particularly his? Nikolai looked deep into my eyes and saw himself a bargain.

"Fine," he spat, "but you won't like it, shadow witch."

"Why's that?"

"Because you're hunting the spirit of Midwinter."

"Did you unleash this thing on me?" I growled.

"Not us, no, but we're familiar with the legend of the Albanian bogeyman, the reanimated corpse of a gypsy, only free in the weeks after Christmas."

You had to be kidding me... The freaking gypsies? I'd run into them at the very first cemetery I'd checked.

I nodded and loosened the knife on his throat. "Now that we're making nice, tell me what this thing is."

"The karkanscholl."

I pointed to the dome of my head. "Karkan skull?"

He laughed. "Skull, ribs, fingers—whatever bones are left."

My face darkened. "Who raised it?"

"A Calabrian Albanian, I would guess. Catholic, Eastern Orthodox. At Vespers, they dig up the body of a buried traveler, clothe it in vestments and bind it with chains. At Compline, they animate it with dirt, and then the ritual is complete. The bogeyman cannot be stopped until it resumes its sleep at Epiphany."

I locked eyes with Kasper. We weren't much for ceremony or church, but after our research we recognized the names of the holy periods and the feast day. Epiphany was January sixth, the first day after the Twelve Days of Christmas.

Which meant a killer was on the loose for all of Twelvetide.

"There has to be a way to stop this... karkan."

Nikolai grinned. "It has never been done in history, or so goes its legend. They're laden with magical chains and armor, their very breath is lethal to lesser animals, and they bring with them the cold."

Which explained the brisker-than-usual winter Miami was experiencing.

"I want specifics," I pressed.

"Those," said Nikolai, "I do not have. I don't run in the circles you do, witch. I only know of the myths printed in books."

"So I need to take this thing on myself, is that it?"

The Russian boss chuckled. "You would be wiser to let it

run its course. Karkanscholls are notoriously unstoppable. And they are famed assassins. It is said that one was responsible for the death of Alexander the Great."

My eyes smoldered. "Yeah, well, one never ran into Cisco Suarez."

I thrust the knife down and sliced through the duct tape binding him to the chair. When he was loose, I helped him up with a boot to the back. Beaumont glared at me in warning, and Nikolai rushed behind the vampire guard.

"We'll talk again," he warned, wiping his shoulders.

"I very much doubt it," intoned Beaumont. The upirs escorted him out, and Leverett turned and left after them without so much as a nod of thanks.

I stepped to the door and watched them hike away. "I've gotten lazy with security," I muttered.

Used to be, back when I crashed here, I had a brigade of zombie thralls watching from the trees. Now that I had the condo and my secured shadow room, I didn't keep anything of importance here and hadn't maintained a protective presence. Now that my secret was out, that would need to change.

"You didn't ask about the bullet," reminded Kasper, after our visitors were long gone.

I returned to Scout, crouched by his side, and gave him a pat. My gaze strayed to the piece of metal I'd pulled from his body, another enchanted round with Cyrillic script.

"Weapon trafficking is the heart of the Russian operation. Beaumont wouldn't have let me mine for that info." I didn't tell him the rest of it, that it was too risky a subject to bring up with Kasper present.

Enchanting ammo was an escalation of sorts, a line crossed. The simple act would instantly put any scribe into enemy crosshairs. Kasper had crossed that line with the Bone Saints earlier today, and he had done it for Milena and me.

If I had gone down that line of questioning with Nikolai, it would only be a matter of time before he would connect the dots with Kasper. Not today, not tomorrow, but one day, it would come to him. I couldn't take that chance.

"Good boy," I said, rubbing Scout's neck. It was large and shaggy, like a wild animal's.

The biker stroked his beard and wandered forward. "All right then. So what about this karkan assassin? You're not the type to sit back during a killing spree and watch a murderer go silently into the night, but if the legend is true..."

"It doesn't matter whether or not it's unstoppable," I said firmly. "I might not know karkans, but I know necromancers, and whoever raised this thing from the ground bleeds red."

"You're gonna go after the master and not the thrall."

"I should've been doing that from the start. And now I finally have an idea of what to look for."

Chapter 20

The next day I learned "an idea of what to look for" wasn't the same thing as "a lead." Meaning, although I could fulfill my curiosity about the karkan, I had little actionable intelligence to find it.

I started by doing the appropriate research. Centuries ago, a host of Albanians fled the Ottoman Empire and landed in the Calabria region of Italy, importing their culture into villages so remote they preserved elements of their history better than their motherland did.

Calabrian Albanians speak a version of Arbëresh that's practically extinct. Until the 1980s, the language's only written form was used by the Italo-Albanian Byzantine Church. These days, most villages don't even speak it anymore, and in-depth knowledge is difficult to track down.

My target was likely a Calabrian Albanian fresh from overseas, still familiar with the old ways, but what did that really get me? It wasn't like there was an Occult Albanian Facebook I could trawl.

I drove by Miami Memorial Park again, back in the Firebird, and, what did you know, it was the one day the gypsies weren't throwing a block party. Scout and I wandered back to the car dejected.

"Okay," I said into my phone, ending a short conversation. "Just make sure he gets back to me." I hung up and frowned. If I didn't know better, I'd say Chevalier was ghosting me.

I hadn't been able to update him on the Albanian angle. I figured he deserved to know since I'd sent him snooping on the West Africans, and at this point it was unlikely they were involved. Ozo Ebu may have had a bone to pick with me, but he was unlikely to be so infatuated with the Christmas spirit.

I set my hands on my hips and eyed the cemetery grounds with half a mind to set up camp until the Roma troupe showed up. Instead I caught a few men in the middle of pointing me out. They were South American, maybe, and dollars to donuts part of the santero network. They looked away, pretending not to notice me, but one of them was immediately on his phone.

I clicked my tongue. "It appears we've been spotted."

Scout sat down and let his tongue hang.

"What do you say? Should we stick around and wait for another shootout?"

The large mutt's tail thumped the ground.

I chuckled and scratched his head. "I wouldn't do that to you again. Let's get out of here."

We loaded up. When I drove by the santeros, I put the

window down and stared to let them know I was onto them. None were man enough to follow me so we were in the clear.

That got me thinking about my santero problem. Johnny Red had been a knucklehead with an ax to grind, but whatever the rest of them had against me, it couldn't be enough to motivate murder. Sure, there was a bounty on my head, but the santeros didn't pack the firepower to take me on. But could I really take that for granted?

Maybe it was time to play a little defense.

I'd been operating on the assumption that no one from the Holiday Village shootout was still alive to question, but that wasn't exactly true, was it? The olive oil lady had dimed me out, and she had a small shop in Little Havana.

It was worth a quick visit.

Not too many cars filled the road but, as usual, the curbs and small parking lots were full. I did a drive-by of the sundries shop. It was part of an aging strip mall with metal bars over the storefront windows. That said, this particular shop had a measure of care put into its facade. A freshly painted exterior, a few potted plants, and a sidewalk chalkboard that probably had an inspirational greeting.

It was good to see the lady taking an active interest in bettering the neighborhood. Too bad she was a traitorous piece of garbage.

From the street, it was hard to tell if the shop was open or closed. Despite the cars crowding the lot, not many people milled about. As I drove the rest of the block, I didn't see a lot of activity at all except for a literal dumpster fire. A patrol car waved drivers around the hazard obstructing the alley. Since the burning dumpster was a safe distance away from the side of the building, I assumed the cop was waiting for the fire department to arrive and do their thing.

I had to drive three more blocks to find a space on a back street sufficiently distanced from the police officer. Scout and I unloaded and began our march, and I got a weird feeling on the street. Usually there were people sitting on upside-down buckets listening to salsa or merengue drifting from open storefronts. There was none of that today. The shops were open but guarded. For whatever reason, the populace seemed more buttoned down than usual.

I turned a corner and headed down the final stretch. Finally, a crowd of pedestrians rushed my way. Momentary relief at the sight switched to alert. These people were panicking. They broke into a run, straight for me.

"Cool it," I said in response to Scout's warning growl.

I braced myself in front of the dog as the people scurried past. "Hey!" I called, stepping in the path of a teenager. "What's the matter?"

"*Una bomba!*" he cried. "Get out of here!" He took after the others.

Scout and I were left alone, looking around. Was someone throwing pipe bombs into dumpsters? Was there an arsonist on the loose?

"Eyes forward," I told the dog, and continued to the shop.

A low whine carried on the wind. It grew louder as a small drone flew from over a nearby rooftop. I ducked against a store's security bars, under the awning.

"Evacuate this area," announced a computerized voice. "Danger. Evacuate this area."

My brow furrowed. Drones were regularly meant for eyes in the sky, but this one either didn't see me or didn't care to look. It sped away on whirring rotors, periodically repeating the same prerecorded warning.

Now I knew what the people were running from.

Ahead, a man in dark clothes stepped onto the sidewalk. He wore a mask and headed away from me. I slowed as I connected his movement as coming from the olive oil shop.

I hurried to cross the street and the man broke into a sprint. I gave chase, glancing at the storefront as I passed. Cursive handwriting on the chalkboard read, "*Lo que es para ti siempre te encuentra.*" "What's for you always finds you."

I canted my head as I ran, sensing something amiss. What a load of—

The sundries shop exploded. Flames and jagged glass flipped me sideways. I landed hard, ears ringing. Scout, already ahead of me, charged back and bit my pant leg, trying to pull me away from the fiery wreckage.

The front door had blown open and I gazed inside.

Shelves and tables had been flattened by something much more powerful than a pipe bomb. No one inside could've possibly made it.

I pushed to my feet. "I'm fine," I snapped, jogging stiffly after the man in the mask. Scout swept passed me, but a pickup truck swerved around the corner with more masked men inside. They were too far ahead to catch. The culprit braced himself in the bed of the truck, gaze lingering on me as they escaped.

Damn it. Why would anyone go after the olive oil lady?

It could've been some sort of santero payback. By twisted logic, she was the reason Johnny Red had marched to his death. But the drones didn't fit that narrative. The santeros weren't a tech savvy bunch, and this announcement was about more than saving lives.

No, this was a terrorist action. The men in the truck weren't wearing patches, but they smelled like militia to me. The Vanguard also lost lives at the Holiday Village. Any investigation into the santeros might've linked the booth to the shop. Maybe they were investigating deeper leads. Maybe they wanted to question an eyewitness about what really happened in the park.

Sirens filled the street, and a fire engine was the first to arrive. It had probably originally been dispatched to deal with the dumpster but turned into the strip mall instead. Where I was. Right in the middle of ground zero.

I turned to leave.

"Hey!" someone called. A cop car pulled to the curb. "Sir, come back."

I cut into the alley and broke into a run. Maybe it was a dumb move, but it was instinct. I just wanted to get out of there, and the out-of-shape officer didn't have a chance to catch me.

Scout and I looped around the building and headed to my car. Only two blocks left, but more sirens joined the fracas. I considered running straight for the car. I considered just turning myself in. I hadn't done anything. Then a whirring noise approached.

The drone hovered above. Instead of the prerecorded computerized garble, a voice sounded like someone over a bullhorn. "I've got you."

I put my hand up to block the camera, reached into a shadow, and pulled out my shotgun. "Be careful what you wish for." I blasted the drone. Birdshot tore it to pieces and it crashed into the street.

But the gunshot just announced my position. I dropped the sawed off and retreated into the residential back streets. It was the long way but hopefully avoided the authorities. After a circuitous route, we had to loop back. I hurried to the Firebird, but a black Explorer swerved into my path. Scout skidded to a stop some ways ahead and looked back. I locked eyes and whispered, "Run." The dog spun around and disappeared down the street.

Federal agents hopped from the truck with pistols trained on me. My hands were already in the air as Special Agent Rita Bell stepped from the passenger seat.

"Cisco Suarez," she bristled, grinning like she'd just won the lottery. "It's time you and I had our talk."

Chapter 21

The feds took me to a surprisingly low-rent safe house: a budget business motel on Flagler one step above taking payment by the hour. The heavily textured carpet smelled a mix of mold, smoke, and detergent, with each receiving honorable mentions in the competition for most offensive odor in an enclosed living space. Special Agent Rita Bell stepped outside for a phone call while three agents leered over me.

They had me sitting on the bed wearing flex-cuffs behind my back. That was their first mistake. In his day, Opiyel the Shadow Dog was known as The One Who Cannot Be Bound. The nickname was earned back when rope was the going binding, with modern metal throwing a wrench into things, but even-more-modern plastic proved just as useless. Given the need, I could slip into shadow and free myself instantly.

Of course, doing so would out me as the Shadow Man, which was the last thing I wanted. But that itself was a valuable point. If the feds really knew what they were up against, they would've used cold iron, a regular pair of handcuffs. This realization gave me confidence that my secrets were still my own and the interrogation was only a temporary setback.

I didn't know two of the agents, a woman and a man, both in their thirties. The third was Carter. Not only had we previously met, but he'd been the recipient of my fist to his face after getting between me and Milena. Carter was built like a tree trunk, a little older and experienced, with a buzz of short white hair atop his head. He was an old-school G-Man, and he was only too happy to have me.

"You're in for it now," he crowed, smirking with his cohorts.

"In for what, a cheap date?" I shot back. "At least put some chocolates on my pillow."

He snorted heartily. "You always talk tough, don't you? You think you're above it all. The police, the lawyers, the law." He leaned close. "I hate to be the bearer of bad news, but we are the federal fucking government, and your ass is ours."

"Is that a no on the chocolates?"

He scoffed in my face, spraying spittle. I clenched my jaw and fought off the urge to headbutt him. He must've noticed.

"Wanna do something, cowboy? Wanna take me on? Ramirez." The woman stepped close and he handed her his pistol. "There we go. Now it's a fair fight."

"You gonna untie me fir—"

Carter planted his fist into my temple. He must've been a boxer in another life because it was a solid blow. It rocked me to the side and made me lightheaded for a second or five, but I resisted the urge to fully lie down. I resumed my straight posture and simpered at him.

"I owed you that one," he said. "Now it's time for a little interest on the top."

The door opened as he drew a fist back and Agent Bell stepped in. "What's going on?" she asked.

Carter stepped away, recovered his gun, and reholstered it. "Just laying down the ground rules," he answered.

She looked to me for a chance to elaborate, but I remained stoic. There was no point getting into it with the FBI. The sooner I let them tell me what I was doing here, the sooner I'd be on my way.

"You wanted to talk," I started. "Let's talk. What do you want to know?"

Agent Bell pulled a chair from the desk and set it across from me and sat. "For one, Cisco, what were you doing in Little Havana today?"

I cleared my throat. I'd been hoping she would skip current business in lieu of old, but no such luck. And that left me in a bind even the Shadow Dog couldn't slip.

I hadn't done anything illegal. There was nothing they could hold me for past suspicion. Which didn't mean I could come clean. I couldn't explain the olive oil lady's connection to the Holiday Village shootout because, on the record, I hadn't been there. Admitting that would get Evan into trouble, since he'd never disclosed my presence in his report.

Now... maybe Rita already suspected. Maybe she had a witness that put me at the scene. To avoid entrapping myself, it behooved me not to lie about it, but I still wasn't going to freely volunteer the information.

"Would you believe I'm a fan of hipster EVOO?" I chanced.

She grinned. "So the sundries store *was* your target."

I sighed. "Don't say it like that, Agent Bell. *Target.* I'm not a terrorist."

"Then give me a non-evasive answer."

I winced. Rita Bell's ire was entirely evident. She'd been hounding me for months, and now that she finally had me it was a full-court press.

"Gladly," I assured her. "That 'sundries shop' may look normal on the surface, but it has a reputation in the magic scene."

Carter scoffed, but Rita's interest was piqued. "Magic?"

"Santero gangs."

It wasn't really the truth, but it wasn't a lie either. Let's call it an educated guess. The deal was, I didn't know the olive oil lady and I'd never been to the shop before. But she'd not only been aware that Johnny Red had been looking for me, she'd known how to contact him. There was enough of a connection that the FBI might dig up some corroboration.

"Santeros," repeated the special agent. "Are you moonlighting on the Holiday Village shooting?"

My eyes widened. "The Holiday... No. This is in regards

to my work on the Quentin Capshaw case. Since the crime scene showed a presence of occult markers, I'm pinging contacts in the underground, trying to stir up proof of anyone having a beef with him." I considered introducing Rita to my stew metaphor but decided against it. She was the bitter garlic.

She watched me without hiding her skepticism. "You expect me to believe that? Are you aware Mrs. Campos was one of the vendors at the Village?"

I shook my head idly like I was trying to remember, and then I pretended I had already answered the question.

"What about the Vanguard Against Parahumans?" she asked. "Are you following them?"

I gave her my best puzzled expression. "Are you talking about those internet LARPers? What do they have to do with... Wait a minute... You think they were responsible for the explosion?" I figured I could throw her a bone even while keeping up the act. "You know, I saw some sort of drone warning people away. Maybe you could trace it and see where it came from." Let it never be said Cisco Suarez isn't a concerned citizen.

"I would, if it wasn't filled with buckshot. The local police found it and are running it down now."

I swallowed down the urge to correct her about the birdshot. Maybe she had set me up on purpose.

"Cisco, have you had any interaction with the Vanguard?"

Okay, this was a tricky one to answer. Did she know something about the shootout or not?

"I'm not psychic, Agent Bell. How would I know if I've ever interacted with anybody that's a member of the militia, or who identifies with who? But no, not that I'm aware of."

She put her elbows on her knees and leaned in. "Does the militia bother you? Are you doing anything about them?"

I wasn't much of an actor and didn't know how to look properly shocked. "If they're blowing up storefronts, of course they bother me, but I'm a consultant, Agent Bell. As far as I'm aware, the police are working on it. And let me stop you right there, because I haven't been in communication with them. Evan's been pulling OT since that happened. In the meantime, I've been investigating the Capshaw case. Which brings me to my question."

"I'm asking the questions," she said.

"What are *you* doing about those explosions? Because, to me, this here feels like a waste of time."

Carter stomped forward to give me a shove. I pushed my body against it, and Rita slapped him away. "Agent," she scolded. He grumbled and stormed to the other end of the room, which wasn't very far. Then again, this room could've been Hard Rock Stadium and it wouldn't have been far enough.

Rita Bell's narrow lips twisted. "Waste or not, you're stuck with me for the long haul. I can do this all day until you level with me."

"At your service," I returned as sarcastically as I could muster. "Apparently."

She bobbed her head in satisfaction and mulled

something over. After a minute of silence, she said, "Tell me about the Shadow Man."

I sighed again. "I don't know what to tell you, Rita, and that's the truth."

"Agent Bell."

"Fine. But you've been wrong about me before. Don't forget you thought I was the Manifesto Killer. I didn't."

Her fingers in the air shooed the thought away like a fly. "That's old news. I'm investigating a new vigilante now. Someone with your experience should recognize the peculiarities with this case."

"Agent Bell, with all this dogged pursuit, you're gonna make me suspect you believe in magic."

"Well, Cisco, after everything you've seen, are you trying to convince me you don't?"

We entered a tense staring contest until Agent Carter sniggered. "What a load. You're letting this guy get to you," he said to his superior.

"Agent Carter, wait outside please." Her eyes were still locked with mine.

"Wha— I... You know what? That's a good idea." The gruff man swung the door wide and stormed out.

"The two of you as well, please."

The other agents looked at each other. "You sure you don't want backup?" asked Ramirez.

"I'm sure."

The two agents departed and closed the door behind them. At this point my eyes were watering because I hadn't blinked for a full minute.

Rita Bell smiled graciously, leaned back, and shut her eyes. Victory! I grumbled about the other agents not being around to see it while I blinked fresh moisture into my eyes.

"Cisco," she began in a conversational tone, no doubt attempting to salvage the interrogation, "you and I don't need to be so adversarial here. Yes, I admit I was off base about Manifesto. And yes, the law doesn't take kindly to vigilantes. But there are those who might call you a hero."

I pursed my lips. "That's a weird thing to call a guy who runs a coffee shop..."

"Your side hustle, Cisco, and I'm not referring to the consulting gig. I believe you know things most people don't. I believe you can do things most people can't. I think you are, or at least are close to, the Shadow Man."

I hissed. "What is this crusade? They're gonna say you're crazy."

"Better to be crazy than a fool."

"They're often the same thing."

She frowned. "Then let's not call it crazy. Let's call it enlightened. Let's call it something I've been tracking the better part of my career, and something I'm so close to I can smell it."

I paused, lowered my nose to my arm pit, and took a sniff.

"Cut the crap, Cisco. You're a fan of olive oil? Well I'm throwing you an olive branch. I need to know the Shadow Man's intentions."

My lips twisted into a scowl. "The Shadow Man's a myth. Sorry to spoil the illusion, but magic isn't real.

Quentin couldn't read minds, otherwise he wouldn't be dead. And if I could do what you think I could do, why would I be wasting my time sitting here?"

Her features twitched. A little disappointment, a little anger, but she cooled off quick enough. "Well, *someone* was on that video at the construction site. *Someone* was with Manifesto when he died. And *someone* dropped this at the scene."

She pulled a plastic bag from her jacket. In it was a burner phone. It was an old one but doubtless one of mine. If it was the same one I thought it was, I'd last seen it in the talons of one of the black owls at said construction site. I now knew the birds to be strixes, the servants of the stiges.

"You implying that's mine?" I asked gruffly.

"I wouldn't dream of it. One of the techs got a little cocky opening this up. Tried to guess the passcode without knowing it was rooted with a boot loader that restores factory settings after two incorrect guesses. The phone's completely wiped."

"Fat fingers," I jibed, relaxing the muscles in my neck. "Sorry, I'm not a computer guy."

She smiled. "If I checked the phone in your pocket, Cisco, would it be rooted with the same security measures?"

"It would take a warrant to find out."

"No need."

I grimaced. The warrant wasn't necessary. She knew it was my phone. She knew I was at the scene, even if she couldn't prove it. My Rita Bell problem wasn't going away anytime soon.

"Is someone making you do this?" she asked idly, slipping her evidence bag back into her jacket.

"Do what, Agent Bell?"

"The consultant business. The interest in magic. Who taught you this stuff? I want to know."

"Watch out what you wish for," I told her, more earnest than evasive. "It's not a safe world out there."

"Exactly why I became an FBI agent," she smoothly returned. "Actually, it's a little more specific than that. My dad was a cop." She leaned back in the chair and crossed one heeled pantsuit leg over the other. "He wasn't a complicated man. The farthest thing from a crude thug, mind you, but when it came to the job he was as straightforward as possible. Clock in, do the work, and clock out. He was my ordinary, everyday hero."

I settled into the story, waiting for the "but." It didn't take long.

"My daddy saw something one day. Something that shook him to his core. He was never the same after that. He wasn't just afraid for his life, he was afraid for the world."

"What did he see?"

"Hellfire. That's how he described it. He said magical flames swallowed someone whole right before his eyes. Hellfire that danced from the killer's fingers."

I scoffed. "Come on. He was confused by what he saw. You know how much those old-school cops favor alcohol."

"It wasn't the drink," she said more sternly than I would've expected. Her cheeks tightened and she took a breath before resuming her cool. "My father had been on the wagon for over a year. He saw what he said he saw. And no one believed him, not even me, his only daughter. Not until he was found in his car two weeks later. The whole thing was burnt to a crisp."

I swallowed down the guilt of trying to play it off as a hallucination. That must've been hard for her.

"I was fifteen years old. My father never got to take me to prom. He never had the chance to see me graduate at the top of my class, or join the FBI. But I never forgot what he said he saw, and what happened to him. I never forgot what I need to do."

I worked my jaw. "Did they ever find the killer?"

She shook her head. "The scene was a mess. The usual accelerants weren't present. The fire chief didn't know what to make of it." She uncrossed her legs and leaned close again. "But I did. I know what really happened, even if I don't. You understand? And so I've devoted myself to taking cases with occult ties. I've investigated mystic groups and practitioners. It's why I was the most qualified to investigate Manifesto. Because, just like you, I'm familiar with these things." Rita Bell looked me straight in the eyes with unwavering conviction. "Now tell me, Cisco, am I crazy?"

My gaze dropped to the floor. It was an awful story. But her desire for knowledge was misdirected. It couldn't bring her father back.

"There are lots of dangerous people doing lots of dangerous things," I leveled, voice gravelly. "I've seen a ton of sick things in my sphere of study. It nearly got me killed all those years ago. But I don't know anything about your father, Rita. I don't know what he was into, or who killed him, or how to help."

She put a hand on my knee. "But you know *something*, Cisco. You can let me into your world. Let me see it as you do." She lifted my chin and I met her willful gaze. "Magic is real, isn't it?"

I fought the lump in my throat, wanting to say something but needing to stay quiet. I didn't know Rita Bell. I couldn't trust a fed.

But then, as a fellow human being, one who'd also been sorely wronged, didn't she have a right to know? Couldn't I give her the slightest bit of closure, the smallest measure of peace, with just a simple nod?

I started to lift my head.

Carter slammed the door open. Rita flinched and spun on him. "I ordered you out of here!"

"You didn't get the call? It's the locals." He held up his phone as a visual aid. His eyes went from me to her to the scooted-in chair. "What are you doing?"

She shook it off and retrieved her cell phone. "Tell me what happened."

"There's been another murder. Just like Capshaw. This is officially a serial case now."

Chapter 22

After news like that, it wasn't hard to convince Rita to take off the flex-cuffs. Considering the moment we just had, if we weren't friends fighting on the same side, we were at least sympathetic victims. On top of that, we were technically coworkers, both linked to the City of Miami homicide investigation of the now-multiple karkan murders.

Sitting in the back of the Bureau Range Rover, I massaged my forehead. If Agent Bell was chasing magic, she could've hardly done better than the karkanscholl. Unlike Manifesto, who mostly came off as a crazed nutjob rando, it would be difficult to explain away a bony zombie wearing chain mail.

I grated my teeth as I pondered December's Cold Moon. Milena had warned us, hadn't she? But then, the moon wouldn't be out until tonight. Something was off about the whole thing.

Evan's text came through when we were almost there. "There's another one that looks like Capshaw. If you move now you can scope the scene before the FBI barges in."

"Too late," I texted back. "I'm already on the way, courtesy of the government dime." After a second I added, "Long story." I didn't bother elaborating and he didn't bother asking.

Soon we turned down a dismal backstreet in Opa Locka. My thoughts darkened as we parked near a rundown shanty of a warehouse that reeked of impropriety. They might as well have put a sign across the entry that read, "Illicit Business Inside." In a way, they kinda did. A blue full moon was spray-painted across the large wall between the office door and the loading bay.

The sun was long in the sky, casting surreal shadows across the warehouse. Stepping outside the vehicle, a chill wind prickled the hairs on my arms. I was gonna need to start rocking a pullover. Until then, there was nothing I could do but grin and bear it.

A wall of eyes met me from behind a police barricade: Igbo and Yoruba gang members with expressions twisted in contempt. If they didn't hate me before, they certainly did now. Coming from the street as I did, consorting with police was a bad look. Cozying up to the feds was downright sus.

I ignored the necromancers and the biting chill and headed inside.

"You weren't kidding," muttered Evan, greeting me and my escort at the door with a flat face.

Special Agent Bell converged. "Are you the ranking officer on the scene? This has obvious ties to Manifesto, and the Bureau would like to take an active part in the investigation."

"Be my guest, but Detective Mullen's in charge. Talk to him."

"I will." She proceeded ahead with the other agents.

I smirked as we lagged behind them. "You're just gonna let them take over like that?"

"The FBI doesn't take over, they offer resources, which, if you haven't noticed, we sorely need. My ass is on fire over the militia stuff, and we're probably gonna need their insight on that too. Uncle Sam's welcome to share the workload."

I shook my head and muttered something about TV being a lie.

"This is a place of business," continued Evan, "so we have a few cameras. One covering the front door exterior. There's two in the backyard, one watching the back gate and a broken one covering the parking lot. The only one inside is watching the office. Problem is, even with all those eyes, none of them saw anything."

We caught up to Agent Bell as she spoke with the old medical examiner attending the body. I hadn't met the ME yet, but he wore a tattered official ID and appeared knowledgeable. If I had to guess, and based on the profile of this case, he was the best in Miami, and the one we'd been waiting on at Capshaw's house. Major Bruce Petty had no doubt laid into the man to make sure he was more punctual with future homicides.

"Look what the feds dragged in," laughed Mullen as he

returned from elsewhere in the warehouse.

Rita's eyes narrowed. "I would urge you to drop that metaphor at once." Carter eyed the detective in cocksure warning.

"What?" asked Mullen with a dismissive shrug. "It was a dumb joke. By your reactions, you'd think somebody died."

The detective was on a roll.

The dead man lay in the middle of the warehouse, apparently having fallen from the catwalk above. His elbow had shattered in an attempt to stop the fall, and his neck crooked at an impossible angle as testament that gravity doesn't negotiate. His mouth was wide open as if gasping for air, and what I would bet money was cemetery dirt was spattered around him in clumps.

This was definitely the work of the karkan, and worse than recognizing the killer was recognizing the victim. A fellow necromancer. Which explained the crew outside.

"Damn it," I said.

"You know him?" asked Evan.

I nodded. "This is Ozo Ebu, boss of one of the West African gangs in this hood." The officers and agents all turned to me as I explained. I pointed to the painted moon on his forehead. "These guys are Igbo and they call themselves the Night Walkers. The blue full moon is their symbol."

"Night Walkers sounds ominous," noted Mullen.

"It is. Their alusi, a sort of patron spirit, is Ogbunabali, which means He Kills At Night."

Mullen snorted. "Looks like this one went the other

way."

My cheek twitched as I considered withholding the next part, but it wasn't like I was getting them into trouble. "Some of the gawkers outside are Night Walkers, I think."

Rita directed Ramirez and Sotomayer outside to go question them. Evan snickered. "Good luck with that, agents."

"Oh ye of little faith," countered Rita.

"It's not faith, it's a law of physics. You won't get a word out of that crew."

She clicked her tongue in defiance, but she would find out the hard way. Rita should've known better after searching for magic her whole life. The Igbo were as tight-lipped as they came.

"Ozo's an honorific," I continued. "See the scars on his face?" Lines, long healed, ran up and down the bald man's cheeks and temples. His arms too. "Self mutilation. It signifies a high rank. Ebu was well respected." I scoffed inwardly. "I guess I was wrong to suspect him of Capshaw."

Agent Bell stepped closer. "What's that?"

"Oh, it's nothing. Quentin and Ebu crossed paths once or twice. I had a sneaking suspicion the former was killed by the latter, but it was nothing more than a bad guess. Ebu was innocent."

But I was still put off by the timing of it all. The Cold Moon wasn't until later tonight. Was Milena crazy or close enough to prescient?

"When did this happen?" I asked the medical examiner.

The old timer scrutinized me.

"He's okay," vouched Evan.

I must've had my rattiest tank top on today because the ME checked with Mullen next. Or maybe he was just the type to cross his t's and dot his i's. The senior detective nodded in turn.

"Last night, easy," declared the medical examiner. "Probably a similar time of death as the first victim."

So Milena was wrong but... I snorted in revelation and turned to Evan. "Yesterday was the Massacre of the Innocents."

Rita crossed her arms expectantly. "And that is...?"

This was where I had to be careful. "Just an observation, agent. Given the timing of Quentin's death, I researched the Twelve Days of Christmas."

"And?" she prodded.

"And, counting today, there are eight days left."

Evan ground his jaw. I hadn't filled him in on the complete story, but he'd worked with me enough that he was as caught up as he needed to be.

Agent Bell frowned between glances at Evan, the body, and me. "So this is what your consultancy buys. Familiarity with the players, their rituals, and the speculation that results." She said it matter-of-factly rather than disparagingly, as if she were taking mental notes.

I, of course, did more than those things, possessing as I did the rare job qualification of practical experience in the field of necromancy. But discussing the empty grave in the potter's field and the existence of the karkanscholl was one bone too many to throw her way. At some point my knowledge would work against me, painting me a disreputable kook.

Rita Bell's father burned alive, whatever the source of the flames. Convincing her people could be raised from the dead was a much tougher sell. But then, she was the one who swore she wanted to believe.

"Okay, expert," said Detective Mullen, "let's hear your cockamamie theory this time. I enjoy tackling difficult problems from multiple angles."

Again, what could've come off as demeaning was said in earnest. I couldn't be too self-conscious about my role here. I wasn't on the case to shield them from the crazy, I was here to explain it. Instead of hiding what I knew from them (and effectively obstructing the investigation), it was best to attack it from a clinical perspective, framing the events through the lens of a killer obsessed with myth rather than an actual myth come alive.

The strategy had the added benefit of being a good litmus test for Rita's receptiveness to the arcane.

"First things first," I announced. "Does Ebu have a knife wound?"

"It's self evident," answered the ME, pointing to the T-shirt stained with blood. I walked around the body to get a better look at Ebu's side.

"Can I see it?" I asked. "The symbol."

White eyebrows creased over his eyes and the ME pulled the shirt away. My face flushed, and I was at a loss for words.

This wound was simpler than Quentin's, but it was just

as unmistakably a message. That much I had expected.

The part that left me reeling was the symbol itself. I didn't know what it meant but I'd seen it before. It was the same scribble Milena had drawn with a sharpie.

Chapter 23

"Cisco?" prodded Agent Bell.

I realized the whole group had been staring at me for upwards of a minute.

This was bad. I couldn't let on that I'd seen the glyph before because it would draw suspicion on Milena. But past keeping a low profile, I was well and truly concerned about how Milena had come by this knowledge.

"What is it, Cisco?" urged Evan.

I shook out of it. "I... I'm not sure what this means..." Milena had muttered something about the moon being high in the sky. "I'm guessing this image, the circle, represents the full moon. And it's tonight at 10:30."

"I'm telling you, this man died last night," said the ME.

"I know. I'm working on a theory that the glyphs represent the reason for their deaths."

"You think something is going down tonight?" suggested Mullen. "Maybe the killer wanted to prevent Ebu from doing something during the full moon?"

"Maybe. I don't know."

"May I suggest the obvious?" cut in Rita. She stepped over and pointed at the blue moon on Ozo Ebu's forehead. "They're both full moons."

That was another possibility. "Is there bloody dirt in the mouth?"

The old medical examiner studied me. "You're the one who picked up on that last time, aren't you?" He nodded. "This one's the same as well. We also have deep bruising on the vic's wrists, arms, and neck that suggest being bound with metal chains."

This particular bruising was more obvious than before. Ebu's marks were darker, meaning the struggle and ensuing damage was worse. The ozo was a powerful man. He would've fought back, and he would've done ten times the job Quentin had. And he still perished.

"No footprints though," added Detective Mullen. "Not yet, at least."

I scanned the room. There were multiple entrances and pathways between rows of boxes and shelves. The large space was a makeshift mechanic shop, including a lift on the far wall. The Night Walkers were petty car thieves who likely stripped down their prizes and moved them upstate.

Unfortunately, the dingy environment made it difficult to pick out details related to the crime scene versus the default level of grime. There were no dirty footprints in sight.

"So this mark could be related to the full moon," Mullen conjectured. "Or the Night Walkers. Or something else entirely. What's your take on Capshaw's mark?"

I didn't answer immediately, and Agent Bell's eyes narrowed. "You have a theory, don't you?"

"I think it refers to hypnotism," I said.

"And you know this how?"

Here went nothing...

"I've done research into Albanian mythology," I said. "They believe in a bogeyman, a spirit of Midwinter that kills over the course of Twelvetide. Whoever's perpetrating these murders believes in this karkan, a killer that may be wearing old robes and"—I cleared my throat—"chain mail."

Mullen's whiskers spread into a wide grin. "Armor. Like World of Warcraft." He shook his head and chuckled. "At least they're getting creative."

"That would exclude this killer being aligned with Manifesto," remarked Agent Bell. "If our new killer does indeed see themselves on the side of magic."

"Not necessarily," interjected Evan. "Sometimes you need to fight fire with fire." He stopped short of revealing that Manifesto had been ensorcelled by demons himself.

The FBI agent canted her head. "What does Midwinter want then?" she mused. "Manifesto announced his intentions. Why are these victims being killed? Vengeance for a wrong committed? Is this justice?"

I ground my teeth and shook my head. "Karkans are rumored to be assassins, so the motives could be anything."

"Which keeps us at square one," grumbled Mullen.

I didn't agree there. I needed to believe we'd made some progress tracking this thing. But Rita was right to look for motive. There was a human necromancer in the city who wanted Quentin and Ebu dead. Why?

I inspected the ceiling. The metal catwalk ran from one wall to the other, right over our heads. It was the obvious spot where Ebu had fallen from. "Can I get eyes on top?"

"Right this way," said Evan. He made a move toward the front of the warehouse where metal steps ran along the wall.

I hiked my thumb the other way. "You mind?"

He paused and shrugged his shoulders. "Either way works."

As we walked away, Rita questioned the ME about cause of death.

"Yikes," griped Evan once we were alone. "The FBI's on you pretty tight, huh?"

"You don't know the half of it. They were in the middle of interrogating me when you called."

"I didn't call," he countered. "I was hoping to give you some alone time first. I'm still wondering how they knew."

It was a riddle I couldn't answer since I hadn't seen who was on the call with Carter. Come to think of it, I wasn't even sure Agent Bell had received a call herself.

"If it makes you feel any better," hissed Evan, "I'm being hounded too. The mayor bitched me out for not keeping tabs on the Vanguard. The thing is, they shouldn't be our problem. They operate out of the Glades somewhere. Before the Holiday Village, they had zero presence within city limits."

"Who has jurisdiction in the Everglades?"

"Who doesn't? The Park Service. The various counties it

spans. Highway Patrol."

"Yeesh. How's anything get done?"

"It doesn't. The politics are worse than every bad eighties cop movie. Which is why I'm requesting the FBI's help." He stopped me and looked around to confirm we could speak privately. "Do you think this karkan business is militia related? Like Manifesto, they hate magic but turn it against itself?"

I hooked my hands in my jeans. "It's hard to argue with the timing, but the whole city's on edge. Any number of crazies could be striking while the iron is hot. The Russian mob just tried to have me killed. And Manifesto was never about Manifesto—it was the black witches."

He winced. "So we're back to the stiges."

"Only as another possible lead we can't tell anyone about."

We continued to the far wall at the back of the warehouse to an alternate set of stairs. The entire structure was built from steel, cut through with a pattern that allowed visibility through each step to the floor. Besides making the structure much lighter, the texture aided in surface grip. There were no footprints per se, but close examination of the edges of the holes revealed small grains of dirt.

"I'll be damned," muttered Evan.

Underneath the first several steps, on the dirty concrete floor, was more cast-off dirt. It wasn't nearly as much as before, which I attributed to the thrall not being as fresh, but it was still there. And still way more than would have naturally been tracked out of the graveyard so many days later.

I scanned the back exits. One door was propped open and led to the back lot. "You said one of the outside cameras was broken?"

"Yes." He followed me to the door. "I know what you're thinking, but it's been broken for a while. Besides, it's pretty easy to sneak through the back while avoiding both cameras."

We stepped outside. He pointed to the first, working camera, that covered a section of the rear fence with the entrance gate. Any cars driving in or out of the yard would be recorded, but there were plenty of other places to hop the fence off camera.

"Where's the other one?" I asked.

Evan led me around the building. His nose wrinkled as a stiff breeze carried the scent of urine and rot. The back lot had multiple junked vehicles in various states of disrepair. It was an oddly shaped corner abutting a large wall. It didn't make sense to break in this way since it was more work and easily enough done elsewhere.

"There," said Evan, signaling the top of the building. An old mounted camera hung limply at an odd angle.

"What good is a fake camera if it's not pointed in the right direction?" I asked.

"Yeah. The owner says he needs to periodically get a ladder up their to tighten the mounting screws. Strangely enough, he swore he had just done that a few weeks ago."

"So the camera could've been purposely knocked loose last night?"

Evan chewed his lip and shrugged.

I eyed the lot and followed the sharp smell around an old VW Beetle with a mismatched door. Flies scattered from the corpse of a black cat. Its skin was shriveled, with fur falling off the body in clumps. It reminded me of the dead bird beside the karkan's grave.

"Gross," said Evan.

I turned in place and fixed on the broken security camera. We were in the center of the back lot and would've definitely been in the field of view of a properly positioned camera.

"What's on your mind?" asked Evan. "You think this is related?"

"I don't know. There's no reason at all to come back this way. The karkan could've snuck over the fence and entered the back door without being recorded. Instead, he came back here and disabled a camera at great risk, and for what? It doesn't make sense."

"We don't know for a fact that's what happened..."

I studied the surroundings, trying to make sense of it, but besides the cat and the camera, there was nothing to suggest the karkan had passed this way. When I spotted a greasy shop towel on one of the cars, I grabbed it, unfolded it, and laid it over the cat.

"How about we head back inside?" suggested Evan as he plugged his nose.

We headed the way we came and returned to the rear stairs, carefully stepping past the soil evidence and making our way to the top. The catwalk stretched across the wide floor. Jensen was crouched above the location of Ebu's body, setting down markers and taking photographs.

"I guess we're making this a regular thing," I joked.

He nodded toward Evan. "Talk to your boy. I was a special request."

"It's not me, it's Petty," Evan explained. "He wants to keep as few eyes on this as possible so the details stay contained and we don't end up with another salacious Manifesto situation."

I snorted. "Good to know he's concerned about optics in a time like this."

"Optics are important, Cisco."

Rita and Carter made their way up the front steps at the opposite end. Mullen, having probably already done the rounds, elected to save his knees and stayed at ground level.

Jensen's evidence markers matched those of the first crime scene. Scrapes and scratches on the catwalk railing that could only have come from metal against metal. More chain marks. This was where Ozo Ebu and the karkan had stood their ground. Blackened scorch marks were no doubt the result of Igbo spellcraft. I peeked over the railing to the grisly scene below. The assassin must've been strong to pick up someone so stout.

"I hope you're not running an investigation without me," warned Agent Bell as she caught up, only half in jest.

"Just doing what we can," said Evan. "We found some dirt on the rear steps."

Jensen's eyes lit up. "I'll get over there and block it off in a minute."

"I don't want you to keep your theories to yourself," said Rita.

"We're not," I replied, "which is why I waited till you could hear the rest of my research." I crossed my arms and leaned against the opposite railing. "Starting six hundred years ago, when the Ottoman Empire invaded Albania, centuries of fleeing countrymen migrated to Italy. Their old culture thrived in Calabria, keeping the old beliefs and myths alive."

"The writing," said Rita.

"They speak a Vaccarizzo Albanian subdialect of Arbëresh, an ancient language that's quickly going extinct. I believe our killer is familiar with this alphabet. It might be the best shot we have at catching him or her, outside of a careless mistake in commission of the crimes."

Jensen set his camera around his neck and grabbed his bag as he stood. "You know, Mother Teresa was an Albanian gypsy." He strolled away down the catwalk to collect his dirt samples.

Evan and I looked at each other. "Learn something new every day," he grumbled.

"So dead myths..." belabored Agent Carter in a sour tone. "You think this karkan is one of them?"

I hiked a shoulder. "It's what they believed."

"Arbëresh," mused Agent Bell. "That's actionable information. We'll put our linguists on it. In the meantime, I'm operating on the theory that the occult inclinations of the victims is the reason they were targeted. While the MO is vastly different from the militia attack at Bayfront Park, the anti-magic sentiment is a common denominator, and one that's sweeping over the city."

Evan winced at her cavalier declaration. I recalled the Magic Pizza shop and had to agree with her. I glanced down at Ebu's body again, wondering what his confrontation with the dead was like. Had the big man fought with his usual self-sure gusto, or had he been afraid that a practice he'd immersed himself in his entire life had finally caught up to him?

"It's a working theory," I agreed. "Two attacks, two dead practitioners."

Evan's lips twisted. " 'Tis the season," he griped.

"Yeah, but is it a season to be merry, or open season on animists?"

Chapter 24

I spent a couple of hours at the crime scene before Evan could give me a ride back to my car. Rita had offered but I was keeping my distance, seeing as she had just kidnapped me. Besides, the talk back at the motel had gotten a little too close for comfort. With the new murder, everyone was refocused on finding the karkan, and I saw no reason to distract from that.

Once I was out of their hair, the police and the feds were free to do their own thing. I, unfortunately, discovered a new problem. I couldn't find my dog.

I marched up and down the residential blocks of Little Havana trying to sense Scout, and he wasn't there. It was the oddest thing.

Echoes of spellcraft are everywhere, but my powers don't have universal coverage. A connection to a thrall only goes so far. It wasn't possible, for example, to activate one of my few drones in the Everglades from the city. I needed to be near enough to feel them. The range of the dog whistle was a good stand-in.

Except, when I put the enchanted silver to my lips, nothing answered back.

I hopped into the Firebird next, venturing out into larger and larger loops of the neighborhood. No dice. The increased range didn't help.

For a zombie, my dog sure had a mind of his own. It made me wonder what exactly my last command to him was. Near as I could remember, I had simply told him to run.

Which meant, by now, with his paranormal endurance, Scout could be anywhere in the city.

I slowed as I approached a red truck staffed by firefighters rolling up a hose. A small house that doubled as a fortune teller shop was blackened with wet soot and still smoked. Someone had done a pretty good job of burning the joint down. While the building still stood, it wouldn't be open for business anytime soon. I ground my teeth and wondered what was happening to my city.

But I couldn't be everywhere at once.

On a hunch I returned to Brickell. I was disappointed as I pulled into the underground parking structure. Scout's presence was undetectable.

Luckily, he wasn't a normal dog that I needed to worry about. He wouldn't be aggressive with anyone. He wouldn't poo on any sidewalks or dig up any lawns. And while he may have appreciated a snack or two, he didn't need sustenance, shelter, or belly rubs. For all I knew, Scout was an outside dog. Maybe he preferred freedom over being huddled in my back seat. I sighed and hoped I was right.

Upstairs in the condo, I found a note on the bar from Kasper. He was covering a shift for Darcy. Which was just like the old man, too. Far from what I'd call a reliable employee, Kasper could barely be bothered to come in for shifts of his own, but when a friend was in need, he was there with bells on.

I smiled at the empty house and considered nuking some leftovers. Then I realized the opportunity. I found Milena in the bedroom so I kicked off my clothes and snuggled next to her under the blanket. She was fast asleep. I considered waking her, but that didn't last long. I hadn't rested much the night before, assassination attempt and all, and I was completely beat. I happily passed out beside her.

In the morning we lay awake for some time in a wordless embrace. It was a comfort to be there for somebody, and they for you. I stroked Milena's hair and only opened my mouth after I could tell she wasn't all there.

"Does it scare you?" I asked.

She rolled onto her back, wearing my Guns n' Roses tee. I rubbed the warm skin of her waist, just above her underwear, and she gave me a kiss. "Everything scares me these days. But it's nice being here."

I pressed my lips together and tried to smile. "Everything?"

"You know, I think I'm a little depressed. It's like Seleste died all over again. It's weird because we're mostly fine. We're happy together, we're healthy, but... *Dios mío*, I don't want to bother you with this."

I grabbed her hand and squeezed. "It's not a bother."

She blinked lazily and her lush lips crooked. "I just feel like the world is getting darker, you know?"

I answered with a reassuring nod, even though the acknowledgment wasn't the most comforting thought. I'd seen some troubling things these last few days, and I wasn't talking about the karkan. The zombie was just another supernatural threat, just another random plot on someone's bucket list.

The real problem was the temperament of the city. Everyday Miami folks were opening their eyes to the presence of magic in their midst. Giving in to their fear and tribalism. Their destructive tendencies.

Someone needed to talk some sense into them, starting with this militia, and I had half a mind to give it the old college try.

"Want me to take the day off?" I asked. "I could give you one of my famous Suarez massages."

She grinned. "As nice as that sounds, I'm too exhausted for one of your massages. Either I can't sleep or my dreams leave me restless and I can't even remember why." She swallowed and stared at the ceiling. I wondered what she saw. "I'm gonna take a long, hot bath with the jets on. Then I'm gonna take another ambi and pass out, if it's all right with you."

"A beautiful woman in my bed is always all right with me." I gave her waist a squeeze. "And nothing makes me happier than you being in my house. Want me to bring anything home for you?"

Her eyebrows widened at the possibilities. "Some guava

pastelitos would be bomb."

"As you wish."

I slipped out of bed and into a quick shower. Since I was feeling like a new man, I put on a fresh pair of jeans with holes and a clean ratty tank top. As I wound the dog-collar fetish around my wrist, it almost felt constricting, like I was putting a helmet on or something. I ignored the sensation and finished off with my red alligator boots. They were pretty scuffed by this point and needed a polish. Maybe next year.

Milena got out of bed to take the bathroom next. Her panties rode up her ass and I watched longingly as she disappeared behind the door. Then she opened the door, slipped out of the tee, and tossed it at my face before slamming the door shut. I grinned and made a mental note to ravish her later.

I locked up and passed by the coffee shop downstairs. It was doing brisk business for a weekday, and I was surprised to find Kasper again on shift.

"This Clarence fellow is pretty good," remarked the biker, hiking his thumb at the new employee manning the espresso machine. "Maybe not the most gregarious guy behind the counter, but he's fast with the orders and makes a delicious cup. It lets me be the personality of the store."

I was impressed to hear that, and reminded that I needed to make some time to work the shop myself. I hadn't been able to see the new kid in action yet.

"Darcy suckered you into covering her shift again?" I teased.

His eyebrows came together. "Actually, she quit."

"She what?"

He sighed sharply. "I figured she told me 'cause she didn't want to tell you. Not sure what kind of spat you two got into, but..." He watched me take out my phone and dial. "Broham, if she didn't call you to deliver the news, she's not gonna pick up—"

The call went to voicemail a little too quickly. "Hey, Darcy, just checking in about Outlaw Coffee. Give me a call back." I shoved the phone back in my pocket.

"So, what happened between you?" asked Kasper.

"Nothing. This is the first I heard about this and it doesn't make sense. Darcy liked this job." I wondered if she'd been planning on quitting for a while. Maybe it was why she'd insisted on hiring Clarence. But that didn't mean anything. We needed the extra help anyway. The shop, despite my best efforts, was getting busier. I recalled the night before last. Darcy was going out with... "Shen."

Kasper perked at the mention. "The Society illusionist?"

"Darcy mentioned them being in town." I couldn't call Shen directly since his number had changed. I could do what Darcy had done and reach Simon, but I regularly changed burner phones and only kept my closest contacts saved. I didn't have his number on hand.

Besides, Darcy would call me back. There was no reason not to. Kasper was wrong about there being a spat.

"Anyway, Clarence mentioned his aunt is looking for a job. I asked her to come in today for an interview. See if we can patch up our staff problem."

I nodded absently. The truth was, business was hardly my concern. The shop was a base of operations that provided an air of legitimacy. It provided me a vote on the building's HOA board. I couldn't care less whether it was profitable or not.

"Sounds great, Kasper."

"That'll give you time to patch things up with the girl."

I narrowed my eyes. "Nothing happened. It's no big deal, whatever it is. She'll get back to me."

"If you say so. Busy day?"

"Boring," I said. "Hopefully. But when you get a chance, I want you to translate that scribble Milena drew. I found it on Ozo Ebu's body yesterday."

His eyes narrowed. "Seriously?"

"Unfortunately. I'll send you the image."

"So Milena was right about the Cold Moon last night?"

I sighed. "Not really. Ebu was killed the day before. Unless something happened I don't know about, last night was uneventful. Our new theory is the moon symbol relates to the Night Walker gang, but we can't be sure. That's why we need it translated."

Clarence squeezed past Kasper and placed a *cafecito* on the counter. "Good morning, Mr. S. One for the road?"

I smiled. "Always." I downed the shot of sweetened coffee that would ensure I had energy for hours. Kasper was right about the kid. The froth was perfect. I held out my hand. "By the way, Clarence, good work."

The young man hesitantly shook my hand. We'd need to work on his grip, but no one was perfect.

Then I started my boring day. No more militia. No more undead traveler. I was just looking for a single Albanian parish member who perhaps took his Christmastide a little too seriously. I started on my list of Orthodox churches in Miami.

That assassination attempt might've been the luckiest break that happened to me regarding this case. Many Orthodox churches were Russian, which explained the mob's familiarity with the subject matter. Once they gave me the lead and I did a little digging, I found other Eastern European denominations existed, including an Albanian one.

The churches themselves were heavily ceremonial, and the priests wore traditional vestments. The first church didn't have anyone available to talk to me, but at the second I met Archpriest Pavel. The Albanian Diocese, he told me, didn't have a large presence in the South. I didn't really consider Miami the South but kept that to myself. There wasn't even a dedicated church in the city, so any Albanian immigrants would likely attend any of the Orthodox choices available.

When I asked about the karkanscholl, well, he never looked at me the same again. He informed me that I had crossed the line from religion to myth, and assured me there was no mention of a karkanscholl in the bible. For obvious reasons, he stopped short of claiming that coming back from the dead was impossible.

That said, my interest in Twelvetide greatly excited him, as too many these days saw Christmas as a one-and-done single-day event. That was far from the truth. Christmas Eve starts at sunset, or Vespers, which coincided with the karkan ritual. Christmastide is a time of thanks and giving, and ends with Epiphanytide, a time of blessings and purification. It made sense in my mind that the karkan would disappear from the world during this period.

But that was all Archpriest Pavel could offer me, aside from pointing to library books concerning Albania. I thanked him and headed on my way.

The last church I wanted to check out was in North Miami. I couldn't help but see the proximity to the Bone Saints as a sign that I should check with them. And as Chevalier had been avoiding my calls, I now had an excuse to pop in and say hi.

And speak of the devil, as I drove up North Miami Avenue, I spotted a few Haitian necromancers hiking up the curb. I slowed my approach and one looked back. He wasn't wearing face paint, but he was definitely a Bone Saint.

As I debated whether to stop, two gunmen rounded the building ahead of them, aimed their rifles with military precision, and opened fire.

Chapter 25

A stream of bullets pelted the Bone Saints. The eldest, a guy in his twenties, shoved the others aside and waved a doll before his body. I winced as the bulk of the burst cut him down.

The other two huddled in an alley. They were just teenagers. The gunmen reloaded their weapons and advanced.

I snarled and stomped on the gas. The V-8 of the Anniversary Edition Trans Am roared to life. The men barely had time to turn their heads before I was on them. I rammed into the first guy and hit the storefront window. The glass shattered and the old car halted sharply. I was thankful it wasn't equipped with an air bag.

I hopped out. The gunman was knocked to the floor inside the shop. The other had somehow avoided the collision. He repositioned on the sidewalk and pulled the trigger.

The Helm of Awe on my open palm burst to life,

projecting a circle of turquoise energy that deflected the bullet. Behind me, pops opened into the Firebird's metal frame. As the gunman swept his aim, I did my best to keep my small shield over it, but he was a good shot. A round pegged my shoulder. I grimaced and pulled my hand up.

Another bullet beamed me in the forehead and everything went black.

My head struck the car on my way to the ground. Grit and glass on the sidewalk jabbed me, and my whole head went numb. Adrenaline prevented the sensation of pain, but my head was swimming. I was seeing literal stars, and they were hard to shake.

"Fucking parahumans," spat the man. He stepped closer as he pulled the empty magazine from his rifle and replaced it.

He wore dark gray tactical gear consistent with Vanguard uniforms, though, as with the others involved in illicit activities, failed to advertise his allegiance with a patch. His mouth and nose were covered with a cloth mask to hide his identity. His rifle pointed at me.

A small knife spun through the air and hit him in the gut. The man doubled over, but the strike didn't put him down. With a painful grunt, he pulled the blade and dropped it to the floor, eyes going past my car.

"You little..."

His head shook. A voodoo chant hit my ears and I could literally feel the spellcraft oozing past me. The gunman jerked this way and that. He swatted at his skin. At something on it.

I rolled onto my elbow and shook my head, refusing to entertain the dizziness. I sprang to my feet as one of the kids slid over the hood of my car, *Dukes of Hazzard* style.

The gunman was under attack from an enchanted psychedelic. He probably thought snakes were crawling all over him. He dropped his weapon and lowered to one knee to recover it. The Bone Saint planted his foot in the man's chest, knocking him backward. He picked up the rifle, turned it on its owner, and fired without a word.

Inside the shop, the other teenager knelt over the man I'd hit with my car. His neck was sliced open ear to ear, and the Bone Saint washed his hand into the pooling blood and wiped it over his face like warpaint.

I stiffened as the first teenager turned the rifle on me.

"Cool it," I said.

He watched me a moment. "For a dead man, you still breathe."

"Don't believe everything you hear."

The rifle aimed my way wasn't a threatening gesture, just poor gun discipline. I put two fingers on the end of the barrel and pushed it gently to the side. I turned back to the twenty-something gasping behind us. I hurried around the car.

Even riddled with bullets, he was still alive, though it was a hard fight. The poppet at his side had absorbed more than half the barrage. Cloth torn and shredded, its innards were seeds spilling to the concrete.

The kids knelt beside him. "Barnabé, you okay?" They dug under his shirt and found the bullet wounds. I pulled a squeeze bottle of toxin to attend to him, but turned to a whining vibration in the sky.

A drone whirled on us.

"Gimme that, kid."

I traded the squeeze bottle for his rifle. The drone buzzed away as I took aim, and it never stood a chance. It shredded apart and tumbled.

"You okay here?" I asked the kids.

They were busily applying my zombie toxin. It wouldn't heal anything, but it would help the process and staunch the bleeding.

"I'll get help."

I hurried to the car and pulled backward into the street, wincing as the bumper bent out of shape. I needed to find a houngan. Voodoo priests knew a thing or two about dealing with gunshot wounds, more than I did anyway, and the Bone Saints' block was a minute away. They had an army of houngans.

But then, there's that saying about fighting fire with fire. The Vanguard weren't stupid. If they were hitting the voodoo gang, they would've sent more than two of their own.

Automatic fire split the air. The fenced-in apartment block the Bone Saints called home came under attack from a caravan of pickups and Jeeps. They drove right through the main gate and took the gang head-on, shooting at anybody unlucky enough to be in the yard.

I veered toward their roadblock and it was like they expected me. Gunfire ripped into the hood of my car and I swerved into a string of bushes. I pointed the rifle out my window and returned a few rounds of controlled fire. As they took cover, I jumped out and advanced on them.

Two men posted behind a black Jeep Wrangler parked crossways in the middle of the street. I pulled my fist down and twisted. The vehicle hopped a few feet into the air, toppled to its side, and landed on the panicking gunmen.

A militia member at the gate turned to me. I dropped to a knee and we simultaneously aimed at each other. We both fired but he was wide. I took him out with half a mag left to spare.

By now there were several dead Haitians in the large yard. Bone Saints scrambled among their building walkways, but a fast-response crew sprinted over the open field. Black men mostly, but some women too, of all ages and stripes. None wielded guns but they were hardly unarmed. Machetes, knives, and clubs waved in their hands as they charged with ruthless abandon.

Gunfire cut into them, but the oncoming soldiers didn't scatter or scramble or fall. Bullets punctured their skin or bounced away as they continued closing on the militia. The horde of zombies was the gang's first line of defense, and their horrific vigor left the Vanguard altogether slack-jawed.

Rampaging thralls met their enemies with slashing blades. One, two, three militia members were struck. But the opening was born more from surprise than anything else. The gunmen regrouped and coordinated their fire. Zombies were tough but they weren't impervious, and they weren't just facing a few ARs. As skin shredded and bone splintered, some of the thralls fell too.

I hurried across the street and popped some shots at the mustering militia, keeping them scattered and disorganized. But I had to run for cover when a few fired back. As my rifle clicked empty, I tossed it to the ground.

The militia adapted quickly to the new threat. Their Jeeps and pickups revved, doing donuts in the dirt and running down the horde of thralls. I was too far away to use my magical powders on them, but the shadow would do. It was a sunny day so I mainly had to work with what was under their vehicles. Which was plenty.

With a kick of power, I knocked another Jeep over. It flipped completely, toppling two riders. Another gun turned my way. I unleashed a whip of shadow and struck the rifle aside. As the weapon was strapped over the gunman's shoulder, he recovered quickly, and I had to latch onto the gun with a tentacle and yank it hard. This dragged the shooter along the ground until he slipped the strap.

By now the field was filling with a sickly green fog. The Vanguard fired upon the ghostly presence, but they were literally shooting smoke. Other sparks and fires shot across the field, and snakes and worms burrowed from the dirt below, causing several to fire into the ground.

I was pretty hardened in the ways of voodoo, but the sheer amount of spooks manifesting from the Intrinsics, in broad daylight, was creepy as hell. This was what happened when one directly raided the headquarters of the largest voodoo gang in Miami.

It was an impressive show of force that even I wouldn't

be able to overcome. Every able-bodied militia member jumped into their trucks and sped towards the exit.

Which was the open gate.

Which I stood in the center of.

A pickup with extra-large wheels bore down on me. I gathered a tremendous force of will and felt the power constrict a bit around the fetish on my wrist. In the sunlight, the shadow was fighting me. I heaved upward and the pickup bounced off its wheels...

And landed right down on them again.

The fleeing vehicle hopped like a monster truck and skidded over me as I dissolved into shadow. They whooshed past and I was in sunlight again, ripped back to physical form. As the next truck came at me, I dove aside and landed hard. The remaining vehicles cleared the yard, swerving and peeling out as they vanished down the side streets of Little Haiti.

The gunfire stopped, and I was left panting for breath in the dirt.

Chapter 26

Hundreds of hissing snakes and spectral creatures went silent. The green pall over the battlefield receded. The snaps and sparks of violent spellcraft subsided, giving way to pained grunts and sorrow. Jean-Louis Chevalier offered me his hand.

"Rise, Suarez." He hefted me to my feet and studied my face curiously. "You have a knot on your head."

I pressed the butt of my hand into the welt where the rifle round had hit my forehead. The pain finally forced a grimace out of me. I checked my hand, satisfied at the lack of blood, before reapplying pressure.

"It'll take a lot more than a bullet to the head to kill Cisco Suarez," I said, although it didn't come out as confidently as I'd intended. I shook the brazenness away. "One of your guys was shot."

I told him about the ambush on the street and realized how inconsequential it sounded next to everything else. But the leader of the Bone Saints diligently sent practitioners out to recover any stragglers and bring them home.

As the field cleared, the size of the human toll was evident. There were plenty of hurt people right here. Plenty dead too. The Bone Saints were a powerful force of scrubs and players. They were strong enough to fend off the assault, but it was nearly impossible to counter the raw firepower of modern armaments used *en force*. Not without some casualties, anyway.

"You've been avoiding my calls," I said.

The bokor wiped blood from a clawed silver gauntlet. "I've been occupied by skirmishes up north. The Yoruba as well."

I bit down. "This is bigger and bolder than anything they've tried before."

"It is the speed of their escalation that concerns me," he replied.

Him and me both. A few days ago, The Vanguard was known only by their viral videos. Now a hit turned into a bombing turned into a full-fledged shootout.

"We need to prepare for the police," proclaimed Chevalier. "In Little Haiti, they wait until the gang shooting is well finished before they approach, but they'll be here eventually."

He marched away and instructed the others on what to prioritize. The hurt were attended to. The dead were left where they were. Then there were the walking dead. A few were finessed from the ground, reanimated to walk off their grievous injuries. Others were left to be disposed of, able to be passed off as freshly killed.

Interestingly, the dead members of the Vanguard were picked up and carried into the bowels of the apartment buildings. Several thralls righted the upturned Jeep, and a boy got behind the wheel and drove for the gate.

I flagged him down. "Hey, kid, what are you doing with the militia bodies?"

He snorted. "When the popo investigate a gang war, they don't ask questions, and we don't give answers. If they find dead white people on our block, everyone goes to jail."

I raised my eyebrows and backed away as he gassed the Jeep onto the street. Massaging the knot in my head, I turned to my own car. The silver Firebird was still a beauty. Across the street in a neighboring yard, nose in, from my vantage it just looked like it was parked.

I headed over and frowned as I converged on it. A couple of rounds had hit the driver-side fender, but I winced at the bullet hole that had popped through the enlarged Firebird decal on the hood. Those bastards were gonna pay for this.

There was worse damage to the front grill and bumper, incurred when I'd headed straight for the roadblock and when I'd aggressively parked through the store window. The smell of coolant was apparent and, at the very least, my radiator was cracked. I would need to call Triple-A for a tow and probably rent a Mustang or something.

At least there was some luck to the whole thing. The Firebird didn't appear to be part of the crime scene. It was parked in a neighbor's yard, likely someone friendly with the Bone Saints, or at least someone who wouldn't cause them trouble. Even if the cops noticed the damage, it appeared incidental compared to the massacre across the street.

After some time the yard was sanitized. Evidence of a shootout was still apparent—that couldn't be cleaned up in a matter of minutes—but the scene now told a different story. It was a narrative of nameless, faceless intruders in one or more vehicles that drove down the apartment block's locked gate and rammed and gunned down innocent bystanders. The weapons belonging to the Saints were nowhere in sight, the zombies long gone, and no dead attackers remained. What happened here now fell safely into the category of drive-by street violence, far away from the concerns of the general public.

And still, the police had yet to arrive.

"They know now," said Jean-Louis, stepping to my side as I watched the scene. "I don't know how they found us, but they did. The Vanguard uncovered the spellcraft they were looking for, and they lived to tell about it. They've seen us. They've seen you. And we're not the only ones they're going after."

I turned away from the carnage. "What do you mean?"

He pulled out his phone. "Are you on Twitter?"

I snorted. "Are you serious? It's a megaphone for idiots."

"That is why I listen, Suarez, and do not speak."

He brought up a phone with a large, wide screen and proceeded to play several minute-long video clips of street violence. Two of them were recognizably Wynwood. The Vanguard Against Parahumans recorded themselves taking shots at outposts of black-nailed upirs and their drunken familiars.

Damn, the militia was more organized than I'd thought. It wasn't just animists; they were hitting vampires too.

Was I allowed to root for those efforts?

"What's their motivation?" I wondered. "To go after everybody?"

"Manifesto was months ago," Chevalier replied. "True believers of all stripes joined the militia."

"But they're just going around shooting people. They're —"

I hissed. I had almost called them vigilantes before realizing the irony.

Was I any different?

Was I any better?

The Obsidian March... the Bone Saints... They were known criminal organizations being targeted by a self-proclaimed protective militia. It made me wonder if I was on the wrong side of things.

But then, no matter the Vanguard's mission, their methods were overzealous. The santeros at the Holiday Village, while troublemakers, hardly deserved execution. Even anyone arguing otherwise would fail to rationalize killing some others, like the herbalist. Nigel was innocent, targeted simply for his avid interest in preternatural remedies.

The final video Chevalier played showed a man in a room with an American flag backdrop. He wore a black ski mask to hide his identity and spoke directly to the camera after introducing himself as a leader with ties to the militia.

"These attacks will continue. We will root you out. We will endure. We are the Vanguard Against Parahumans. This is our manifesto."

The video cut out. It was undeniable now. The militia was taking cues from a dead serial killer, continuing his crazed work on a larger scale.

"I don't get it," I muttered. "If these guys just admitted to committing a host of crimes, wouldn't they be arrested?"

"The video was posted anonymously to the dark web," he explained. "It's spreading on legitimate sites by groupies not actually connected to the militia. Official Vanguard accounts have remained silent. They're not using names or organizations to link their acts, just the hashtag #VAP."

I scowled. Social media was being used as a buffer to give the militia deniability. It was still a risky play. I couldn't see how ambiguity would protect them after they killed people in the streets. I had to get in touch with Evan about this. But then, even the police were having trouble finding the Vanguard.

"Parahuman is a new word," I said, canting my head. "Kind of useful, actually."

"The vampires aren't human, Suarez."

"No, they're using it wrong maybe, but we're human."

"Not to them, we aren't."

My face darkened. "I'm talking about others like that wolf cult I fought a while back. Just because someone's changed or cursed... Calling them subhuman just seems, you know... mean."

Jean-Louis studied me a long moment. "This is about

the girl, isn't it?"

"Don't bring Milena into this."

"You never told me how you saved her in the Nether."

I turned my scowl on him. "Magic, dummy. Now I suggest you drop it."

I was, admittedly, quick to anger, though it was understandable for everyone's tensions to run high. I was pissed off and beat up and just wanted to get out of here.

I quickly mentioned the dead cat I'd found at the scene of Ebu's death, killed by the karkan's famed poisonous aura. If anybody in this city knew magical poison, it was Jean-Louis. He had one of his guys unload the cat from the trunk of my car. It was still wrapped in the greasy shop towel, although I'd cast a charm on it to somewhat halt the decay.

With our business done, I backed out of there. "And try picking up the phone once in a while," I grumbled.

I marched for the sidewalk, passing several Bone Saints getting their home in order. The gang member I'd talked to about the police walked by.

"Hey kid, where's that Jeep?"

"Five blocks down."

"And the keys?"

He pulled them from his pocket. I held out my hand, and he turned to his leader. Chevalier sighed and nodded, and the kid tossed them my way.

Chapter 27

I didn't know anything about Jeeps. This one was a little older and lacked a top. That made driving in the crisp winter air a bit uncomfortable. I padded around for an extra coat but was relieved I didn't find one. It was bad enough I might be driving a dead man's Jeep, I didn't want to be wearing his jacket too.

I hadn't really planned on a destination outside of abandoning my tour of Orthodox churches. Before I knew it I drifted back into Brickell. I tensed as I spotted two militia members in the middle of a crosswalk. Unlike the soldiers in Little Havana and Little Haiti, these wore uniforms of gray camo with visible patches of a red shield. Official Vanguard. Oddly enough, they held fishing poles over one shoulder and AR-15s across their chest.

Their weapons were safely anchored to their bodies, pointed down, and not in active use. It was a strange sight in Miami, like they were just hanging out at the local fishing hole, except that fishing hole was the swank Brickell corridor of high-end restaurants and shops.

A few more men waited at the corner and eyed the Jeep as I drove past. Their attention fell into the curious category more than suspicious, and I concluded that they didn't recognize me or my hijacked ride.

A block and a half down, I pulled to the curb, watched them in my driver's door mirror, and exhaled. By all outward appearances, the men weren't causing trouble. They nodded and waved at passing pedestrians, and proselytized if anybody paused long enough. Maybe the fishing hooks weren't so far off. This was a fucking public relations goodwill tour, not an hour after orchestrating a deadly gangland attack.

This... was an opportunity.

Instead of declaring war on this army, was it possible to break bread? It was a difficult thought to entertain, and one I had no idea how to approach Chevalier with. Hell, I hadn't even thought of it until witnessing their incursions against the Obsidian March.

That vector opened up a whole world of possibilities and common ground. I began to wonder if the Vanguard could be reasoned with. What if I could show the vampires for the human-trafficking parasites they were? The enemy of my enemy? The militia might rally with us. At worst, they would redirect their rage.

Either way, no more humans killing humans.

This, of course, ignored the minor complication that quite a few humans were already dead, some of them by my hand. Breaking bread is hardly appetizing when it's covered in blood. And here I was, driving one of their dead or wounded compatriot's vehicles.

Ultimately, the environment was too volatile for me to just stroll right up and introduce myself now. These boys were too close to home to risk instigating anything. But maybe I could tackle this from another angle.

I dialed Evan's number and watched the mirror.

"You were there?!?" were the first words out of his mouth, usual incredulous tone included.

"Of course I was there. Why else would I be calling? Wait—which shootout are you talking about?"

"It doesn't matter!!! You were there for one of them."

I clicked my tongue. "Guilty as charged. But you can't expect me to sit back while people are being gunned down in the streets."

"Did they come after you?"

"I wasn't the target. I'm just lucky, I swear."

"It's not luck, it's the crowds you roll in. Anyone in the parahuman community is at risk."

"You're using that word too?" I bristled.

"What? It's a good word." He sighed. "This whole thing's a shit show. I'm being pulled ten different directions."

"Well, how about one more? What would you say if I told you the Vanguard set up a checkpoint in Downtown Brickell?"

He grunted. "The City's mustering a presence, but there's not much we can do. We're spread thin and most of them aren't breaking the law."

"Last I checked, Miami doesn't allow open carry."

"No, but there are exceptions on the books that practically allow it. Long guns in a vehicle are okay. Any are legal for hunting and fishing trips."

Which explained the fishing poles in the bustling intersection. I dropped my head into my palm. "You can't be serious."

"It's the law, Cisco. We just enforce it. And speaking of which, I've got to go coordinate with the gang unit. But that's *my* problem. Do me a favor and don't get distracted from the karkan case."

I snorted out a laugh. "Hey, I was doing that all morning. It's kinda hard to focus when the militia points rifles at me."

"I'm not blaming you; I'm trying to compartmentalize. The police are scrambling on this. We're coordinating with the feds. In the meantime, Rita is running with our serial murders. Mullen's a capable detective, but in my absence I'd like to have the City's consultant keeping an eye on things."

"Okay, got it. What do you need?"

"You haven't visited Drop Team Central in a while. Come check us out. We've set up a manhunt for your killer."

I pulled into the street and made a U-turn back to central Downtown. "I'm real close. See you there."

I hung up and avoided eye contact as I once again passed the militia checkpoint. I couldn't believe the boldness of announcing themselves in broad daylight after the violence they'd caused, but I supposed that was how plausible deniability worked.

I crossed the river and weaved between high-rises until I found myself at Evan's nondescript police office. As it was nearing the end of the workday, finding a spot on the street wasn't difficult. I walked the extra block and entered manhunt headquarters.

The large, communal room fit half a dozen desks for DROP team officers to share space on alternating shifts. As lieutenant, Evan was above the common rabble and held residence in one of two private offices in the back. The other had been converted into a conference room.

The office was a hive of activity, and not at all what I was expecting. Officers in black BDUs lined up and traded SWAT gear: plastic shields, batons, gas masks, and bulky nonlethal firearms.

"Look what the cat dragged in," laughed Booker, testing the fit of his bulletproof vest.

"Is that a cop saying or what?"

He flapped his lips. "Don't take it out on me 'cause someone gave you a black eye."

"Wha—? I..."

I poked at the knot on my head. The bruise had likely bled down over my eye socket. It was lucky the round hadn't popped me an inch lower. Then I'd be in the market for an eye patch.

"Here he is," called Evan, exiting the rear conference room. His vest was complemented by dual shoulder holsters securing twin Colt Diamondbacks. He was such a show-off.

I made my way over. "You making arrests?"

"Just making our presence known. We need manpower all over the city. For now we're beholden to the gang unit."

"This is past gang violence. Don't the Wynwood hits overlap with your ongoing investigation?"

I was met with a scowl. "Operation Black Out hasn't developed fast enough. Our intelligence isn't actionable enough for a warrant. We're not in the driver's seat."

"And the mayor?"

Evan glanced at his team and took me aside in a lowered voice. "I'm trying to get a special dispensation to tackle it, but Major Petty has the mayor's ear and I don't have my usual leeway on this. Orders are orders." He hiked a resigned shoulder. "My team isn't autonomous right now. But no worries, we're looking into hitting these guys where it hurts. It's just gonna take time. Until then, your team is in there." He pointed a firm finger at the conference room. "It'll give me peace of mind to know you're tracking down our other problem, which may or may not be related."

I conceded a nod, but Evan never saw it. He was already on the move, signaling to his crew.

"Mullen, you drive."

The name caught my attention, but instead of a grizzled detective answering, it was another eager soldier in a SWAT uniform. Mullen Senior's son headed outside followed by a squad. Within seconds, the entire DROP team filed outside, with Evan moving last.

I was only alone a moment.

"Hey cowboy!" called an agent from the conference room door. "You waiting on an invitation?"

Special Agent Carter. The stocky old timer always reserved a cocksure grin for me. I pretended he wasn't there and pressed past him into the back room, expecting a few people but finding a packed house.

There was the FBI, of course: Rita Bell, Carter, and the two junior agents, Ramirez and Sotomayer. MPD stalwarts Detective Mullen and the crime scene tech Jensen were expected. Less so were the pair of City of Miami uniforms and Major Bruce Petty, the head of the Criminal Investigations Section. Which made about four buzz cuts too many in this room.

"I would ask why you look so crestfallen," remarked Petty. "Then again, I would be too if I was a supernatural consultant." A few of the officers and agents snickered at my expense.

I was surprised the medical examiner wasn't here too, but then his job was at the morgue with the victims.

"There's been a reshuffling of personnel," Petty continued. "The DROP team has been reassigned. As we're shorthanded, I'm taking command of this investigation for the city. Mullen will be my stand-in, and we're sharing everything with the FBI."

I nodded, surprised I was still here. The prescient major picked up on my thought.

"You might wonder why I haven't terminated your contract, and you have Special Agent Bell to thank for that. She has relayed, to my complete and utter stupefaction, that you've been helpful thus far."

I was gonna shoot back with a snide response, but he

leaned on the conference table and addressed the crowd before I could find the right balance between "fuck you" and "sir."

"As I was saying, this panic in the streets is a direct result of Nathan Bartlett Jones aka the Manifesto Killer. The last thing we need is another maniac inspiring the hearts and minds of the Bakers. I want this killer brought to justice, and I want this thing under wraps without any surprises. Are we on the same page?"

Everyone nodded. The major excused himself without further fanfare and headed out with the pair of officers. Agent Carter followed him to the door for a word, leaving the conference room decidedly less ornery.

"You all heard the man," said Mullen with a sigh. "Let's get to work."

Chapter 28

Even though the long table could seat an easy dozen, only the veteran Mullen was taking a load off. Pictures and files stretched across the tabletop, splayed out for examination in related clusters. The walls had opposing whiteboards, one side with notes and taped-up pictures of the victims, the other with decidedly less information on possible perpetrators. Because Ozo Ebu was a gang leader, the heads of rival gangs were automatic suspects. Listed also were persons who had grievances with Quentin, who was a public figure. Finally, the FBI had compiled a list of known speakers of Arbëresh. It was small and included a member of the church I hadn't been able to visit, one Charles Goncharov.

None of it looked very promising.

"These names aren't right," I dissented. "No offense, but I see a lot of West African occultists, a lot of middle-aged men who were duped by Quentin Capshaw's parlor tricks, and a handful of academics." I put my back to the whiteboard and crossed my arms. "No one here believes in the karkanscholl enough to model their kills after it."

"We can't say that for sure until we run everybody's psych profiles," countered Rita.

"Crazy's not the same as occult-inclined."

She canted her head. "I admit these are long shots, but it's possible our killer consulted with one of the academics, or that they can shed light on our clues."

Jensen was the next to take a seat. He looked like he'd been on his feet all day. In front of him were several photos of Ebu's warehouse, including the dirt clusters I'd found.

"You're serious about this stuff," he said. "The magic, I mean."

Rita pulled her head back defensively. "Why shouldn't he be? Haven't you ever seen anything you couldn't explain with science?"

He blinked a questioning gaze her way.

I sighed and made eye contact with the junior agents before settling on Jensen. "Listen, all we need to worry about is that *someone else* is taking this 'magic stuff' seriously. We're just here to clean up the mess."

"I get that," said Jensen, though he seemed unconvinced.

Carter returned to the room, slipping his phone in his pocket. "What does he think?" he asked gruffly.

Rita frowned. "He doesn't like them either. And he's right. All our possible suspects belong in one discrete victim pool or the other. There's no crossover between Quentin and Ebu. Aside from their interest in the occult, the two men are practical opposites. White, black; wealthy upbringing, immigrant running the streets; famous, unknown."

"Isn't the occult enough of a link?" peeped Ramirez.

"It might be, but there still needs to be a commonality for discovery. If you're going on a killing spree, why start with these two? How would our killer have come across them and not others?"

Carter nodded. "Serial cases always break that way. If the yahoos don't mess up by getting pulled over for a broken tail light, it's their MO that does them in."

Agent Bell took it from there. "In other words, we're missing a connection between Quentin and Ebu that we haven't made yet. If we find that, we're one step closer to our karkan."

Mullen blew his cheeks wide. "Could be territory," he offered. "Some crossover in Opa Locka."

I took a deep breath. There was a difference between keeping some juicy details to myself and actively impeding a federal investigation. I knew of a link between the two men, though I had to be careful not to incriminate myself in telling it.

"I picked up some information on the street that might be helpful," I announced, knocking my knuckles on the whiteboard list of gang leaders. "The West African belief diaspora extends to voodoo and Santería too. There's a lot of overlap in the underworld. Shared values, shared stakes. They share a lot of rumors too."

That got the attention of everybody present. For some reason I was glad I didn't need to reveal this to Major Petty, though Mullen had been quietly listening the entire time and would surely relay everything I said. I had to trust he would have my back if it came to it.

"So we know Quentin Capshaw was making a public spectacle of himself for a while, and the entire time he was holed up in Opa Locka. Some people suspect he paid off their local police for protection." I nodded to Rita. "We now know he was also an FBI informant."

Detective Mullen's forehead twitched. "What was that all about anyway?" he asked. "What was he doing for you?"

The special agent swallowed uncomfortably. "Unfortunately, that's confidential."

"Balls to that," he retorted. "We're supposed to be sharing information here, aren't we? How are we expected to produce links if you keep secrets from us?"

"It's not that simple," she muttered defensively. Carter's face developed an edge and he stepped forward.

"Everybody," I snapped, trying to catch this train before it derailed. It worked, and I lowered my voice to ease the tension in the room. "Agent Bell was trying to catch the Shadow Man. We all know Quentin claimed to know his identity, but that's bunk. He had nothing. It was all a bluff."

Jensen perked up. "You have a theory?"

I shrugged. "Same as you. He doesn't exist."

"Now wait just a minute," argued the crime tech. "Magic might not exist. The concept of some mythical vigilante might be ridiculous... but *someone* was in that video at the construction site."

Mullen often worked with Jensen and he backed up the

tech's point with a nod. "One way or the other. I don't care if what we saw were special effects or camera glitches, someone real is responsible for the myth."

I sighed and pushed past that. "Whatever. The point is, Quentin was bait. Not only protected by the FBI but by allegedly corrupt locals. Quentin had finally achieved a measure of fame he was uncomfortable with. And according to the street, even Ebu attempted to deal with him."

Rita took a heightened step forward. "The Night Walkers spoke with Capshaw? About... the identity of the Shadow Man?"

I rolled my eyes in overdramatic fashion. "Of course not. He doesn't exist. But Quentin was convinced he did."

"That asshole!" hissed Rita. "He never told me he was approached."

"How about some respect for a dead informant?" chided Mullen as he leaned back in his seat. He didn't care about Quentin, really, but it was a free shot at the feds and their screwup.

Rita was too incensed to respond. She stared at the floor like she'd been played a fool, which was a stronger reaction than I'd expected. Carter met each of our faces, trying to catch up.

"How do you know all this?" asked Ramirez. "We questioned the Night Walkers and couldn't even get real names."

I snickered. "Next time a city detective tells you witnesses are gonna be tight-lipped, you should listen. The point is," I belabored, reining things in, "Quentin and Ebu *did* know each other. And if Quentin had crooked cops on his payroll, maybe he had gang members watching out for him too. Maybe they had other deals we didn't know about."

"No," intoned Rita, voice deep and shaky, "it's simpler than that."

She snatched a dry-erase marker from the table, grabbed an eraser, and wiped out the list of gang members. In their place she drew a square and wrote the word *Killer* inside. She followed it with three empty circles and another square at the end.

"Here's our chain," she expounded. Rita drew an arrow from the killer square to the first empty circle. "This is our first victim."

She wrote *Quentin* inside the circle.

"And three days later..."

Another arrow, another name. *Ebu.*

Detective Mullen sat up straight. "Cause and effect."

"That's right," said Rita. "Ebu wasn't premeditated. One led to the other. And we're trying to figure out who's next." She drew an arrow from Ebu to the final circle, which was left blank.

I crossed my arms. "Okay, but what's the last square for?"

She grinned with the cool collection of a magician about to make their big reveal. "Our killer deals in myth. We know that. The karkan is a mythical assassin. Why assassinate a hypnotist and a car thief?"

I shook my head. I never liked mental exercises and

didn't see the point in asking the same question using diagrams.

Rita stepped across the board, dragging the marker in the air past the empty circle until it landed in the center of the last square. The end of the chain. In its center she wrote *Shadow Man*.

We all blinked for a moment.

"Our killer is looking for one target. A target that most definitely exists," she urged. "The killer came up behind Quentin and wrapped a chain around his neck. Yes, there was the ritual to consider, but there was also a purpose for not killing Quentin right away."

Mullen scooted closer to the table. "To squeeze him for information."

"Right. And what information did the whole city believe he possessed?"

Jensen smiled. "The identity of the Shadow Man!"

I groaned, and Rita's eyes lit up.

"So Quentin has a chain around his neck, he admits he doesn't know anything. But Ebu had approached him and offered to sell him the real identity. *Quentin knew* that *Ebu knew*."

Carter pounded his fist into the table. "And then the killer knew."

Rita nodded excitedly. "They're dominoes. The assassin is hunting the Shadow Man. He'll go from victim to victim until he finds his mark. The main question now is who did Ebu name?" Rita traced the arrow from Ebu to the next link, looping the marker around the empty circle several times in emphasis. "Who's one step closer to knowing who the Shadow Man is?"

I fidgeted in place, reeling from the dual revelations. First was the one thing I'd been desperately avoiding, which was having a room of dedicated law enforcement personnel actively and seriously discussing the Shadow Man.

Second was perhaps more unsettling. Rita's theory rang true, and if that was the case, there was an unstoppable killing machine hunting *moi*.

And we might as well skip that last circle and go straight to the final square because Ebu had known I was the Shadow Man.

"We need to pick up the gang leaders and lieutenants," instructed Rita. "Starting with the Night Walkers, but the Haitians and santeros too, like Cisco said. Someone is likely to share Ebu's secrets."

Mullen chewed his lip. "That's good work, special agent —I'm not making light of it—but what are we talking about here? What could Ebu possibly have known? The secret identity of a superhero?"

"He's a man," replied Jensen.

"Sure, and maybe it was Ebu himself."

"Ebu wouldn't have tried to drop the dime on himself by contacting Quentin," countered Rita.

"Okay, fine, so it was a rival in his gang or one of these West African outfits. What're you gonna do, pick up every black santero on the street? They won't talk to us."

The special agent shook her head. "The Shadow Man's not black."

"Oh, really, and you know that how? Because right now all signs are pointing in that direction." Detective Mullen grew a little heated and took to his feet. "I can understand our killer being white. Serial cases usually fall that way. But what basis do you have to claim the race of the Shadow Man? Is there more information you're keeping from us? You work up a profile we don't know about?"

Rita met his eyes with fierce defiance and silently bit down.

"That's what I thought!" he snapped. "Is the FBI here to assist, or here to run their own investigation?"

She again refused to answer his challenge, which only infuriated him more.

"Listen, lady, we're not some Podunk city you can push around. I can say with full confidence that I've worked more murder cases than you. Your fancy suit and fancy badge don't hold any sway with me. And if you want to continue *assisting* in my case, you better look up that word in the dictionary." He yanked a pack of cigarettes from his coat and stormed out the doorway.

The conference room was quiet as Mullen slammed the station's front door on his way to the sidewalk. Everybody avoided eye contact. With Miami's lead detective excused from the room, we all waited on Rita to announce the next steps.

She cleared her throat, more sullen than before. "We don't know for sure what Ebu knew or didn't, but the best we can do is scoop up those closest to him and, as Detective Mullen mentioned, those in rival gangs as well. Someone will talk to us because, if they know anything, they might be the next name on the whiteboard."

And there was more of Rita's savviness coming into play. She wasn't so naive as to believe that she would receive full cooperation from the players on the street, but survival instinct was the strongest motivator there was.

I grumbled loudly. As much as I hated to put a damper on a good plan, somebody had to state the obvious. "Talking to the gangs is gonna be difficult for a while. With the recent shootouts, the mobilization of the gang unit and police everywhere, the whole city's on edge. Sending armed feds to pick up paranoid gangbangers holed up with weapons... You're gonna get more people killed than we're trying to save."

Carter hissed. The veteran might have been hard-boiled, but he'd been on the job long enough to see the obvious. Rita didn't say anything and just stood in place with her hands on her hips. Dealing with the militia and the karkan at the same time quadrupled the logistics, and the FBI strategy of rounding up suspects would lack the manpower supplement of local law enforcement.

"Maybe Lieutenant Cross can spot us some team members," suggested Carter.

"Maybe," she muttered. "But we'll need the cooperation of the gang unit to get this done in time."

"What's our timetable?"

"A day," I cut in. "Two if we're lucky. Our karkan seems somewhat constrained by ritual."

Ramirez had been silent in the back. "What happens if

we can't swing police support by then?"

"Then someone else dies." Rita turned to the door, took a breath, and said, "Time to make peace with Detective Mullen, because we're gonna need all the support we can get."

Chapter 29

I retraced my route back to Brickell, though things had changed in my short absence. Four City of Miami black and whites were parked at the intersection of the Vanguard checkpoint. Militia members amicably chatted with police on the sidewalk. The body language on both sides was firm but friendly. Even so I got the feeling the demonstration was being dispersed or, at the very least, controlled.

Fewer cars drove down the strip and populated the swanky curbs than I would've expected. It was like everybody felt the discordant air right through their bones. Maybe it was media scare tactics or simple common sense, but people were smartly avoiding public encounters, perhaps opting not to go out at all. And who could blame them? Explosions weren't conducive to shopping sprees.

Another police car pulled onto the road behind me. I only made it a block until he flashed his lights. I gritted my teeth and slowed the Jeep as I considered a plan of action. It was late in the day but not yet dark. With the top open, the cop probably already got a good look at me when I passed. The conditions weren't ripe to run.

Yet I was being pulled over while driving a stolen vehicle.

I delayed stopping over the next block by turning on my blinker and trawling for a good space. The act would've been more convincing if there weren't so many parking spots available. Ultimately, I decided to play this one cool. If you were an illegal militia operative involved in a shootout, you wouldn't report your Jeep stolen, would you?

I pulled over near Beaumont's restaurant, right behind a gray Hummer. The windows were pretty dark, but the low sun highlighted a lone driver waiting. Carbon must've been opening for dinner.

I watched through the rearview mirror as I entered that abominable waiting period where the cop toys with his computer and decides whether to give you a ticket or worse. I pulled my cell phone low and texted Evan on the sly.

"Pulled over at Carbon. Not my Jeep."

A friend on the force came in handy at times. I tapped the screen with my finger, willing my friend to hurry. It looked like the officer who pulled me over was running my plate, which could put us at odds before he ever saw my smile.

The officer cracked his door open and he spoke, though it wasn't to me and he was alone. There must have been a radio or phone out of sight. I ground my teeth at another tense delay, reactivating my phone's screen as it went black. Still no reply.

The police car's door swung wide and then slammed shut. The red and blues shut off and the Shamu pulled onto the street. Our eyes met as he drove past. They were more inquisitive than anything.

After he was safely out of sight, I leaned my head back and laughed. My text to Evan: "Now THAT is service. Thanks, bro."

Crisis averted. Next time I'd just rent the Mustang. With a calming breath, I hopped out of the Jeep and headed into Carbon.

The restaurant was indeed doing business, and I was greeted by a sultry hostess. "Right this way, Mr. Suarez." We strolled toward Beaumont's back table. A few others had already been seated with guests but the place was mostly empty and, due to the demonstrations in the neighborhood, I expected it to stay that way. The hostess led me to the corner booth and poured two glasses of wine.

I stopped at the table. There must've been some mistake. Leverett was MIA.

"Please sit," said the hostess. "He'll be with you shortly."

She turned to go and I didn't sit. I was just about to check the kitchen when a waiter placed a silver tray in the center of the table. Lemon and sage garnished jumbo oysters on ice. The man prepared two place settings and quickly excused himself. Service without a smile.

My phone buzzed so I held my tongue and slid into the booth. It was a text from Evan.

"What happened?"

"It was perfect," I typed. "The cop didn't even get out of

his car."

A moment passed. Then, "You out of the woods? I didn't do anything."

I set the phone down and blinked at the food. If Evan hadn't gotten me out of a confrontation with the cops, who had? And why did I have the feeling it had to do with the fact that Beaumont seemed ready for my arrival?

I upturned an oyster into my mouth and pulled on the glass of wine. I wasn't good at patience, but I strained it for a good ten minutes before it just about ran out.

"Just in time for dinner," announced Beaumont as he emerged from a nearby curtain along the wall. I'd never been back there and figured the area connected to the stage. "No, don't get up." The vampire slid into the booth and nodded at a distant waiter who immediately disappeared into the kitchen.

I licked my lips and poured another glass of wine. When the waiter approached and set two steaks down, I was salivating.

"I apologize for taking the liberty of ordering for you. I played it safe and got you the same dish you enjoyed at your friend's anniversary dinner."

I wasn't sure what all the wining and dining was for, but I was too hungry to complain. I took a knife to the rib eye and dug in.

"Is the Russian business settled?" I asked offhand.

Beaumont was precise with his dish. He sliced his steak into juicy morsels before drowning it with an entire ramekin's worth of demi-glace. I questioned the ingredients of a vampire's steak sauce and was all too happy I didn't have any of my own.

"Just as I said it would be," he answered.

His voice was dry. The dinner was rushed. The entire act was stilted, as though the facade of fancy food and drink was making up for something.

Leverett Beaumont was a conundrum. In a lot of ways, he broke the mold of a vampire living topside. He came off as a genuine guy, even a concerned friend at times, and I reminded myself that people like him did things for personal gain.

As far as any awkwardness between us, it didn't take a rocket scientist to figure out. I was pissed about him following me, he was pissed about me going off the reservation. Until that moment in time, Beaumont had always treated me as an ally. Not an equal, per se, but a friendly party. The second he intruded into my cookhouse and ordered me to stand down, he made it known I was just like every other person in his organization. I was an underling.

Only I'd never agreed to be an underling.

"I expect the police didn't give you too much trouble outside?" he asked.

My eyebrows went up. "That was you?"

He held a delectable piece of meat up on his fork. "You're hardly the only one with connections."

I winced. His protection angered me, yet I leaned on it time and again. Watching Emily and Fran, traveling with Trinh and Lago, and now even the police. I was concerned about Beaumont's ambition and slighted by his liberties, which made my next request hurt even more.

"We might need to step up our eyes in Brickell," I said. "We're operating on a pretty good theory that the karkanscholl will be coming this way."

His eyes lit up. "Ah, yes, the mythical assassin of Alexander the Great."

"It's not the same one. At least I don't think it is. The problem is, it's after me. Someone sent it to kill the Shadow Man."

He shrugged as he chewed. "They're not the only ones after you. The Vanguard announced the same intentions."

"They know who I am?"

"Not exactly, but they have a description. It's only a matter of time."

His tone carried an air of blame to it, like it was my fault for defending the Bone Saints, or being caught at the olive oil store, or enjoying downtime at the Holiday Village. Like it was my fault for being recorded by Manifesto and allowing the myth of the Shadow Man to germinate in the first place.

And he wasn't wrong in the technical sense. I *had* taken those actions, and they *did* have very real consequences, but that kind of math lacked all the moral variables. Lost in his sober business acumen was any acknowledgment of right and wrong. Lost was the fact that, if I could do everything over again, I wouldn't change a whole lot.

Because I'd saved lives.

Sure, I wasn't perfect, but I was concerned with more

than profit. I'd tackled the threats in this city better than he had.

"A price on my head is nothing new," I muttered. "Drug cartels, the Obsidian March, Manifesto, Stygian witches. I woke up in a dumpster running for my life. Having the local gun club queue up doesn't change anything."

"You're taking on the world again," he warned.

"Actually, I was considering doing the exact opposite for once." I took a labored breath. "These guys, the Vanguard Against Parahumans, I was wondering if we should approach them."

He arched an eyebrow and continued eating.

"They're just people," I continued. "Assholes, maybe, but they're scared. They have no idea what's going on. They're playing parts in a movie script that Manifesto wrote."

"Which should tell you how disconnected they are."

"It does, but can't we show them they're wrong?" I set my fork down. "I want to talk to them."

The vampire boss took a sip of wine and shook his head. "That's crazy."

"Why?" I spat. "You make deals with the Russian mob."

Unlike me, Beaumont didn't raise his voice in turn. "The mob is tamed by money. Mutual business interests. The militia, on the other hand, attracts zealots and malcontents, each competing to out-crazy the other at a moment's notice."

"But what if—"

"No, Cisco. You're not a general playing war games."

I worked my jaw. "What's that supposed to mean?"

"Open your eyes," he snapped. "You're a soldier and they're trigger-happy. They'll kill you on sight, or at least try their best."

I ignored his condescending tone in the interests of the greater point. "They're hitting the Obsidian March," I grated. "You seriously telling me you haven't thought about having them on our side?"

Beaumont took another sip of wine and resumed eating. After a minute of silence, he said, "It would be a short-term gain. It's no benefit to me for the Vanguard to go after the March and fully understand the presence of upirs. We might be allies at first, but soon enough they'd come after me as well." Leverett waved to the waiter. "Take these away."

I wasn't quite finished but my plate was taken. When the waiter left, Beaumont continued.

"These militiamen are murderous zealots. If they know about us, they'll take us down with them when they flame out."

"Flame out? That's a bunch of people you're talking about. People with a legitimate grievance."

"Now you're sympathizing with them?" he snorted. "What grievance could they possibly have?"

"I don't know... Maybe people deserve to know the truth?"

His eyes narrowed in warning. "That's the last thing people deserve."

I exhaled sharply, growing hot at the state of things.

"Maybe, maybe not. I'm just saying we're not the thought police. It's not up to us to decide for them."

Beaumont wiped his lips with his napkin and stood. "That's dangerous talk, Cisco, and selfishly focused. Your kind would crucify us."

"And who asked you to crawl up from the Nether?"

His eyes flashed with anger. "I trust you'll see yourself out."

Chapter 30

Things weren't only contentious inside the steakhouse. With the increased militia presence around town and the stepped-up police patrols, mere travel was risky. Thankfully, Chevalier promised to keep an eye on my car so that I didn't have to return to Little Haiti.

It was pretty late at night when I hit the road again. As expected, the Vanguard had mostly dispersed. The police still made themselves known by cruising through hot spots, but tensions had sufficiently relaxed.

Darcy still didn't answer the phone, and I found myself driving mostly to think. Despite lacking a destination, I passed by Miami Memorial Park, now closed and empty. My gut feeling was that the gypsies were lying low. Maybe they recognized the signs of the karkan—hell, maybe they were the ones who summoned it—or maybe they were just allergic to all the people with guns too.

With lighter traffic due to the day's craziness, the drive itself was actually pleasant. I'd finally had the foresight to don a hoodie, but the open-air cabin eventually proved too much to handle in the unusually crisp weather. Maybe I needed a cool trench coat like the hard-boiled wizards in books. Then again, this being Miami, snow would be the real magic. Let's face it: I was a Caribbean kinda guy. After half an hour the chill got to me, and I was ready to pack it in.

But the shadows had other plans. They twitched in response to a proximate familiarity. Scout wandered somewhere on the verge of my range. I rubbed my hands and blew them with hot air. Then I leaned back into the seat, calmed my mind, and felt for my dog.

The sensation was so faint that, at first, I was playing a game of Hot and Cold. The leather collar prickled my wrist. I turned the wrong way a few times, losing the signal and doubling back, before I felt him strongly enough to bear directly at him. And as I closed, I realized exactly where Scout had gotten off to.

The nearby potter's field where the karkan had climbed out of the ground.

It was nearly midnight so the surrounding public park was closed. I hiked to the spot in the fence where it was easiest to slip through unseen. In the distance were occasional flickers of lights from the police station parking lot. Fortunately, most personnel were too busy patrolling the streets instead of lounging around the station to notice my late-night graveyard tour.

A quick survey of the cemetery was stunted when I spotted my pooch lying motionless on top of the grave.

"Scout," I voiced, sending my will into the adrift minion.

Spellcraft flooded him and sent him to his feet, wagging his tail. He rushed over and I hugged him as his tongue lapped my cheek.

"A little manic depressive, don't ya think?" I chided. "You take a bullet for me one day and then run off the next."

I was only half kidding. At this point I couldn't deny the dog had more personality than most thralls. I rubbed his ears.

"I bet that little head of yours is already trying to figure what trouble you'll get into next." I paused and considered my words. Why not, then, give him a little help?

Scout, after all, had already proved his usefulness. If he was gonna stick around, I might as well make things more official. I slipped the dog collar from my wrist and a weight left me. I frowned and rubbed the sore skin, surprised by the wash of relief like I'd been hampered by a low-key headache, rooted in my brain for days, and it had finally eased.

It made me ponder the purpose of the fetish. Simple manipulations, like bending shadow or sinking into it, came naturally to me, but any instance of turning the darkness against its nature, of making the ether tangible, was a meaner feat. Used to be, without the dog collar, I couldn't perform those manifestations at all.

But I'd recently been disarmed, so to speak, by an Obsidian March boss. He had me on the outs, stripped of my fetish, and I was forced to kill him using nothing but raw fortitude. And ever since then, funneling the Intrinsics was a different experience. Easier in some ways but more hampered like a sinus congestion. It was a hard concept to grasp beyond thinking, on some fundamental level, that the fetish was now holding me back.

Spellcraft is rooted in belief but its implementation is part muscle, part practice. Taking off the fetish was like removing the training wheels from a bicycle. The action came with curiosity and doubt and maybe even a bit of fear, but going without was the only way I'd level up.

"And besides," I said, finishing my thoughts aloud, "we can't have you getting lost again."

I placed the spiked collar around Scout's neck. Whether he was more headstrong or not, I'd have a better bond with the dog while he wore it. The fetish was so ingrained with my workings that Scout would never be lost to me again.

His tail waved happily at the attention.

"Okay, doggo," I said, looking around. "Now what exactly are you doing here?"

He spun back to the grave and put his nose to the dirt. This time he was careful not to disturb it.

My eyes widened. New runes had been traced over the forgotten traveler's grave. A pair of symbols. The necromancer had been here.

I put my knee in the dirt and took a picture with the flash, cops be damned. This was a huge break. But it could be anything, including a signal or a trap.

I'd already asked Kasper to look into Ebu's rune so I sent him the new ones too. And then I realized, because of

Darcy's continued absence, he'd pulled a double at the coffee shop today. The old man wasn't even used to making it through a single shift without a nap and a beer, so the day's work had knocked him out. He wasn't likely to see my message until noon tomorrow.

Unless I decided to wake his ass up.

Scout whirled on his paws and barked. His hackles shot up and he lowered his head into a threatening growl. He was facing a pair of sad, brittle trees that could barely hide a squirrel, though the dog was well past his days of chasing varmints.

I let the shadow sink into my eyes. Interestingly, Scout's shone with a soft blue light like the Cold Moon. And ours wasn't the only magic in the cemetery.

The pall of darkness among the trees surrendered to my spellcraft, revealing a dozen necromancers fanning out to surround us. The West Africans had used some type of glamour to conceal their approach. A woman holding a copper sword boldly led them. Oxtail wands shook like rattles, sending threatening sparks skyward.

Since my last run-in with the Nigerian gangs in Opa Locka, I'd read up on them. This group wasn't Igbo but Yoruba. They called themselves the Children of Oya, named after their mother orisha. Oya, the patron of winds and storms, of death and rebirth, possessed an impressive cross-section of powers.

"So it is," said the head woman with one hell of a vicious snarl, "sometimes the hunter is caught in his own snare."

Chapter 31

Clouds passed over the nearly full moon and the field darkened, as did the faces of numerous opponents.

I called out loudly to let them know I wasn't afraid. "Samira, I presume?"

The leader's eyes twitched. "You know my name."

"I have no beef with the Children of Oya. How'd you find the grave?"

Samira nodded toward a boy barely out of childhood. "Komivi talks to the gods," she said matter-of-factly.

"That must come in handy."

Her eyes stared evenly. "Make light if you like. The orishas led us to this place. What about you?"

I shrugged and pointed to the dog. "The nose knows."

They snorted in contempt at the beast. I wasn't sure if they objected to dogs or thralls. Come to think of it, I'd never seen a Yoruba zombie. Maybe they didn't partake in the practice.

"What do you know of the karkanscholl?" demanded one

man.

"Relax," I said, seeing where this was going. "I'm investigating, just like you."

"Or giving it more instruction," he countered.

A few pointedly eyed the runes at my feet, mere inches from the growling dog baring his teeth.

I took a deep breath. "Let's settle down and compare notes," I urged. "This isn't my work. If I'd wanted Ebu dead, I would've killed him myself."

A few of them stiffened. Anger splayed across their faces. None of them were members of the Night Walkers, but the West Africans banded together for mutual strength.

"Damn it," I muttered. "I shouldn't have said that. I'm sorry. That's what this is, don't you see? This is what they want. Maybe this is what he"—I pointed to the grave —"wants. For us to fight each other."

That kind of us-against-them sentiment usually got people to listen, but it rarely did all the convincing on its own. The Yoruba remained skeptical.

"I swear I didn't kill him," I added.

The loudmouth was about to respond but Samira interrupted him with a hand signal. He backed up a step and glowered but didn't say anything else. Clearly, they held their leader in high regard.

"How do we know that?" she asked.

And they were amenable to discussion.

"It's simple," I answered. "The karkan is hunting the Shadow Man. I'm not the hunter, I'm the prey. So really, it's not healthy to be surrounding me right now."

The woman released a smarmy chuckle. "Sounds rather convenient."

"Trust me, being hunted by a professional assassin is anything but. It's the reason I'm in this boneyard in the middle of the night."

"And why should we believe your claims?"

"Because the karkan went after Quentin to get to the Shadow Man. The only person Quentin thought might know was...?"

Her thick lips curled into a frown. "Ozo Ebu."

"And Ebu knew my secret, so I'm next on the list."

She groaned and it sounded eerily similar to my dog's low growl. "Do you think so little of us that we would sell you out so easily?"

"Don't give me that line," I spat. "I know Ebu tried to sell my identity to Quentin."

Samira's eyebrow arched. I wasn't sure if that meant she'd known and was impressed that I did too, or if that meant it was new information. Regardless, she didn't deny it.

"Business is business, shadow witch," she returned. "Ebu may have decided to profit off you, if it served his interest. You were well worthy of his ire." Her eyes narrowed to slits. "But, under the threat of certain death, before a dogged killer, Ozo Ebu would've only opened his mouth to spit in the karkanscholl's face." Samira raised her chin as she finished her statement, as if it were a self-evident truth.

I wasn't sure I saw it that way.

Now, obviously, the Yoruba knew Ebu and the ways of

the Igbo better than I ever could. Maybe what she said was true and the ozo had some twisted sense of street honor that I never credited him with. Hell, for all I knew, maybe he was ripping off a desperate Quentin with false information. Another grift of the elite, another example of the street procuring what it could by any means.

The way I saw it, Ebu's true intentions were unknowable at this point, and they didn't matter. I could hardly let my defenses down in the hope that he hadn't sold me out. Survival of the fittest was the rule of the jungle, concrete or otherwise.

"So then," I announced calmly, pretending to be settled by their claims, "we've traded a pair of truths. That Ebu didn't sell me out, and that I didn't sic the karkan on him. Now let's discuss a pair of demands. You demand vengeance for the death of an ally, and I want to protect myself. What say we join forces?"

I was met with a slew of hardened faces.

"Perhaps it is true our interests align," said Samira callously, "but you belittle the Children of Oya if you think we can't protect our own."

"I never—"

"You're finally at our mercy, shadow witch," she growled. "If Ebu were here now, would he go on his way, or would he do his best to take you down again?"

"Maybe he would see the bigger picture," I returned.

"He gave up his fight for the bigger picture last time, and has now lost his chance forever."

Even though the clouds had long past, the area

continued to darken. Shadows crossed over my face. They drooped down my shoulders like honey and roiled over the grass like a clinging fog.

I had no intention of fighting but had every right to defend myself. I couldn't help but regret the poor timing of removing my fetish. A brawl with a dozen practitioners was a risky forum to test a shaky hypothesis.

Adding to my uncertainty was the glowing smoke drifting from Scout's eyes. Against the blackest black, they shone light-blue, lighting the grass.

Edgy faces appraised the dog. They knew what he was, but not exactly. I wasn't entirely sure I did.

"Don't think because I'm outnumbered, I'm helpless," I warned.

The leader of the Children kissed the hilt of her sword and ran her tongue along the copper all the way to the tip. "We would be disappointed, shadow witch, if you were."

Blades and wands twitched nervously. Scout pawed the ground. The encounter was technically still in the chest-bumping stage. That meant there was a chance to draw them down. The best way of accomplishing that in the face of an overly hostile enemy was flashing superior firepower.

I held my left hand low to avoid sparking a battle. Intrinsics tickled up and down my arm as I stretched my fingers. It felt unnatural, decadent even, to channel them without the fetish. The itch was gone, but it was replaced by something uncertain. A wavering of faith.

I bit down and willed a tendril to rise from the ground behind the gang. Just as it did for a young student practicing at Martine's old cookhouse, the power manifested itself, slow and steady. With a stronger force of will, additional arms peeked from the ground. I didn't risk pulling enough juice to cover every single one of them, but I had a good half of the gang in my sights.

And they started to take notice.

Some sidestepped from the spellcraft. Others shifted in agitation. I had to make it known that every single one of them was vulnerable, even the ones in the back. *Especially* the ones in the back. If we were gonna throw down, it was every man and woman for themselves.

Survival of the fittest is less about the fittest and more about survival. And apprehension began to crack their masks of surety.

Samira held resolute and readied her copper sword. Rather than allow her to incite them to action, I squared her with a scolding glare and took a single step forward.

My alligator boot scuffed a glyph in the dirt, interrupting the seal of magic. Soil shot up as a chain exploded from the ground and latched onto my wrist. It wrapped around the exact place my fetish used to be, and all my shadows simultaneously winked out.

Everyone sucked in taut breaths. No one spoke as the chain pulled tight against the grave, almost like someone down there was fishing for necromancers and found a bite. I tugged in response but the binding didn't give in the slightest. This was a thick chain, heavy, like what might have been wrapped around Ebu's throat. Much worse was the fact that, with it clamped on me, I could no longer pull at the Intrinsics.

The Yorubas spun in place, searching for my shadowy tendrils. Relieved glances started to embolden them once again.

I cracked an unsteady smile. "Now, now, now, ladies and gentleman, let's think about this before we do anything rash..."

Samira's copper sword jutted skyward. "Get him!"

The Children of Oya snapped into action.

Chapter 32

A streak of light fired my way.

There wasn't time to think. There wasn't time to try and fail. Clamped with some kind of superpowered cold iron, my available options were severely limited. I dove to the dirt and landed on the karkan's grave with a thud. Magic rushed overhead, and Scout guarded protectively over my prone form.

"You heard the lady," I fumed. "Get 'em, boy!"

The Alaskan shepherd bounded an easy ten feet toward the Yoruba leader. She met him with the sword, and Scout's jaw fearlessly clamped down on the blade. Electricity crackled across the copper. He yipped and lost his grip. But before she could smile, Scout chomped down again. Like a dog catching a Frisbee, failures only motivated him more, and the next shock of lightning didn't shake him so easily.

I meanwhile found it troublesome to push to my feet. With my arm against the ground, the chain had only been slack a few seconds before retracting deeper into the dirt.

Now it was a struggle simply to pull back to waist height. I gritted my teeth and braced my legs under me, screaming as I power squatted.

A knife jabbed close. I ducked beneath my bound forearm, and I was relieved to see the protective tattoo flare and disarm my opponent. I'd need to thank Kasper later for the ink because it may have been the only magic I had. I swung a wild haymaker in response but my reach was limited. The Yoruba hunter retreated.

Oxtails whipped the air, and the soil shuffled beneath me. More chains would really put a damper on things, but the metal wasn't theirs. This, I knew, was the karkan's magic. So what was coming out of the ground next?

Oh no. It was spiders.

A hundred spots of black and red wriggled at my feet. I stomped them madly and pulled the chain as far as I could, but it wasn't far enough. As my boots smashed the ground, I danced in the circle constrained by the chain.

Scout finally ripped Samira's sword free and flung it to the grass. The copper was bent and resembled a used-up chew toy. The dog growled and advanced on the leader as she drew a wand.

Another Yoruba sword came for me. I blocked it with my forearm, but this was no ordinary weapon. Powerfully enchanted, the blow actually hurt. Which gave me an idea. I shook spiders off my leg and, when the next swipe came, twisted around and held the chain in the path of the blow.

The sword struck my binding. Intrinsics exploded, burning both our outstretched hands. As the fire cleared, the top half of the copper blade lay molten in the dirt. The chain glowed red too but cooled, as if fresh from the forge. It hadn't even chipped.

"Huh..." I muttered. As I examined the chain, a line of spiders crawled along it from the ground. "Oh, hell no."

The priest holding the half sword swung it at me in anger. His strike was high, an attempt to avoid the chain, and clipped me. Pain raked my shoulder, proving the weapon had some magic left.

Like a crazed madman, I rubbed the wound with my free hand, scooped a dose of fresh blood, and incanted as I brushed the midsection of the chain. Charging spiders rushed over the slick gore in haste to reach me. They sizzled and popped like they were in the microwave. The trick was so effective I took a time out of the fight to hop on each leg and coat my boots too.

But the Children of Oya were just getting started. Being pinned in place against so many of them was dizzying. I weaved in and out of their blows, too occupied even to direct the dog. Thankfully, that didn't seem necessary. Scout lunged in and out of view, tackling and biting all on his own.

Look, I was too busy to even make a joke about fighting with one hand tied behind my back.

Fists fortified with spellcraft struck me from all sides. I fought back where I could, punching and kicking. My body was conditioned against this, making me stronger than the average bear, but I was unable to instill my counterblows with shadow. No matter how tough I was, the gangbangers would eventually wear me down. They were coming at me with lethal force and I was playing under MMA rules.

I had to clear some space.

Dancing around wriggling spiders, I zipped open my belt pouch and grabbed a handful of everything I could. A pill bottle, a couple of plastic Easter eggs, a baggy of bone dust. I crushed them open and swatted powder all around me. It didn't matter if it was a psychoactive, sedative, poison, or even recreational—if it was a powder I added it to the cloud.

Two Yorubas priests caught clumps on their faces. One went down screaming about imaginary snakes, and the other wouldn't win any more beauty pageants. Fallen comrades were yanked to safety as the gang regrouped. They, like me, were well familiar with the two main drawbacks of using powder as a weapon: it only traveled so far, and it didn't last forever.

For my part, my skin tingled and I coughed before I pulled out my cloth mask. I was lucky it was still knotted because I didn't usually do this one handed. I slipped it over my head to cover my nose and mouth. Instantly, the air was like a breeze in the middle of the Atlantic, miles away from the pollution of civilization. It took a few of those breaths to recover while those closest to me hurled up their dinner.

That was my space. The next thing I needed to deal with was this chain. Not only did it pin me in place but it prevented the best of my crowd control and defensive spellcraft.

I tried to form a darksword but the Intrinsics didn't gather enough for a sputter. The sword, though brilliant, was still a manifestation of shadow. That was off-limits because of the iron.

I didn't dare give it a go with Scout's teeth. He was doing a bang-up job of scattering the enemy, and I'd seen what happened to the copper sword that struck the metal.

Why not, then, try a little human ingenuity?

I stomped out a spider-free zone and reached into the ground and retrieved my sawed-off shotgun. One gang member braved the cloud of magic, spotted the gun, and retreated. That was well and good but the last thing I wanted was to kill them. I turned the weapon on the chain, looked away, and fired.

Birdshot ricocheted and buried in the ground. I winced, thinking it had been loaded with fireshot. Not a problem. I dug into my belt pouch and retrieved two cylinders. One was a road flare and the other was a custom shotgun shell in a red tube. Bingo.

I quickly loaded the weapon and tried again. The resulting bark was impressive but, besides lighting the ground on fire, didn't do much. Well, a heap of burning spiders might disagree. I pulled the chain to maximum extension to avoid the growing flames.

And then the unused road flare on the ground caught my eye.

This trap was karkan magic. Necromancy. I couldn't be sure what powered it, exactly, but there was a decent chance it was a spirit. Maybe I couldn't get rid of the chain with brute force, but I might be able to banish whatever spiritual energy powered it.

I lit the flare, spiked it into the ground, and reached into my belt pouch for another. I had just finished the third arm of a budding pentagram when Scout yelped. He flew through the air and landed twenty feet away, two knives protruding from his hide.

Damn it all. The Children of Oya had only backed away to focus on him. And now they were making me angry.

As I grabbed another flare, a hurricane blast blew me off the ground. I snapped in place at the end of the chain and dangled like a sapling unwilling to uproot. A horde of spiders disappeared with the gust, but the cloud of protective powders blew away too. Biting wind pelted me and shredded the hoodie. The fire blew out. Random equipment that had spilled from my pouch tumbled through the air. My heart sank as the staked road flares wiggled loose and catapulted away. When the windstorm ended, I slammed face-first to the dirt for good measure.

Honestly, it was worth it to get rid of the spiders.

But now my pentagram was out of the picture. I didn't have another full set of flares to create a new one, and this environment was too hectic to light a slew of birthday candles.

Scout twisted his head around and reached for the knives in his side. He wasn't the limberest of dogs, but he snagged them both from his body. With the second one still in his teeth, the predator targeted his prey. The Yoruba he charged dropped his jaw and stood dumbfounded as ninja dog bore down on him.

"Drop the knife!" I commanded.

Scout leapt. The blade fell from his jaws mid flight, and he tackled the priest with good old-fashioned teeth.

I was swarmed from all sides again.

Rather than fight the reach of the chain, I stepped into my trap to slacken the links. I quickly wrapped a length around the nearest Yoruba's neck, spun it tight—hopefully not too much—and used the incapacitated priest as a shield. With my back to his, I dodged and kicked. When someone came at my side, I turned their own teammate into the blow.

Now that I forced them to funnel at my front, I drew the shotty again. I attempted to reload it one-handed and that broken copper sword knocked it out of my grip.

No more shotgun, no more powders, no more flares... I was fighting a battle of attrition, and I was losing.

As more blows rained down on me, the chain squeezed tight. The caught Yoruba passed out, and I begrudgingly decided give up my shield. I unlooped him and kicked him to the dirt. I grabbed the bottom of the chain with my free hand to free up more slack and sent a quizzical glance to the ground. How deep could this thing possibly go?

"Scout," I called, signaling to the base of the chain. "You like digging holes, don't you? *Go ahead and dig!*"

The dog eagerly hopped off a battered gang member and set his paws to work, quickly upending massive amounts of dirt. The yard darkened again as an unusually small storm cloud gathered right above us. It crackled with energy and the Yoruba backed away. This was gonna hurt.

"Enough of this, dead man!" boomed Samira, swiping a gash in her arm.

My eyes darted to the hole in the ground. Already two feet deep, and nothing but chain. My gaze shifted to the shotgun.

"I don't want to kill you," I warned.

With the slack still in my hand and the added length freed up by digging, I was able to inch closer to the shotgun. It was a few feet out of reach.

The Yoruba collective laughed. Most of them were beat up pretty good but, thus far, no one had been seriously wounded.

"The only one dying tonight," Samira scornfully derided, "escaped the grave a long time ago."

She thrust her wand into the air. I dove for the shotgun but hit the limit of my leash. A thick spear of blinding light slammed the ground. Scout jerked upright and stiffened. Electricity crawled up the metal chain, flowed into my arm and torso, and exited into the ground through my legs. A vicious crack of thunder broke the night, my entire body snapped straight before collapsing, and everything went black.

Swirls of black ash drifted into the air against the backdrop of distant car alarms. The Children of Oya massaged their pained ears. Samira fell to her knees and panted in exhaustion after expending such great energy.

I didn't feel too hot myself. I squirmed in the dirt. After my fall, the chain had gone taut again, resetting my progress to the shotgun. Any hope I had of reaching it was over.

Scout had taken the brunt of the blast and hadn't gotten up. I was ninety-nine percent sure the electricity couldn't kill him, but then I'd never been so close to such a supreme act of nature. Oya, the goddess of tempests, sure didn't play around.

"There, you see?" asked Samira, smiling in delight. "The Yoruba can defeat you."

I locked onto something behind her. "No," I rasped.

"The Children of Oya can defeat the karkan," she continued. "You thought us weak when we are strong. And you... You are pitiful..."

"No," I warned.

"And alone..."

Two glowing red eyes materialized behind the woman. "Never alone," corrected the Spaniard.

Samira spun around, leading the wand into a strike. An unseen force struck her. The Yoruba leader stumbled several steps and landed with a thud beside me, gasping for air. The conquistador's armored body faded in to frame his skull.

The priest with the broken sword moved for him. The wraith's head turned with flaring eyes, stopping the man in his tracks. He struggled against the ghost's power, arm trembling as his own sword inched toward his neck.

I pushed to my hands and feet. "Don't kill him."

The Spaniard flicked a hand. The broken blade slashed upward but only grazed the man's forehead, leaving a long, jagged cut.

A woman on his other flank came at him holding a doll. He locked eyes with her and she shook under his awesome power.

She spat defiantly. "We learned to defend against the likes of you."

Impressively, the priestess rebelled against his will. She spoke a curse and twisted the doll's neck backward. The Spaniard's skull and helmet snapped as it mimicked the motion.

Everybody gasped. Samira sat up, but I took the moment of distraction to wrap the chain around her neck before she could stand. The rest of the gang tensed. For a long moment, nobody dared move.

Then the Spaniard's head spun back around to us like an owl's, desiccated fingers affixing it in place. He glared at the woman with the audacity to attack him. A low grumble filled the night, and he raised his gaze and arms to the moon.

A whirlwind of brilliant fire engulfed his body. It rushed around him in a chaotic blaze. Likewise, the doll in the Yoruba's hand burst into flames and scorched its wielder. The woman screeched and discarded her ruined weapon.

The fire died as suddenly as it had started, and the wraith addressed the crowd.

"You are but children, like your namesake," he snarled. "You believe yourselves invincible because you are too naive to understand the danger you are in." He scraped his old side-sword from its scabbard. "You each deserve to die for your impertinence... but perhaps less is more." He advanced on the trapped gang leader and put the sword to her belly.

"No," I growled, pushing fully to my feet and pulling the noose tight.

The Children of Oya inched forward. As frightened as

they were, each was ready to defend their leader in the face of certain death. That taught me something about them. It also increased the chances of Samira's words being genuine: Ozo Ebu hadn't surrendered my name to the karkan under threat.

I held my bound hand up as the woman gasped for breath. "The chain," I urged the Spaniard.

Hellish orbs studied me a full minute as the Yoruba woman struggled for air. "I never knew wisdom, Brujo," he finally said. "I pray this is it."

His sword sprung.

The ghostly blade sliced the heavy chain in two. It crackled and disintegrated. Samira collapsed, and her followers descended on us. I threw my hands to my sides and commanded every ounce of unbridled power that had been denied me by the iron. The Intrinsics blanketed me in darkness that not even the full moon could pierce.

And then it exploded outward in a sonic boom that blasted every last Yoruba to the ground.

Chapter 33

I slept in later than I would've liked the next morning, probably because the house was empty and no one was around to wake me up. There was a note on the nightstand though. It was from Milena.

"Went out for a bit. Still never got my *pastelitos*."

Oops. The pastries had completely slipped my mind. After the scuffle in the potter's field, I'd grown weary with the Children of Oya. They'd only backed down due to force, which was typical of the street players, and I was better off leaving them behind. Besides, I'd gotten a new clue.

I sat up gingerly as every single muscle in my body was stiff. Even stretching for my phone required loosening up. After the fireworks last night, the screen was cracked and wouldn't illuminate.

I grunted and trudged to the PC in my office. Luckily, the phone's storage hadn't been compromised. I plugged it into my computer and copied the image over. I stared at the picture on the monitor but couldn't make anything of the dead language.

I still wasn't sure what to make of the previous night's events. The new glyphs and magical chain were proof the necromancer had visited the grave since Vespers. My best guess was my previous digging was discovered and the new glyphs were a trap activated in an attempt to keep me around, maybe forever.

After the wild episode, I doubted anyone would ever return to the scene of the crime again. Still, I had taken precautions. I sent one of my pigeon thralls to sit watch in a tree. I was way too far to connect and see through its eyes, so instead I sort of left it on record. In case it saw something worth playing back.

I donned new clothes that weren't ripped and burned, grabbed the image from the printer, and headed down to Outlaw Coffee & Colada where Kasper joked with a new woman behind the counter. She was a little on the pudgy side, with salt-and-pepper hair and a beaming smile. I propped an elbow on the counter as their laughter died down.

"Cisco!" chimed Kasper, who I hadn't seen this excited since being surrounded by unclothed nymphs at a silvan wedding. "Let me introduce you to your newest employee. This is Clarence's aunt, Mabel."

I couldn't be bothered to look too professional, but I shook her hand. "Nice of you to join us on such short notice."

"Oh, it's my pleasure. I've been looking for a joint with a

good aura for some time."

I fought raising my eyebrows and nodded. "We've got good coffee too."

"I'll trust your word on that, Mr. Suarez. I don't partake. Caffeine interferes with my energy."

"Er," interjected Kasper somewhat tepidly. "She's never actually been a barista before. Or knows that much about coffee. But Clarence is a natural and has promised to show her the ropes."

"That's right," Mabel agreed. "Besides, a place like this really sells good vibes. We just serve coffee on the side."

Kasper happily nodded along.

"I can't argue with good vibes," I said. "Anyway, I'll let you get back to it. I just wanted to drop something off." I slid the folded piece of paper across the counter to Kasper. "I was hoping you could take a look at this and translate it for me, if possible."

The tattoo artist unfolded the printout and studied the symbols without regard to Mabel leaning over his shoulder. Kasper noticed my worry. "Don't mind her, broham. She's open-minded about this stuff."

"I'm Pagan," added Mabel. "Gaia loves us all, am I right?" She giggled. "You know, Kasper mentioned he'd been in a scuffle or two with you."

"He did, did he?" I glared at the loose-lipped old man as my newest employee went to her purse.

Kasper steamrolled past the implication that he'd said anything of consequence. "I'll get right on it, broham. It's almost lunch. Clarence is coming in to train his youthful aunt. It shouldn't be too busy today since it's New Year's Eve."

I couldn't believe it had been almost a week since Quentin had been killed.

Mabel returned and presented me with a brown feather. "This belonged to a majestic eagle," she explained. "Judging by that black eye of yours, you could probably use it."

I flashed a terse grin and accepted the gift. What was I supposed to do with an eagle feather? Still, Kasper might've been onto something. An employee with a side interest in woo-woo wasn't likely to judge our... abnormalities. I couldn't see a reason to not give Mabel a chance.

"Milena passed by," said Kasper, changing the subject. "She grabbed a *café con leche* on her way to check up on Darcy."

I tensed at the news. For some reason I figured Milena was staying closer to Brickell. "An actual coffee," I grumbled. "How nice that sounds."

Kasper and Mabel smiled without picking up on my hint. I mean, I was only the owner of the establishment and no one else was here. It seemed the least they could do, and Clarence would never stand for this.

Kasper took my annoyance for concern. "Don't worry about Milena," he nudged. "She needs to get out of the house, get some sun, and visit a friend."

I stretched my sore neck. "I'm not really sure you can call them friends, but you might be right. I guess I'll catch you later."

I held up the eagle feather and thanked Mabel as I left

the shop. It was only when I was below ground climbing into the Jeep that I realized just how much I needed caffeine.

Scout's tail thumped against the seats as he jumped to the front row and licked my face.

"Whoa, boy."

I'd forgotten I'd left him here. He accepted my pats to stem his persistent attack. Then I nudged the hundred-pound dog off my lap. "You ride shotgun."

Scout was pleased as punch to take his post, and as we hit Brickell Avenue his head stretched over the door. It was another chilly day but, as there wasn't a cloud in sight, the sun did an admirable job battling back the cold. It and the dog warmed my soul, both sorely needed comforts these days.

The lampposts were stripped clean of their red-and-gold decorations. Shops already displayed New Year's signage in their flashy windows, a sure sign that capitalism was embracing the next buying opportunity and putting Christmas in the rear view.

Someone should tell the karkan the world was moving on.

Speaking of change, I was pleasantly surprised to find the militia absent this morning. It probably had more than a little to do with the squad cars stationed every other block. It was still an improvement.

Society was crazy like that, able to move past a tragedy and keep grinding. Not judge ourselves too harshly. Push past grief in order to live life. It was a valid coping mechanism, and there was no doubt in my mind that Bayfront Park would shed the memory of the shooting and go full steam ahead with the New Year's Eve bash tonight.

Though I dwelt on the hopeful resilience of mankind, a more cynical part of me also knew the celebrations would be a prime target for a crazed militia. But the police weren't stupid. They knew that too. Any gathering of that magnitude would have an army of good guys watching.

I skipped I-95 in favor of drinking in the scene at street level, and I was glad I did. Driving north of Downtown takes you through neighborhoods less-affluent than Brickell, where the view isn't nearly as rosy. Today was no exception. Less police protection, a sparse population of wary citizens, and more vandalized shops.

The people may have been resilient, but so were the factions who would break us. We had to be adamant not only in our hope, but in our fierce defense of everything we loved.

And then there's Wynwood. To locals it's a thriving art scene and a place you can still score truly interesting food and drink. To the greater outside world it's a photogenic Instagram hub to hit on your beach vacation. To Cisco Suarez it was a vibrant neighborhood marred by the recent incursion of an upir criminal organization.

Missing today was Wynwood's usual troupe of hipsters in the streets, though many of the small shops and restaurants appeared open. As I passed a notable vampire dive bar, the door opened and a familiar figure strode out in high heels.

I turned my head away and drove as Tutti finished her conversation with black-nailed bar patrons. She didn't know I was in a black Jeep these days so I slowed at the next block and turned.

Tutti was an under-nourished waif and piece of trash that made my skin crawl. I could never tell if she was going behind Beaumont's back or not. Seeing her here triggered my warning sensors, but that alone wasn't unusual. Shiftiness was a general trait of vampires, and I wondered if something suspicious was afoot.

I pulled to the curb and leaned back in the seat, thinking. Scout watched me, ready to take orders. I sighed loudly.

In the past, I would've urged Beaumont to reconsider his alliance with the girl. It was a song he'd heard before, and his side of the dance was assuring me he knew what he was doing, that Tutti's connections to the March made her invaluable, and that she could be controlled with power. Instead of keeping that track on repeat, I decided it better to investigate on my own. Maybe I'd finally learn something the Frenchman didn't know.

I leaned over and opened the passenger door. "Go follow her, boy."

The Alaskan shepherd obediently hopped to the sidewalk and let out a "ruff."

"And be careful," I added. "Follow but don't be seen."

The dog turned and sped back to the corner to regain visual contact. It was a risky task because Lago had recognized him as a thrall earlier. Though I hadn't worked with Scout long, I had confidence he was up to the challenge.

I sat back in the seat and watched through Scout's eyes. Tutti was alone now, leaning against the wall and smoking. When she flicked the butt away and went for another one, it became clear she was waiting for someone. A little more patience rewarded me with the answer to my question.

A beautiful Asian woman in a yellow dress greeted her outside. She was more than familiar, though it took me a full minute to realize it was Trinh all gussied up in fashionable club wear. That was odd as she'd been watching Evan's house. But then, with the increased patrols in Brickell, maybe there was no longer a threat to look out for.

The two vampires were opposites in many ways. Tutti sported blonde pigtails and was weathered for her age, while Trinh wore her black hair down and her smooth skin was not only supple but toned with muscle. Tutti was taller than her Vietnamese counterpart and had multiple piercings to contrast with Trinh's many tattoos. The starkest difference, though, came in their personalities. Trinh was reserved but capable, more than able to handle herself in a fight. It wasn't that Tutti couldn't scrap, but she lacked the finesse of a trained warrior and used boastful threats to make up for her lack of confidence.

I watched the two women chat like old buddies, wishing I could read lips. Even then, Scout would probably need to get closer, and that was too risky with Trinh present. She'd come face-to-face with Scout before and would ID him on sight.

Some men came outside the bar and Tutti handled

introductions. Beaumont's people, meeting Obsidian March bosses, with Tutti as the go-between. What was going on here? They laughed snidely at some remark and retired inside as a group.

I dug for my phone, but of course I'd ditched it at home with a broken screen. I caught myself reaching for the glove box next before realizing this was the Jeep. My stock of burners was in the Firebird.

My teeth ground together. Patience, Cisco. Patience and restraint. Clan Beaumont necessarily pledged allegiance to the larger Obsidian March. It was part of the game Leverett needed to play to stay alive. While I'd never dipped my nose into his contacts before, regular meetings seemed a reasonable occurrence.

This wasn't my business, at least not yet. I shifted out of park and sent Scout a mental command to keep at it.

Chapter 34

Little Haiti didn't have the police presence Brickell did. Nevertheless, there was a Shamu parked right in front of the battered-down front gate of the Bone Saints apartment block. A ripped length of yellow police tape lay in the grass, and several residents congregated around the outside of their respective buildings.

Missing from the picture were the zombie thralls and armed patrols.

I considered phoning Evan for some help with the police before again realizing I no longer had my phone. Man, was this what the future was like? Always feeling naked without constant contact?

Honestly, I wasn't sure how much Evan could do for me anyway. The gang unit was calling the shots these days. It was probably best to avoid the police entirely, which got me thinking... That was exactly the thought Jean-Louis Chevalier would have. I doubted he was inside.

I parked across the street behind my silver Firebird and

switched cars. I grabbed a brand-new phone from the glove compartment and started my ritual of programming in my usual contacts and letting them know my number changed. My first text, as usual, was to Milena.

"New phone. *Besos.*"

I continued filling in my close contacts from memory while pondering what to do next. I paused on Darcy's number. I'd been meaning to call the moody teenager but would probably get her voicemail again. If Milena was visiting the girl, maybe I'd take a back seat and allow women's intuition to handle this one.

I had just saved Kasper's contact when I noticed the business card in the center console. I picked it up and flipped it over. Special Agent Rita Bell, FBI.

A young boy knocked on my window. I rolled it down and he held up a stick.

"Give me your money," he said.

I blinked at the shoddy weapon. The boy couldn't have been more than nine. I carefully set down the business card. "Kids these days don't want candy anymore?"

He shook his head. "Money."

I cracked a smile and looked around. It was a poor neighborhood but this felt engineered, like the kid was proving himself for a bet or something. "What if I say no? You gonna use that thing?"

The kid gnashed his teeth into the cutest snarl ever. "I will if you're a cheapskate."

I put a hand up while reaching in my jeans. I unfolded two bills, peeling the one from a five-dollar bill. I offered the dollar but the kid reached into the window and snatched the fiver.

"Too smart for me," I said.

The kid nodded. "This way." He strode away and waited for me behind the car.

I grinned. Of course. I locked up the Firebird and followed away from the parked squad car, went down the main street a block, and then turned onto another residential street. The kid shrewdly scanned the area before ushering me to the porch of a beat-up yellow house. I turned around at the door but the kid was already sprinting away with his ill-gotten gains.

Chevalier greeted me at the door. "I am popular these days."

I snickered. "Tell me about it."

"I appreciate the warning about the police, Suarez."

After the meeting at Drop Team Central yesterday, I'd let Chevalier know the FBI were looking to pick up gang leaders. I shrugged and stepped inside. "It wouldn't do to have you picked up by the gang unit. It's not like you know anything." There were four more soldiers in the house with him. Bokors and a houngan. "Do you?" I added. "Know anything?"

He shook his head. "I cannot concern myself with the karkan now."

"Even though he could be coming after you?"

"It is not."

I snorted. "Ebu might've given him your name."

"He didn't. Ebu was an intractable bastard. Nothing

could be forced from him."

He shared that opinion with the Yorubas, lending even more credence to it. It was entirely possible the karkan had gained no new information with the latest kill. That would hopefully delay further killings. A literal dead end, as it were. Hmm, the lack of progress could explain the necromancer's recent visit to the grave.

"Tell me you at least looked at the cat," I said.

The bokor teased his lips into a smile. "I did, but there's not much to glean. The poison is airborne. It enters the bloodstream through the lungs and acts as a sedative. The brain then goes through a calcification process. Similar disorders produce fatigue, cramps, seizures, and dementia, with one marked difference."

"The cat was dead," I muttered.

He dipped his head in acknowledgment. "Much like other magical poisons, its onset is sudden. This one is lethal to small animals. It continues working on the dead, further drying and calcifying the corpse until running its course."

I grimaced. It sounded like an awful way to go. "How do we use this knowledge against the karkan?"

He hiked a shoulder. "Poison is poison. It won't work against the karkan because it's dead. But I did find something else about the cat. It was fed upon, and the bite marks appear human."

"The karkan sampled the goods? What are we talking about here, a zombie that needs to feed?"

"That is unlikely," answered the bokor, and I tended to agree.

In general, there was no purpose for an animated thrall to feed. They were automatons who took orders. That said, any given zombie could eat, especially if instructed to do so. And it wasn't uncommon for some quirks leftover from life to be carried over into death. Case in point was Scout enjoying the odd treat or three.

"So our assassin fancies the occasional snack," I mused. "But the crime scene... I found the cat in the back lot, away from the entrance. The only reason the karkan had to go there was for the cat. In order to do that, it went so far as to take out a security camera that was already broken."

Chevalier's lips pressed tight. "What are you thinking?"

"The karkan went out of his way to get to this cat. He was in the neighborhood, staking out Ozo Ebu, and his poisonous aura kills a stray and effectively distracts him from his mission." I hooked my hands on my hips. "Is the karkan compelled to feed?"

"It's possible. A reflex of some sort. The animal was barely eaten, so the feeding wasn't about sustenance."

"That gives us an opening. Remember how we killed the asanbosam?"

"The African vampire was impervious until it fed on a thrall with corrupted blood." He clicked his tongue. "But asanbosams are Nether fiends, flesh and blood, however spoiled. The karkan will not have the same weaknesses."

"What about engineering an antidote?"

"Suarez, you ask too much. It is a long shot at best, and one that is hardly necessary. Quentin and Ebu didn't show signs of the poison. They weren't calcified, they were interrogated. It's possible the noxious gas weakened them, slowed down their vitals, but no more."

"And you're sure about that?"

"It is what I do, Suarez."

I trusted his skills but was annoyed by his detachment. "So that's it, then? We forget it and move on?"

His voice rose to match mine. "As I said, I have concerns more pressing than the karkan."

I turned away from him to stare out the window. Right, the militia. Everything regarding the karkan was somewhat theoretical, even the question of whether I was his prime target. The Vanguard, on the other hand, presented a very real and very serious threat, as a handful of dead Bone Saints would attest.

To be honest, my attention was constantly split as well. The Vanguard's attacks had grown bolder over the week. Yesterday was Little Haiti; what was today? City police, county sheriffs, and federal agents were after the paramilitary group. On the surface, they were someone else's problem. Hell, they weren't even supernatural types.

But I couldn't shake the feeling there was something I could do to defuse things, with or without Beaumont's blessing.

And it's not like I was neglecting the current karkan business. Agent Bell was interviewing gang leaders, Kasper was researching the cemetery runes, and I had a thrall waiting if he returned. With this dead cat thing fizzling out, I was regrettably out of leads.

Maybe Jean-Louis realized he was being indifferent to

my plight. "Suarez," he said, joining me by the window, "why is this thing hunting you? Was it sent by the hellions?"

I idly shook my head. "I don't know, man. All this funny business is keeping me from even thinking about the Stygian witches. Maybe that's the whole point."

Alarm bells went off in my head. I shut my eyes and flushed my mind with shadow. Scout's perspective blinked in.

We watched Tutti in a back alley that must've been blocks from the vampire bar. Her hips swayed right up to a group of militants dressed in gray camouflage. A pickup with an extended cab was loaded with troops and supplies, and they performed weapon checks.

"Shit," I announced, "Tutti's coordinating with the Vanguard as we speak. They're gearing up to attack an Obsidian March bar."

"Good."

"No, not good."

Jean-Louis arched an eyebrow. "Better them than us."

"You don't understand. If Tutti's behind this, there's something in it for her."

"And? Let them destroy each other."

"I can't. I have to go talk some sense into them before they do something they can't take back." I marched to the door.

"Suarez," he called, "why intervene in their affairs? Your actions would put an abscess on a boil."

I grimaced. "That's just gross."

"It's a common saying."

"No, it's not." I shivered at the mental image. "Look, I have a friend in there."

Scout was watching both women. If Trinh had exited the dive bar, I would've known. She was in danger.

"I've asked you for too much already, Jean-Louis. Catch up or don't, it's up to you, but I'm gonna try to stop a war before it gets off the ground."

Chapter 35

I tore ass down Miami Avenue, weaving past light traffic between glimpses through Scout's eyes. As much as I wanted to call the DROP team in on this, there was no time. This strike was about to go down and my pitch to save a vampire would fall on deaf ears.

The Jeep screeched into the Wynwood back alley as the militia started their march. Tutti broke away from them, apparently not joining the fight. Scout traded glances in opposite directions as he tried to keep eyes on both, but I was gonna need to make a decision soon.

As for me, there was no more point in being discreet. I skidded to a stop and slammed into park at the dive bar's back door. And, as stupid as it was, I rushed inside the dank interior. A handful of bar patrons jumped to their feet as my boots scraped to a stop on the unfinished concrete.

Black fingernails, every one of them. No santero hustlers, no innocent bystanders. Maybe that was one silver lining of the very public violence of late: the only people still going out were the ones who were looking for trouble.

Only this time, trouble had found me. I hated fighting vampires in tight spaces, and several of them closed around me. The *coup de grace* was that Trinh was nowhere in sight.

"Wha...?" I scanned the dark environs, wondering where my damsel in distress had gone off to.

"What do ya think you're doing here?" asked a tough voice, ironically the shortest and least physically intimidating guy in the bar.

"I... uh..."

The largest guy present appeared all three hundred pounds of a bouncer. Black daggers grew from the tips of his fingers.

The door to the ladies room popped open and Trinh stepped out with a bemused expression. "Easy!" she tempered. "He's... with me."

The short guy snorted. "He's not welcome in this place. You know what happened the last time he was here?"

She lasered him with a stare. "I know you hid in the kitchen during the whole affair."

The jab left him momentarily speechless.

"Put your claws away," I said, firm enough to mean it but as cordial as I was willing to be with this scum. "I'm not here for a fight."

I closed my eyes for a split second to get an update on the Vanguard's position. I ordered Scout to abandon Tutti. Then I grabbed Trinh's arm and pulled her back into the women's room. She backed up against a dirty porcelain sink. The space was cramped, and my elbow banged against the empty paper towel dispenser on the wall.

The close quarters made me question how much I really trusted the vampire because she could slice me in half if she really wanted to. She lifted her chin and seemed to take my smell in. "You better have a really good reason for putting your hands on me," she said in an indignant tone.

"This place is about to get hit."

Her finger went to my lips and she pushed me back into the metal dispenser. Her arms and stomach were tense. "Keep your voice down," she whispered sharply.

My brow furrowed. "Wait, this is the plan?"

"Of course it is. We're waiting for their up-and-coming boss, Hayden. He's making waves after the death of Magnus, and he's a little slippery for our tastes. Once Hayden's here, I get out and they strike. What are you doing here?"

I pushed her off me, back against the sink, hand on her hips to keep her at bay. "I'm here because the Vanguard's not waiting. They're moving in as we speak."

Her eyes pinched tight in amusement, but her face softened. "My knight in shining armor, huh?" Her fingers tickled my chest for a tender moment before she bashed me back into the paper towel dispenser, this time denting the metal. Her face hardened. "I don't need animists keeping tabs on me."

I shifted off the wall, keeping my hands between us as she did the same.

"There's no point killing a few nobodies," she assured. "The militia is waiting for Hayden."

I closed my eyes and checked the scene outdoors. Scout was just catching up as the militia split into two groups and sent one around the building. "I'm telling you, they're moving in hot and heavy. We have thirty seconds before they breach."

Her eyes only challenged mine for a few seconds. Trinh had worked with me before. I didn't play games or politics, and she knew it. Perhaps she took a moment to assess my motives, but that was all she needed. She turned to the door. "Damn, this is what happens when you enlist amateurs for professional wetwork."

"Or maybe Tutti doesn't want to cripple the Obsidian March as bad as you do. Maybe she wants you dead too. Did you ever think of that?"

She huffed, defiant on that point. "There's no time to weigh theories. Those men are armed with armor-piercing rounds and trained to hit center mass." She pushed outside the restroom and strode to the back door.

"Wait," I said, concentrating as Scout edged nearer. "They have the alley covered." I stepped around belligerent March members to peek out the front window. "They're at the front too. It's too late."

The big guy followed my gaze without a word. It was the little one who spoke. "What's going on?"

Trinh bit down and sighed. "The Vanguard Against Parahumans intends to kill us all. Cisco came to warn us."

Vampires who I hated with all my being looked to me with newfound respect. I glared at Trinh and joined her in the center of the room.

"We need the bodies to draw their fire," she whispered. "Otherwise we won't get out alive."

I shook my head. I didn't like it. There were too many people involved, too many variables. I wasn't sure who deserved to die or not. All I knew was, once the shooting started, it didn't matter. This would be a bloodbath.

"Maybe we don't have to fight," I hedged.

Trinh scoffed. She effortlessly dragged an antique porcelain refrigerator from behind the bar and upturned it in the center of the room for cover. "I never took you for a hopeless romantic. There's no avoiding it at this point." She pulled a karambit into each hand. The curved blades resembled eagle talons ready for prey. In the shadows all around me, obsidian claws extended.

"Screw this," I muttered. I marched to the front door and pounded three times. "I'm coming out," I announced. "Unarmed." Before anyone could respond, I opened up and slipped out.

Five men in gray camo trained their rifles on me. Only a couple had helmets, but they all wore cloth masks over their faces. None of their uniforms were emblazoned with red shields. Instead, empty strips of Velcro adorned their shoulders where their Vanguard patches should've been. They were dressed for trouble.

I had my hands up and moved slowly, giving them no reason to jump the gun, so to speak.

"You one of them?" asked a man with brown-lensed shooting glasses.

"He's standing in sunlight," answered another.

Technically I was in the shade from the tattered awning above. For an animist who drew power from the shadow, it paid to be aware of my surroundings.

"I'm one of you," I said. "This is a mistake. You're being used to fight someone else's war."

A few partially lowered their weapons but remained defensive. "We're being shown a second sight," argued the man in the sunglasses. He hadn't lowered his rifle.

"I don't know what you've been told..." I started.

"They're monsters in that there den," stated one man coolly, "and we're gonna take 'em out. You're either part of the solution or part of the problem."

It was jarring to hear a bunch of uninitiated humans speaking so matter-of-factly about Nether fiends, but then everybody who knew found out one way or another. Ever since Manifesto hit the news, public consciousness has been increasingly aware of magic. And with fortune tellers being burned out of their businesses, the realization was clearly not welcome.

The team leader in the sunglasses clocked me. "He was the one those shamans wanted. At Bayfront Park."

Crap on a stick. The Vanguard had interrogated olive oil lady. They'd seen me with the Bone Saints and their drones. Beaumont had warned me about this.

"Are you with that voodoo gang?" asked another. The guns came up again.

"I'm not in any gangs," I said sharply. "I'm only here to stop the violence. I don't want anyone to get hurt."

"You know what the guys inside there do?" asked

Sunglasses.

I grimaced. "Damn it. Yes, you're right. They're monsters. I've tangled with them myself." I stepped closer, right up to the edge of my shadow. "I'm trying to help you guys. We need to talk."

"You're Shadow Man."

"No." I swallowed. "It's complicated. But I care about this city every bit as much as you do."

They laughed. "This city is a cesspit of freaks," groused one.

"It's Gomorrah," said another.

Sunglasses trained his rifle on my heart. "I don't care if this city burns to the ground. We're here to protect humanity."

He pulled the trigger. A double tap of rounds went through shadow and popped through the establishment's door. It was controlled fire, designed to put me down and conserve ammo for the next target. All five men recoiled at my apparent disappearance.

A limb of shadow lashed ahead and grabbed the shooter. I materialized and yanked him toward me, wresting his weapon away. Two more muzzles flashed. I ducked behind the still-surprised team leader and spun the rifle around, opening fire.

At that point, body shield or no, the other men had no options. With nowhere to run, all rifles let loose, tearing apart their own man.

My return fire was unhampered.

I swept a barrage across them all in a smooth motion.

Two crumpled in place, another dropped his gun and stumbled, and the last took a round in the back as he sprinted behind a car on the curb.

I didn't press my advantage. With the strike team down and out, I kicked the ventilated team leader off of me. As he fell away, I snatched his brown sunglasses and twirled them onto my face before backing inside the bar. My eyes magically adjusted to the gloomy interior.

Trinh squatted behind the refrigerator with an I-told-you-so smirk. I started to shrug, but the front window exploded in a hail of gunfire. I dove to the floor. Splinters and shards filled the room in a celebration of confetti, and I army crawled behind the fridge with the vampire.

The back door kicked open and a bar of sunlight filled the room. My new brown lenses kept the man entering in focus. I discharged my weapon and hit him with a burst, center mass. He fell back outside. His allies scattered as he crawled away.

"What good are armor-piercing bullets if they don't go through bulletproof vests?" I complained.

"They're wearing steel plates over their chests," explained Trinh, repositioning to a crouch in the restroom doorway.

"Good to know," I grumbled, wondering how many of the people I already shot were still alive. It would have been a relieving thought if they weren't trying to kill me.

A plastic bag wrapped with duct tape came through the broken window and pattered on the cement.

"Bomb!" yelled the big vampire.

I knelt behind the fridge as the explosive shook the building. Vampires tumbled and the room filled with smoke. Coordinated militiamen rushed in the front and back entrances.

Trinh hopped out behind the men, slashing open one's hamstring and planting her knife into the base of another's skull. The Vanguard man taking the rear discharged his weapon but she flipped away, tossing her second blade. This one wore a military helmet with a GoPro attached, so the knife clattered harmlessly off what would've been his temple. He advanced behind a barrage of bullets.

Meanwhile, the suppressive forward fire of the men attacking frontside stopped. Smoke swirled outside and enough cleared to see a handful of upirs in various states of transformation. Claws were extended, heads and shoulders were carapaced over with black bone. The big man was missing an arm and a piece of his skull but pushed to his feet with a growl.

I came up to shoot and everyone opened fire at the same time. I took a militiaman out. A pair of vampires exploded as armor-piercing rounds found their hearts. As the weapons turned on me, my rifle clicked empty and I ducked.

"Reloading," called one of the men.

The big guy rushed him, but the other dropped to a knee and fire protectively. The vampire twisted away from the bullets, doing a lap around the bar until the man's magazine ran dry. By then the first militia member was locked and loaded. As the big man bore down on them, a new mag loosed on him, exploding his heart.

The little guy flew out of nowhere, proving that brawn is often overrated. He slammed into the shooter, sweeping him off his feet and propelling him like a rocket. Together they took the front door off its hinges and landed outside. The man's entrails didn't all go along with him, as daggerlike claws had opened his gut. The upir reached high to finished the job, but the sunlight reverted him to human form. A soldier covering the front exit mowed the unsuspecting vamp down. The little guy collapsed, lucky to have avoided a heartstrike, but he was too damaged to escape a reload. The man kicked him to his back, fired on him point blank, and was rewarded by a spray of blood and ash.

Two vampires tag teamed the other militia member inside. He didn't even get a shot in before they ripped him to shreds.

Trinh slid past me, avoiding another barrage. I put my shield up to cover us both while we flipped to the opposite side of the fridge. Three men including GoPro fired mercilessly from a tight formation, hitting everything in sight. Trinh peeked out with her pistol and kneecapped one, drawing further fire. The men rushed forward to cut the angle of our cover. I grabbed Trinh and sunk into shadow as bullets sparked off the concrete.

There'd been five Obsidian March vamps in the bar. While formidable in close quarters, they'd been ambushed with what I considered superior tactics and force. Shooters working in unison, using rounds capable of penetrating upir carapaces, and trained to shoot the hearts. Although some militiamen had made the fatal mistake of getting too close, the bullets had done their job.

"Targets down!" yelled GoPro. "Let's evac!"

The few remaining militia members rushed out the back door and yelled, "Clear!"

Trinh turned to the window first, and with the guns and screaming silenced, the whirring of the approaching drone was all too obvious. She tried to get up but I forced her shoulder to the ground. "This is gonna be loud," I said.

She cocked her head questioningly and I pulled her back into the shadow. A heavy drone drifted in the open doorway, moved to the center of the bar, and went boom.

Chapter 36

The phone in my jeans pocket buzzed and I stirred back to consciousness. My body was constricted in place by the rafters of the building that had collapsed on top of us. I wasn't sure why I was in physical form or why I'd blacked out.

The air was thick with dust, leading me to believe I'd only been asleep for a minute. I really hoped that was the case, otherwise we'd have lots of questions to answer. I coughed dirt from my throat.

A body shifted beneath me. "You mind?"

Darkness seeped into my eyes, framing opalescent yellow cloth. My face was somehow buried in Trinh's crotch.

"Not that I don't appreciate the offer," she added, "but I get plenty of that at home."

She twisted under the rubble but only smothered my face more.

"I can't breathe," I said.

"Don't talk," she snapped. "That... tickles."

I held back for all of two seconds before my lips burst

with laughter. Which only made Trinh squirm more.

"Okay," she muttered, "you had your fun."

Her entire body snapped over with black plates of armor, which was decidedly less comfortable than her lap. Trinh gripped a heavy wooden beam that rested on the bulky refrigerator. That old appliance might have just saved our lives. Using superhuman strength, she forced the wreckage aside.

Enough space was created that I could pull away and take her in. It was amazing to me. One second I lay on a beautiful Vietnamese hottie, the next she was in her true form: a monster with milky white eyes wearing nothing but hip holsters for weapons.

"Still like what you see, big boy?"

"That's an awful Marilyn Monroe impression."

Her foot was pinned under a chunk of concrete. I nudged it so she could wiggle into a crouch and take a look. She winced at what I thought might be a broken ankle. It was hard to tell when she was all sealed up in obsidian.

"That was a big bomb," I said, only afterwards realizing how unhelpful the statement was. "I mean, we need to get out of here." I was on a roll.

Trinh tested the broken roof over us. We were still beneath enough rubble and smoke that hardly any daylight pierced through. She braced against a large ceiling panel as I gathered a cushion of shadow.

"Ready when you are," I said.

She nodded and heaved upward as I released my spellcraft. An entire section of roof blasted aside. Sunlight blinded me and I covered my eyes, wondering what had happened to my cool new sunglasses. I'd never owned a pair of shades I didn't lose within a month. This had to be some kind of record.

When my eyes recovered, Trinh was back in human form, wearing a yellow dress that perfectly framed her body. Even after the bomb, the dress was spotless and unripped. As she stood, the pressure on what was *definitely* a broken ankle forced her to lean on me.

"Wait a minute," I mumbled. "Your clothes are an illusion."

That was common for Nether creatures who hid in human guise. Instead of needing a change of clothes every time they transformed, it was more practical to rely on their glamours.

"That meant... when my face was in your..."

Her eyes narrowed. "Let's never talk about that again."

I couldn't wipe away my stupid grin. "Did I just make it to third base?"

Her hand clutched my throat and squeezed my voice box.

"Got it," I eked out. "There were no bases. I struck out. In fact, I never even left the dugout."

Her top lip curled ever so slightly, like maybe I was too endearing to kill.

"Cisco?" called a deep voice from the edge of the rubble. It was Booker from the DROP team. He crawled over the rubble and offered his hand to help us out.

"Aren't you a sight for sore eyes," I said. We picked our

way to safety.

"Should I be worried you're here?" he asked.

"We weren't here," Trinh corrected.

He chuckled. "Right." The big man beamed as he took her body in. "It's nice to meet you. And you are?"

"Leaving."

Trinh tried to step away but nearly took a fall. I caught her waist and pulled her against my side.

"Take it easy," I urged. "We all know you're a tough girl and can take care of yourself, but it wouldn't kill you to lean on a friend for a few minutes, okay?"

She worked her jaw as she stared into the distance.

"Booker," called out a middle-aged officer as he approached. "These survivors?"

My face went flat at the possibility of being interrogated by police.

"Nah," answered Book. "These jokers are rubbernecking." He spun to us with an authoritative shove. "There's no free booze here. Clear out unless you want a ride to County."

"All right, all right," I grumbled, playing my part and nodding my thanks.

We trudged to the Jeep, doing our best to hide Trinh's limp. I lifted her into the passenger seat and rounded to enter my side. I pulled away at a measured speed, treading the needle between desperate to leave and wanting to stick around. At the end of the alley, I set the whistle to my lips and blew. Scout loped over from across the street and met us with an ecstatic bark before hopping into the back and panting happily.

"You still have that thing," said Trinh without a degree of excitement.

"That *thing* might've just saved your life."

She regarded the large dog as a soldier might regard a hunting knife or some other useful tool. I supposed it was better than disdain.

In the middle of pulling out, I slammed on the brakes and stared across the street. "No way."

The vampire tensed and grabbed a knife. "What is it?"

I pointed to a billboard. "Taco Bell has fries now."

She smacked my shoulder, and it hurt a lot more than when Milena did it. "Are you always a child?"

I blew a raspberry in denial. "That's what *you* are. You sure you can't go for a quick bite? I mean, it's not human blood, but there's a cup of nacho cheese."

She rolled her eyes and crossed her arms. "I'd like to leave the scene of a crime, actually."

I huffed unreasonably loud and begrudgingly turned away from the main street. Another siren approached from somewhere, but I was pretty sure it was Fire Rescue. I weaved in and out of various blocks to make it difficult for anyone to follow.

"What are you gonna do about Tutti?" I asked.

"What do you mean?"

I stared at her incredulously.

"We still don't know that she betrayed me."

"Okay."

Trinh was in denial. Maybe she underestimated Tutti.

Maybe the two were besties now. The only things I knew for sure was that Tutti was only in it for herself, and she played to win. I was about to talk some sense into Trinh when my phone buzzed again. It was what had woken me up in the first place. I hadn't checked it yet so I answered while I drove.

"Cisco," breathed Milena. "Finally! I just came from Darcy's apartment."

I didn't know where the telekinetic lived, but it was somewhere in the Design District, which was nearby.

"Did you see her? What did she say?"

"She wasn't there, but some people were. I think they were watching the place."

I hit the brakes and the Jeep left black tire tracks as it screeched to a stop. "Where are you now? Did anyone follow you?"

"I don't think so. I'm at my place in Midtown."

I didn't like that she wasn't locked down in Brickell, but Midtown was nestled between Wynwood and the Design District. I could see why she might hole up there after being spooked.

"I'll be there in five."

Just as Trinh had adjusted to the harsh stop, I jammed the gas and she flew back against her seat. In a matter of minutes we were up the elevator and knocking on Milena's door. She opened up and threw her arms around me. I held her tight as Trinh limped inside past us.

"Oh, it's you." Milena shut the door and locked it. "Nice dress."

"It's—" I stopped short as Trinh flashed me a glare. "Uh, nothing."

Milena arched an eyebrow. "Anyway," she said to Trinh, "I don't think I properly thanked you for helping us in the Nether before."

"Don't mention it," said the vampire as she sat heavily on the couch. "How're you feeling?"

Milena's lips pressed tight. "I'm alive, I guess."

There was that sudden awkward silence that happened when people who didn't really know each other overshared. Skipping small talk worked for me.

"Who was at Darcy's place?"

Milena shook her head in frustration. "It's pretty bad, Cisco. Darcy wasn't there, but some guys were. I think they were watching the apartment building, but I snuck past them."

"That was dangerous."

"Please. After fighting off ghosts, gnolls, and a mermaid assassin, this was a piece of cake."

"She has you there," remarked Trinh.

I simpered mockingly to show her just how welcome her commentary was before turning back to my girlfriend.

"They didn't recognize me, so aside from a few catcalls from the movers, it was probably a good thing I did this instead of you."

"What do you mean, movers?" I asked.

"That's what I'm trying to tell you, Cisco. When I first got there, I saw the men loading Darcy's furniture into the moving truck. I thought, *'Wow, she's just up and leaving her place. How empowering.'* But then I saw the men watching her building. And Darcy wasn't moving out so much as *being* moved out. She wasn't there. And she's not being robbed. The front office officially confirmed the apartment was available."

Trinh had an impressed look on her face, but Milena's savviness didn't surprise me. I pulled out my phone and dialed the teenager, expecting it to hit voicemail again, and was surprised to find the number now disconnected.

What the hell? This had officially crossed into the realm of a full-fledged mystery.

"The guy that directed the movers took some of her personal effects into a car. Check it out."

Milena handed over her phone. The first snapshot was of a pair of lugs carrying a sofa. The next showed a Chinese man in a tidy suit carrying some of Darcy's spell tokens. My lips curled.

"That's Shen Santos," I spat. "Card-carrying member of the Society of Free Peoples and potential grade-A asshole."

"I tried to get more details from the front office," she mournfully explained, "but they won't give information on tenants. Do you think Darcy was kidnapped?"

I worked my jaw as I cycled through pictures of stuff being loaded into vehicles. Besides limited furniture going into the U-Haul, Shen placed a garbage bag into the trunk of a large gray Hummer.

My face twisted in rage. I'd seen that exact truck on several occasions, always parked right in front of the hippest steakhouse in Brickell.

Chapter 37

After I was confident no one had followed Milena, I left the girls in the apartment. Trinh needed the rest, and they were safe together. Besides, a little of Milena's softness returned at the sight of a familiar face. Trinh wasn't a bubbly person, but a little bonding time with Milena couldn't hurt.

Armed with Darcy's ex-address, I drove by the place. The movers were long gone by now. I returned to Brickell and kept eyes on Beaumont's restaurant for a while, but there were no signs of the gray Hummer.

I was naturally stewing in anger, which got me thinking about my investigative stew all over again. The Society was an ingredient I hadn't added to the pot, and one bound to change the flavor profile of the whole shebang. I couldn't decide if they were mushrooms or eggplant or what. All I knew is they weren't welcome.

The Society of Free Peoples is an outfit of animist businessmen who function like a cartel. They're not evil, per se. By their own admission, the Society was formed in the early days of the country as a way of advocating for animists and advancing their interests. But don't think B-movie antagonists. They're not an ancient council of wizards who get their rocks off policing magic. Rather, they keep each other's financial pursuits positioned at the head of their respective markets.

They're a capitalistic venture, no different from hundreds of other businesses, special interest groups, and lobbies. As long as you hand-wave the spellcasting bit. This means the Society cares more about image and profit than trivialities like right and wrong. And their insistence on controlling the narrative can be obnoxious. As with any titans of industry, you can expect the big guys to bully the small.

Instead of surrendering to rage, I set my thoughts on more productive ventures. Beaumont and the Society were notoriously calculating; in order to play on their field, I had to be as well. So instead of barging into Carbon during business hours, I bided my time and got some tacos on a street-side table, tossing Scout the odd bite. It wasn't a pan-seared steak with truffle butter, but it was comfort food, and the company was a hell of a lot better.

By the time I returned, the gray Hummer was parked in the reserved spot in front of Carbon. It wouldn't do to make a scene in front of guests, so I waited and watched. I passed the time by staring at my phone. The call from Darcy would no longer be coming, and with Milena, no news was good news. I hadn't heard from Kasper all day and realized why. I'd programmed his number into my phone but never texted him with mine. I corrected that in hopes he had an update on the runes.

Scores of diners filed from the restaurant over the closing hour. The valet guys packed it in, running into the restaurant to deliver the last set of keys to the straggler. Twenty minutes later, I figured it had to be the owner of the gray Hummer because no one else was leaving. The coast was clear for me to get some answers.

"Come on, boy," I said, leading Scout across the street. "You're coming with."

This time there were no misgivings about taking a dog into a fine dining establishment. We pushed inside, marched past the abandoned host stand, and found the entire dining room dark and empty.

I was hit again by the feeling that something was out of place. What was it about emptiness that was so unsettling? Scout released a low, throaty growl, which was a validation of my gut feeling. I drew power into my eyes and studied the room. Nothing appeared amiss at first glance.

I tip-toed toward the kitchen, knowing it impossible that my presence was undetected even while hoping for a little luck. Scout's ears perked at the curtain leading to the back room, and he growled again.

I patted his head to keep him quiet. Beaumont usually did his backroom business in the kitchen, but he had been backstage earlier. I'd never actually been back there and altered my destination. Inching forward in complete silence, I pulled the heavy red curtain aside.

The familiar, public part of the restaurant had a long bar

that spanned the host area to the corner window, but apparently there was an extra-secret bar in the back. The seedy lounge vibe was strong, with several booths, freestanding card tables, and a cozy corner bar. The opposite corner featured couches and chairs snuggled beside a crackling stone fireplace. Leverett Beaumont sat cross-legged on a plush chair with a martini on the mid-century end table. His white formal coat was folded over the armrest, leaving him in a blood-red button-up and loosened bow tie.

His fingers unsteepled and signaled the seat across him. "By all means, join me."

Scout's throat rumbled and the vampire's eyes snapped to the dog at my feet. It was good to see I still had a few surprises. I advanced to the center of the room, cautiously examining the surroundings. If a strange feeling had nagged at me in the front of the house, it was turned up to eleven back here.

"A drink?" he offered.

"I'm not staying long."

His eyebrow twitched at my tone. "You realize you're breaking several health codes by bringing that mutt in here."

"We'll keep it our secret," I returned. "Just like this place. I've never seen this bar open."

"I intended it to be a public lounge, but then I got my hands on an actual lounge and decided to keep Carbon respectable. I use this room for sensitive business matters and as a green room for the musical talent. But you're too late if you're looking for a free show."

"The Vanguard blew up an Obsidian March bar today."

My forwardness took him off guard. He pressed his lips tight. "I heard."

"I'm guessing you also heard Tutti pointed them to the place."

It took Beaumont a minute, but he eventually grinned. "The answer to your question is yes."

Now I was off guard.

"I secured a deal with the militia in order to protect Brickell," he revealed. "I don't need to remind you how that protects your interests as well. And if I hurt the Obsidian March in the process, well, nobody's crying over them."

I had to admit, I was angry at being kept in the dark. "What happened to contact being dangerous?" I demanded. "To keeping a low profile?"

"I can no longer afford to do that. As conservator of Miami, my presence must be known, and I can't have my authority challenged."

"Conservator?"

Beaumont picked up his martini glass and took a sip, his gaze never leaving me.

My hands went to my hips. "Tutti screwed up. You know Trinh was in that bar, right?"

The dog lowered his ears and spun around. I followed his gaze as Tutti stood from her hiding place behind the bar. How had I missed her?

"You're not talking about me behind my back, are ya?" she asked coyly.

"I was trying to," I snarled.

"The Vanguard was overeager," Beaumont clarified. "Tutti says they went in too fast."

"That's horseshit. Why would they jump the gun and risk hurting their inside connection?"

"The real question," asked Tutti pointedly, "is what do you think you're doing spying on us?"

I turned back to her. I didn't like not being able to look at both of them at once. "Why should I trust you if you don't trust me?"

Leverett set his glass down and crossed his hands in his lap. "Keeping you in the dark isn't a failure of trust, Cisco. It's compartmentalization. There are methods of getting things done that you excel at, and matters of diplomacy which I do. But that begs the question, what were you trying to accomplish in Wynwood today?"

I let Scout fixate on Tutti and took a step closer to the boss. I'd already caught him admitting to one lie. I might as well test that trust by catching him in another.

"Besides saving Trinh you mean?"

He bit down uncomfortably and betrayed himself with a gaze at Tutti. "She's alive?"

Tutti was nonplussed by the news, as if I'd taken the wind from her sails.

"Don't look so disappointed," I said.

"I'm disappointed," he sternly replied, "in Trinh being left behind." Leverett cleared his throat. "It seems I owe you my thanks."

I took another step toward him. "I'm not here for your

thanks. I'm here for the Society."

Once again he was surprised. For a guy like him, in such a short period of time, his head must've been spinning. Leverett killed off his martini in a final gulp. "It's time to show you that trust goes both ways. Although it seems you're already aware, the Society is indeed with us."

The entire room rippled. The thickness of the air popped and sagged as reality wove away. Multiple animists stood along the walls, including Shen Santos who dispelled his extravagant illusion of emptiness.

Chapter 38

Scout whirled in a circle, barking and baring teeth. I might as well have done the same. I'd worked with Shen before. Three others I didn't know. And there was the last, Simon Feigelstock, Society enforcer and big-money lawyer.

Shen was a clean-shaven young man with spiky black hair. His confident smirk betrayed a bit of resentment against me, probably for having stuck with Darcy when he didn't. At the same time, he had no reason to really hate me. None of them did, but I wasn't naive enough to think they wouldn't turn on me the second it benefited them.

Simon was the big cheese here. Though balding and in his late forties, he had a thin physique and was at the top of his game. Pinstripe suit, jumbo cuff links, tan wingtips— Simon was the type of guy who could back up every bit of his extravagance with magical muscle. His strength, supreme command of anything related to lightning, was thanks to an old Sumerian god, Ishkur the Thunderer.

"You weren't supposed to come clean with him," berated

Simon.

The vampire boss calmly met the accusing glower. "Our agreement does not stipulate me lying to my associate."

The animist enforcer snorted. "Come on, doesn't *associate* sound a bit official? The entire reason we're here is because he doesn't want to join the band."

"My ability to work with others is precisely why you value me."

"So that's why the Society's in town?" I cut in. "Working your connections?"

Simon shrugged. "That and the Manifesto mess. Those aftershocks are still rumbling all over South Florida."

I addressed Beaumont. "Are you a card-carrying member of the Society now?"

"Him?" Simon cracked up. "No. He's not a human or an animist. But we respect everything Clan Beaumont has accomplished. This is a 'you scratch my back, I scratch yours' situation. Very similar to the one we had with the *Agua Fuego* cartel. You remember them, don't you?"

I ground my teeth. "Peas!"

Simon pulled his head back and gave me a strange look. "I beg your pardon?"

"I just figured out what ingredient you are in my beef and potato stew. You guys are the mushy peas. Unoriginal, unnecessary, and all you do is clog things up."

The enforcer sighed. "Are you done?"

I faced the vampire boss with crossed arms. "What are you doing with mushy peas, Beaumont?"

"I'm the new conservator of Miami," he said plainly.

Title aside, I didn't know why I hadn't seen something like this coming.

The Society had always desired a handle on South Florida. They're a northeast outfit and—let's face it—things are different down here. Connor Hatch's Caribbean influence and political allies got the job done in the old days. With the Obsidian March filling that void, there'd been no forthcoming candidates to side with the Society.

Not besides Cisco Suarez.

"Let's face it," expounded Simon, "Leverett here entered the game with high marks. He made a deal with police to keep the militia out of Brickell. He's friendly with several acceptable crime families."

"What about the unacceptable ones?" I growled.

"He has the Obsidian March on the run, doesn't he?"

I grimaced, unable to deny how satisfying the recent hits against the vampires were compared to the glacial pace of the DROP team investigation. Though it would be a lie to claim I was completely comfortable with Beaumont's rising star.

"So you're hungry for power," I said in rebuke.

"This has nothing do to with power," answered Beaumont. "And everything."

My brow knitted.

The vampire sighed. "Cisco, the more power I have, the more people want me dead. This danger isn't appeased with beneficence, or helping others. These acts are often seen as signs of weakness to be taken advantage of. When it comes down to it, someone, somewhere, wants what I have. I'll always be a target. The only way to fend off continued aggressions is to grow even more powerful."

I grumbled to myself, mainly because I didn't have any specific criticism of what was happening. I'd known what Beaumont was, and my alliance with him had strengthened both of our positions. That meant that all this time he'd been offering me protection, I'd been lending him local credibility.

"Come on, man," encouraged Simon with a grin. "You look like you're jealous we appointed him conservator instead of you."

Shen chuckled. "Aren't you the one who said you didn't want the job?"

"That's true," said Simon. "You did turn us down. But I'll level with you, Cisco: Leverett is a better businessman. You... you're a wild card, a loose cannon, and a ticking time bomb all in one. After that nasty Shadow Man business, I warned you about being damaged goods."

"I don't give a shit about the conservatorship or your fucking Society," I spat. Everybody paused breathing as I took a measured step towards the shifty lawyer and leveled him with a glare. "I'm here for Darcy."

He blinked for a moment before recovering with a smirk. "Is that all? Darcy left on her own."

"Bullshit."

He laughed incredulously. "Think about it, man. She joined you because she had a crush on you. She would've followed you to the ends of the Earth if you let her. But you didn't return her affection." He canted his head in thought.

"I really think you could've convinced your stripper girlfriend to go for a nineteen-year-old, but that's just me."

I growled at him in warning.

"Either way," he hurried, getting back on track, "you can't expect Darcy to follow you around forever. It's unfair to her."

"Yeah, 'cause you've got her best interests at heart."

"Hey, I'm just middle management," he quibbled. "But, I will tell you that we protect our own. And Darcy's with us now. No amount of... chest thumping is gonna change that."

I worked my jaw. While I didn't take his words at face value, they still stung. "I want to talk to her," I said.

Simon chewed his lip before looking to Beaumont for assistance. The upir airily shook his head. He knew me too well to get in the way of a friend. And, as stubborn as Simon was, he did too.

"Fine," he said. "In the interests of our new relationship with Clan Beaumont, and seeing as you're an outside contractor for them, I'll set up a meeting."

"That's a bad idea, Simon," warned Shen. "You said—"

"What matters," he interrupted, "is what I say now. Cisco's proven he can play ball in the past. Despite his gruff exterior, he can be reasonable, right?"

Shen pouted. "He's proven he does whatever he wants."

I scoffed. "Says the guy who abandoned Darcy after a run-in with a serial killer."

He turned crimson. "I wanted to take her with me!" he fumed.

"So you finally resorted to kidnapping."

Before Shen could respond, Simon threw his hands up. "That's enough you two! A little jabbering's expected, but don't act like children. I've already agreed to your request, Cisco. Let's leave it at that. But..." Simon pointed a stern finger my way. "I won't force the girl to do anything she doesn't want to do. And that includes speaking with you."

I turned on my heels and marched out. "She'll talk to me," I told them.

And I was confident of that too. No matter what Darcy had going on, no matter what hurt she may have felt or what obligation she had to the Society, I just couldn't see her splitting without saying goodbye.

Not unless I had missed something big.

Chapter 39

It had *not* been my day.

I lounged in the Jeep beside Kendall Indian Hammocks Park, nursing a plastic coke bottle with some rum in it. Between the dead cat being a bust, failing to talk sense into the militia, Darcy moving out, and the revelation about Beaumont's new working relationship with the Society, I had a lot on my mind.

And I was a worker, waiting in the darkness near the potter's field for a break in the case. A pigeon thrall was watching the grave and Scout was posted down the gravel road making sure nobody snuck up on me. All there was for me to do was bundle up in layers, watch the clock as midnight approached, and take another swig of my highball. It was my own private party.

Happy New Year.

Not only had it not been my day, but it wasn't my night either. The potter's field had no registrable necromantic activity.

I woke up to a zombified dog licking my face. Scout backed away from my shove and panted happily, not having slept a wink all night. There were a couple of hikers in the area, but from his attitude it was clear the dog wasn't warning me of danger. If anything it seemed like he just wanted company. I ruffled the fur of his neck.

Stretching forward in the seat with a wide yawn, I discovered several notifications on my phone. A missed call and three voicemails. Once again I'd snoozed through the morning and had to play catch-up.

The first voicemail was Milena letting me know she was safe at the condo. The call came in the early a.m. and made me wonder what she'd been up to all night. But she was a big girl and it was nice to hear she was thinking about me even when I was in the field.

Next up was Evan with a few updates. The operation at DROP Team Central was fully staffed and Rita wanted me in the office regularly to strategize. Which sounded like buckets of fun. He apologized but reminded me that the FBI's good word was keeping me on the case, and I should do my best to keep them happy.

Evan then said he wouldn't be around much as his team was on loan to the gang unit. I'd already seen Booker in Wynwood so it wasn't hard to imagine the guys stretched across the city. He mentioned reaching out to other police departments in an effort to track down the Vanguard's home base, but they were mostly waiting on federal resources.

And it wouldn't be Evan if he didn't finish with a word of

caution. There were metric shit-tons of police in the streets, he emphasized, and tensions were higher than ever. It would be best not to do anything too spectacular, which was code for letting the Shadow Man out.

The last voicemail was the call that had woken me up. Kasper reported some kind of breakthrough with the cemetery runes. I called him back first.

"Broham," he said, voice lowered, "I just called you."

"Yeah, that's why I'm calling back."

A blender went off in the background and Kasper covered the speaker and said some muffled words. I thought someone else spoke before hearing my patio door slide shut. Judging from the sound of wind, Kasper was on my balcony.

"I think I've finally got something," he relayed. "For a while I couldn't make heads or tails of some of these symbols. Some of them are words and some are similar to hieroglyphs. You know, that's why Milena's moon symbol looks like a moon. But it's more than that. Remember, she drew that symbol around the same time it may have been carved into Ebu, only her symbol was more pure. The version the killer did had a horizontal line through it, like a strikethrough."

"We saw that before," I said, "on the rune drawn into Quentin's arm."

"That's right, but until now the strikethrough has only been on the victims. One of the two new grave runes had it, and I think I finally realized its significance. We've seen the naked version of the symbol before, or at least part of it, around the original ring of symbols you photographed. It's

San Silvestro, a church in Rome."

I frowned. "Except this new version of it is crossed out?"

"I think it's a way of powering down the glyph. The original was part of the circle, a set of instructions for the karkan, and the new command was a way to cancel it."

"So you think the strikethroughs drawn onto the victims are a way of closing the loops, of canceling them out?"

"It would make sense," he said. "Quentin's rune referred to hypnotism or hypnotist. Ebu's rune is a little harder. The circle represents the moon. If you ignore the horizontal strikethrough line, the vertical lines mean something similar to zenith."

"Milena said the moon was at its peak." I grumbled and wondered how she'd been able to draw a symbol from a mostly dead language. "What about the second rune on the grave."

"That's the one that gave me fits," he said. "It didn't make any sense at first, but I considered the strikethrough and the combined symbology of Ebu's rune. I realized this glyph wasn't one word but two, overlapping into one meaning."

"What does it mean?"

He took a breath. "The first word doesn't have a direct translation. Near as I can tell, it means boss, or authority. I found one instance of it meaning warden."

"Warden..."

My balcony door slid open and shut. Kasper covered his microphone and thanked someone before loudly slurping a frozen drink through a straw. Then I heard a clap and a woman's laughter.

My eyes creased. "Kasper," I said coolly, "are you boinking Clarence's aunt?"

"What's it to you?" he asked defensively. "She's fun."

I rubbed my forehead and wondered if I needed a lawyer. "What about the other symbol?"

"That one was easy. Not that I can figure out what it means."

There was a splash in my pool. "You're not making sense," I said.

"Of course I am. The word's easy to read; I just don't know what it means in context. The symbol's a bell, and it's almost always used when referring to church bells or churches. Considering the Byzantine usage of this script, that ends up being a lot. So I'm digging for some church authority like the Pope or whoever's in charge of San Silvestro."

It was good work but part of it didn't sit right with me. I didn't put much stock in complicated conspiracies involving ancient organizations. Why go through the bother when there were plenty of more tangible reasons to kill someone?

I recalled my initial impression of the ring of glyphs around the karkan's grave, even before I'd made the connection to Twelvetide. I'd thought of the numbers around a clock. That wasn't right either, of course, but there was a chronological parallel: a calendar.

Twelve days was the karkan's mission. Christmas, Childermas—the arms of his clock pointed to days not hours. San Silvestro wasn't a church, he was a saint, and his feast day was New Year's Eve.

"Were any deaths reported last night?" I asked.

"What?"

"The karkan. Do we know if there was another victim?"

"I haven't heard anything."

It was the late morning. Whether I would've heard from the police about a new body could've gone either way, but I was starting to suspect nothing had happened last night. The glyph had been canceled. The karkan was ordered to stand down on Saint Sylvester's Day.

But it was also given a second instruction. A separate rune, not one signifying a day but instead...

"The runes on the victims are monikers," I realized. "Quentin was the hypnotist, crossed out when he was killed. Ozo Ebu was the head of the Night Walkers, the leader or 'zenith' of the blue moon gang."

Kasper switched back indoors. "I see where you're going with this broham, but who does authority church represent?"

"It's simpler than that. Boss, authority, warden... They're all words for police."

"Sure but..."

"What about agent?" My voice lowered an octave. "*Agent Bell.* The church bell represents Rita Bell. She's the karkan's next victim."

My mind raced. Ozo Ebu might've been a dead end for the assassin, or maybe not. Either way, both Quentin and Ebu had known of Rita's involvement tracking the Shadow Man.

But if she was still looking for him, how would the karkan benefit by going after her? Something didn't make sense about the monster's sudden reprogramming, but I couldn't deny the obvious link to Rita.

I didn't have time to work the problem through in my head. I'd wasted enough waiting and watching.

"Kasper, you translated some partial runes from the original ring. It was how we found the word massacre. Were there any others that stood out?"

He cleared his throat. "Well, there was Twelvetide. And one was solemnity."

"That's it. Today's the Solemnity of the Mother. I gotta go."

I hung up before explaining details. He was with a woman twenty years his junior—he would get over my slight. The Solemnity of Mary, the Mother of God, was an important feast day. If we were splitting hairs, it was observed by Roman Catholics and not the Eastern Orthodox Church, but there was a lot of overlap and syncretism when it came to religion and spellcraft. I had no idea when the karkan would strike next, but today was as good a bet as any.

I went to dial Rita and immediately realized my bind.

I didn't keep Agent Bell's number reserved to memory, and we hadn't spoken on my new phone. It hadn't been a priority since I'd kept her business card handy. It was right in the center console of my Firebird... in Little Haiti.

Crap.

I shifted the Jeep to drive and peeled out. The fact that I

was in a hot car didn't stop me from speeding. I called Evan as I drove. It went to voicemail so I hung up and redialed. On the second voicemail I left a message. "I need Rita's number now. It's important."

I stepped on the gas and considered other methods of getting in touch. There was the public FBI office. I could call and go through their operator, but that didn't seem worth the time. It was just before lunch so traffic wasn't bad. I would be at DROP Team Central in five minutes. All I needed to do was get to Rita before...

When was the last time I'd seen Rita alive?

I could've been wrong about the timing. Maybe the karkan did strike last night. Maybe Rita was already dead. I wasn't sure where she was staying, though my first stop would be the cheap motel they'd interrogated me at. She wasn't sleeping in that room but it would make sense to find her nearby.

I bit down and continued to the station. Once downtown, I parked behind the FBI-issue Ford Explorer and rushed into the building.

Rita and Carter spun to me as I skidded to a halt, breathless. "You're alive," I said.

They blinked.

"Of course we're alive," hissed Carter. "We're the FBI. And you're late." He muttered something to himself and retired into the conference room.

I glanced around the tranquil office, embarrassed I'd worked myself up for nothing, and approached falteringly.

Agent Bell furrowed her brow. "You look like you've

seen a ghost."

"I get that more than you think."

She hiked a shoulder. "Carter's right, you know. He can be a dick, but what does it look like to everyone else when our star consultant doesn't show up for work?"

I shook my head, flustered. "It's not like you gave me a heads up until this morning."

"Only because you disconnected your phone."

I didn't have a retort for that. In the interest of not experiencing another scare, we exchanged numbers. I didn't like handing the FBI my burner number. With it she could track my phone and my location, despite my security precautions. In this case it was a necessary evil.

"Look," I said haltingly, "this schedule thing is new to me. It's not like I was dicking around for fun. I'm working angles too."

"Care to share?"

I bit down. There was only so much I could say without essentially admitting her suspicions about me were true. Which I wasn't prepared to do. Animists don't get far in the real world by announcing themselves. For all the Society's quirks, it was one facet of the secret organization they'd nailed.

"Today's New Year's Day. The feast day of the Holy Mother."

She blinked. "That's all you have?"

"It's... all I have. But it's significant."

She studied me a moment before nodding and leading me into the conference room. Carter and Jensen were each perusing their own sets of files. They sat at opposite ends of the table, as if sharing air space was too much of a distraction.

"Well if it isn't Harry Dresden," said the crime scene tech as he pulled his gaze away from his photos.

I arched my eyebrow and looked around, confused. "What?"

His face went flat. "You're kidding me. You're a supernatural consultant and you don't read the books?"

I slowly wagged my head, unsure of his meaning. "I was... out of the country for a long time."

His eyes widened as if he'd just stepped in a steaming pile of dog poo. "Oh, your abduction. Sorry. I guess you didn't have a lot of time for pop culture after being kidnapped by a blood cult."

I chuckled nervously and looked to Rita, hoping for a swift change of subject. My time in South America was a hazy cover story for being a zombified hit man. It was better not to share details that could be picked apart, especially in front of the FBI.

"Can someone tell me what I'm doing here please?" I asked wryly.

"Work," droned Carter. "You might have heard of it. It's what productive members of society, i.e. other people, do with their time."

I narrowed my eyes, secretly pleased he'd taken the bait and shifted the focus in the room.

"We've been coordinating with the gang unit," explained Rita, pointing to crossed-out names on the white board.

"Since our last victim was a member of the Night Walkers, we targeted them first. Unfortunately, the few members we picked up yesterday were low level. They were no help at all."

I crossed my arms and leaned on the back wall, figuring silence was better than an I-told-you-so.

"We also passed by the stomping grounds of the Bone Saints. Have you heard of them?"

I raised my eyebrows and blew a raspberry as I pretended to scour my mind. "Bone Saints... Haitians who paint their faces, right?"

Rita nodded. "I thought they were right up your alley. The gang unit performed two sweeps of their compound, but we haven't located their leadership."

I hiked an unsurprised shoulder. "Anyone who's a possible target of the karkan is bound to make themselves scarce."

"Especially if they know something," she pointed out. "Which brings us to the biggest complication of our task. It's hard enough to convince these outlaws to trust the feds. How are we supposed to appeal our case if we can't even find them?"

"You ask me," said Carter unprompted, "this is well-deserved street justice."

"That's one way to miss the point," remarked Jensen with an eye roll that was meant to be noticed. "Quentin Capshaw wasn't a gang member."

"But he had dealings in the street," returned the hardened agent. "I'll bet you two-to-one odds that, when the truth comes out, we'll find Capshaw brought this on himself."

Rita sighed loudly. "That may be, agent, but the evidence must bear out the conclusion, not the other way around. Gang violence is a likely culprit and we're currently following that line of inquiry. Until then, I want the three of you to play nice and come up with new leads." She started to walk out of the office.

"What are you doing?" I asked pointedly.

"Interviewing a person of interest the gang unit picked up."

"Are they coming to us?"

"Nope. This one had a warrant. I'm headed to the federal detention center."

I followed her into the main office. If Rita was marked by the karkan, the last thing I wanted was her wandering the city on her own. "I'll go with," I volunteered.

"It's not necessary. This is mostly procedural and probably a waste of time."

"And eating shit in this office isn't? Look, I have gang contacts. I can contribute."

"Fine," she said gruffly. "It might be fun to watch you work."

We headed outside, but my grin was short-lived. As we neared her SUV, several cops dealt with a barking dog in a black Jeep. They had the vehicle surrounded and were attempting to extricate a large Alaskan shepherd from it. By their apparent jumpiness, I was guessing a couple of them had already almost lost their fingers. One officer fired a stream of pepper spray at Scout and was answered with a resounding howl.

"Officers! Officers!" I sprinted over to the car and Scout sat and happily wagged his tail. I threw up my hand to halt any displays of affection. "He's just a dog. I can take care of this."

I pulled the silver whistle to my lips and gave Scout a silent command to head into the alley. His large ears turned away from me, his tail went between his legs, and he bounded from the back seat to the asphalt and across the street.

The cops blinked stupidly at me. "Was that your dog?" one asked. Then their faces hardened. "Is this your vehicle?"

"Never seen it before in my life."

"How'd you do that with the dog?"

I wagged the whistle at them. "It's a dog whistle."

"Can I see some ID? This Jeep was reported stolen."

"It's not mine. I drive a silver Trans Am. She can vouch for me." I hooked a thumb at Rita. "She's FBI."

They suddenly noticed her, and she confirmed my statement. They didn't seem to know her directly but took her at face value despite no identification being presented. I guess Rita just had that vibe.

"Don't worry about it then," said one of the officers. He scanned the street as a large group of pedestrians filed past. "I have the feeling we'll have a lot more to worry about today."

"You and me both," said Agent Bell as she thanked them. We returned to her car. "So where is your Trans Am?"

"It's, uh, in the garage." I waved my hand in the opposite direction. "I was thinking we'd ride together."

She narrowed her eyes and nodded. "Fine, hop in."

We waited as a crowd passed before we were able to pull out, but the full view of the situation grew apparent as we drove several blocks. Scores of citizens strode down the sidewalks, bike path, and whatever spaces they fit. It would only be a matter of time before they spilled into the streets.

"And I was hoping this would be a big fat nothingburger," muttered Rita.

My expression was blank. "What wouldn't happen?"

"The Million Militia March. Vanguard sympathizers have been spreading the word. Where have you been all night?"

Chapter 40

The gathering protesters were a far cry from the empty neighborhoods of days past. There wasn't any looting or burning, but it was clear the day was just getting started.

I scoured social media. #VAPMMM was trending.

"A New Year, A New Day."

"I walk with the Vanguard Against Parahumans. Do you?"

"One in a Million Militia March."

Several videos were linked. My jaw dropped as I watched the back door of a Wynwood dive bar kicked down from the vantage of a GoPro affixed to a helmet. The militia member rushed into the dark hallway as a fellow soldier sprayed bullets at an antique refrigerator. The view advanced and swiveled to a shiny black beast with claws. It was dark, but not enough to hide the inhuman horror caught on camera, at least for the split second before semi-automatic fire ripped it apart.

The video cut to a man in a room of security feeds.

Behind were large glass windows and a dark sky, indicating this was filmed last night. The speaker was the same leader from before, except this time he started the video by pulling off his ski mask. Though fairly young, he had a head of nearly white hair.

"This is Landon," said the man, "and we've had enough. As you can see, we're up against pure, unhinged evil. They come at us wearing the skins of humans. They appear as friends. But we can never let our guard down."

The man took a measured breath. The gravity of his words were not lost on him. "The Vanguard will never back down. For every one of us that falls, three more join the fight. *You* are part of that fight if *you* are on the side of humanity."

Landon smiled grimly, coming off as a handsome, middle-aged straight talker. "Tomorrow is a new year, and a new day. Join the fight. March with us. They can't stop a militia a million humans strong."

The video ended with the hashtag but no other directions. There was no goal other than getting out, no destination other than the streets. This was about rallying the city to a cause.

Hundreds, maybe thousands, of marchers would cross Miami unchecked. It had been almost a week since the Holiday Village shooting and the increased police presence. With the release of this shocking footage, maybe the locals were finally sick of being scared.

Agent Bell turned into the nearby lot of FDC Miami, and I put my phone away. The federal building was a tall stone structure with minimal windows and stout square columns along the base. Decorative flairs were sparse save for the large brass-colored seal of the Federal Bureau of Prisons above the entry, with matching brass bowls and handrails in the plaza. It looked like something modern-day Egyptians might build.

The detention facility served as a prison for the US Marshals service and those awaiting federal trials. I'd never been inside because the Miami Police Department didn't usually have business here except, perhaps, as couriers. In this case, the gang unit had been kind enough to deliver Rita's prize to a secure facility. While the move seemed a favor on the surface, the dump-off probably had more to do with liability than anything else. Babysitting gang members for the feds wasn't high on the list of a city cop's priorities.

Rita warned me about the metal detectors so I begrudgingly left my belt pouch and implements of spellcraft in the truck. That included the silver dog whistle. I kept the belt and skull buckle on until I passed through the machines and the guards deemed it wasn't dangerous. We took the elevator to the second floor and made our way through a holding office where Rita picked up a manila folder from the front desk.

"Person of interest is Samira Awesso, a suspected lieutenant of the Night Walker gang."

I snatched the file photograph in case there was a mistake. No such luck. They had Samira in custody. I stopped in my tracks.

"Uh... Samira's not a lieutenant, and she's only a friend

of the Night Walkers. She's the undisputed head of the Children of Oya. Yoruba, not Igbo, but West African."

Rita was so taken aback by the news, she forget to castigate me for grabbing her file. "Wow. I suppose even the good guys get lucky once in a while. Let's go see what she has to say."

"About that... Samira and I aren't really on speaking terms."

"So? She's in handcuffs."

"What I mean is I'd only distract from the goal of getting information. She'll clam up the second I step in the interrogation room."

Rita's lips twisted into a sour expression. She snatched her photo back. "I thought you said you could help."

I shook my head. "Sorry, I thought I could. For what it's worth, I don't envy you having to deal with her alone."

Rita snorted. Instead of cowing her, my statement inspired defiant confidence, but live and learn. I waited in the hallway as she entered the interrogation room alone. Unfortunately, this wasn't one of those professional rooms with two-way mirrors. If there was any surveillance of the interview, I didn't have access to it. I couldn't do anything but wait on the sidelines, like it was take-your-child-to-work day.

Oh well. At least I knew the karkan wouldn't be getting to Rita in the middle of a secured federal detention center.

I briefly wondered what Samira might reveal about the karkan and my involvement, but the interrogation wasn't likely to result in much. If Samira saw me with Agent Bell, sure, her anger might prod her into calling me out. But the head of a Yoruba death gang being dragged in by the police for questioning? I'd seen stones bled for more.

Somewhere around an hour into it, Major Bruce Petty stormed by without a word and entered the interrogation room. It was a concerning-enough development to clench both butt cheeks, and I could do nothing but wait in full tense glory until Bruce and Rita exited ten minutes later.

"This is a fishing expedition," berated Petty as they stopped beside me. "You don't have anything."

"That's not entirely true," she responded. "Samira confirmed Cisco's theory that this isn't based in Caribbean voodoo."

"Great, so we know just as much as we started with."

"Might I remind you, major, that your detective of choice is working the case right alongside me and might be a better target for your displeasure."

"Don't be so sensitive, Agent Bell. I'm not calling anyone out, but it's my informed opinion that we're not moving fast enough. Unfortunately, this Million Militia March is a complication. I need to reserve my resources for one more day before I can begin to alleviate manpower. Don't you have federal boots at your disposal?"

Rita grumbled. "We had them on deck, but they were diverted to a task force to find the militia."

"What task force? Why wasn't I notified?"

"You'd need to ask the ATF. I don't have full details."

"The ATF?" Petty's head looked like it was about to explode. "Call them off. The Vanguard militiamen are average joes. They don't want to hurt anyone. You saw their video, right? They're self-styled patriots. I'm in the middle of drawing them down. The last thing we need is a federal powder keg. Let me handle the politics."

"What politics?" I cut in.

He did a double take as if just realizing I was there. "It's a city matter."

"The militia's swept up popular support," I grumbled. "People in gray fatigues are filling the streets."

"Which is exactly why this needs a delicate hand." His face flushed red. "I don't know why I'm discussing police matters with you, and I don't know why you're arguing. I swept them out of Brickell, didn't I?"

I blinked. "*You're* the police contact. *You* made a deal with Beaumont."

"So what if I did?" he rebuffed. "The department takes care of our donors. Beaumont put in a good word for you, so I wouldn't bite the hand that feeds."

Now I flushed. "I'm not a lapdog, Petty."

He replied with a cocky scoff. "Don't think I don't have my suspicions about you too, Suarez. Trust me on this one: it's better to be a harmless pup than a wild stray. As of this moment, I think of you as a moderately successful if flamboyant police consultant. It would behoove you not to become more interesting to me than that."

"Is that a threat?" I snarled.

"Take it for what it is," he said. "A little friendly advice to stay in your lane."

"Gentlemen!" barked Rita. "Enough with the dick

wagging!"

"Like you're above it," scoffed Petty. "It doesn't matter that you're a woman, you're FBI. You think you have the biggest dick of all of us."

She jerked her head back and eyed him coolly. "Then you'd better hurry home and dig the penis pump out of your closet, because the federal government is *not* backing away from the militia. And if you have a problem with that, you can take it up with the deputy director. I believe I can get you an appointment."

He sneered for a good ten seconds before backing down. "No need, Agent Bell. By all means, waste federal funds on another Waco if you like. But if this task force intends to play police within spitting distance of *my* city, you'd better seek approval from the mayor *and* the chief. And good luck getting those appointments."

The major stormed back down the hall from where he'd come. As soon as he was out of sight, Rita deflated like a balloon. Keeping up that tough exterior must've been a full-time job.

"I don't get it," she muttered. "We're all after the same killer, aren't we?"

"I'm not sure what we're after anymore."

She put her fingers to her temples. "The last thing we can afford right now is a breakdown in local relations."

"He's just blowing off some steam," I tempered. "Besides, I do my best work when everyone's against me."

She rolled her eyes but cracked a smile, only partially able to fend off my encouragement. "You're right," she said.

"I'm just hungry. I skipped lunch and could use an early dinner. I'll drop you back at HQ and—"

"No!" I cut in a little too energetically. With the karkan hunting her, I couldn't let her out of my sights.

She eyed me peculiarly.

"I... I mean I could use a bite too."

We made for the elevators. "Thanks for the invitation, but I prefer to eat alone. It helps me think."

"Come on. Two heads are better than one."

"I have no doubt that's true, but I have a couple of errands to run. Rain check?"

She tapped the call button and I waited with crossed arms and a pout. Rita wasn't going along with the plan, leaving me with few options. I could secretly tail her, but she wasn't born yesterday. The chances were high a trained federal agent would spot me, and this uncomfortable conversation had nothing on that one.

Besides, that plan assumed *I had a car*.

I pouted all the way to the first floor and out of the building. In her Explorer, I took a moment to collect my personal effects. She started the engine, and I had to say something to stop her.

"Okay, listen to me, Rita. I gotta talk to you."

"It's Special Agent Bell," she reminded.

"Whatever. Let me come clean about something."

She stopped fiddling with the sun visor and gave me her undivided attention. At this point, I was only getting out of this by giving her a little of the truth, but I had to minimize it as much as possible so she wouldn't put me in cuffs or get me fired.

"Last night," I started, "I found a cemetery that roughly matches the dirt from the scene of Quentin's murder."

She glared. "You discovered this last night and waited till now to tell me?"

"It was more of an early morning thing. Listen to me. I found a grave with a symbol traced in the dirt. A symbol similar to the ones found on the victims. The translation is the phrase: Agent Bell. I believe the killer is targeting you next."

She didn't say anything for several seconds. "That's ridiculous."

"Is it? The killer's looking for the Shadow Man. They hit a dead end with Ebu, but you were connected to Quentin."

"But I'm a fed."

I chortled. "You think that matters to this kind of crazy?"

She licked her lips and swallowed. "Whose grave is it?" she asked timidly.

"A gypsy traveler's, probably."

She shifted to drive. "Take me there."

I shifted uncomfortably in the seat, but there was no turning back now. After I gave her directions and we were on our way, she went to her phone.

"Don't make it a crime scene," I urged. "These runes are proof the killer visits the grave. If you tape everything off and flood the cemetery with cops, any chance of luring the necromancer in will be ruined."

After a little thought, Rita saw the wisdom in my plan. Still, she didn't want to leave everything to me, so she split the difference. She called Agents Ramirez and Sotomayer and had them meet us at the potter's field. They combed the place for evidence even though I warned them none would be forthcoming.

Our visit was longer than I would've liked, but Rita came to the same conclusions I had, just on her own time line. She decided we needed to watch the site overnight. I could only protest weakly because she didn't know about my hidden sentry and I wasn't about to tell her. In the end, she compromised by assigning the two junior agents on alternating shifts in the distant police station parking lot. That backed them away from the park and cemetery, keeping activity where it wouldn't be suspicious.

It was a solid, conservative plan of action that had absolutely no hope of being successful.

Chapter 41

Some time later, Rita and I sat in a cafe. Our table was already cleared save for two cups of coffee and a sealed white box of guava pastries. See? I was a good boyfriend. And since I was so good, I was considering a reward. Milena wouldn't need the whole box, you see. Perhaps I could sample a *pastelito* or three.

"I don't get it," bemoaned Rita after a protracted silence. "According to your theory, the glyph is an instruction, an order to come after me. If that's the case, who is the killer instructing?"

I shrugged. Some things were easier to believe than others. "Our guy is crazy, right? The symbols cut into his victims, the dirt shoved down their throats—it's magic to him. The adherence to the ritual is what's important. So if our killer believes he's raising the dead, maybe he goes to a graveyard and traces lines in the dirt."

Her expression was skeptical. "Is that what you believe?"

I swallowed and glanced at my empty cup of joe, mouth

dry and wishing for a refill. "Are you suggesting this is a two-man job?"

"You know what I'm suggesting."

Our eyes met. "That a necromancer raised a legendary assassin from the dead to kill the Shadow Man?"

"He exists, Cisco. Of that I'm positive. And the killer... There's no denying he's infatuated with a bogeyman. Screw what the official reports will ultimately say. Screw what the general public believes. You and I know there's more out there. Is it really that far-fetched that we're facing something unknown by the laws of physics?"

My teeth ground together and my gaze returned to the mug. "What you said before, about your dad dying in a fiery blaze of real magic... How far are you willing to take this?"

"What kind of question is that?" she snapped. "I have an obligation to take this all the way."

"And what if you find what you're looking for? And I don't mean scrawlings of a dead Albanian language, I mean actual, tangible spellcraft. What if you encounter it? What do you do in the face of its existence?" I shoved the mug aside and sighed. "What difference does it make?"

Agent Bell worked her lips. She wasn't naive enough to think these questions had easy answers, but pragmatism did little to stymie the fire in her eyes. She put her weight on her elbows and leaned close to me. "The difference is *I would know*. That's all I want, Cisco. To know the truth. After my history, I deserve to know the truth."

Her cell phone rang. Rita waited until the third chime before pulling away and answering.

"Yes," she answered curtly, "just finishing my one square meal of the day... Of course I'm still working it. None of us stop. Agents Ramirez and Sotomayer? They're—"

I desperately waved her off finishing that sentence.

She took a stuttered breath. "They're done for the night. No, I'm not with them. Sure, I can handle this alone."

She leaned back, propped up her elbow with an arm rested over her chest, and listened. The restaurant was nearly empty, but enough people called out and chanted in the street that I could only overhear bits of chatter from her phone.

Rita's eyes widened. "I'll be right there." She bounded from the table and stowed the phone. "Jensen has new evidence of the killer," she relayed. "A blood sample."

"Blood? Where'd he get it?"

"I don't have all the details, but it's like you said: the killer's obsessed with ritual."

I nodded. "Well, let's go."

We left cash on the table and headed back to DROP Team Central. The drive was slow going because the streets were full of jaywalking protesters. Their numbers had more than doubled with the setting of the sun, causing us to stop every fifty feet. It was officially crazy time.

"Jeez," I griped, "this is getting worse than I thought."

"You ever been to New York for New Year's Eve?" she asked. "This is nothing."

"This isn't Times Square, and the party was last night. Today's the day to nurse a hangover at home."

The vast majority of marchers appeared to be normal

people. Revelers wearing party hats and carrying drinks. Families lugging coolers and lawn chairs with kids in tow. There were some troublemakers, lone wolves wearing all black, fans of general anarchy, but out of all their impressive numbers, I only picked out a handful of people who might've been legitimately tied to the Vanguard Against Parahumans.

This wasn't a march, it was a movement.

After Manifesto and the violence in the streets, New Year's Day was the release valve Miami needed. People stormed the streets in force, banding in sheer numbers for safety, and daring any evil to befall them. It was somewhat inspiring while also leaving a queasy feeling in my stomach. I would feel a lot more at ease once the night was through.

The street the station was on wasn't heavily populated by protesters, though small groups constantly cut through to the larger downtown thoroughfares. We parked in a well-lit area and hiked down the sidewalk. A couple holding Tiki torches strode past.

Rita covered her nose. "Is that citronella?"

I chuckled. "You see the size of the mosquitoes we got in Miami?"

Carrying a torch was one thing, but lugging around a scent like that had to be torture. But then, the choice to hit the streets tonight wasn't the result of extensive planning.

We pushed inside the station to the sounds of an argument between Jensen and Carter. The two had succumbed to the close quarters over the last few days and discovered they weren't compatible. Rita hurried over to stifle the situation while I remained by the open door for a last look outside.

Scout was nearby, his presence constant if a little hazy. Maybe he was off on his own again. I gave him a signal with the whistle and eyed the stragglers in the street before shutting the door.

"I told him he doesn't need to be here," complained Jensen. "You said you didn't need help, right?"

Agent Bell gave the tech a funny look. "Until the killer's in cuffs or a casket, we could use all the help we can get."

Jensen spun to me as I approached. "Oh great, you too?"

"What's the matter?" I joked. "You were hoping for a little alone time with Rita?" I winked as obviously as I could.

Rita's lashes flickered and her voice went monotone. "It's Special Agent Bell to everyone in this room."

Everyone was irritable and had bags under their eyes, including me. I peeked into the back offices. "No DROP team?"

"Haven't seen them all day," answered Jensen.

"They're no longer part of this investigation," said Carter with an edge in his voice.

I studied him a second. "Yeah, well, you're in their house so don't get too comfortable." I set the unspoiled box of *pastelitos* on a nearby desk.

"What say we all act like the professionals we are," interjected Agent Bell, "and get right down to it? What do we have on the blood?"

"Right." Jensen moved to a central desk in the main room. A cardboard box the size of a basketball rested beside the computer monitor. The tech tapped on a photograph of a dirty alley. Sunlight from earlier in the day glinted off red blood that was traced on the very same package. "I think Cisco's onto something with the Christmas runes. We found this mere hours ago." All eyes shifted from the photograph of the box to the actual box.

"Who's the vic?" asked Rita in a stilted voice.

The tech shook his head. "There's no sign of one."

"Then whose blood is it?"

"If this guy believes he's casting blood magic, then it might be the killer's. But Cisco's our expert..."

Everyone watched as I inched toward the box. I had no hope of deciphering the glyph and instead focused on the motive. Why would the killer change his MO yet again? Unless there were previous packages we'd missed.

Unlike in the photo, the box was now opened, cut in a way as to preserve the bloody symbol. The box was empty.

"What was inside?" I asked.

"That's the weird thing." Jensen moved to the opposite end of the desk and rested his gloved hand on a hardcover book. "It's a King James Bible. I performed a cursory examination of the pages, but it's not marked up. None of the pages are dog-eared. It looks like it was picked up new in a bookstore."

"It's a code," deduced Carter. "This guy wants us to solve his game."

Flashbacks of Manifesto. Nathan Bartlett Jones was the eponymous serial killer who'd enjoyed media attention and toying with cops. He'd sent letters to the press and created an elaborate treasure hunt for the public based on a complicated cipher.

For some reason, I never expected the necromancer to follow in those footsteps.

"Where'd you get this?" I asked.

Jensen shook his head. "An alley about ten blocks from here. There was nothing there."

"No, I mean how'd you find it?"

"Major Petty brought it to my attention, actually."

"I thought the major was giving us another day," said Rita.

"It's not like that. It came to the major's attention and he suspected it pertained to our case. I think he's right."

"He found it himself?" I prodded.

Jensen laughed. "Doubtful. It was kicked up the chain before he booted it to us."

"By Detective Mullen?" asked Rita.

"Nah. One of the uniforms, I think. What's up with the Twenty Questions? Does it matter which police officer found the package?"

"Chain of custody," answered Rita. "I don't like being late to the party."

"I get that," he agreed. "The way I hear it, the officers didn't know what they were looking at. There was no body, no crime. We're lucky somebody had the smart idea to inform a supervisor. Otherwise this might've ended up in a dumpster and we'd have nothing."

Agent Bell crossed her arms. "Okay, so what do we have then?"

Jensen grew cagey. "It's a developing situation."

"Which means you have squat," berated Carter.

Jensen nodded to the computer sitting between the evidence. "We're running an early analysis of the blood against possible matches. Known convicts came up empty, so we've broadened the search. I was hoping we could tap into the FBI's database for this one."

Rita nodded. "Carter?"

"On it."

The veteran moved to the PC and went about authorizing the search. Everyone watched, but it quickly became clear this wasn't as simple as pulling Google results.

"How long are we looking at?" I asked.

Rita sighed. "It's a process. Even after authorization, the database needs to weed through a lot of partial hits."

"I figured as much," said Jensen. "Catching a serial killer is a marathon, not a sprint." He looked us over and clapped his hands. "Since this is officially a party, what say Cisco and I go across the street for some coffee? And then while we discuss the contents of this box"—he pointed to the Bible —"we can explore the contents of that one." The tech pointed squarely at my box of guava pastries.

It wasn't a bad idea, though I would pick up more pastries across the street. "Let's hit the road," I rejoined.

"We just had coffee," pointed out Rita.

I hiked a shoulder. "So? I could use more. Between this and the other thing, it's gonna be a long night."

Carter eyed me and I realized he wasn't privy to the sting at the potter's field. Good thing he was distracted enough with the federal search that he didn't ask questions.

"Fine," said Rita. "I'll go with. We can walk and talk."

"Actually," said Jensen, "Cisco and I can handle it. You should brush up on my initial report, see if anything strikes you before I color your expectations with my theories." Jensen slid a few pages of handwritten notes across the desk.

Agent Bell went sullen. "Start with the facts, huh?"

"I learned a lot from Mullen," he said with a prideful shrug. "Let's go, Cisco."

The two of us headed out to the sidewalk, where we waited as a small crowd passed in the street.

"Where is Mullen anyway?" I asked. "For a lead detective, I haven't seen him around much."

"He's working angles," said Jensen.

"A bloody package is a big freaking angle," I pointedly returned. "Does he know about this lead?"

"I left him a message but he hasn't gotten back to me. Don't worry. He's no stranger to working nights. He'll be here."

"I guess you're right."

As I took a step onto the street, a bitter scent filled my nose, and it wasn't leftover citronella. I turned back to the building and spotted a bundle barely protruding from the alley.

"You're gonna love this place," beamed Jensen. "It's this way."

"Hold on." I skirted to the side of the building and crouched beside a dead terrier. It lacked a collar and could've been a stray, but it was young and displayed no visible signs of death. I peered down the dark alley.

"Well, that's gross," remarked Jensen right behind me. "We can call city services later."

I stood sharply. "Get back inside." I marched for the front door.

"What?" asked Jensen. "No... What about the coff—"

I grabbed his arm and dragged him along. "Inside. *Now.*"

"Hey! What're you doing?" He frantically pulled away from me. "You're crazy, man!"

I didn't have time to explain something he wouldn't believe, so I shoved him inside very much against his wishes.

"Let go of me!" he yelled.

I shut us inside and locked the dead bolt. Rita and Carter snapped their heads at us, and I gently released the crime scene tech.

"Look," I said softly, "we need to stay inside. Trust me."

"Why should I?" demanded Jensen, rubbing his bicep where I'd squeezed too hard.

I sighed. "How many cases have we worked together, Jensen? I have a good instinct for this stuff. Just trust me for a minute."

But he wasn't the one I needed to worry about. Carter stomped forward looking for a fight. I hit the light switches to the main overheads. The room went dark except for a couple of desk lamps and the light from the open door of the rear conference room.

"What's going on?" demanded Agent Carter.

"I don't know," said a frazzled Jensen. "He just snapped."

"I didn't snap. We're in danger."

Carter's eyes narrowed and he reached for his sidearm.

Rita cautiously approached. "What did you see?"

"Noxious odor. Dead animal. Those are the signs of the karkan."

Jensen blinked. Carter slackened. "Are you kidding me?"

I moved to the windows one by one, peeking through the blinds and making sure they were locked. There wasn't much need as steel grates covered them tight. "This isn't a joke. Something's out there and it wants to come inside."

Carter's gun pointed at me in a flash. "Drop that weapon."

I stiffened, realizing I'd instinctually drawn my sawed-off shotgun from the shadows. I held it by the barrel pointed downwards, so it wasn't in a position to shoot.

"Carter," I said firmly, "I'm arming myself for defense." I skipped over Jensen and turned to Rita. "As should you."

"Cisco..." she whispered, "where'd you get that shotgun?"

"It was around."

"That wouldn't happen to be the 20-gauge I was looking for a while back?"

Crap. Once upon a time, Rita had found evidence of a shotgun with links to the Shadow Man. Until now she hadn't actually linked that weapon to me. Until now.

"Does it matter?" I seethed. "You need to draw your weapon and call off your agent. *Now*."

"Damn it if she does," spat Carter. "I'll tell you one more time: drop your weapon."

I bored holes into the ranking federal agent. "Rita, do I

need to remind you who the karkan's coming after? Do I need to translate the glyph again?"

"What glyph?" asked Jensen.

Rita's face twisted as she fought a battle inside her head. "Shit. Carter, draw down. That's an order." Rita drew her pistol as well. "Cisco suspects I'm the next target."

Carter's weapon sagged to the floor. "What? You can't be serious..."

"He found a grave matching the cemetery dirt. He—"

Something loud banged in the alley, forcing us all to flinch.

"We need to get out of here," whined Jensen.

"Too late for that," I said. "Is there a back door?"

He weakly pointed to the back hallway. My eyes landed on Carter and I canted my head, asking for permission to move without getting my head blown off.

He grumbled and held his aim low. "Go ahead."

I hurried to the back, to one of those emergency exit doors that was officially supposed to remain closed but was jerry-rigged to open for frequent smoke breaks. The alarm might not have been active, but the mechanism was locked tight. I returned to the main room.

"Stand away from the doors and the windows," I instructed. "Keep your eyes and ears peeled. Jensen—" I realized he wasn't standing with the others and took a second to locate him crawling under the heavy central desk. "Okay, that's good."

The FBI agents joined me in the center of the room. "Who exactly is coming for us?" asked Carter.

"I guess we'll see for ourselves. The real question is, who else knows that we're here?"

"They're after me," whispered Rita.

"Would you guys make some sense?" snarled Carter.

But he got all the explanation he needed when a decorative window above the front door shattered under the weight of an intruder.

Chapter 42

We ducked behind cover as a barrage of glass careened to the floor. A mangled body bundled in robes buckled on contact and settled into a motionless heap. Stray screams from outside drifted through the broken window as someone riled up the protesters, but the interior of the station was quiet, all weapons cautiously pointed at the broken figure surrounded by glass.

Carter fought through the darkness with a squint. "Is that... another victim?"

My shadow sight was well adjusted to the dim surroundings. The figure, a woman, lay crumpled in the entryway, wrapped in several layers of brightly colored cloth. Decorative reds and yellows with a base layer of white. The Intrinsics weren't spiking with magical activity.

"It's a distraction," said Rita, turning her weapon to the back hallway.

We rose into guarded stances, guns clocking the recesses of the room. I advanced to a front window and peeked outside. Feet scampered by amid hoots. Chants carried on the wind, but only the dancing shadows of streetlamps were visible. I turned as Carter approached Jane Doe.

"Looks a little small," remarked the agent. "A child maybe?"

I approached from the other side of the victim. Rita warily traded glances between us and the rear exit. She was focused on the killer, not the handiwork.

"We should call this in," said Carter. He paused. "Ugh, what's that smell?"

He reached for the shawl covering the woman's head. It didn't look like a child to me. The victim was both lithe and bulky, but it was difficult to tell with the layers of robes. Pant legs underneath the dress ended in decorative hems that dressed bare feet thick with dirt.

"Carter," I alerted, but it was too late.

Right before he touched the shawl, the scraping of metal betrayed the ambush. I was already sending a billow of shadow forward. It plowed into the agent and sent him backwards as a heavy metal chain swiped his previous position.

"It's the karkan!" I yelled.

The short barrel of my shotgun flipped forward as several more chains exploded from the robes. I dove away with a hasty trigger pull. A cone of fire burst forth, chunks of birdshot digging into the fire-resistant carpet.

The karkan, however, had darted up and away from the blast. She landed on light feet, in a wide stance, and assessed each of us.

She was not what I expected. Not burly but diminutive, not a child but elderly, covered in robes and fanciful metal pendants. Only her forearms and feet were uncovered. While she wasn't masked, the top half of her face was obscured by an intricate metal shawl, as if a crown had melted and sagged over her eyes. Yards of ghostly chains snaked from her robes and curled at her feet.

"FBI!" cried Rita, both hands on her pistol in a shooting stance. "Don't move."

Desiccated lips curled into a cruel smile. I aimed the shotgun. The karkan thrust her arms up and flipped backward, animated chains spraying outward. My shotgun kicked high and went off, lighting the darkness with a fiery blaze. Rita's and Carter's weapons barked, and the room went dark.

A chain snagged my shotgun and wouldn't let go. It tugged somewhere into a distant darkness even my enchanted eyes couldn't penetrate. The karkanscholl herself was gone.

"Where'd she go?" snarled Carter, angrily climbing to his feet. He aimed at the shadowy end of the chain and fired, but the bullet just hammered the wall.

The metal tugged and my boots gave way inches at a time. The assassin's actions were telling. Unlike the other guns in the room, my ammunition was custom-made to deal with supernatural threats. The voodoo-enhanced fireshot may have been an actual danger to the karkan. If that was the case, there was no way I was going to let her have it.

As my boots once again slipped, I called the shadow into

the floor. The carpet grew tacky and held my soles tight. When I stopped, the chain tugged harder, but Cisco Suarez was no slouch. I retained my grip, all the while scanning the corners of the room for our uninvited guest.

"Little help," I grated.

The air beside me whistled as a rapier snapped the chain in two. My weight shot backward, but my boots were still stuck to the ground so I couldn't catch myself. Realizing my predicament too late, I unceremoniously crashed on my butt. The armored Spaniard materialized.

"What the fuck?" snarled Carter.

Gunshots rang out, this time at the wraith. Carter and Rita both let fly at the skeletal figure, who by any measure was a good deal more horrific than the karkan. The bullets passed through his weathered armor like air.

"Stop firing!" I yelled, scrambling away on the floor and waving the Spaniard off. He nodded once and vanished, but Carter emptied his magazine for good measure.

"How many of them are there?" hissed Rita.

I cursed myself for calling the Spaniard too soon. It was a heat of the moment decision—the only thing I knew that could cut the karkan's magical chains. It wasn't that I couldn't use the wraith, but the mere sight of him might do more harm than good.

I brushed the amputated length of chain off my weapon as Carter reloaded his. Jensen peeked out from behind the desk and I waved him back under. I racked two more enhanced fireshot cartridges into the side saddle and another in the chamber, and then I turned to take aim.

The assassin was right next to me and caught the sawed off in both hands. I growled and twisted. The short barrel made it difficult for the karkan to control despite her preternatural strength. I took the superior angle, pulled the trigger, and fire raked my opponent's side. She released the weapon and flipped sideways, landing smoothly on her feet.

The white robe and red sash covering her right side had partially burned away, revealing a shiny breastplate below. So that explained how she was both small yet bulky. I didn't know if the armor was magically enhanced or not. My birdshot was and it had left little dents but hadn't penetrated.

I bent open the sawed off and loaded another cartridge. The karkan quickly closed the distance. She grabbed both halves of the weapon before I could close it. We struggled for control. Two more chains grabbed the ends of the weapon and she yanked.

My trusty sawed-off shotgun snapped in half.

The karkan's open palm slammed into my chest, knocking the wind from me and sending me over a desk and a half before I tumbled hard to the floor.

Now that she was an easy target again, gunfire rang out. The assassin flinched and sidestepped where she could, attempting to avoid direct hits without ever seeming overly concerned. One of the rounds punched through the exposed breastplate. Instead of blood, loose soil dripped from the hole. If the karkan was affected by the damage, she pretended otherwise.

Carter's jaw dropped. "What the hell?"

Before he could find another mag, the assassin lunged. The heavy chains binding her did the opposite of weighing her down. She in fact used them to jump and maneuver like some kind of killer octopus. The zombie touched down right beside Agent Carter, grabbed his arm, and flipped him overhead. He crashed down atop the desk Jensen hid under, knocking the monitor and evidence away. His pistol spun in place on the floor.

The FBI agent attempted to get up, but a length of chain slapped him down, breaking bones and ripping up the hardwood desk in the process. Jensen grunted. The karkan watched and waited. Carter didn't get up.

The monster's gaze snapped to Rita next, ornamental headdress jingling. "Agent Bell..." she rasped.

And I realized the expert assassin had been holding back against me and Carter. We weren't the targets. She had come in, disarmed and dealt with us, and now her prize was in sight.

This was a backwards position to be in, going after the beast and ignoring the master. Necromancers were glass cannons. They usually let their thralls do the fighting for them. Taking on the karkan was doing things the hard way.

Yet I still had no idea who had revived this bogeyman from the grave. Major Petty was a major asshole, but would he turn on other law enforcement agencies to flush out the Shadow Man? Then there was Detective Mullen, who had to suspect more than he let on when it came to supernatural matters. But to this day he'd never betrayed any interest in the Shadow Man. I had to trust my close working relationship with the man.

The DROP team abandoning their headquarters was suspicious as well. Was this diversion of resources intentional or a legitimate need by the gang unit? It wouldn't be the first time someone in Evan's unit worked against him.

But the days of academic study and strategic deliberation were over now that we were face-to-face with the famed karkanscholl.

"Don't move," urged Rita, pistol quivering.

A chain whipped forward and wrapped around her waist. Rita emptied her pistol to no effect, and the karkan pulled.

Once again, the Spaniard appeared just in time, striking the metal binding apart. Rita pulled away, and the grizzled conquistador turned to his foe. "You do not belong here, old one."

The karkan's head canted. "And who, pray tell, are you?"

The wraith's glowing orbs flared.

I hurried over to the demolished desk and assisted Carter to the floor. He had an awful welt on his head and was still woozy, but at least he was awake. Rita rushed over as I helped Jensen squeeze out from under the wreckage.

"You're bleeding," I said.

The crime scene tech looked down to see spots of blood over his ribs staining his T-shirt. "It's nothing," he said. "Don't worry about me."

"This is crazy," growled Carter.

I nodded. "Okay, new plan. You and Jensen head outside. The karkan doesn't want you."

"I'm not leaving Agent Bell," protested Carter.

"Don't be stupid," she told him. "You're hurt."

"And you're gonna die," he said.

His eyes watered from a growing pungent scent. The air was nearly toxic and I had just now noticed. The karkan's poisonous fumes were gathering, sneaking up on anything that breathed. It wouldn't kill us, but I had yet to know if there were other ill effects.

"I get the sentiment, Carter," I said, "but your weapons are useless here."

"I'm NOT leaving," he said firmly.

We stared hard at each other until Jensen piped up. "Um, I'm not a hero. I'll leave." The tech was covering his mouth and nose, and the others followed suit.

"We have to go together," urged Rita.

I worked my jaw and peeked above the desk to watch the unfolding scene.

"This is not your fight," rasped the karkanscholl, chains menacingly scraping the floor.

"And what makes it yours?" asked the Spaniard.

Lips curled in response. "I come to the call."

The wraith drifted forward ever so slightly, "Yes... you do. I see now. You and I are not so different." His eyes glimmered. "You are nothing like the mindless thrall I was led to believe you to be."

The metal charms hanging from the karkan's shawl twinkled as she chuckled. "You presume much to compare yourself to me. You've seen many lives, yet I've haunted for millennia."

The skull accusingly peered at her. "And still we are both ghosts no longer fit for this world."

I moved away from the others and dug some zombie powders from my belt pouch. The wraith was a damn good distraction, but not enough of one to sneak people out either door without notice. So far the karkan hadn't killed bystanders, but she might in order to prevent the escape of her target.

Which was why retreating with Rita was a problem. Anywhere she went, no one else would be safe. If it were up to me, everyone else would run and she'd stick by my side.

Except Agent Carter would never go along with it. The man was a stubborn hard-ass. The only way to separate them was through trickery. Get everyone safely outside and then shake them.

Until then I had to turn this distraction up to eleven. I blew into my silent whistle and bit down as I scraped a blade across my palm, pooling it with blood.

"Your bespelled blade may be able to break my chains," said the karkan as I slowly maneuvered around her, "but it won't be quick enough to catch me."

The Spaniard drew his flintlock pistol and looked down the barrel. "I am aware."

The karkan tensed and I saw my shot. I dove into the shadow and lunged for her side. She spun, discovering the deception quicker than I'd hoped, but my fist was already mid swing. Her arm met mine with an expert block that stopped my blow cold. Fortunately, the puff of powder I'd palmed sprayed an amorphous cloud over her face. She recoiled and let loose a ravaging scream while her skin burned.

We now knew she could feel pain.

It also gave us an opening, one distraction snowballing into another. The Spaniard's flintlock sparked and whatever unholy ammunition it used pounded through dangling charms and into the unguarded karkan's head. She dropped to the carpet, mouth agape.

My other hand, the one that was bleeding onto a handful of cemetery dirt, rammed into her mouth as I invoked a familiar spell. As the assassin had symbolically done to her victims, I snuffed out the Intrinsics that animated a walking corpse.

Rita was the only one standing from behind the desk, pinching her nose closed. She clearly had questions about what I'd just done, but the presence of a spectral conquistador split her attention. She reloaded her weapon.

"What the hell just happened?" demanded Jensen, pushing past Carter to get a view of the carnage. He blinked in awe at the apparition.

The karkanscholl lay motionless, fanciful headdress hanging away from her withered face, revealing an overtired crone with a gaping bullet hole for an eye. Dirt drooped from the open socket.

Rita huffed with adrenaline. "Is it done?"

I furrowed my brow. I couldn't be sure. Ever since she'd arrived, the karkan had rebuffed my ability to detect her magical tethers. In fact, whatever spellcraft powered her didn't give off any energy signature at all.

The corner of the corpse's mouth twitched. "Is that all you've got?"

A chain clutched my neck and squeezed.

Chapter 43

It wasn't just me under fire. Every chain in the karkan's arsenal exploded outward from her robes, multiplying and snapping and stretching.

Two came for the Spaniard. He sliced one and feinted at another before another chain diverted his way. Rather than be overwhelmed, he vanished. A single chain snagged Rita, and Jensen ducked behind the desk again.

I tried to pool shadow into my fists, but the iron around my neck prevented the flow of magic. The karkan flipped to her feet, headdress once again falling over her face, and she grinned. She was so close when she spoke, I felt the grains of dirt she spat from her teeth.

"I never liked warlocks," she carped.

Her fist came down for a knockout blow. I raised my arm bar, sparks fluttered weakly, and her blow was deflected. Her other hand swept in under my guard and once again slammed into my chest. I lost my feet but was held by the chain. It was like the graveyard all over again except now I was in danger of cracking my neck.

I fell hard. Gunshots rang out. Seemingly of its own accord, a chain whipped the gun out of Rita's hand. Then it joined the one around her waist by also wrapping up and pinning her arms to her side. The karkan grabbed the leash around my neck and yanked hard, lifting me to kneel at her feet.

"I've seen more magicks in my lifetimes than you mortals can comprehend," she taunted. "I was sacrificed to spellcraft, risen by spellcraft, and I have been the exterminator of those who would use it since the dawn of time."

My eyes watered as I battled the pain. By now the office had filled with a brown haze. The stink coming off the karkan was intense, and it physically burned my eyes and lungs. Jensen broke into a fit of coughing.

The wraith blinked into existence mid swipe. The karkan hopped over my head and landed behind me. The Spaniard teleported to her flank, but she kicked me into him, keeping his blade at bay.

"Who are you to defend the living?" she spat.

Before waiting for an answer, she swung around me with a low kick that hit his side. I blinked in amazement as the wraith buckled. Chains came for him, but he parried them with his side-sword.

The karkan showed black teeth. "You guard yourself well. But how well can you protect him?"

She tugged the chain, constricting my windpipe. I gasped for breath that wouldn't come. It was all I could do to keep my neck from snapping.

The wraith darted forward and the chains came for him again. Despite hacking at them, they continued to extend in length, continued to come at him. The karkan stayed behind me, preventing him from access to the chain around my neck. He couldn't free me without exposing himself to attack.

"Stop this!" he demanded in a heated voice.

The karkan laughed and pulled me to shield her body. The noose slackened and I breathed in sickly air. "Stand aside. Let me finish my business in peace, and you both may live."

The denuded skull cocked eagerly, careful of the scraping chains on both flanks. "You fail to understand my power, old one. You are strong, but you're only a spirit. I walk with one foot in the Murk, where you are vulnerable. And I have no need of going around your defenses." The Spaniard lifted his sword to a ready position. "I can go through them."

He lunged straight forward, ignoring the chains... ignoring me. There was no deflection or feint or spin. My eyes widened as his rapier punched right through my ribs and into the karkan's. I felt nothing but a chill through my heart, while the assassin's breastplate popped and her chest ripped open.

The chains went limp, and I finally had enough play to collapse to the floor. When I tried to work it off my neck, I met resistance. I blinked in awe and looked up.

"A masterful stroke for a lesser opponent," remarked the

karkan.

The Spaniard's skull trembled with one part disbelief and two parts rage. He twisted the side-sword through the bogeyman's heart, gnawing up her steel armor.

It was then I realized, the karkan wasn't a zombie, yet she wasn't a ghost either. Not exactly. We'd run into something like her before when we'd faced Emily's dead father. The Spaniard had frightful power over ghosts because of their tie to the Murk, but once housed in a corpse, they were protected. The karkan, if anything, was a revenant, an embodied spirit immune to the Spaniard's pull.

"It has been ages since I've encountered such an opponent," exclaimed the assassin. The charms hanging from her face twinkled. "It is an honor to destroy you."

The loose chains on the floor wrapped tightly around the wraith's arms and torso. He recoiled but was unable to escape their clutches. They winched the Spaniard in, pulling him within an arm's length. With his hands bound, she was free to pull the shimmering sword from her chest and discard it. She then placed a naked palm on the conquistador's breastplate.

And. He. Screamed.

I struggled against my leash. The chains binding the Spaniard crackled. Heat flared against my skin as the wraith radiated with orange light. His armor glowed, his gloves burned away, and the flesh from his fingers charred. Fiery red eyes toiled with growing desperation.

And here I was, stuck without spellcraft.

I'd finished off the only powder I was confident would do

anything. Hallucinogens and spells that fed off fear were unlikely to harry the accomplished assassin, so I was down to pure pain. Useless against a mindless zombie, perhaps, but this one was anything but.

The Spaniard was in danger of immolation. The room rumbled as a budding force pushed him away from the karkan, strung up on chains like a tangled kite. His helmet and breastplate went molten orange. His bare teeth spread wide in agony, and I watched as the very foundational magic that held the wraith together began to unravel.

I pulled the last roadside flare from my belt pouch, struck it alight, and jammed the incendiary cone of fire into the assassin's gaping eye cavity.

She stumbled backward and clawed at her face with a panicked screech. These things might not look like much, but they burn at over twenty-five hundred degrees of intense heat. Right now that fire was focused entirely within the karkan's skull. The chains slackened enough for me to finally loop it off my neck. A thrum of power washed through me.

The others were more tightly wrapped and couldn't free themselves. The Spaniard was a sorry sight, still pulsing with destructive energy. His dress sword was on the floor beside me. I imbued my hand with shadow and picked up the ghostly blade.

The karkan yanked the flare from her head just in time to see me slash the three chains funneling destructive magic into the wraith. The sudden release sent a wash of energy rippling outward in a sudden explosion. The nearby windows blew out. The wraith took off like a rocket with a fuel leak, barreling through the metal cage reinforcing the window, traces of his materia prima smoldering as he faded to nothing but ash.

The karkan and I were struck with a concussive blast that tore apart a ring of desks around us. The two desk lamps cut out. When the fire died down, the room went blacker than before.

Darkness was my friend, but the spinning... not so much. I'd been tossed and tumbled like a stray alligator boot caught in a commercial dryer. It's not that I cared about me so much. I was resilient. It was all the other articles of clothing tumbling along with me.

I rolled to my hands and knees, bracing on all fours and still barely keeping my balance. A quick scan of the room didn't turn up Rita or the karkan, even with my enhanced shadow sight.

Quiet was good. Quiet was workable. I just hoped the others had been far enough from the blast to not take the beating I had at ground zero.

I crawled forward a little too gingerly. A glance out the destroyed window showed the wreckage left behind by the defeated Spaniard. A path of molten materia glowed along the street, the equivalent of supernatural road rash, but it faded to nothing before reaching the far building, almost as if the wraith had vaporized.

I shut my eyes and willed the darkness to wash into me. I'd been keeping a low profile as far as visible spellcraft was concerned because of present company, but it was a luxury I was ready to abandon the instant it was necessary. I couldn't let the others die for the sake of anonymity. Hell, an undying revenant and a cursed lich—they'd already seen too much.

Still no Rita so I crawled to the others. The boost of magic energized my system like a cocktail of Red Bull and adrenaline shot straight to the heart. I rounded the charred desk to find the guys huddling behind it.

"How's everyone doing?" I grumbled.

Carter sat awkwardly. His collarbone looked broken. "A little woozy, but the pain helps."

I sneered against the growing toxins. "The karkan's poisoning the air. You should be fine; it's not lethal."

Not lethal, no, but breathing it in was probably affecting me more than I realized, so I pulled out my mask and wrapped it around my nose. As much as I wished I could provide relief to Carter and Jensen, I was the one doing the fighting. The first breath of truly fresh air rejuvenated my senses. My head cleared.

"It's you," whispered Jensen in awe as he stared at my mask. He had spittle on his chin from coughing so much. "You're the Shadow Man..."

Carter's eyes widened, and I winced.

Great. There was no living this one down.

"You're talking crazy," I said halfheartedly. "It's the fumes."

My weak explanation barely registered. The good news, at least, was that Carter was still conscious, and the blood stain on Jensen's shirt hadn't spread. Neither of them were mortally wounded.

"I'm gonna find Rita. If you get a chance to run, take it."

After a few more bountiful breaths, I slipped my boots beneath me and shoved up.

The karkan had similarly regrouped. She was two desks over, standing behind Rita, who faced me as well, ankles bound, hands tied behind her back, with the last chain wrapped around her neck. I imagined Quentin Capshaw's final moments of life to be comparable.

"Move," warned the karkanscholl, "and she dies."

I snarled inwardly. The accomplished assassin wasn't looking her best. Her robes were torched and torn in several spots, her breastplate was ripped to hell and hung loosely, and a few chains limped sluggishly behind as she dragged Rita to a safer distance. A stream of mud painted her face from chin to eviscerated eye, resembling a long-dried tear.

The karkan placed a palm on the FBI agent's shoulder and spoke into her ear. "You know the identity of the Shadow Man." Her lips quivered hungrily. "Tell me."

Rita's eyes darted my way. Fuck, she did know. I gathered shadow into my fist and took an unassuming step closer.

The assassin yanked Rita hard. The poor woman's eyes almost popped out of her head. I dispelled the magic and lifted my hands. "Wait." I struggled for something else to say. "Just wait."

"You've fought bravely, necromancer," commended the karkan, "but you must see the truth. I can destroy you as I did your wraith. You have a decision to make: only one more dies, or everybody dies."

I swallowed and looked down at the wounded men. Jensen was still watching me with awe. When I met Carter's eyes, they hardened with a suggestive nod. He was ready to do something stupid, and I wasn't far behind.

But what attack would succeed while the karkan had Rita in such a tenuous position? One failed strike against a highly agile assassin and the chains would finish the job. The effort wouldn't rise to an afterthought.

The karkan produced a short knife from a fold of her robe and cut the buttons off Rita's shirt, exposing her stomach. "I am an artist, Agent Bell, and you are my latest masterpiece."

The knife bit into Rita's skin. She grunted through clenched teeth. The wound wasn't mortal, but we knew it to be the precursor. The karkan used the surface level of flesh as a canvas, tracing a symbol I was already familiar with. She was going to nix Agent Bell as she had the others.

But not before she squeezed her victim dry.

"Tell me," urged the karkan, "and I will make it quick. Painless."

Jensen stood and opened his mouth. I shoved him down as the karkan's head snapped to the new entry in the room. A large Alaskan shepherd had hopped through the dismantled window. Scout angled low and growled menacingly at the assassin.

"That smell," piqued the karkan. "Yes... I remember you." Scout flanked her, drawing her attention from Rita to him. Away from me. "You escaped me once." The karkan pulled the small knife to her side. "You will not get away from me this time, little morsel."

The chains at her feet snaked, but they were too languid to be a threat. The assassin glared at her malfunctioning weapons. They answered with only a wiggle, and a snarl overtook her face.

"You're wounded," I gloated.

The bogeyman ignored my insult, as she was entirely infatuated with Scout. The dog's paws brushed the carpet as he circled, searching for an opening. The karkan spun cautiously. The chain around Rita's ankles started to unravel. It was one of the few that still worked, one she could spare to go on the offensive.

The room went hazy again, and Scout's growl died down. He lapped at the air as if having trouble swallowing. The chain that was ready to strike paused and backed away before once again wrapping around Rita. I searched the floor for the Spaniard's blade but didn't see it anywhere.

"Ah," cooed the karkan in a lilt, "it's a little musty in here for you, isn't it?"

Scout blinked and attempted to shake off the vertigo before toppling over. He tried to rise but couldn't find his feet. Once, twice, and again before resorting to whines. The karkan turned to me with a smile. Then she gazed at Rita as if deciding what to do.

"The flesh is best when fresh," she said longingly.

We'd seen this before. At the body shop, the karkan had taken out a camera, leaving unnecessary evidence of her passage just because she couldn't resist the urge for a quick bite. And now, even when in a tactically superior position, the monster couldn't fight her nature.

"A taste, a taste," she said melodically, nearly prancing toward the downed pet.

Shadow drooped from my hand, hidden low behind the desk. Jensen and Carter stared as the Intrinsics folded over and brightened into glowing amethyst.

The monstrous bogeyman was so eager to feed that she didn't notice my spellcraft. She bent over to take a bite when Scout suddenly pounced, sinking his teeth into her neck. All one hundred pounds of fur were instantly and viciously wagging her back and forth like a deer in the jaws of a Florida alligator.

I charged through the shadows, materializing a stride away from Rita. I leapt and sliced my darksword down, attempting to recreate the energy signature I'd felt while gripping the Spaniard's spectral sword.

It worked.

The chains ripped like flesh. The karkan uttered an agonizing howl and tore the dog away, opening her neck to an avalanche of cemetery dirt. She heaved with all her might. Scout bounced off the far wall, tumbled, and rose to his feet. His head and half his body shook, spraying loose dirt on the floor, and Scout bared his canines.

"The thing about zombie dogs," I said with a snicker. "They have a knack for playing dead."

I put my arm around Rita's waist and yanked her back into the shadow. A length of severed chain was quicker and had snagged her wrist. All my strength was wasted as I crashed back into the physical world. I brought up my darksword as another chain reached for my leg. The thrumming energy shaved a few links away before I turned it on Rita's binding.

The karkan may have been wounded, but she wasn't content to sit back. She closed the distance between us in a blink. Far from being down for the count, fists pummeled my gut, then face, then back to my gut. My sword sputtered as I went dizzy. Before I could recover, a kick to my temple sent me spinning. I landed with a raised arm to fend off further assault, but the assassin ducked away from a leaping dog. A free chain caught his waist and slammed him forcefully to the ground.

With my arm raised defensively, I noticed it was slick with blood. My chest and cheek had open wounds. The assassin's double-fisted blows weren't just punches—one of her hands still palmed that knife. And its simple blade had somehow cut right through my enchanted skin.

The assassin turned back to Rita. Carter charged her unguarded back holding a heavy chair overhead. She spun in a flash, barely missing him. He wobbled sideways. The chair tumbled to the floor. His eyes snapped to Rita, hands plugging a fountain of blood at his neck. The karkan hadn't missed. Rita cried out as Agent Carter's legs folded under him.

"Now," seethed the monster, "you *will* name the Shadow Man, or your life will end in unimaginable pain."

I struggled to stand as the karkan stomped toward the chained FBI agent.

"It's him!" cried Jensen, hopping to his feet quicker than me. He was practically hyperventilating as his finger singled me out. "He's the Shadow Man. Isn't it obvious?"

I grimaced. "Shut up, Jensen."

"There's no need to kill her," he stressed. "Cisco's the Shadow Man. Let her go."

I stared at the idiot. He thought he was saving her, but he was doing the exact opposite. Once the karkan got what she came for, Rita's life was forfeit. Jensen was so harried by the spellcraft and the toxin that he had no idea what he was doing. His shirt rode up over his wound to give me a better view of the damage.

The karkan cocked her head at the new player in the game. "Agent Bell is my charge."

"You don't need her anymore," urged Jensen.

The karkan grinned. "This isn't about need, it's about the call. My work must be finished." She flipped the knife ready in her hand and faced Rita, futilely struggling against the magical bindings. "Now, now, dear, it appears I have no further use of you."

"Wait!" I yelled, leaning on the desk to stand. "You were right," I said.

The karkan's lips curled in pleasure.

I took an uneasy breath. "You were right," I told her. "We don't all need to die. Only one of us."

Jensen's eyes went wide as I plunged my bronze knife into his heart.

Chapter 44

"Cisco!" cried Rita, eyes frantic.

I had to hand it to her. Most people in her position would be a sobbing mess right now. After witnessing impressive magic and having her coworkers killed by a supernatural menace, she still hadn't broken. But the look Rita gave me as I dropped Jensen's limp body to the floor gutted me. His heart pumped for another minute, spilling the last of his life in an oozy mess.

"How could you do that?" she scolded.

But the gambit paid off. The assassin's blade stayed for another moment. The karkan's head tilted in amusement.

"Yes," she agreed coyly, "what have you done?"

Energy intensified in my veins. The shadows grew slick and danced over my skin. "I've removed your motivation," I answered.

The karkan tittered uncharacteristically. "You are mistaken, necromancer. I have come for the call. Agent Bell is to die, and I am to carry out her sentence."

I sneered as the very night blanketed me. The ruckus in the street, the dead bodies, the leftovers of the Spaniard—they all faded away as the world darkened.

"Even if I'm the one you seek?"

Her cheek twitched. "Even so. Tonight is Agent Bell's solemnity. You have a few days yet. Don't you see, Shadow Man? Necromancer? Even with my master dead, I still heed the call."

Rita blinked down to the crime scene tech. She was starting to get it.

"See," I said, flipping Jensen's corpse to his back and pulling the knife from his chest, "that's the thing. I might not know much about Albanian runes or holy feast days, but I know blood magic when I see it."

I crouched beside the dead crime scene tech and pulled up his shirt, exposing the glyph he had carved into his own side. The wound was messy and scabbed over, flesh cut almost a week ago and periodically reopened. I, frankly, hadn't the slightest idea what it said. But I did know how to cancel it out.

As had been done to Quentin and Ebu, and on the grave when Jensen must've canceled the assassin's old instructions in order to redirect her to Agent Bell, I carved a horizontal line through the glyph of power.

The karkan staggered backward as if struck, off-balance for only a second. When she regained control of her faculties, she stood up straighter and looked around the room anew. "The spell... It is broken..."

The three chains binding Rita Bell carefully unfurled.

The karkan ignored the woman completely as she took in her dark surroundings. Rita sprinted to Carter and dragged him by his shoulders behind me. I stepped forward to guard them.

The bogeyman's charms jingled as she unstrapped the old breastplate and dropped it at her feet. "I am... no longer compelled to carve your skin, necromancer."

"No hard feelings then," I growled. "Isn't it about time for you to get going back to wherever you came from? I dispelled you."

"Not me, no. You dispelled the magic binding me. I have some time yet." She cocked her head. "Only the time is now mine..."

My eyes narrowed. Had I just set this monster free?

The karkan strolled nonchalantly toward the front door. I stuttered in place, confused and angered by the slight. The shadows around me billowed.

"It is too bad," mused the karkan with a farewell glance. "I was looking forward to the fight." She turned her back on us.

"Hey!" I called back with a throaty growl. "I wouldn't want to disappoint you."

I lunged, batted away the chains rising to her defense, and slammed her with a fist of darkness. The shadows detonated and the karkan erupted through the shattered door. She flew through the air and slammed into the concrete wall of the office building across the street. She crumpled to the sidewalk.

My eyes widened at the excess power I'd expelled.

Usually something of that magnitude would've come with blowback, would've harmed those I was trying to protect. Instead I marveled at how well the Intrinsics had been coaxed into a single target, extreme focus that only magnified the blast.

But as destructive as the spell was, the unstoppable assassin lived up to her legend. She bounded to the air, showing her teeth, chains whipping wildly as she took a determined step toward unfinished business.

Gunfire sprayed the ground and popped her, causing slight flinches. The shouts in the street intensified. Chains danced to the air and struck at oncoming bullets, but another shooter opened fire.

The karkan staggered as a third shooter joined the chorus of ARs. Semi-autos clustered into an onslaught that even the deft karkan and her chains couldn't rebuff. Like a scarecrow in a violent hailstorm, her robes pattered against relentless entry wounds.

Undead or not, there was only so much damage physical flesh could take. The karkan gave me one final gaze before backing into the far alley. She spun on the balls of her feet and fled.

Paramilitary soldiers in gray camouflage converged on the alley in unison. They used team tactics that prioritized safety, firing from cover and keeping their distance. A few started to give chase but were called back. The karkan was too fast.

These weren't weekend protesters. They were militiamen, the Vanguard Against Parahumans acting as advertised. Before I knew it, the men regrouped and filed into the police headquarters, weapons hot.

"We're FBI!" called Rita, still shaking from adrenaline. Her arms and neck began to show bruising.

In the absence of a threat, the militiamen pulled their rifles away from us. It went without saying that I'd dispersed my cloak of shadows.

"Who's here?" called a Vanguard member. "What was that?"

"A killer we've been tracking," muttered Rita.

I kneeled beside her to check on Carter. "She ambushed us."

A man with beard stubble stepped forward and examined the bodies of Carter and Jensen. "Well, I hate to be the one to tell you folks, but that killer wasn't human. You're extremely lucky to be alive right now."

I blinked back befuddlement and traded a glance with Rita. She nodded, wiped a tear from her cheek, and stood. "Thank you. I— You're right. That thing was a monster."

"We need you to tell us about it, miss. Can you show us some ID first?"

Militiamen returned from clearing the back offices and hallway. A quick shake of their heads signaled their failure to find anyone else. The man with the stubble was their boss.

"Special Agent Bell," she answered, humoring them by flashing her badge. "He's with the local police."

I didn't have an ID, so I made a show of checking if the crime tech was alive and being really upset he wasn't.

The man bit down and nodded. "We support our officers if they open their eyes and support us. We're going to save this country, and you can help us do it."

Chapter 45

Rita took control of the scene, but it was only symbolic. The Vanguard outnumbered and outgunned us. They seemed to innately distrust the federal agency and rebuffed Rita's attempts to clear them from the building. When her request grew more forceful, they outright refused to leave.

"The police have to know the truth," they asserted. "No offense, but we're waiting right here for their full response. Our mission is to stand witness and make sure what happens gets properly reported."

Talk about a kink in the ironwork. See, Rita had her suspicions about magic before. Now she was an avid believer who could never be convinced otherwise. But even she was aware of the utter ridiculousness of filing a federal document that claimed an immortal Albanian bogeyman had risen from the dead during the Twelve Days of Christmas.

Pinning the whole affair on Jensen would've been the simplest play. Say he'd killed Quentin and Ebu and taken

Carter by surprise at the station before a lowly police contractor took him down. That would've been an open-and-shut case for the feds and the City of Miami, and it would've been as near to public justice as we were likely to see. Then, with a little bit of moonlighting, I would have the freedom to find the karkan.

Instead, the Vanguard was asserting the public's right to know that some unstoppable being had fled the scene of the crime. And they were expecting—no, demanding—that we recount our true experiences to the bosses up the food chain.

I snorted at my surprise by the interaction between the karkan and the Vanguard. I'd been so worried about the meat that I'd forgotten about the potatoes. This level of exposure and publicity was a whole new ball game for Miami, and I was conflicted about it in more ways than one. I wasn't sure I could deny that the Vanguard Against Parahumans had a point.

But... we obviously couldn't tell the truth, the whole truth, and nothing but. So it worked to our advantage that the paramilitary contingent knew very little about what actually occurred indoors.

The emergency response was quickly incoming. We were central in the city, and in a police station for chrissakes. Considering the adversarial mood, it was easy to remain tight-lipped about events for a few minutes. We called 911. Rita talked to the feds while I tried Evan, but he didn't pick up. I paced up and down the line of destroyed desks, studying the militiamen.

I needed to find someone I could talk to. Someone who wasn't a zealot.

I approached a man with a ponytail and nodded at the weapon held across his chest. "Is that a bump stock?"

He snickered.

"You're really gonna brandish that in front of police? Those things are illegal in Florida."

"It's not a problem," he answered. "We have an understanding with MPD. They know who the true enemies are."

I was taken aback by how openly he'd admitted what would normally be a scandal. By this point they'd gleaned I was a contractor and didn't pay me special notice one way or the other. I supposed that was a blessing in disguise.

Sirens filled the streets, somewhat impeded by the crowds of pedestrians blocking traffic. Still, the emergency response time was impressive, and a crew of law enforcement and EMTs arrived. As identification was passed around, militia members were asked to wait outside.

A starker-than-usual Detective Mullen was assigned the case. Rita and I ran through the incident three times for the record, and then he set about interviewing the militia witnesses. Major Bruce Petty made a quick appearance, but he was pulled away, citing growing unrest in the streets.

Even Evan could do nothing more than hear the details from me over the phone. By the time I finally got in touch with him, I half expected him to abandon his assignment and race over with lights and sirens active, but my friend stoically remained at his post on the other side of town.

After a long night past the midnight hour, with festive protests-slash-celebrations audible in the distance, Rita and I sat in the back alley sipping Styrofoam cups of cheap coffee from the pot in Evan's office. About a hundred cigarette butts surrounded the popular stoop.

She hung up her phone and slipped it into her jacket. "Sotomayer and Ramirez still don't see anything."

She was hoping the karkan would show her face back at the grave like a vampire sleeping in a coffin. It wasn't gonna happen, but they had orders not to engage just in case.

"It just doesn't sit right with me," I grumbled. "Instead of being revealed as a traitor who murdered law enforcement, Jensen's dying a hero. No one will ever know the evil he committed."

The FBI agent sighed. We'd come to the decision together, despite the difficulty of it. With the Vanguard attesting that a killer escaped, including Jensen in the mix would only complicate matters. With multiple eyewitnesses, we'd had to provide supporting statements of a well-armored opponent who'd taken gunfire, who wielded chains like whips, and was fast with a knife. No mention of the potter's field was necessary. There was no necromancer mastermind casting spells over a thrall, there was just another victim. It was cleaner that way.

"Jensen was one of their own," replied Rita. "If they knew you killed him, some would never accept your explanation. The department would be skeptical of an impossible truth, and you'd be put in cuffs and investigated." She flubbed her lips.

It was the same case she'd presented earlier. Honestly, I could take or leave the part about protecting myself. That would work out one way or another. It was protecting the integrity of the case I was worried about. Or was it the need to hide the truth about magic? Whose interests was I really serving?

"I just can't believe it was Jensen," she hissed.

I took a bitter sip and canted my head. It surprised me too. Not that it should have. The crime scene tech was around dead bodies all the time. He made a perfect necromancer.

He wasn't Albanian, though. Or Roma for that matter. Then again, spellcraft is about knowledge and belief; heritage is hardly a requirement. Simon Feigelstock didn't have ancestors in Ancient Sumer. I powered the Helm of Awe without a drop of Viking blood. Syncretism combines various beliefs into one. For example, an outsider, like Jensen, drawing upon feast days from Catholic and Eastern Orthodox theologies.

In some cases, belief itself was optional. I was intimately familiar with Opiyel the Shadow Dog, I spoke blessings in the Baron's name, but the defensive runes Kasper painted on my skin channeled Norse spellcraft from a god I'd never honored.

Runes, like enchanted items, acted as physical substitutes for belief. The symbol, painted with Intrinsics but grounded in the world, did all the heavy lifting for the animist. It, then, was no surprise the karkan wasn't raised by a Calabrian Albanian but an outsider utilizing runecraft.

Armed with identical knowledge, I'd broken the spell using nothing but the glyph.

"It was a hell of a risk you took," she said, "plunging that knife into his chest... What if you were wrong?"

"I worked it out once I saw the glyph he carved into himself."

"Right, because you know blood magic."

I licked my lips. "The other day, in the conference room, you admitted to having some knowledge of the Shadow Man. You were adamant that he existed. The karkan didn't have that information, but Jensen did because he was there with us. So he went to the grave, canceled the previous San Silvestro directive, and overwrote it with a new instruction to go after you. You were the next circle that would lead to the square."

I frowned. Jensen had also apparently noticed that the grave had been tampered with. He'd laid a trap for me, but that was another story.

Rita studied me with a strange expression. I wasn't sure how much she comprehended, but I didn't elaborate. I was still fuming over Jensen.

"It was pretty smart, when you think about it. He kept himself close to the case the entire time. He was the one who called you back to DROP Team Central tonight using some manufactured evidence as an excuse. He even asked if you were alone first. Remember he didn't want Carter here? And he had no idea I was shadowing you all day."

She watched me askance. "If Jensen had gotten his way, I would've been alone with him. He would've handed me the report, excused himself to pick up coffee, and left me for the karkan. I wouldn't have stood a chance."

I chuckled sourly as I thought about that coffee run. Jensen had insisted Rita stay in the office. He'd also thrown Carter to the wolves as collateral damage, but for some reason he'd asked me along.

Jensen hadn't known I was the Shadow Man. He hadn't intended to kill me. We'd worked several cases for the city together, and I supposed there'd been a level of mutual friendship between us. All that goodwill was flushed down the drain as soon as he knew I was the Shadow Man.

But Jensen's plan went south as soon as I noticed the roadkill outside. Even then, I had to drag him back into the station, kicking and screaming. But he had called some audibles himself. In the end, he even tried to save Rita by calling me out, as if he didn't want to hurt anyone if it wasn't necessary. I stopped myself from pointing that out since I refused to say anything good about the traitor.

"We still don't know why," she said.

"Why what?"

"Why he wanted to kill you."

I flexed my jaw, downed the disgusting coffee in a single gulp, and rose to my feet. "Can we get out of here now?"

"Before you admit you're the Shadow Man? Before I tell you I know for sure now?"

I didn't answer. Things were developing ultra-fast now. I just needed time to think, time to sleep, wake up to a new day and see what dominoes were left standing.

Rita's lashes fluttered in resignation. "Yeah, we can leave.

I'm betting you need a ride home."

She offered her hand and I helped her up. After all the excitement, both of us were cranky and tired and sore all over.

I'd been officially exposed to a federal agent now. It was only one, and I knew she could be discreet, but there would undoubtedly be repercussions in the future. Jensen hadn't succeeded in killing me outright, but exposing me might just be the beginning of the end.

I grabbed the back door but Rita put her hand over it before I could open. "Will the karkan continue killing?" she asked me.

"I don't know," I said as honestly as I could. "I suppose she's free to do whatever she wants now."

Rita gritted her teeth and removed her hand from the door. "That's what scares me."

We limped back through the station like a couple of retired seniors on the beach, oblivious to the parade of wild Spring Breakers. Well, not oblivious exactly, but uncaring. The medical examiners, the techs, and the police all frenetically started what would be a long night.

Ours was done.

I waved to Mullen on the way past, concerned about the single-minded killer that was now on the loose. Ironic, in way, that the karkan was officially a retired undead hit man. It wasn't such a far cry from yours truly.

If it's our choices that shape us, what does it mean when we have no choice to begin with?

My eyes lit up before I left the station, and I dug under

the wreckage of several desks.

"What are you doing?" asked Rita.

I retrieved a ripped and smashed box of *pastelitos*. Somehow, the food left inside was in worse shape than the packaging. My face fell, and I grumbled under my breath.

Chapter 46

There were no paramilitary murder sprees overnight. No karkan rampages. The New Year's Day Million Militia March was crazy and packed and loud, but the holiday and protest came and went without descending into chaos.

Or so claimed Lieutenant Evan Cross. He had Saturday morning off before another long night shift. In between sparse time with his family, he stopped by the condo to get the lowdown on the events at DROP Team Central.

"I appreciate that you kept the destruction out of my personal office," grumbled Evan after I recounted the true version of events.

"Not so fast," I told him. "The biggest atrocity by far was whatever came out of your coffee maker. You need to invest in some serious equipment."

"Exactly why I suggested meeting at your coffee shop," he returned. Evan was understandably grumpy about missing all the action, but I was worming my way into him.

As far as meeting in Outlaw Coffee & Colada, Kasper

was currently on shift with Clarence's aunt so I was avoiding the place. "No thanks. You should see the way those two behave around each other. It's like they're teenagers again."

With Evan brooding on a barstool, I sat with Milena on the couch, massaging her feet. She sucked her teeth. "I think they're cute together."

"They're probably scaring away all the customers. Which might be for the best. When I opened the coffee shop I didn't realize how much time it would take to actually, you know, *run* a coffee shop."

My girlfriend rolled her eyes and patted my leg. "Boss of the year over here." She scooted closer and rolled to her side so I could work on her back too. "You know, maybe I'll pick up a shift there."

She stared off into the distance with a smile, and my mood brightened. While I didn't think Milena would enjoy customer service long-term, a little public interaction could be beneficial.

"Hate to break it to you," said Evan, digging into the fridge for a beer, "but the tips you make at the coffee shop won't be anything like dancing."

"Pig!" she laughed. And then I laughed too. "Anyway, I quit my job at the strip club."

My laughter cut out. "Wait, what? When did that happen?"

"We were away from Miami for two months, Cisco."

"Yeah, but I figured, a job like that, you could just pick up where you left off."

"You can. And after a few days of rest, I got a little stir

crazy and tried to go back..." She sighed. "It's just not for me anymore."

Evan took a long chug of beer and pretended he wasn't there. I just widened my eyes, unsure what to say.

"I bet you're stoked to hear that," she said.

I shrugged. "What, that you're all mine? Was it ever a question?" I winked.

"I'm serious!" she asserted.

"All right, all right. I don't know. I'm cool with whatever you want. Are you happy with the decision?"

She took a moment, then turned to me and nodded. "I just feel like I don't have anything more to prove, you know?"

"You certainly don't need to prove your sexiness to me." I squeezed her butt cheek.

"I was also thinking," she said, "I might be without income for a while... I think I might sell my condo."

My face brightened. "Really? That's great! Move in here!"

"I don't know. This joint is woefully understocked with *pastelitos*."

I snorted. "You're really not gonna let me live that down..."

"And you'd probably complain about my hair all over the place."

I grinned and leaned in. "I love your hair all over the place." We kissed.

Evan cleared his throat. "Weren't you just complaining about public displays of affection?"

"You're still here?" I grated.

"Too bad," Milena purred. She twisted seductively and stood. "I suppose I'll just have to soak in a hot bath all by my lonesome." Her lashes fluttered dramatically, and she strutted to my room with so much sway I'm surprised she didn't fall over.

Evan blinked. "She's too much."

"Isn't she great?"

He set the half-full beer on the countertop. "Welp, I know when I'm no longer wanted. I should get back home too."

"Enjoying some private time of your own, huh?"

"If you mean I'll be passed out in bed with a pillow over my face, sure."

"Long days and hard nights," I commiserated, walking him to the door. "Guys like us need to find tranquility when we can."

"I think there's actually light at the end of this tunnel. Vanguard activity is receding."

"Sorry if I remain unconvinced."

"I thought you wanted these guys in our corner. I'm telling you, they might be turning a new leaf. We have officer outreach happening. The department blanketed the city with police. Everyone's on their best behavior."

I crossed my arms and leaned against the open doorjamb. "You say that, but the real problem is separating the bad apples from the good. Talk is useless if it doesn't reach the right people. And at some point, culprits will need to be arrested for those murders. That's a tough ask."

He shrugged. "Maybe they came to their senses."

"Or maybe Major Petty has a gentleman's agreement with their leadership."

Evan scoffed. "Always the pessimist. Isn't anyone good enough for you?"

"Sure, and she's naked in my bathtub. I'll see you later." I slammed the door in my best friend's face, locked it for good measure, and did twenty quick push-ups.

I cracked open the bathroom door to a waft of pleasant steam. Milena's clothes sat on the floor as she ruffled her toes on the plush rug. She faced the mirror, underwear riding up her ass. The tub was filling and my pants were halfway off before I noticed she was just standing there.

I inched up slowly and put my arms around her. "What's the matter?"

She flinched as if I'd surprised her, and then took a solemn breath as she held up a black hand mirror. It was the one gifted to me by the gorgon after we... uh... consummated our deal. It was old, strong glass in a frame of intricate obsidian, but after hours of study I'd found it to be purely ornamental.

But it was an ornamental mirror with emotional baggage.

"This thing..." she croaked.

I rubbed her waist. "Yeah. It looks nice, doesn't it?"

The sound of the running water filled the silence.

"What do you think it's for?" I asked. "Eden was pretty cryptic about it."

"It's not for anything good," she assured.

I took a measured breath. "I understand if you can't fully

trust the gorgons—"

"No, Cisco, it's not about the past, it's about right now. This... thing... I can feel it."

Her hand trembled and I held it tight. I gently pulled the mirror from her grasp and examined it. It was just a fogged-up mirror. I opened a vanity drawer, slipped it inside, and pushed it shut.

"There, is that better?"

Milena turned to me slowly and leaned in. "Yes."

We held each other a few minutes until I had to pull away to turn off the tub. I swirled the water. It was the perfect temperature. Milena unhooked her bra and let it drop to the floor. She blinked seductively, and did a little wiggle as she slipped her panties off. My God that should be illegal.

"I may be out of a job," she purred, "but I still offer private dances to select clientele."

"All right," I sighed. "How much is this gonna cost me?"

She slapped my chest for ruining the moment, but that was impossible. Nothing could ruin this. My girlfriend lovingly slipped my tank top over my shoulders, kissed my chest, and traced her lips down my stomach.

With a low moan, she stood and pressed her soft flesh to mine, breathing with anticipation. I could feel her heat, her desire, and I decided right then and there to make this agonizingly slow. I took her hand and led her into the water.

Chapter 47

I spent the day at Miami Police Headquarters on Second Avenue, an unimaginative four-story building that kind of looked like a 1980s brutalist spaceship if you squinted. Because of my association with the department, the debrief of an attack on the DROP team station turned into a full day of work and a grade A waste of time. On the bright side, as a consultant on the payroll, these were billable hours.

The real value of the proceeding was connecting with various members of the police force for updates. I chatted with Detective Mullen a fair bit. There were some open questions, such as why Jensen had never contacted the lead detective about the new evidence. Of course, the real reason was because it wasn't evidence at all. The whole thing had been a ruse orchestrated by Jensen to get Rita vulnerable and alone. The officer on the scene had found the package in an alley due to an anonymous tip, likely sent by the crime tech himself. Still, despite the occasional minor discrepancy, there was never any feeling in the department that one of their own was in the slightest way culpable. It helped that there was a tangible enemy at large.

Major Bruce Petty was in and out of various meetings. He glared at me more than anything else. He was still angry with Rita from the day before and avoided both of us for good measure. To be fair, the influx of new federal agents into the city put a lot on his plate.

As a fed, Rita was twice as popular as I was. Eventually, we found a moment to step aside and talk.

"After the death of a fellow agent," she explained, "the FBI is taking no more chances."

"I met the other team," I said.

"Those are just the operations folks, the first ones in who set up a task force. There'll be more agents in the coming days. And that's not all."

I exhaled nervously. I had never dealt with this level of law before, and though my involvement was isolated, I was a named player in this operation. I was noticeably uncomfortable with the whole affair.

Rita didn't empathize. "Now that I've witnessed what we're up against, I've reinforced our cemetery surveillance with extra security. I wonder if you shouldn't be there as well."

"The karkan's not returning to the grave," I said. "Not yet, anyway. But it's the smart play. She felt the results of focused, modern weaponry firsthand. She wouldn't invite that kind of trouble unless it was necessary."

"So you're just gonna do nothing?"

"There's nothing I can do in front of..."—I waved at

literally everybody around us.

"That's not an excuse to sit on the bench."

"Who said that? Look, I have my own problems. If the karkan shows, we'll know about it. What else can I do?"

She gritted her teeth. "We have the full power of the federal government at our fingertips. I talked to a friend in the ATF. They're mobilizing against the Vanguard. If we really need to, I may be able to call in a favor and get some real guns on our side."

I arched an eyebrow. "Interesting. Talking to the locals, it seems they think the threat is already neutralized."

"Far from it. Groups like this, they consolidate power and influence until they reach a tipping point. Action has to be taken early in order to save lives. The United States treats threats from fringe movements extremely seriously. The Vanguard already resorted to killing sprees. They have to be found before it happens again. It's not an if, it's a when."

I nodded, finding it hard to disagree with the sentiment. "How can you make arrests when they're in hiding?"

"We don't have much in the way of contacts within the organization, but we've gleaned snippets. The ATF has narrowed down their location to an area of the Everglades in Central Florida. It's a large swath of swamps and heavy tree cover, obscured from satellite imagery, but it's only a matter of time. They're doing helicopter flyovers. To support a group this large, visible roads or other infrastructure must exist somewhere. This is ending now."

Her words had grim undertones. Operations like this

don't end cleanly. There were too many zealots in the militia, and the worst part was they weren't all wrong. They were killing child-trafficking vampires for chrissakes.

I wondered how much the FBI shared with the police, and how much would make its way back to Beaumont and the Vanguard.

I wondered if it mattered.

The militia had opened their campaign with a public massacre. Didn't that make them their own brand of monsters?

Rita checked her watch and nodded me out. "Let's go. We're done for the day."

I looked around. "That's it? No award ceremony or anything?"

"I'm afraid all you're winning is the simultaneous respect and disdain of your fellow police officers."

The DROP team wasn't around, and I didn't want to introduce myself to any more feds than I had to. While I'd been kicking around the idea of confronting Major Petty about his relationship with Beaumont, it seemed a wasted effort. Petty was too important to admit anything. This was the wrong time and the wrong place for that. Hell, I was pretty sure he was the wrong guy too.

In the hallway, we quietly waited for the elevator, having run out of things to discuss. The mood grew awkward. I should've seen it coming, but the long day had relaxed my guard.

"Are we gonna talk about that other thing?" asked Rita.

"Hmm?"

"You know, the identity and purpose of a certain unnamed Shadow Man."

The elevator door opened and she filed in. I stared a few seconds before huffing and pulling away. "I don't know what you're talking about. Go on ahead. I wanna use the steps."

She opened her mouth to reply but the door started closing. I waved her off stopping it, and she hesitated just long enough that it shut.

I sighed and stretched my neck and shoulders. This whole thing was a mess.

Jensen's betrayal revealed my need to keep my secrets close, even among those I considered allies. As a consultant, I'd crossed paths with the crime scene tech on numerous cases, including a dustup between a golem and a wounded dragon. Every single time I had played it straight, just an ordinary guy investigating occult wackos. If I had made the simple mistake of revealing my powers during any of those cases, of trusting Jensen, then he would've realized my connection to the Shadow Man from the start.

And I might have never seen the karkan coming.

Curiously, Jensen had been playing the same game. He'd likewise hidden his identity, playing the scientific skeptic from the start, all the while dabbling in necromantic and who knows what other circles.

The karkan was no longer a threat, at least not to me. The larger question was why Jensen had sicced her on me in the first place. This wasn't about Cisco, it was about the Shadow Man, which ruled out the black witches bungling from beyond. They knew my identity and wouldn't have gone on the whole magical mystery tour.

Hell, what did I know? About the only genuine takeaway I had here was not to trust anyone outside my inner circle, and that included Special Agent Rita Bell.

That night I did what I could to get answers. With Scout unable to pick up the Spaniard's scent, I retreated to my cookhouse and attempted some fact-finding necromancy of my own. Ghosts weren't always readily available to talk, and even when they did they weren't fonts of information. It was a big world, and finding the right people who knew the right people, whether living or dead, was like playing the lottery.

There were no jackpots that night.

It was too bad, too. The Spaniard had seemed to recognize the age and majesty of the karkan. The two had some kind of sick mutual respect for each other. It was possible, if unlikely, that the wraith could fill in some blanks for me. As long as he wasn't missing or dead, of course.

If those glowing red eyes were to turn up anywhere, it should've been right here, in the isolated Everglades we once called home, in the middle of the night, in the middle of nowhere.

All my inquiries were answered with the void.

Chapter 48

And that's how the next couple of days went. No karkan, no militia.

Maybe there was something to Evan's belief in heavy policing contributing to law and order. The Vanguard had not only refrained from any more raids, they disappeared altogether.

The rest of the city, too. After a busy Christmas season, a public scare, New Year's Eve celebrations, and the Million Militia March, the populace was burned out. The protests, the fires, the unrest—it all evaporated. I had never seen so much damage stuffed back into a bottle so fast.

But then, Miami had a cold wind blowing through it. We were still in the midst of Twelvetide. Even though the karkan hadn't killed anyone, her presence nagged at me like leaving the house with the oven set to murder.

So on the surface things were chugging along like always, but there was more to the story.

All the militia raids, the video of the upir being gunned

down—these were victories but also calls for retreat. The Vanguard had burned too hot too fast. The silence only meant they were planning. And they weren't the only ones.

Burn bright, fast, and you end up with an army of feds in relentless pursuit. The ATF and FBI wouldn't honor a deal negotiated through Major Petty. Politics are a bitch to navigate, but put enough chum in the water and the sharks will eventually work it out.

And it was on the eleventh of twelve days that the unlikeliest of sharks contacted me. You see, despite what I intimated to Rita, I wasn't one to rest on my laurels. It was just that, sometimes, it took a while for the street to pull off its outlaw magic.

I took a ride to the warehouse district in Miami Springs, strolled up to an old cream-colored Cadillac Sedan de Ville, and opened the passenger door. Two Haitian faces I didn't recognize looked up at me.

"Oh... Sorry."

I peeked past them into the back seat and found Jean-Louis Chevalier. I closed the door and opened the one behind it to slip inside.

"Why did I think you'd drive yourself?" I asked once I was comfortable. The back seat had a surprising amount of legroom.

Unlike the guys in the front, Chevalier had painted an ebony skull on his face in the style of the Bone Saints. If he was ready for war, I was willing to bet there were other bokors nearby.

"He don't look like much," said the driver to the gang

leader.

"Maybe not," I replied, "but I can tie a cherry stem into a knot using only my tongue."

The man's eyes in the rearview mirror bored holes into me. I winked, angering him further. "You best watch that tongue lest you get got."

I sighed and turned to his boss. "Are you seriously telling me you couldn't find a driver who can keep his mouth shut?" The man reached to his waist and I said, "Don't or you'll be sorry."

It wasn't a gun he'd reached for but what looked like the femur of a large rodent. A voodoo fetish. Between his choice of weapon and the fact that he paused, heeding my warning, the driver wasn't a complete idiot.

"Enough," bristled Jean-Louis. "I asked Suarez to come. If you challenge him, you challenge me."

The driver looked away from the mirror. "No worries, boss man." I guess I wasn't gonna get to see what that fetish could do.

Chevalier's eyes were peeled to his window. I wasn't sure why we were here. It was a normal business day, with workers loading trucks on various properties, with enough cars driving by and extraneous activity that we didn't stand out.

"So what are we doing here?" I asked.

Jean-Louis put a finger to the window. "Two blocks that way."

The car sat opposite a salvage yard, and around the corner some ways down was yet another warehouse property with several delivery trucks. The bay doors were shut and no one was outside except for a worker taking a smoke break.

"You watching the Marlboro Man?"

"He's been smoking for over an hour."

My eyes narrowed. "He's a lookout."

I squinted but we were too far away to discern details. The man wore a jacket and gloves, though, which was consistent with someone planning on being outside for longer than a few drags.

"What did you find?"

Chevalier pulled away from the window, tired. It was evident he'd been at this a while. "The Vanguard has been troublesome to locate. Upstarts from out of town, no street presence, no criminal ties."

"You trying to tell me they're upstanding citizens?"

"They are killers who would see every last one of us dead."

I flexed my jaw, unwilling to deal in absolutes. If I could only get to their leadership and talk some sense into them before things got worse.

"There were too many dead ends hunting them down," he continued, "so I decided to take a new route."

I peered at the smoker again. "He's not a militiaman..."

Jean-Louis grinned. "The Bone Saints aren't the only organization hit by the militia. That incident in Wynwood, the one you sped off to, gave me an idea."

I tensed. "You made a deal with the Obsidian March?"

That smoker. Even if I'd been standing right next to him, his gloves would hide his black fingernails.

"If I had made a deal," rebuked Chevalier, "would I be parked two blocks from them?"

I swallowed my ire and let him finish.

"The vampires are also searching for the Vanguard, but they are a larger operation than we are, with more resources. They put feelers out, and these feelers are known by the street. It was only a matter of observing before they turned up." He knocked the glass with his knuckle. "Inside that warehouse is a team of upir leadership, one calling himself Hayden."

I sneered. Hayden was the up-and-coming March boss Trinh had mentioned to me. Beaumont's strike was supposed to take him out and cripple the March for the foreseeable future, except Hayden never showed and the Vanguard went in early.

"What's Hayden up to?"

Chevalier smiled. "You should ask who he's up to something with. Right before I called you, I watched a member of the Vanguard go inside."

"A prisoner? Are the vamps interrogating the poor guy?"

"I don't think so. The man has grievances with his own organization. We believe his name is Victor. He was close with the two men Lieutenant Cross killed at the Bayfront Park. From what I understand, Victor is angered by the Vanguard's inaction on New Year's Day."

"He's selling them out."

"Amusing. For an organization that preys on unrest, internal strife will be their undoing."

Which was exactly the opening I was looking for. As

long as there was disagreement about the extent of the Vanguard's aggressions, there was a chance to steer the organization in the right direction, to help them go legit.

"If Victor wants violence and he's going against the leadership," I said, "then whoever's in control doesn't want blood in the streets."

Jean-Louis looked at me pointedly. "Does this look like control to you?"

"So they're being betrayed. It happens to the best of us."

His face hardened. "The Vanguard is a collection of drunken, murdering, weekender psychopaths. You want peace with them? An accord? You are nothing but a parahuman, one to be extinguished."

I shifted in my seat. "They're misguided..."

The edge in his voice didn't soften. "They made their choice, Suarez, as soon as they drove through the gates of my block and pressed their triggers." The painted skull on his face made his features stark. Chevalier and the Bone Saints weren't looking for a peaceful solution to this business.

And it was hard to blame them. Anytime someone had come for me or mine over the last few years, it was open season. A man has to take a stand when it comes to family. And while mine had thus far been lucky, the Saints had spent days burying or reanimating their own.

Harsh eyes in the rearview mirror met mine, and I gave up trying to convince them. The car's occupants were a captive audience but not a receptive one. Rather than infringe on their goodwill in inviting me here, I took a long breath, checked the warehouse, and let the silence ease the budding resentment.

After some time, another man exited the warehouse, but it was just the one. He wore gloves and what looked like an orange ski jacket. The man relieved the other, who returned inside.

"I don't even own a jacket," I muttered.

After a long while of not speaking, Jean-Louis said, "These are strange days, Suarez." He took a breath and turned to me. "Is it true? One of the dead men the newspapers are calling a hero was the necromancer responsible for Ozo Ebu's death? You killed him?"

I returned a grim nod. The newspapers had been running salacious headlines about the police station raider getting away, about the FBI's manhunt, and a few puff pieces about the dead heroes. Most thankfully focused on Special Agent Carter, a longtime veteran of the bureau. If you can believe it, I actually missed the guy.

"It was all Jensen, and I got him."

The ends of his lips upturned. "And his pet is now at peace?"

"The karkan wasn't a mere thrall."

"Regardless, without a purpose it will wither into nothing. It is the way of things."

Someone was in an introspective mood today.

And it must've been infectious. Sitting in a car and waiting did that to a person, I guess.

Purpose is just a philosophical stand-in for survival. That's what most people wanted. Security, protection, opportunity. The FBI and City of Miami had different ideas how to achieve it, but they had the same purpose. Clan Beaumont was looking out for its own. Even the Vanguard, at least a significant portion of them, likely believed they were serving the public good.

Good intentions make the world go round, but one good intention running into another often ends in war.

"I can't sit on the sidelines and watch the bodies drop," I grumbled. "That's what will happen if the vampires strike the militia."

"The first shots were already fired," he stoically replied. "Do you really believe you can do anything to stop it?"

"Ability has nothing to do with trying." I gritted my teeth. "And what if the Obsidian March wins? Doesn't that mean we lose a powerful ally in the process?"

"Your definition of ally has always been strange, Suarez."

I didn't point out that we were currently in the car together. Friendship hadn't always been our status quo. "Fair enough, but the Vanguard aren't Nether fiends. They fear what they don't know, and there are a lot of good reasons for that." I pointed to the vampire standing watch. "Said Nether fiends being the prime example."

Chevalier watched the window without reply.

I grunted. "A war like this will make bigger headlines than anything the karkan did. We need to be smart about this, Chevalier. What's the greater threat: the militia or public opinion?"

He turned to me. "I realize the danger of public opinion all too well. The Vanguard are experts at manipulating it, and they are turning it against us."

"Which is why we need them on our side. And not just them. *Everyone.* The police, the feds, the Society, the marches, the silvan circles. Enemies are in plain sight, Jean-Louis. *Everywhere.* They're coming from the shadows, from the Deep, and their eyes are on us, man. We're in *their* sights too."

I leaned close with a spark in my eyes. "If we just took the time to look around, we'd see more friends than enemies. I'm as serious as I've ever been. We need to work together. We need to emphasize our commonalities. We all just want life, don't we? That's *our* purpose. It needs to start somewhere, and it might as well be with the two of us."

The bokor behind the painted skull glanced at the men in the front seat for a long moment. Then his eyes turned back on me. "I've been waiting for that, Suarez."

"Waiting for what?"

"For you to get your head out of your ass."

I blinked back befuddlement.

He snickered. "If you keep making noble speeches like that, you just might change the way things are done in this city."

I huffed. Chevalier was still being cryptic, and I wasn't going to let him escape that easily. "This militia..." I pressed. "They're not as powerful as they seem."

"I'm not talking about the militia," he spat. "The Vanguard is done with. I speak of our future, of my faith in you."

That stopped me short. Jean-Louis Chevalier knew the

pulse of the street. He felt the same things I did. Supernatural incursions into Miami were escalating, yet only a few of us were in a position to notice or care. These times were far from normal.

The stiges, the encroachment of Hell, the void of power in Miami—they were all dire problems that weren't going away. Survival wouldn't be granted to those who stand alone.

"So," announced Chevalier with a wide smile, "it seems you would tie your sausage with mine."

I grimaced. "What? I didn't say *that*."

He snorted. "It sounds better in Creole." The Bone Saints laughed.

I grinned uneasily. I think I got what the gang leader was saying, but I could have done without the sausage metaphor.

The mirth in the car suddenly cut out.

"There, that's them."

In the distant loading yard, a team of several well-dressed upirs exited the building. They escorted a man wearing a backward baseball cap. Victor wasn't a prisoner, he wasn't being pushed around or treated disrespectfully. As a matter of fact, he shared a laugh with a few of them, probably about a sausage metaphor.

The entire crew loaded into two white vehicles that resembled FedEx trucks without the branding. A dozen vamps. The man in the yard opened the gate, locked it after they rolled out, and joined them in the trailing truck, making it a baker's dozen. Not too shabby a contingent, but far from invincible.

I reached for the door, adrenaline coursing through my body.

Jean-Louis pulled my shoulder back into the seat. "This isn't a fight, Suarez. We stay quiet, we watch, and we follow."

The driver started the Sedan de Ville and unassumingly turned onto the street.

"Wait a minute!" I called out. "You seeing this?"

The driver hit the brakes. Chevalier's head moved on a swivel.

"I can't believe I've been sitting here the whole time," I muttered, "and just now noticed."

"Damn it, Suarez, what is it?"

I pointed at a sunbaked billboard in the distance. "They make Coca-Cola with coffee now."

The occupants of the car hissed, and we pulled after the Obsidian March.

Chapter 49

We cruised Alligator Alley across the width of the state. It was as boring as a divided interstate can get, all nondescript flatland punctuated by occasional rest stops. Instead of continuing to Naples on Florida's west coast, the vans cut north on a small state road and passed through Immokalee, best known for its Seminole Casino.

The drive continued through some of the more remote areas of the Everglades. Past wide-open sawgrass prairies and miles of farmland, it was hard to believe we were only a few hours out of Miami.

We finally stopped in a city I'd never heard of named LaBelle, inland of the sleepy town of Fort Myers. LaBelle was a strange place that was somehow small yet impersonal at the same time. Everywhere I looked were tractor trailers, farm equipment, and service shops supporting the business of agriculture, treading the line between agrarian and industrial.

Hayden and his team of vampires made a pit stop for gas

before settling at a homey diner. I wasn't sure how much upirs needed to eat, but they were likely humoring the lone human among them. Some of them stayed with the trucks while Victor and others went inside to sit.

As much as I could've used a chicken-fried anything, I would be recognized by the Obsidian March on sight. Instead I patronized the dive bar with a big window across the highway. The fish and chips were greasy and the fries soggy. I sat at the bar and washed them down with a cerveza.

Some of the Haitians used the bathroom, which was when our follow cars first caught up to us. I counted five, if that was all of them, full to the gills with Bone Saints. Even without the face paint, the parade of them coming through attracted attention in this town. But they disappeared as quickly as they arrived, hitting the road and stowing somewhere out of sight again, while they waited on Chevalier's word to continue the road trip.

I was long done with my plate and working on my second beer. Chevalier waited in the car as the time stretched, the diner securely surrounded. There was nothing to do but relax until Hayden made his next move.

"Funny meeting you here," said Darcy, standing two stools down.

I'd been so focused on the window she'd snuck right on top of me. I turned to scope the interior out. Simon Feigelstock leaned against the far wall with crossed arms and a lawyerly smile. His pinstripes were the classiest thing for miles.

I regarded the teenaged adult at my side. "How'd you find me?"

She snorted. "You don't think Cisco Suarez can take a road trip without the Society noticing, do you?"

My face darkened. She'd used the name of the group inclusively, even if the word came out with a tinge of bitterness. "That's not as comforting as you think," I said.

"Hey, you wanted to talk."

I spun the stool to face her. "And you didn't? Why mysteriously disappear like that? You think I'd try to stop you?"

"Will you?" She peered deeply into my eyes. It wasn't a challenge or a warning—just a question. Maybe even a hope.

I glanced at Simon. The Society enforcer wasn't just here to contribute a winning personality. He was watching Darcy, making sure she played by the rules.

I lowered my voice. "What do they have over you?"

Whatever expression she held faded into disappointment. She shook her head. "It's not like that, Cisco."

"Then why suddenly rejoin the crew?"

She hiked a shoulder and turned to the bar. "A shot of whiskey, please." She placed a fiver on the counter, and in a place like this they gave her change. Darcy gulped half the shot and puckered her lips against the bite. "I'm an adult," she squeaked through a grimace.

"Obviously," I said with an eye roll.

She set the glass down and turned to me, keeping her distance at two stools. "This is something I need to do,

Cisco. I don't expect you to understand, I don't expect you to be excited about it, but I do expect you to leave me alone. Okay?"

When we'd first crossed paths, my impression of Darcy was one of subdued ambivalence. I always figured she was unhappy with her place in the world, with where she'd ended up, and she'd accepted that as her lot in life. But recent months had seen a sea change. Darcy professed how much happier she was. She joked, she laughed, she smiled. While her life wasn't exactly normal, it had finally achieved a desirable baseline.

My heart sank a little when I detected that resignation seep back into her voice.

"Just tell me you're not doing it for..."—I grimaced as Simon beamed—"them."

She met his eyes across the room and turned back to me. "Cisco, you need to believe me when I say this. I'm doing this for me, okay? Like I said, this is something *I have to do.*"

My eyes narrowed at her emphasis.

The quiet guy from Chevalier's passenger seat entered the bar and approached, drawing her attention.

"I need to go," she said. Darcy fumbled with the change and left a couple of bills and a spattering of coins beside the unfinished shot of whiskey.

"Wait... Darcy..."

"They're on the move," whispered the Bone Saint. Across the street, Victor and the vampires loaded into the van.

Darcy winked. "See ya on the flip side, cowboy." She

backed away with one hand in her jacket pocket and the other firing a finger gun.

A single coin from her pile slid across the bar and settled in front of me. Darcy rejoined Simon.

"Suarez..."

"Only Chevalier calls me that," I snapped, hopping to my feet and leaving some cash on the counter. As I did, I surreptitiously palmed Darcy's coin. We hurried to the door.

"What, no thank you?" admonished Simon.

I ignored him.

"Asked and accommodated," he called after me. "Remember that."

I slammed the door to drown out his smug taunts.

"Who was that?" asked the Haitian.

"Nobody."

The denial didn't stop him from reporting the incident to his boss before his car door was closed. Chevalier sneered as I sat.

"Are you running a game on me, Suarez?"

"I'm not running anything," I grumbled. Then I pointed to the highway. "Your mark is getting away."

Chevalier suspiciously eyed the bar as we pulled away.

After a rest that should've done us good, no one found themselves in good spirits, least of all me. There was nothing to be done for it when we were this close. All we could do was drive on.

We left LaBelle in the rearview and headed to wilder country. The highway was an old scar intersecting dense vegetation, and I was finally beginning to understand the difficulty of locating the Vanguard. Victor was really leading Hayden into the heart of their operations.

But then the trees gave way to farmland. The trucks turned off the state road and we had to continue past so as not to draw suspicion to ourselves. Chevalier had another of his cars follow at a distance while we doubled around. After a good fifteen minutes on the back road, instead of a dense Everglades compound, the trucks parked beside a quaint farmhouse with a wide expanse of land. We stopped short, pulling to the side of the road ahead of the waiting follow car.

"This is a residence," I said, slightly annoyed.

The swamps and tree growth I was expecting were far from these suburban plains. The property had a modest house and barn, but there was no room for a militia. An idyllic horizon harbored nothing but bulbous clouds.

"Maybe it's his house," said the driver.

That theory was dashed as soon as a man creaked the screen door open with the barrel of a shotgun. We all squinted at the proceedings.

The homeowner called out, not appearing to recognize the vehicles. Victor bounced out with a friendly wave. The man lowered his shotgun as Victor approached, and they locked hands.

"What do you suppose they are saying?" asked Chevalier.

"I don't know. This isn't on the up-and-up. I can't see a thing from this distance."

"He must be a fellow Vanguard sympathizer."

The two men had a casual familiarity as they chatted, but they didn't appear to be good friends. Victor beckoned the homeowner to the van. He parked the shotgun over his shoulder and helped roll up the back access door.

Claws slashed the homeowner's throat out. Victor flinched at the suddenness of it. He looked away but didn't run, which meant he'd more or less expected the carnage. Hayden's crew unloaded and a grunt dragged the body back into the house.

I reached for the door and Chevalier grabbed me. "We can't let them know we're here, Suarez."

"Fuck that. They killed him."

"Death comes to soldiers in war."

"Those are vampires violently entering a human household," I hissed angrily. "Excuse me for making a distinction."

I brushed him off and pushed out of the sedan. It felt like there was a mile between the house and me. The other cars doors opened. The driver brandished his bone fetish.

"They're leading us to the base," snapped Chevalier.

"It was a mistake bringing him," remarked the driver.

The leader of the Bone Saints appealed to me. "Do not sacrifice the location of the Vanguard compound for the death of one man, Suarez. What's done is done."

The two follow cars parked behind us emptied of gangbangers ready for a fight.

"There might be more people in that house, Jean-Louis. I won't sit back and watch the Obsidian March slaughter them."

"Look around," he snarled as his people approached me. "This is a Vanguard outpost. I can't let you go when we're this close."

I balled a fist at my side. "Chevalier, you head a gang in Little Haiti, but I know you better than your reputation. Things don't always fit nice and square in a box, and there's a difference between criminals and monsters. I'm getting a closer look at that house because I have to, and if you get in my way, well, I'll have to do something else."

I glared daggers at them. The last thing I wanted was to make enemies of the Bone Saints, but they were only in this for revenge, and the price was too high.

"You told me you were waiting for me," I added. "You see something in me. I know it. I feel it too. But if we're gonna do this..."—I cleared my throat—"tie our sausages together, I need to do it with a clear conscience, with a chance for everyone. Now... I'm going in there."

I turned away. The driver took a step before Chevalier spoke with heavy resignation. "Let him go."

I heaved a sigh of relief and broke into a sprint along the fence line. At an old break of weathered wood, I hopped into the property and bolted for the farmhouse. With the delivery trucks empty, I used them as cover. Anyone watching from the windows of the house wouldn't see me.

I hauled ass to a small cherry tree, crouching and reaching into the shadow beneath. I pulled out a shotgun missing its barrel.

Damn, the karkan had broken my trusty sawed off. I'd

had this thing a dozen years and would need to begin the lengthy process of prepping a new gun for safekeeping in my shadow box. For now I would have to do without.

I grumbled and scanned the large yard. Then I hauled ass to the side of the truck and peeked in the open bay. No upir armory, unfortunately. I moved to the passenger door, pulled up on the step, and peeked in the window. Bingo. I stealthily opened the door and recovered the pistol from the console. It was an old SIG P210. I did an ammo check to find the mag wasn't full and the rounds were standard.

Against vampires, this was slightly worse than useless. Call me old fashioned for taking it anyway.

Resting on a sizable crawl space, the house's windows were above my head. I snuck around to the side porch that had a door with an attached window and checked inside. Faded curtains partially hid a dim kitchen. The linoleum had a smear of blood where a body had been dragged. As I adjusted the angle of my view, two obsidian monsters came into view, crouching over and feasting on a young girl that was barely a teenager.

Chapter 50

The wood frame shattered under the weight of my boot, and the upirs spun around, milky white eyes gleaming, blood dripping from slurping mouths. The poor girl was opened up and missing most of her internal organs.

The vamps lunged. I blasted shadow into them, flinging them backward into the counter. I advanced and ripped down the curtains hanging above the sink, sending a wash of sunlight over them that partially reverted them to their human forms.

I punched the pistol into their crowns, cracking skulls and knocking them back. Claws came up and I kicked them away. I pounded a vamp's face in, deforming his nose and cheeks as I kept at it. These things didn't bleed, but they sure as hell broke.

A snarl came at my back as a third upir entered the kitchen. A tendril of shadow caught his neck and yanked him to the floor. Jaws tightened over my calf and I screamed. I put the pistol to the vamp's temple and pulled the trigger one, two, three times before he released me.

The other one lunged blindly, unable to see because his eyes were caved in. I easily dodged but tripped backward over the dead girl, landing in a wash of slick blood. The third upir on the floor grabbed me close. I put my hands on his chest and shoved away snapping jaws. Violet thrummed between my fingers, and a sliver of shadow pierced his chest.

The vampire exploded, chunky bits of a recently fed heart painting the kitchen and my front side. I spat the viscera from my lips and spun to the others as ashes swirled in the air. I stomped over and, before they could recover, exploded two more hearts.

I growled and turned out of the kitchen, stepping over the girl's dead mother.

Several vampires in armored carapaces waited for me in the living room. While there was a large curtained window, the angle of the sun prevented direct sunlight from seeping through. I must've been a sight myself, covered in the blood of their friends. I advanced on them and a couple more filed in behind me.

This was it. The nightmare scenario. Close quarters... surrounded by multiple fully armored upirs... and I didn't mind in the slightest.

"You're all going to die," I seethed.

Slick faces grinned back. "You're welcome to try, wizard."

They all sprung at once. I dropped down and punched the floorboards. Shadow exploded in a twisted ring of jagged tips, covering all sides of me and spearing the most eager vampires. Besides the strikes being painful, the two that took hits directly to the heart were momentarily stunned.

Not dead, though. In order to rip them apart, I'd need to get in close.

My darksword moved like a whirlwind, going for the enemies I'd merely grazed. Claws were aggressively clipped. A head was cleaved clean through. I slammed my hand up and sent another flying into the wall, propelled on a jet of darkness.

Razors raked my back. I grunted and slipped into the shadow, darted aside and appeared behind my attacker. The purple blade ruptured his back. The vamp had enough time to look down at the tip of the sword protruding from his gut before I ripped it up through his lifeline.

The first of the vampires detonated, filling the rest with rage. They came at me in anger, and I dissolved to escape the scrum. Another ruptured before he knew what hit him. Then a latecomer entered the room and ambushed me from behind. I barely twisted away from her claws, instead getting bashed on the head and dropping to the floor.

I swept an alligator boot behind me. The bitch jumped the attack and readied her talons once more. I moved toward the shadow, but a handhold on my leg prevented retreat. The darksword sliced his hand off, but the interruption had given them an opening. The woman speared my stomach, obsidian dagger sinking a good two inches before I escaped into the floor.

I reappeared with another burst of knives. The darkness blanketed me, cutting upward and outward, and the reward was a flurry of screams. I took a leg off, flipped around and embedded my blade into another exploding heart, and slashed horizontally to fend off assault from all sides.

The melee continued fiercely, hole in my gut not even registering. The vamps began to fight defensively. It was a necessary tactic as they had nothing that could block the darksword that mowed through their black armor like a lightsaber. Instead of parrying, the three remaining feinted and dodged, playing Keep-Away while waiting for opportunities to occasionally slash my exposed back.

I took a nick or two, but my ability to shift through shadow was a wild card. Given enough targets, my attacks were unpredictable enough to keep them guessing. They moved fast and it took a few tries, but eventually I surfaced close enough to dust another one.

That left two of them. Well, two of them standing. The one missing half his head was still alive, heart unpierced, twitching disturbingly on the ground. Even I wanted to put him out of his misery.

Before I could deliver a knockout to the tag team, a new crew entered the living room. Two humans and two monsters. I twisted the pistol from my belt and pointed it at the newcomers, only one of which was truly human.

A man with dirty-blond hair held a pistol to Victor's back. Larger than usual upirs in beast mode flanked each side. I was thinking bodyguards. I stepped aside to keep a wall at my back, while the two I'd been fighting hungrily licked their teeth.

"This is who you want," said the man with the gun.

"Come get him."

No one moved a muscle. Well, again, except for the guy involuntarily twitching in semi-death throes. He got a pass on account of missing a frontal lobe.

I swallowed and studied each opponent. They completed the original baker's dozen. Unless there was a hidden nest somewhere, there were no more surprise vampires. The pair I'd been engaged with was disciplined enough to halt combat at the flip of a switch, which was all the worse. I wanted them acting like animals, dumb and angry. Much easier to pick off that way.

My lips twitched in displeasure. "Hayden, I presume?"

He grinned. "Then you know about me. Good, that makes introductions—"

"You should be thanking me," I interrupted.

His eyes cinched cautiously. "Why's that?"

"Because I'm the guy who gave you your promotion."

He chuckled but I confidently stepped forward.

"The reason you're the new boss is because I ashed your old boss, Magnus." One of the vamps growled and I nodded. "Remember him, do you? Well, Hayden, I hate to say it, but management hasn't been pleased. We're gonna go a different way. Time for a sudden demotion."

He sneered. Fear was evident even though he apparently had the upper hand. Why else announce himself so calmly?

"That's not what's gonna happen," he said evenly.

He pulled the pistol from behind the militia member in an over-orchestrated trick I saw coming a mile away. My palm flew up, bursting outward with turquoise energy as his gun barked.

Although my shield was only two feet across, I'd grown frighteningly good at positioning it against incoming fire. The round hit the half-dome of energy near the center.

The tendon in my arm tugged as if I'd hit the funny bone. Red sparks burrowed into my shield. It flickered, and the bullet propelled through. The round exited the shield at a slight cant and punched into my shoulder.

My insides suddenly burned as if stuck with a hot poker, and I howled.

Hayden fired again and I wasn't ready for it. The bullet screamed into my hip, clattering against bone and making my legs wobble. Against the fierce agony, I managed to fade into the ether as more gunshots rang out, one after the other. Hayden released Victor, a fake captive, and watched with curiosity as he carefully aimed and repeated firing.

The bullets tore past me, failing to pierce the veil of my spellcraft, but managing to hurt all the same. Below me, one of the rounds that had penetrated bounced to the floor as it was expelled from my incorporeal body. Cyrillic etching in the metal glowed with fresh blood. The other bullet was lodged into my hip and wouldn't shake loose.

Hayden's magazine ran dry. I materialized, darksword flickering in my hand... and collapsed. The vamps pounced, slicing me up as a consequence of holding me down. The funny thing was, all I could feel was the bullet. It was like I was dying.

"We got the bastard!" cheered Victor, happy the ruse was successful.

It's not that I ever thought he was a good guy, but his presence had staved off my bloodlust long enough for my fortunes to flip.

"I knew we could count on you," said Hayden encouragingly. He cracked his neck from side to side and paced around me. "Now, what to do with the famous Shadow Man..." He beamed at me. "Believe it or not, this is a conundrum. Word in my ranks is you actually saved a handful of my people in a bar last week."

He took a halted breath. "But then, those idiots invited me into a trap and almost got me killed. I rewarded them for their incompetence." He paused over me. "While your crime is different, I'm afraid the sentence is the same."

"Screw you," I grated.

"You see? You're treating me like Magnus already, and you never even bothered to get to know me. I'm not like them, the old-timers. I'm a modern businessman." He wagged his pistol. "This guy is mostly for show, although it's admittedly a good show." He chuckled at his own joke and produced a satellite phone in his other hand. "This is the guy, though, that provides the real victory. Communications, networking. It's the future of our species."

"Call someone who gives a fuck."

One of his bodyguards kicked my head and had me momentarily seeing stars. Hayden sighed as if displeased by the brutality.

"It didn't have to end this way," he belabored. "I would've been willing to deal. Nothing is beyond negotiation." He smiled musingly. "I know you've grown infatuated with one who left our flock, the Frenchman. While he may be lost, he has the right idea, and the Obsidian March is following suit, charging headlong into prosperity. We're growing connections all over the city and beyond. Legitimate business interspersed with... well... you know." He chuckled coyly about the teeny matter of the human trafficking.

I defiantly pushed against the claws holding me down. "You guys are sick. You're a disease."

"I've been told you were a hard-liner. Now I've seen it for myself." Hayden waved the sat phone for emphasis. "But, unlike you, the federal government is not above bargaining."

I blinked back bewilderment. "What did you do?"

Hayden laughed and paced away. "I'm gonna take over your city, Cisco. I've been planning it for some time. And the difference between us is I'll take all the help I can get."

I showed my teeth, finally starting to overcome the pain. That was the easy part. Shaking off the vamps holding my arms behind my back was the next obstacle. The shadow couldn't release me from their clutches.

"So you'll do it now?" interjected an eager Victor. "I wanna be turned."

The rising star of the Obsidian March spun to him with a smile. "It was a promise," Hayden agreed. And then, with a huff, he said, "Unfortunately, it doesn't work that way. Upirs make familiars, not other vampires."

Victor's face tightened. "But you said—"

"What I had to."

Hayden nodded to the bodyguard at the militiaman's back, and a black claw severed his head from his neck. Victor's corpse collapsed beside the still twitching body of the debrained vampire, creating a grotesque juxtaposition.

The floorboards of the old farmhouse began to rumble, and the sound of whirring motors filled the air.

"Ah," crooned Hayden, "they work quick, don't they?"

He moved to the window and opened the curtains. The entire house shook as a black helicopter blazed past. Two more followed in quick succession. White letters on their side read ATF.

I finally understood the sat phone. "You have federal contacts," I fumed. "Once your patsy told you where to find them, you brought the ATF down on the Vanguard. This isn't a vampire war, it's an annihilation."

Hayden beamed with pride. "You see," he gloated with a grin, "you *do* understand business... when you put your mind to it."

Chapter 51

Gunfire rang in the distance. Everyone in the room but Hayden flinched. He calmly checked the window.

"Ah," he said, pleased, "reinforcements are here." He flashed me a contemptuous look. "Mine, not yours."

I shoved against the claws holding me down. Dozens of firearms broke out in repeated bursts. Stray bullets chipped the wood exterior of the farmhouse. Harried yells joined the chorus. An explosion, a colorful light show, and the green fog of pestilence filled the window.

Hayden's face grew serious as he moved from window to window, peering through the unnatural pall that fell over the property.

"What reinforcements?" I demanded.

His words were confident, but his twitchy eyes betrayed concern. "Do you know how much commuter traffic LaBelle gets on the average day? Your posse did a good job of tailing us unseen, but once we stopped at the diner it was beyond obvious. You don't really think a hamburger and fries takes an hour and a half to eat, do you?"

My face fell. "You called more vamps." The Obsidian March was a large outfit with resources all over the southern portion of the state. I struggled to lift my head enough to see out the window, but the weight on my back was too great.

Hayden pulled a new mag and reloaded his pistol. "Our organization has dealt with gangbangers before. Voodooists are troublesome thorns, but with the right tools—in this case, superior armaments—any thorn can be picked."

I ground my teeth as the gunfire died down. The screams silenced. The supernatural fog in the window cleared, and the smile on Hayden's face stretched from ear to ear.

"There you go," he said, masking his relief. "See for yourself."

The vamps hefted me. It was painful to get up and I leaned on them for support. Whatever was etched onto those bullets worked like a poison against my zombification enchantments. I needed to neutralize it or I'd be a lame duck.

Standing, I now had enough range of movement to get my hand to the wound in my hip. I bit down and stuck my finger into my flesh, scraping for the piece of metal lodged in my bone.

They brought me to the window, and my spirits sank. Dead Bone Saints littered the field. The car I'd come in on was shot up with bullet holes and on fire. A few mercenaries held small arms on a bleeding Chevalier as they shoved him to the front door.

I grimaced as they entered. One of the black-nailed upirs stood watch at the open front door while the other joined us in the living room, doubling the count of able-bodied vampires in the farmhouse from five to ten. And that didn't count whoever remained outside.

The look of grim defeat in Chevalier's eyes almost broke me. He'd wanted to hang back but I had insisted on rushing in.

"Are they all dead?" I asked frantically.

Jean-Louis didn't meet my eyes. It made me sick. Between the guilt and the hostile spellcraft churning in my gut, I felt like throwing up.

"Carraway," exclaimed Hayden. "Report please."

The newcomers traded glances. The man holding Chevalier pushed the prisoner forward. "All threats have been neutralized."

Hayden's pistol shot up at the pair. Everyone froze.

"It's okay," assured the vamp behind Chevalier. "If he makes a move, I'll kill him."

"I don't care about the bokor," assured Hayden. "In fact..."

He pulled the trigger and Chevalier's head bounced. He dropped like a lead weight. Blood drained from the hole in the side of his head.

"Bastard!" I screamed.

Spellcraft flooded my fist but a fierce blow batted me down. A single claw stabbed my wrist and pinned it to the floor. I twisted in agony as my magic withered away.

It took a few moments to command the pain, to notice

that nobody had moved yet. Despite the hostile dead on the floor, Hayden's pistol was still raised, aimed at the one who'd dragged Chevalier inside.

"What... what are you doing, sir?" asked the man.

Hayden's eyebrow arched playfully. "It's very simple. You see, you're not Carraway."

The vamp looked to the others again. He sighed and nodded to the man at the door. "Fair enough."

The illusion drifted apart like dissipating waves of heat, and I blinked back a portion of the vertigo I was feeling. The man at the door wasn't a vampire, he was Shen Santos managing an elaborate deception. The vamp that entered with Chevalier reverted into Beaumont, and another woman, Tutti. The remaining two newcomers were Beaumont's personal guard. I recognized them among the same group that had interrupted my interrogation of the Russian Bratva boss.

Thankfully, the bullet hole in Jean-Louis Chevalier's head vanished, and he watched me from his position on the floor, still playing possum so as not to repeat the experience for real.

Hayden sputtered and spun to the window. All his people did, really, which included the claw staking me to the floor being retracted. I inhaled sharply and fought the pain as I wobbled on weak legs and moved to the window.

No bullets, no bodies, no burning car. Just a crew of twenty bokors and a Society strike team.

Shen saluted to Beaumont from a safe distance. "I got you this far." He glowered at me before retreating outside to rejoin his people. The illusionist never was much of a fighter, but damn if he hadn't come through this time.

Hayden's cheeks clenched in anger. "Where's my strike team?"

"Miles from here," answered Beaumont, "and in pieces. They were undisciplined and fired at friendly targets. What was I supposed to do? Now, may we speak as businessmen?"

I surveyed the crowd. The quaint farmhouse was no longer so quaint. There was no love lost between the two upir clans, but I suppose it was business before pleasure. Hayden took a deep breath and lowered his pistol.

"I'm sorry, Suarez," offered Chevalier now that it was safe to speak. "They surrounded us before we could intervene."

Beaumont's mouth crooked. "Don't apologize. For a drug dealer, you've proved both loyal and cunning." He turned to me. "Your friend volunteered to come in with us in case things got dicey."

I met Chevalier's eyes and nodded thanks. We weren't out of the woods yet, but damn if we didn't just get a do-over. "So this is why the Society was following me," I said with a humorless chuckle. I quietly worked my fingers closer to my bullet wound.

Beaumont splayed his hands in surrender. "I did warn you to stay out of it. I'm afraid the politics of rogue militias are beyond your pay grade."

"That include your deal with the police?"

He grinned. "I think current events have displayed that I don't have a monopoly on those. What have you done,

Hayden?"

The vampire boss scoffed. "The same as you. I used my contacts to remedy the situation."

"Removing the militia was not the agreed solution."

"It's not your place to question me, Leverett. Your vassal clan is subservient to mine."

The Frenchman's eyes narrowed. "Nothing lasts forever."

I dipped my finger into my wound. By this point I was dealing with five kinds of pain—as long I didn't pass out, it didn't matter. I hooked the bullet with my finger and winced as I tugged it through torn muscle.

Hayden's eyes lit up. "Oh? Is this display an attempt to renegotiate our agreement?"

"The agreement was with your predecessor," Beaumont pointed out.

"Yes, and very fortunate for you. My terms wouldn't have been so kind."

Just as I pulled the round from my body, another gunshot rang out. My back surged with fire. I collapsed in searing pain after Hayden had shot me again.

The vampire boss shoved aside a muss of dirty-blond hair. "I'm the one in charge," he asserted.

Leverett Beaumont casually raised his chin. "Are you sure about that?"

Hayden looked over Beaumont's allies. Tutti snickered ruefully. Chevalier's eyes pointed me to her in warning.

"I've secured power on three fronts," explained Beaumont. "The police representing authority, the Society representing animists, and the militia representing humanity."

"I'm sorry to see the ATF break your trifecta," gloated Hayden. "Support of humanity is unnecessary. And laughable, I might add. They would gun you down the second they saw your true form."

"Is one form truer than another?" he retorted. His hypothetical question garnered sideways looks from the vampires in the room, even Beaumont's own people. "The Obsidian March has chosen to live in the shadows. I make the choice to join society."

"Join?" Hayden harrumphed at the thought. "You'll never be one of them."

Leverett's face went red. "I've given everything to South Florida! I represent order, and protection, and a continuation of our species. What do you represent? Stealing deplorables? Growing a network of sodden drug dens? Living afraid and in the dark?"

The accusation angered Hayden in turn, probably because Beaumont hit close to the mark. "Is this display of yours supposed to intimidate me?"

Beaumont showed sharpened teeth. "It takes a wise man to be intimidated, Hayden. Take a look outside. The human animists have sided with me. The voodoo gangs detest your street antics. The last of your reinforcements were dispatched."

The Obsidian March bodyguards shifted uncomfortably. The vamps holding me down lagged in their attention, though the new bullet was doing a good enough job of babysitting.

"You're surrounded," finished Beaumont, "on an island all by yourself."

The prideful boss' eyes gleamed. "The Obsidian March is never on an island. We are a force to be reckoned with, and your bluster does not frighten me for a moment."

"From now on the Obsidian March will behave," returned Beaumont, "because they will cede leadership of the state to me."

Hayden's eyes widened in amusement.

The Frenchman was amused himself but had the grace to be subtle about it. "I've made deals with the local police, Hayden. Deals that your clan has repeatedly failed to close. I've secured police protection for the Obsidian March and Clan Beaumont, and I've notified Eliza of my success atop your failures."

His open mention of the police in his pocket garnered my undivided attention. Hayden's confident demeanor didn't waver until the woman's name.

"Eliza would never accept you," he countered. "You're an outcast."

Beaumont nodded in concession. "Be that as it may, I'm a productive outcast. The police can either protect you or destroy you, and I'm the one that has their ear. Trust me, when Eliza hears of your latest blunder with the Vanguard, she'll have no choice but to rely on me."

Hayden's eyes lit up playfully. Something was wrong.

"It's just business," finished Beaumont. "I'm sure you understand."

Hayden raised his gun, but his hand wavered.

"That's not smart," warned the Frenchman. "Going against Eliza's word has repercussions. For both of us."

"The only word she'll hear is mine. Tutti?"

Beaumont blinked. Tutti flapped pink pigtails behind her shoulders, pulled a gun, and switched sides.

"Sorry, Leverett. It's been fun," she teased, "but I'm a fickle woman."

"Keep your aim on Cisco," ordered Hayden. "If Leverett's people make a move, shoot him."

I snarled as Tutti straddled me and pointed the pistol at my head. "Don't take it personally, slugger." She put a heel on my chest and pressed me to the floor.

Chapter 52

Beaumont was as still as a viper, only moving his eyes as he took in the new dynamics. It wasn't that we were horribly outnumbered—I counted six vampires to four—but the current pointing of the guns didn't favor our side, particularly Beaumont and me.

That said, there was a force to be reckoned with outside the farmhouse. I didn't know what upir agreements held who responsible, but Hayden couldn't execute us and easily walk away from the Society and the Bone Saints. It was the only reason we were still alive.

The vampires on me backed off as Tutti took watch. In some ways I was in a worse position, but without their hold there was a chance I could slip into the shadow. That was a big if, of course. *If* the bullet didn't interfere with my spellcraft. *If* I didn't get shot up with more rounds. And *if* I could even shake it out.

"Now," said Hayden, attempting to regain control of the negotiation, "you'll find I have more friends than you think.

The Haitian thugs outside? They won't make a move while their leader is captive. And if the Society was willing to make a deal with you, they'll do the same with me."

Beaumont's eyelids twitched.

"It doesn't really matter which of us walks out of here," explained Hayden. "One pull of my trigger, and your clan is over and done with. Tutti knows your ins and outs by now. Rebellion on your part only ensures the rest of your people are hunted to extinction. Unless... You'll accept defeat here and now, agree to crawl back into the hole you came out of, and accept my new terms. Or Tutti will do something permanent."

The waif waved her gun at me. Beaumont clenched his jaw, clearly irked by Tutti's betrayal. If it was meant to make him back down, however, it failed. "You overestimate my sentimentality," he warned.

Hayden chuckled. "Is that any way to speak of a former lover?"

"I was talking about Cisco."

I swallowed.

Just how far was Beaumont willing to go to secure victory? He was a crime boss, like a few others I'd butted heads with in the past. Sure, he had loftier goals, goals that sometimes aligned more with my own, but he was willing to play dirtier. His use of the Vanguard as a weapon proved that. It would be negligent not to wonder if I was just another one of his pawns.

"Go ahead," Beaumont told them. "Shoot him. See if I care."

"Thanks, asshole," I muttered. I guess I had to take my shot now or never.

Hayden grew visibly agitated by the Frenchman's refusal to back down. His lips tightened. "You don't think I will?"

"If you do, you're dead. To the Society, one vampire may as well be the same as any other, but don't think for a second they'll forgive you murdering a talented practitioner under their wing. They've invested a lot in him already."

Hayden's eyes darted to me with newfound uncertainty.

"You have one chance of coming out of this alive," Beaumont stressed before uncharacteristically raising his voice. "*Now stop pointing that gun at me.*"

The pistol wavered. "Eliza will protect me," urged Hayden. "Me and mine, we walk out of here. We can deal with Miami later."

"There's no later," Beaumont returned. "I'm running Wynwood now."

Hayden trembled with rage. He wasn't even being allowed to retreat with a modicum of respect. But what could he do, really? If Beaumont was willing to sacrifice me in order to garner Society sympathy, there were no other cards for him to play.

Not here and not now.

Hayden was an up-and-coming boss with a bright future, but it was clear by her mention that Eliza was the real power running the show. Maybe she was in another city, maybe she was holed up deep in the Nether. It didn't much matter. Crime families had a hierarchy, and Beaumont had apparently secured victory before ever stepping foot in this farmhouse.

"Fine," snapped Hayden. "I agree to your terms." He fitfully lowered his gun.

Beaumont grinned. "I wasn't asking."

Tutti swiveled away from me. I lunged and grabbed Chevalier before plunging into darkness. Flesh ripped but the shadow triumphed. We became massless as all hell broke out.

Tutti set her pistol to Hayden's back and fired twice. The vampire boss coughed and stumbled, gun clattering to the floor.

"Sorry, Hayden," cooed Tutti. "It's not you, it's me."

She fired again and ruptured his heart. Every vampire in the room with a gun pulled it. Muzzle flashes danced above us. Blood painted the walls as the enchanted round lost purchase in my body.

I released Chevalier and emerged behind the bitch that had staked my wrist to the ground. My fist punched through her armored chest, to her utter shock. I grabbed her beating, bloody heart and I crushed it.

One of Leverett's bodyguards fell to a barrage of bullets. Tutti gunned down one of Hayden's. I slashed through another vamp. Beaumont took a hit in the shoulder, and the last bodyguard knocked Tutti's gun away. A rush of sickly smoke flew into the upir's toothy mouth. Chevalier's pestilence immediately infected the fiend, who collapsed long enough for me to plunge a darksword through his heart.

Hayden and his people were down, but that hardly

pacified things. Everybody spun and squared off, unsure who was friend or foe. Leverett grimaced as he clutched his shoulder.

"It's done," he cried, painfully lifting his wounded hand. "It's done."

I blinked, taking in the room. The whole thing had been a bluff. Beaumont had never meant for me to die, and Tutti, who'd been the one holding the gun on me, was on his side the entire time. She'd been protecting me.

No one in that farmhouse living room moved a muscle. Except for the incessant twitching of that headless vampire.

"Would somebody freaking put that guy out of his misery already?" I snarled.

Chevalier grinned wide and laughed. Tutti smiled, recovered her weapon from the floor, and did the deed. The room was awash in sticky blood thickened with ground ash. None of us were a pretty sight, but it was finally over.

Beaumont hung his head for a moment for his fallen bodyguard. The other, unharmed, helped him up. Leverett managed to notice I was half dead. "Are you gonna make it?" he asked through pain.

"Oh, I'm golden," I said dryly.

He nodded. "Spread the word, Tutti. To all your old Obsidian March connections. Hayden went off script. I'm now the head of any and all upir clans in the state."

"Sure thing, sugar pie." Tutti leaned into me and licked the blood from my neck to my ear, none of it mine. "I would never kill you without having a little fun with you first. Like a cat with a mouse. You know that."

"Tutti..." bristled Beaumont.

She offered him a conciliatory pout and strutted out of the farmhouse with her hands on her hips.

"That was a little ruthless," I muttered, "even for you."

Leverett checked his shoulder in annoyance. "Yes, well, interesting times and all that."

His man helped him outside, and I sagged to the floor.

"Suarez?"

I pulled a bottle of salve from my pack and squeezed it onto my wrist wound. Tears ran down my cheeks as I clutched my arm against the burn. I addressed the bullet wounds next, and a funny thing happened. Besides hurting something fierce, the feeling of toxins running through my system quickly diminished. The magic of the remedy was countering the magic of the rounds.

"There are more of us than them," said Jean-Louis. "I should not have let them get the drop on us."

"The Society is a multi-state outfit with all the best recruits. You see that illusion? We didn't stand a chance. " I grunted as I applied more good poison to fight the bad.

Chevalier watched me, interest piqued, before picking up one of my discarded bullets and examining the mystical script. "You realize, the Russians likely engineered these specifically to take you down."

I grimaced. "All's fair in love and war."

Then I wicked some blood on the floor and found the embedded bullet that had done Hayden in. I dug it from the hardwood and exposed the same Cyrillic symbols on it.

"Beaumont's using enhanced ammunition too. It's good

against animists and vampires."

Chevalier's eyebrows went up. "And who knows what else." He eyed the window. "That man is not your friend, Suarez."

In the yard, Beaumont shook hands with Simon Feigelstock. I gingerly limped to the window. "It was a bluff."

"He sicced the militia on the Obsidian March and started this war. If he did that, what's to say he didn't point them at me as well?"

I met his eyes. Chevalier had openly wondered how the Vanguard was able to come up with enough organized intel to effectively strike his compound. The accusation rendered me speechless, and I watched Beaumont through the window pane in a new light.

He had gone behind my back, twisting my idea of contacting the militia into something callous and tactical. He'd lied to me. With the police too. Each move was an active choice to keep me out of the loop.

The farmhouse shook as another ATF helicopter rumbled by. The gunfight had been an illusion, but the federal raid wasn't. In the end, Hayden had been spot on: where his gun failed, his phone succeeded. I had problems upon problems to deal with, but the low-flying aircraft highlighted the most pressing concern.

Somehow, I had to outmaneuver the feds.

Chapter 53

The Sedan de Ville drove past a field with three landed helicopters. Personnel trucks parked ahead. Federal agents unloaded and began constructing a base camp around the Vanguard's Everglades compound. From our vantage, this was just a remote rural road and a nondescript double-tall chain-link fence. So far, at least, the ATF was respecting the militia's private property.

The road was blocked and our lead car was met by gruff agents ordering us to turn around. No one was allowed in or out. We didn't attempt to convince them otherwise. I was covered in buckets of blood and couldn't even let them see me. We had no choice but to comply. The situation now amounted to the modern equivalent of a medieval siege.

"Nothing can be done in daylight," remarked Chevalier.

Although I wanted to stay close, the Bone Saints were a criminal organization with a severe distrust of law enforcement. They insisted on returning to Miami and reminded me of my nagging wounds. As if I needed a reminder. The hip smarted, though I could get by with a slight limp. The shoulder was numb after my treatment. The wrist injury was the kicker. It wouldn't stop bleeding. While I was lucky no veins were cut, it needed treatment.

So Miami it was.

The gang stopped in Little Haiti and brought me to a houngan, a voodoo priest with healing capabilities. Once I was wrapped up, Chevalier brought me to my condo and came upstairs. Only Kasper was around.

Jean-Louis and I, especially, looked like we'd gone to hell and back. I tossed my scabbed-up shirt in the trash while Kasper marked me up with runes to speed the healing process. Instead of providing immediate relief, his spellcraft assisted the healing process. I'd feel a lot better in a day or so. In the meantime I would grin and bear it.

"The Society again," said Kasper with a dismissive grunt. "They seem to be getting a little handsy lately, don't you think?"

"Clan Beaumont as well," added Chevalier. "Their partnership will only embolden both."

I massaged my forehead. "Where's Milena?" I asked, deflecting the conversation to something more pleasant.

Kasper hiked a shoulder. "I think she wants it to be a surprise, but she's busy packing up her apartment in Midtown."

"Already?"

He grinned. "Women are worse than vampires. Once you invite them in, you'll never get them to leave."

"What if I never want her to leave?"

He chuckled. "Then you hit the jackpot, I guess. Speaking of which, she said she'd be the whole night and, well, I was wondering if I could have the place to myself for a movie night with Mabel?"

"The place is yours. Jean-Louis and I have a date with the Vanguard."

"Actually," interjected the bokor, "I've reexamined my priorities."

I stared back. "You're not going?"

"The Bone Saints no longer have a reason to intervene in the militia's affairs. We didn't exact our revenge, but the Vanguard has plenty to contend with instead."

"No reason to get your hands bloody," I translated.

"I would suggest you follow the same wisdom."

It was probably for the best. I was thankful for their help but glad to see them bow out. Chevalier and I didn't see eye-to-eye when it came to the Vanguard. Bleeding heart that I was, I still believed some of them could be saved.

"I guess it's gonna be another long night for Cisco Suarez then," I announced.

"Well all right, broham!" cried an ecstatic Kasper with a clap on my shoulder to signal he was done with his runes. I shuddered under the pain of him hitting my wound. "I'm looking forward to a long night myself!"

I thanked him for his non-offer of help. The old biker had too much of a hop in his step to notice my sarcasm. He retired to his room to trim his beard or whatever, leaving me and Jean-Louis, beat up and covered in blood, in the middle of my swanky living room.

"So this is where the infamous Cisco Suarez holes up."

I snorted. "As if you didn't already know where I lived, just in case."

The bokor shrugged, as if it didn't matter which version of events was true.

I checked the soles of my boots and sighed. "You don't have a handy spell to get blood out of carpet, do you?"

"Are you certain you should go back out there?" he asked. "You and I are bloody enough."

"I'm not looking for more."

"You would defend killers."

"And what are we?" I stifled a hiss before it let loose. "Listen, I need to do what I need to do. I think you know that. Thanks for bringing me this far. Not only for finding the militia compound and looping me in, but..."—I swallowed—"for what you said about me. For having faith."

His painted set of teeth grinned over the real ones. "Suarez, we live in a city torn apart by violence in the streets and power plays in government halls. The problems I had coming up, my struggles and my responsibilities, are far outside your experiences, yet you and I—we are not so different, I think. In the way we see things. In the way we believe things should be."

I worked my jaw as he spoke, waiting for the ball to drop.

"I do not wish to see you succeed in saving the militia, but I won't stand in your way. Among the police, the federal agents, the vampires, and all the others, it is your judgment I have the most faith in. And who knows?" he added with a chuckle. "Perhaps, in the end, Miami is best served by an outlaw."

I saw him out, wishing I could be as certain as he was. I'd initially screwed over Miami necromancers by releasing the Spaniard. Things had worked out, of course, in the end. And there was that phrase again. *In the end.* To receive a vote of confidence from someone like Chevalier said a lot about doing what it took to make things right. The Bone Saints had set their differences aside. Maybe the Yoruba and Igbo and santeros could too. Maybe we could band together and strengthen the city rather than see it torn apart by fear and distrust.

And maybe I was just making it up as I went.

Alone at last, I pushed into my bedroom for a quick shower and a change of clothes. As I unloaded the contents of my pockets to the nightstand, I was perplexed to find a weathered brass coin with the words "Fort Lauderdale Swap Shop" on it. The other side read, "No Cash Value." I hadn't realized at the time, but the coin Darcy had slid over to me on the sly was an arcade token.

Man, that seemed like ages ago. This was a clue, no doubt, but I was exhausted and couldn't immediately make anything of it. I set the coin down and moved into the bathroom.

The water washed away the blood, but it was a hollow feeling. The last time I was in here, it wasn't just the shower that was steamy.

I occasionally mulled over how much I sacrificed just to do the right thing, but I wouldn't have it any other way. I had a nice life and there was more to look forward to. Milena would soon be a permanent member of this household. Things weren't so bad.

I dried off and wiped the fog from the wall mirror. Red eyes scolded me. I lurched around, banging my knee on the counter and dropping the towel in the process. It fell to my feet leaving me buck naked, fists raised to...

Nothing.

I glanced around the empty bathroom, sure that I'd seen the Spaniard. It was just me and my thoughts, though. At least until I turned back to the mirror.

Red eyes smoldered in the glass, skull cocked, blackened armor fading away to nothing. The conquistador could barely materialize in the mirror, and he appeared weak.

"Tell me that's you and not my guilty conscience seeing things," I groused.

"Don't be a fool," he rasped.

I frowned at his absence in the real world, turned back to the mirror, and leaned in. "Are you dead? Like... a real ghost now?"

"I was always a ghost, and I was always more. Just like the karkan." His old teeth ground together. "Would you mind?"

His head dipped and I followed his eyes. I was stark naked. I scooped up the towel and tied it around my waist. "I thought the dead were beyond prudish concerns."

"I'm not dead yet," he growled. "But I was nearly obliterated. I'm no longer whole."

"How did this happen?"

"You were there, brujo."

"I mean, I always thought of you as invincible, right up there with Connor Hatch."

He peered at me in annoyance. "You're referring to the jinn you defeated and locked away in the Nether."

"I didn't say Connor was unstoppable, just unkillable. It's just that, whatever made you was some seriously old and powerful magic. How'd the karkan do what she did to you?"

He sneered. "Her magic is older and stronger."

The Spanish conquistador was somewhere north of five hundred years old; the karkan claimed to have lived thousands of years. I couldn't even begin to understand that kind of magic.

"Brujo, she cannot be defeated."

I shook out of my reverie. "The necromancer's dead. I released her from the spell and she ran. I'm on something else now."

I apprised him of recent developments. Restating things helped solidify what I needed to do, even if I didn't know how to do it.

"The Vanguard isn't gonna surrender and hand over their guns. For all they know, the ATF could be infiltrated by vampires. Considering Hayden was the one who called them in, that wouldn't be so far off base."

"There is no end for the Vanguard but death," rasped the Spaniard. "They chose their path, even as they didn't know what they took up arms against."

"You sound like Chevalier," I muttered. "The Vanguard wasn't all wrong. They went about things the wrong way, sure, but there's something there worth saving. That's why I need to sneak into a compound surrounded by federal agents, find sympathizers in their leadership, and talk sense into them."

"And then what? Convince them to be jailed for the rest of their lives? Your government will not treat them lightly for the blood they spilled."

"We'll cross that bridge when we get to it."

His visage withered. "It is a bridge you must cross alone. I cannot help you, not unless you require assistance from the gloam I find myself in..."

I considered his offer. Ghosts generally shifted to the Murk after the passing of their corporeal bodies. While only a temporary rest stop, some spirits stick around longer or even cling to the real world.

The Murk is a spiritual counterpart to our world, extremely hostile to the living, that can be accessed through mirrors, literal windows to the dead.

"Maybe you're onto something," I mused, opening the vanity drawer and finding the obsidian mirror resting peacefully.

As night fell, I prepared. Another dose of zombie toxins to get my wounds comfortably numb. I dressed warmly and in all black so as not to draw more suspicion on the Shadow Man. Evan was busy with police matters, and I was so desperate for a number two that I almost called Rita Bell. Almost.

Jensen had taught me the value of keeping my inner circle small. I barely knew Rita. With her Bureau responsibilities, I couldn't say for sure where her priorities lay.

So I got my truck and I got my dog and I hit the road.

Chapter 54

The Everglades are a different beast at night.

The weather cools and the humidity sticks to everything like a wet blanket. A kind of darkness rarely seen in the city settles over the prairies and swamps, bringing the desolation alive as pairs of reflective eyes shine in the moonlight. The bugs, too, come out to play, dancing and singing and sputtering across every square foot of muggy air. Small mammals huddle together for safety as cold-blooded predators slither through their natural habitat.

A chill wind blew tonight, away from the heat of the city fires, away from the warmth of civilization. The breeze was a foreign intruder, unseen and unwelcome, penetrating every inch of the Glades as if a natural part of the terrain. I had the impression it might never leave.

The dirt road leading to the paramilitary compound was a no-go. The ATF's quick response team had multiplied to over a hundred agents, each armed with a rifle and wearing tactical armor. A command tent set up behind a line of armored SWAT-style vans housed team leaders on computers and radios. Up the road, local police manned a barricade, themselves acting only as a buffer to redirect curious onlookers, many of whom piled behind the obstruction or watched from parked cars.

In a matter of hours, this had become a full-blown circus.

I parked off the main road, far ahead of the gawkers, and hoofed it close to a mile with a backpack. Scout's ears perked as he eagerly cut through the thick grass. This was a blast for him, out in the wild at night. He resembled a true wolf, not just in size but in unabated hunger for the hunt.

I ducked as a drone whirred outside the main gate. Three ATF agents took aim and fired, knocking it from the sky. It crashed to the ground without fanfare and, more notably, without an explosion. Those might have been the first gunshots of the night, but so far the Vanguard wasn't instigating a fight. They were merely attempting to get overwatch of the unfolding situation.

I skirted far around the main hive of activity, through denser tree coverage and murky sloughs. The compound was sizable but not prohibitively so. Walking the fenced perimeter would be a simple affair if not for the embedded ATF guards.

Those watchful eyes would make it difficult to sneak in. I perched behind a thick tree and observed from a distance, getting a feel for any patrols or openings in the line of security. It would be a tough go.

The darkness and tree coverage were welcome, but the compound was circled by a high-security fence lined with razor wire. The foliage ran up to and, in some cases, past the fence line, which had helped hide the location from satellite view. I was betting, from the air, the compound didn't look as big as it was, nor nearly as secure.

The trained federal agents surrounding the property mostly faced the compound instead of back at me, but it would only take a stray glance to be exposed. Once I got past them to the fence, every single one would have eyes on me. And even if I somehow did get by the ATF unnoticed, there was the militia to contend with. The Vanguard was nowhere in sight, but you could bet they had a series of snipers watching the perimeter. Good intentions be damned, they wouldn't take kindly to an animist breach.

The worst part of the scenario was the possibility of my presence igniting widespread violence. Aside from an unlucky drone, both sides were displaying trigger discipline. If I made it inside the gate and the Vanguard opened fire, the ATF would almost assuredly respond in kind, sparking a shootout and defeating the whole purpose of my intrusion.

Which led to the crux of my problem: How could a practitioner of magic convince witch hunters to douse their torches?

A twig cracked behind me. I sunk into shadow as Rita Bell hiked through the trees and laid eyes on my dog.

"Cisco?" she called out quietly.

I sighed and materialized. Even adjusted to the darkness, it took Rita's eyes a moment to place me.

"How did I know you'd be here?" she asked with derision.

"I don't know. How'd you find me?"

"I saw your truck make a U-turn at the checkpoint. I followed and found it parked off the street."

"How'd you know it was my truck?"

"I didn't, but when I checked the bed I found a dog tag with Quentin Capshaw's phone number on it."

I sighed. "You keep Quentin's number memorized?"

"When you spend hours going over phone records, things get burned into your brain."

"Freaking FBI," I harrumphed.

Rita didn't rest on the achievement. "You knew about the militia siege and didn't call me."

I hiked a neutral shoulder. "You didn't call me either."

Our frowns extended into drawn-out silence. Neither of us trusted the other.

"Is the FBI running this thing?" I asked.

"No, it's the ATF's show. They gave our team a courtesy call." Her hands went to her hips. "You're just going to rush right in, aren't you?"

"I'm trying to save lives, Rita, if they're worth saving. This thing looks like Waco all over again."

"The Branch Davidians set their compound on fire, Cisco. They were end-of-days believers who created their own apocalypse. I don't get the same vibe from the Vanguard."

"Those guys hadn't gone on public murder sprees either. There's no way the ATF sits on this for long. I give it twenty-four hours before guns are blazing."

"You don't know that. Even after the Waco shootout,

the following siege lasted close to two months. Policies have changed since then to be even more conservative. Our guidance is no dynamic entry until all other options are exhausted."

My dismissive smirk showed her the stock I put in federal guidelines. Maybe it meant I had more time to work, but it didn't stop the fact that I had to work. "Rita, I'm going in there, one way or another."

We stared at each other hard, but not for long. The special agent huffed and set a determined look on her face. "What do you need from me?"

I arched an eyebrow, finding her more curious every time we met. "I don't suppose you can clear a section of the perimeter guard?"

She chuckled. "At this point, nothing can pull the ATF off this."

"Then all you can do is stay out of the way."

It was a little blunt, maybe, but it was the straight truth. Rita was one of the feds, at the moment the only faction less welcome within the compound than I was. Besides, playing fast and loose would likely result in her losing her job, if not her life. I couldn't ask that of her.

"So that's it then?" she asked defensively.

"That's it, Rita. You don't need any part in this."

"Fine. Do your thing. I'll keep watch." She paced to her own tree and leaned against it with crossed arms.

"Rita..."

"It's Special Agent Bell, Cisco, and I'm going to stand watch so you aren't ambushed. Now if you're going to do something, you should get to it."

I set my eyes on the fence line and grumbled. She was really gonna sit there and watch, no doubt to witness exactly what I was capable of. The Shadow Man, under a spotlight. If I really needed to, I could shake her. I could run. Then again, she could kick up a fuss and blow my operation.

Putting her to sleep was a better option. It would certainly solve the here and now: blow some powder into her face, sing her a lullaby, and then focus on the mission. Unfortunately, doing so might make a dangerous enemy of her once she woke up. Rita had seen and withheld too much already. I couldn't afford to be on her bad side.

Besides, as I mentioned, she'd already seen my magic. She knew what I was. It was time to drop the act.

I pulled the obsidian mirror from the bag and set it on the ground. Scout trotted over as the image of a skull faded in behind the reflective surface.

"You are sure about this, brujo?" asked the withered ghost.

"It's the best idea I can come up with."

"That's not saying much."

"What? I'm a font of good ideas."

"Without a physical presence, I cannot pull your body in and out of the Murk at will. If it becomes too much for you, I can do nothing."

I'd traveled through the Murk before, though it was more apt to say I was dragged by the Spaniard, kicking and screaming. It wasn't an experience I wanted to relive.

"My mind will be elsewhere," I assured. "I got the idea

from my time as a zombie hit man." I turned to Rita. "Uh, ignore that." I leaned close to the mirror and lowered my voice. "My body was used for countless atrocities, but my spirit was in Coaybay, awaiting resurrection."

"If you say so. This would be easier during twilight."

"No can do. We need the darkness."

He tightened his jaw. "Then ready the spell."

I set the mirror into a ditch running against the tree's thick root. The low placement was vital to keep the light from distant eyes. I arranged multicolored birthday candles around the mirror and struck them with a match. Rita watched on as I sliced my forearm and squeezed blood onto the glassy surface at the center of the ritual.

The black mirror twitched with contact, which I'd never seen happen before. Then again, this wasn't your garden-variety ritual we were attempting. As I funneled the Intrinsics from my blood to the Murk, the Spaniard incanted from the mirror world, working the spell from the opposite side.

"When I get in there," I reminded, "be gentle. It'll just be my body. Be careful not to sever my connection to the thrall. Otherwise I might really be stranded."

In truth, if my connection was violently severed, I wasn't sure what would happen. The wraith, always one for exacting spellwork, nodded.

"Okay, boy," I said, beckoning Scout closer to the mirror. "It's your turn."

"Are you... getting a view inside the compound?" asked Rita.

I snickered. "Something like that."

I waited as the Spaniard finished his magic with one palm on the mirror and the other on the dog's head. I closed my eyes, faded to shadow, and fell forward. The last thing I heard with my own ears was Rita Bell's astonished gasp.

Chapter 55

I opened my eyes, only they weren't truly mine. My head canted low to the ground, tongue lolling from my elongated snout. Beneath me, the candles burned around the mirror. A glimpse of the Spaniard lugging my old body faded and disappeared.

"What the—?" Rita lurched forward in shock.

My shaggy head fixed on her. She blinked cautiously and took a breath, eyes settling on me. My ears perked.

"Cisco?"

I barked.

Driving thralls was a part of my standard toolbox. It's a handy way to get a close look while maintaining a safe distance, not dissimilar to the drones the militia utilized. But a drone wasn't good enough tonight. Sneaking a dog into their compound wouldn't convince the Vanguard to join my side.

Tonight, I had to actually get in there myself. A human. Someone who could reason with them.

And so I had to settle on the old art of spirit transference. Separating my spirit from my body, an achievement possible only due to the wraith's mastery of the fine line between the physical world and the Murk.

But getting my spirit inside the compound by hitching a shadowy ride on Scout was only half the battle. I couldn't rematerialize without a body, and that body couldn't hitch along. The shadows didn't work like that.

Technically, the darkness under a moving object isn't one shadow, but a million of them, each layering atop the next. If I really push it, I can slide maybe fifteen feet max. It's why I can't hitch a shadowy ride under a moving car. Manifesto had gotten away from me once that way.

So, instead, my body was taking a detour through the Murk, carried in the arms of an almost dead but undying skeleton, while my spirit avoided the maddening environment by remaining in the here and now.

"This... can't be happening," swore Rita with only partial conviction.

I sniffed her butt.

"We're trained to shoot dogs if we need to," warned the FBI agent.

I retreated with a high-pitched whine. This human was no fun. I loped ahead to the compound.

This experiment was new to me. I trotted, dexterous in form but clumsy in experience. Walking on four legs would take some getting used to. I focused on putting one paw ahead of the other and nearly tripped up. After a few stops and stutters, I found I operated more effectively when I didn't actively think about what I was doing, when I moved by instinct. It was sort of like riding a horse. I had the reins and picked the direction, but I let it worry about the pot holes.

Spellcraft wasn't available to me in this form, yet things were somehow... enhanced. I'd driven dogs before, and cats, and birds, and just about anything under the sun including Florida alligators. I recognized the various differences in each animal's senses. I knew their strengths and limitations.

Scout? He was different. The usual flood of smells came with the package, of course, but his eyesight was superb, almost like my magically buffed shadow sight. And that was nothing compared to what I could smell. A mental map of my immediate surroundings populated with a flurry of sights and sounds. Which illuminated my first obstacle.

ATF agents dotted the perimeter, with a pair taking a break while sharing a puff of stinky tobacco. Blending into the shadows wasn't an option, not magically anyway, and I was a sizable dog. A working dog at that. If the feds saw what looked like a giant German shepherd, they would assume I belonged to the Vanguard and was a threat. I'd be captured or put down.

Luckily the brush was thick and I was fast.

I waited for my opening and barreled between cover, jumping onto a slanted tree and running up its steepening length until it was nearly vertical. I hopped to a branch, and then another that twisted into this one, and walked right over the razor wire.

Getting down the second tree was a harder proposition,

and I suddenly sympathized with climbing cats biting off more than they could chew. But you don't become a zombie dog without being able to take a few licks, so I lowered my forelegs and unceremoniously plopped to the grass.

The noise alerted an agent. I stayed low while a flashlight scanned the area. Eventually it clicked off. This was the Everglades, after all, and it was suspicious if you *didn't* hear occasional scurries in the brush.

Finally, I turned my head to the inner buildings. There were three of them, maybe, though a couple had several perpendicular wings, stout and tall like castle walls. High windows opened to darkened rooms, though no militia members were stupid enough to post right inside them and make themselves visible. If they were manned by snipers, they'd be deeper inside.

The strategy was safer but limited the angles of their sight lines. As the fence line was well spaced from the windows, the snipers had eyes on the ATF, but their awareness of the ground closer to the walls was limited.

The exterior wall lit the yard unevenly. The building was aging and some of the lights were out or had ineffective bulbs. Yet another point in my favor.

The scent of a kennel carried on the cool breeze. If I could smell other dogs, they'd be able to smell me soon enough, at least if the wind changed. The presence of dogs within the gates was surprising since I had yet to see any. I had to be careful around them. Animals were more likely than humans to recognize my charade.

Holy shit a squirrel! I darted out from cover and tried to run the little bugger down, but he hopped onto a tree and scrambled up the bark. I skidded in the yard, wresting control of my animal instincts.

Damn, I had to be more careful. I picked out the darkest path to the wall and abutted against it where I was least likely to be seen by anyone inside. At this point the agents might notice me, but they'd just see a dog in the yard for a few seconds until I disappeared. I trotted along the wall and turned under an arch leading to a gravel-trodden vehicle depot.

Jeeps and trucks like the ones that had raided the Bone Saints were lined up facing a dirt road in the rear. Two men futzed under the hood of a car, but the rest of the vehicles looked in traveling shape. Excluding the pit bull lying on her tummy at their feet, the yard was otherwise empty. My first thought was to approach the trucks and use a door mirror to escape the Murk, but the dog and the swirling courtyard winds were problems. I gave them a wide birth, scanned the interior walls, found an open door, and snuck inside.

The stagnant scent of dozens of humans filled my nose. The smells lingered in the poorly ventilated interior, recent intermingling with old. It was impossible to get an idea of how many militiamen were close. Suffice to say this wing of the compound was most definitely occupied.

I loped down the hall, being as unassuming as a hundred-pound wolf-dog can be. As two men hefted a heavy crate from one room to another, I ducked behind a bookcase loaded with tools.

"It's about time they're givin' us the heavy stuff," said a scrawny, scruffy man.

"Don't get your hopes up," tempered the other, a heavier dude with a blotchy tan. "This is a last-case scenario."

"Should be the first case, you ask me. This is redline territory. Anyone stupid enough to step foot on our private property deserves ten of these bullets."

They dropped the box in a far room and returned for another.

"It's a good thing you're not in charge then," said the more even-tempered of the two. "Landon doesn't want more blood on our hands."

The scrawny one snorted. "Too late for that, partner. Landon thinks he can talk his way out of anything. That might be the case for a little public malfeasance, but look outside. You think talkin's gonna do squat now?"

His cohort grimaced. "It might've. If Victor's crew hadn't shot up half of Miami." They disappeared with the second box and took their time inside. It sounded like they were opening the crates.

The mention of Landon was interesting. He was the one who'd identified himself in their video. I remember having the impression that he was calm and intelligent. If he was their leader, and he preferred negotiation over guns, then he was my earpiece. If only I knew where—"

"Hey," called the scrawny man, now in the hallway and approaching. "I thought you said all the dogs were locked up."

"All but Betsy," came a distant voice.

I froze, wondering how best to act like a dog. I sat at attention on my hind legs.

Dirty teeth sneered. "You ain't supposed to be inside, boy. Now git."

I craned my head around him. I didn't wanna go back the way I'd come. That just led to the yard, to Betsy and the other dogs. I needed to go deeper inside, find a bathroom with a vanity mirror or something.

Before I could act, the man's boot shot up and grazed my snout. I hopped backward and the man raised a threatening fist.

"Are you deaf, boy? I said git!"

My eyes narrowed and my lips curled up. This guy was a peach, wasn't he? Some instinct welled inside, urging me to teach him a lesson. Was that my sense of justice or something else... a presence? Some leftovers of the dog?

But this was the last thing I had time for.

Since I was keeping my distance, the man wound up his leg for another kick. He swept forward. I sidestepped and his overcommitted boot drew him off-balance. I pounced, my weight nearly equal to his, crashing into him, simultaneously using him as a launchpad and knocking him on his ass. He cursed and tumbled as I charged down the hallway, screams echoing after me.

I sprinted without thought, bounding down the next major corridor. I passed two more militia members in various rooms, including what I assumed by the smell was a locked bathroom. I had to give this one a pass.

I barreled through the building's main entryway at the

front. Voices echoed from another room, and I darted up a staircase to a hopefully less-populated second floor. Stuffing myself into an alcove, I waited in silence. I never heard more than distant grumbling downstairs. I was safe.

Stepping softly through the building, I tried to get a sense of the place. People spoke beyond a closed door. With my snout at the base of the door, I smelled a few men, tobacco, and gun powder. My ears perked at mention of their leader.

"Landon's not dicking around right now. He's in the tower with overwatch. He'll tell us if it needs to be done."

Dissenting opinion over how to react to the ATF followed, which seemed to be a common theme in these walls. Not surprising given the circumstances. Things sounded touch and go, but there was enough repeated respect and support for Landon that I knew I had to find him.

I moved to an exterior window at the end of the hall overlooking the compound's front yard. I hurried around a bend in the hallway and found another window cracked halfway open. The remaining wing of this building cut through the center of the property. Beyond, the next building over was long and wide, its central feature a large foyer with a spindly tower jutting above. It wasn't all that high or all that grand, just a third-story addition, but was the highest point in the compound.

If Landon was in the tower with overwatch, that was where I'd find him.

A door popped open and I spun around. People were

coming. I put my paws on the overhanging sill, shoved the window up with my nose, and hopped outside onto the first-story roof. I moved along the wall until I hit the final wing, just the low roof with no second floor. It was my private walkway, away from prying eyes, straight to the tower.

As I trotted along, a group of militiamen in the inner yard passed out car assignments. I reached the end of the building without problem and received another stroke of good luck. A huge pile of firewood stacked against the wall assisted my descent to the ground. I darted across the yard and entered the central building with the tower.

Whereas the first structure was larger with more natural living spaces, this one seemed built specifically to congregate large groups. I entered through the back of a large commercial kitchen that fed into a mess hall, surprised by the lack of militia members. But then it was hardly chow time. A main corridor led toward the central tower, but I scanned the edges of the cafeteria to be thorough. My nose found the large bathroom in the corner.

I shoved the door open, the unmistakable scent of fresh blood overpowering my senses. Someone had been hurt here. I turned the corner of what opened into a large military-style bathroom with urinals on one wall and stalls on another. Crimson pooled over small square tiles. One of the stall doors was sideways on the floor, and a pair of boots protruded, unmoving, from within.

I followed my nose to the other wing where the sinks, and hopefully mirrors, were. A member of the Vanguard crumpled to the ground right in front of me, neck twisted backward in an eerie death gaze. My head spun to the karkan.

She stepped up onto a sink and hopped over a man swinging a machete. Bare feet lightly rapped the tile as a chain snaked around the man's neck. She pulled it taut and hefted him over her back as his breath cut out. He reversed the blade in his hand and stabbed backward, but she caught it and broke his wrist for his trouble. It clattered to the floor as he gagged, trachea crushed. The assassin dropped the last body to the floor, amid several others, and froze as she turned to me.

She licked her lips. "Now this is interesting," she purred.

I wanted to scream but it just came out as a bark.

The charms over her face clinked aside, revealing her empty eye cavity. "No, you won't trick me this time. You're the same hound, but not the same, are you?"

My head snapped to the line of mirrors above the wall of sinks. She twitched as she noticed my gaze.

"So the necromancer crosses my path once again. And what do you have to say about it?" She cocked her head and coyly waited for an answer that wasn't coming. "Worry not then. I'm doing what needs be done."

I couldn't stop her, not like this.

"These men, I've heard their manifesto. They wish to kill the likes of us, to rid the world of magic." She cackled at the absurdity. "I may not have long for this world, but I intend to show them, with my final moments, what magic can truly do."

There was no guarantee the spell would work quickly

enough to catch her, but I had to try. I hopped toward the first mirror.

"No!" she snarled. Her chain lashed out and split the glass to shards. She raked the other mirrors in succession and, when that was done, the chain came for me.

I leapt over it and closed the distance. Jaws clamped down on cloth that ripped away. A solid foot caught my side, propelling me into the wall. I flipped to my feet with a snarl, but the karkan had turned and run. I raced after her and crashed into the door just as she pulled it shut.

Damn, I was a fucking dog. I couldn't just grab the handle and pull it open. Several attempts to bite it failed, as I needed to lean my weight into the door, which held it closed.

I turned tail and checked the shattered pieces of mirror. Some of the shards were large enough, but they were covered in blood. A certain level of "purity" was required for the delicate spellwork, and I moved from shard to shard, hoping to see the Spaniard's face materialize. After a minute of disappointment, I hurried back to the door.

I couldn't properly get hold of it. My human brain couldn't overcome millennia of evolution. Cisco Suarez, thwarted by the lack of an opposable thumb.

I hurried back to the machete, took the handle into my jaws, and jostled it into a secure bite. Back at the door, I set my paws on the wall, slipped the knife into the handle, and pulled. It was about as inefficient a method of opening a door as I could think of, but strength wasn't my issue. I had strength in spades.

The door pulled open. I yanked hard and slipped through. The mess hall was still empty, but gunshots rang out down the main corridor.

I bolted toward the action, passing a downed militiaman with a rifle. Holes opened up the wall above my head. I darted forward. Men in the adjoining room shouted cries for help. Someone got to an alarm, and speakers blared.

The karkan was cleaning house.

My instinct was to charge in and attack, but as a dog that was pointless. Instead I hit the stairwell. I could no longer save everybody. If I could manage to get to Landon, to convince the Vanguard of the real danger, then just maybe I could save enough of them.

The steps led to a third-floor tower behind double doors. They were shut tight and I had no chance of opening them. I retreated to the second floor and checked the open rooms. Militia members checked weapons and charged past me. Their property was breached, the alarm was sounded, and they were going to war.

"They're coming," warned a woman exiting a room.

"But the TV," said another in tow. "The ATF hasn't moved."

"You think that's really live? That's what they want you to think."

They rushed to the stairway and I moved into the emptied room. There was a bed, a chair, and a flat screen showing live helicopter coverage of the ATF siege.

The guy was right—the ATF hadn't breached the compound yet. That said, the alarm and gunfire spurred them into action. Bradley infantry vehicles mobilized at the main gate. Troops gathered into tactical squads.

I growled, literally. After all my careful advances, I couldn't have foreseen the karkan crashing the party. I grabbed the power cable in my teeth and yanked it from the wall. The screen went black. I pawed toward my smooth reflection in the glass, and a pair of glowing red eyes greeted me.

The spell took only a moment. I felt a dissonance of place and the harsh bite of the Murk against my raw flesh. My body careened upward as I ascended from the dog and tumbled out of the TV and onto the carpet.

Chapter 56

"Ugh," I groaned, head reeling. "It's about time."

I turned to the screen and jumped at the sight of the skull, eyes nearly extinguished. The mouth opened to speak, but a crack fractured the screen from top to bottom, bisecting the Spaniard and causing him to immediately vanish.

That didn't look good. I wasn't sure what was going on with the wraith, but I hardly had the time to investigate. I was serious before about him being a tough son of a bitch. If he had survived centuries in the powder horn, he would get through this, in one form or another.

"Guess it's just you and me, boy."

Scout's tail pounded the carpet.

I didn't have a weapon and the men didn't leave any behind. I also wasn't a dog anymore. Dressed in a black hoodie while the compound was under threat of attack made me a suspicious figure, but I didn't look anything like a federal agent. I would just need to take my chances in the hallway.

I made for the stairs with a measured march, recoiling from the railing as gunshots peppered the ceiling. Several men charged by a level down, seemingly having the karkan on the run from focused fire. I turned upstairs and pushed the tower door.

It didn't budge.

I kicked at the heavily reinforced obstacle to little effect. It was a take-your-stand kind of door. I looked around for a gun, and then just knocked. "Open up!"

"Who is it?" returned a voice.

"Your best chance at coming out of this alive. I need you to open the door before this gets worse." I tested the edges to get a feel for where the lock was. I guessed heavy-duty latches in the floor and top of the frame.

"You're trespassing," said a man. "Leave or we'll shoot."

"Assholes! I'm here to save you."

The lights suddenly cut out. Not just here, but all over the property. The men inside cursed. "I told you! They're on the move!"

Things were quickly spiraling out of control, though in this case the darkness turned out to be a benefit. "Wait here, Scout." I dissolved into shadow and slipped through the ample seam under the door. I solidified into a room with glass walls that highlighted the beauty of the Everglades wilderness. Three people turned guns on me.

"Wait," I said, hands raised. "I'm unarmed."

"Who the fuck are you?" asked a slightly familiar man with long hair.

"I'm not a fed," I answered. "And I'm not that thing downstairs killing everybody."

They exchanged concerned glances. One lowered his pistol to clutch a wound in his side. "You know what it is?" he asked.

"It's a monster."

Behind them, a control panel of blackened TVs was quiet. Stacked crates were packed with hay that hid their contents. The glass walls of the tower opened to a three-hundred-and-sixty-degree watchtower-style balcony. With the power out, the yard was a mass of shadow beneath a painted sky framed by uneven trees.

I checked the door locks. Reinforced steel posts. Good thing I didn't waste time trying to bash my way in.

The three militia members were a ragtag group. The wounded man was the one I'd seen on video. His stark white hair made him easy to identify. I had no doubt he was Landon, the one I'd come to appeal to.

The man with the long black hair was openly hostile, which may have explained why I swore I'd seen him before too. I just couldn't place him. The third was a burly woman, no doubt ex-military.

"Are you fighting it?" asked Landon. It was a good sign that his weapon wasn't trained on me, but he was the only one.

"I don't know how effective fighting is, but I'm here to try."

Long Hair sneered, rifle trembling ever so slightly. "And what does that make you?"

I swallowed. There was no way to explain shifting through the door without coming right out with it. "It was magic. But I'm on your side."

His rifle steadied. "You're a parahuman," he spat.

"I'm a human, and I'm your only chance."

Landon set a hand on the man's shoulder amid a staccato of distant reports. "I think we need to hear him out, Frank."

"No!" he snapped, shrugging him away. "This is what Victor warned us about, Landon. Getting in bed with the Other Kind."

"Victor," I grumbled. "Victor sold you out. He gave up your location to a pack of vampires who called in the ATF."

Both their faces went hard. "Impossible," asserted Frank. "Victor wouldn't do that. He..."

"He did it," I swore. "And they tore him up as a reward. If you want to take on an enemy—a *real* enemy—I can tell you all about the Obsidian March. I've fought them. I've *been* fighting them."

Frank's face fell. "My brother's dead?"

I blinked. As his face formed a scowl, I recognized, too late, the family resemblance. That's why Frank looked slightly familiar.

I had said too much.

"No," he growled. Frank took a step forward and shook the gun in my face. "How do we know you didn't kill him? You're the one who led the ATF here!"

I stepped back, hands still up. The gunfire downstairs subsided, but repeated bangs spread to other areas of the compound. Muzzle flashes lit the yard outside the tower.

"Frank," warned Landon coolly, "you're not in command here."

"And what about Victor, huh? What happened to *his* command? He was the one who led us against the Haitians and the witches. Where were *you* during those raids?"

The woman swallowed uncomfortably as the men argued. I couldn't get a good read on her. She had a good poker face. I could tell she was well trained though. Her rifle didn't stray from me, but she kept her distance. Unlike Frank's, her aim wasn't wavering.

The lights came on. Not as fully as before. They were clearly part of a backup system, but they got the job done. The Vanguard had gotten their generators started. Amid the dim lighting, the security feeds blinked on. Although the compound exterior was still dark, night-vision cameras illuminated Bradley infantry vehicles advancing. Several shootouts with ATF positions erupted.

The feeds stalled the argument as everyone watched in horror.

"Guys," I urged with the utmost severity in my voice, "you can't fight them. There's an unstoppable monster in the building, and you're surrounded by overwhelming force."

"Says you," muttered Frank.

I sighed. "Don't do it. Don't kill yourselves. There's no need to die."

"We don't plan on it," said the woman.

I dropped my hands to my side in exasperation. "What about your mission? If you die in a federal raid, how does that get the word out? This is what the Obsidian March wants. They want you to go down against your own kind, limiting their exposure to the outside world."

Landon grimaced. "He has a point."

"He's a witch, Landon!" yelled Frank. "*He's one of them!*"

"Don't be an idiot," I snapped. "I've killed more vampires than you have members in your militia. I've saved countless kids from their clutches. And I'll keep doing it." I stepped forward lightly. "I'll keep fighting them. And I'll work with you guys, because I *am* one of you guys. I'm a man who wants to protect the city from the monsters and the things that would replace us."

Even Frank didn't have a gruff retort to that. The trio of militia leadership mulled over my words with hard faces. Landon winced as he gripped his side. His face softened, and he holstered his pistol.

"We need to think about the Vanguard, Frank," he decided. "Not you, or me, or Victor. We need to think about the mission." He bit down. "And the people who have dedicated themselves to it. Put down your guns."

The woman blinked at Frank and hesitantly lowered her rifle. Frank wasn't so amicable.

"What do you suggest we do?" Landon asked me.

I worked my jaw. It wouldn't go over well, but there was no more time to waste. "I'm sorry, Landon. I tried to get to you before this happened. I tried to stop this, but there's nothing else to do now. You need to turn yourselves in."

"What?" snarled Frank. "THAT'S your big plan?"

My cheek twitched. "The karkan won't directly take on

coordinated fire. If you enter the ATF's custody, there'll be too many agents for her to fight."

"If we surrender to the ATF," he countered, "we'll need to throw down our weapons. We'll be sitting ducks."

"You either have two enemies or none," I urged. "Think about it. You have the power to tell your people whether or not to die."

"They'll do it!" insisted Frank.

"But should they have to?" cut in Landon. "What if we went peacefully?"

"You want us to go to prison?" asked the woman, aghast.

"We have the legal system," hedged Landon. "We put down our weapons, we call for surrender, and the government has nothing to hold us on." The leader of the Vanguard unstrapped his pistol and symbolically placed it on the table. "Now who's with me?"

Scout released a series of frantic barks. "Time's up," I warned. "She's here." We all turned to the door. I closed my eyes.

I growl as the karkan licks her lips, a casual stroll up every step. Her robes are red with blood and she holds a knife in each hand. Chains drag weakly up the stairs behind her.

I lower my head and bare my teeth. The karkan lunges and—

Frank's rifle rapped my head. "No spells from you, witch!" He forced me to my knees with the gun to my head. Scout's yelp was followed by several crashes.

"Frank," snapped Landon. "This isn't the way."

The men stared hard at each other.

The leader lowered his voice. "I said back off."

Frank's jaw tightened. He pulled the barrel of the rifle away and stepped back.

Landon took a long breath, looked both of his people in the eyes, and nodded to himself. Then he approached the PA system on the table.

"Don't do it," urged Frank, crestfallen. "What about our oath? The Vanguard will never back down."

Landon smiled weakly. "I remember our words, brother. But we aren't surrendering to the Other Kind. We're bringing our fight to a new stage. Our audience will be the federal government. Maybe it's okay to lose a battle if it means winning the war." He picked up the microphone and inhaled.

Gunshots raked his side. Landon cried out and went down. The muzzle of Frank's rifle smoked and a familiar sneer crossed his face. "I'm not losing this battle," he swore. He turned to the woman. "What say you?"

She swallowed again. "I'm good, sir." Her rifle trained back on me.

I stood in place, nearly shaking in rage at the sheer stupidity I'd just witnessed. Landon gasped on the floor as his two lieutenants callously ignored him.

Frank picked the microphone up from the floor, put it to his lips, and clicked it on. "Attention brave patriots of the Vanguard. This is the moment we've been training for. The feds are on the vampire payroll. Witches have breached the compound. Kill them. Kill them all. Fight to the last man, and may God bless the Vanguard."

Chapter 57

My teeth grated so violently the noise filled my head. This. Fucking. Idiot. Any hope of a peaceful resolution to this raid had just been flushed down the toilet.

"Now," said Frank decisively, "I'm going to do what Landon should've done the second you magicked your way in here." He raised his rifle.

The edges of my lips curled and I balled a fist at my side. "Try it."

The double doors crashed open. The reinforced locks split the thick door post apart. The karkan's dry lips cracked into a wide smile.

I dove into shadow as a pair of rifles went off. The karkan rolled forward under their fire, chains whipping out and knocking both guns loose. Frank's weapon was on a strap around his shoulder. As he tried to recover it, the revenant's boot hit him square in the gut and upturned him through a row of monitors.

The woman's gun bounced to the far window. She drew

a combat knife and slashed. The heavy chain came back and tried to take her head off, but she ducked and thrust the weapon forward. The karkan sidestepped and caught her arm with her side, jerking up at the elbow. The woman cried out as ligaments tore. The karkan planted a blade into her neck, cutting her cries short.

I appeared across the room as she spun around. A blast of shadow knocked her off her feet and propelled her into the window. It spiderwebbed where she bounced. She landed below in a three-point stance.

"You are not my enemy, shadow witch, and I am not yours."

"You're killing people."

"As are they. Why do you make the fight yours?"

"Because I can."

Spears jutted from the wall and floor, crisscrossing on her position, but the karkan dove forward. A pair of chains swept at me, one high and one low. I faded through the space between them, dashed straight for the monster, and landed a haymaker across her jaw. Metal charms ripped away from her scarred face and she hit the floor.

A chain slithered close, but a burst of violet from my hand sliced it away. I reversed my attack, but the karkan's other chain yanked her away like a tentacle. My darksword dug into the floor, barely missing her.

"You would do well with Twelvetide," she needled. "What if I were to offer you a place?"

I pointed the blade her way.

My body dispersed as automatic fire split the air. The

karkan's snapped chain deflected a barrage as she slipped to safety.

"You see that?" she cried. "They would just as easily kill you, even while you fight for them. You'll die here."

Frank reloaded. Black wings extended behind my back as the glare from my sword reflected in her eyes. "You first."

I charged, hopping the chain that came for my feet. Instead of slicing down at it, I rolled forward and grazed her shoulder. The karkan screamed as the Intrinsics ripped a hole in her ancient flesh.

I dove into the shadow once more, but even with magic it was difficult to keep up with her. I appeared and she bounced away, except this time, she landed with Frank at her back, and he timed his fire just right.

The karkan shook violently as bullets ripped into her back. One hit the base of her skull and she was rocked forward. My sword flared as I pounced with an overhead strike.

A chain snagged my ankle. The darksword came down, cutting into the monster's back, but it extinguished as I drove it in, and the only thing that landed hard was my fist. The chain lurched me aside, and I felt the Intrinsics drain away.

Frank turned his rifle and fired.

Rounds pelted my side as I tumbled behind the table. Bullets whizzed past and I landed hard, pulling at the cold iron pinning me to this world. Frank skirted the table as he pushed another magazine into his gun. "There," he said, "you're not so slippery." He readied his aim.

A small blade hurtled through the air and plunged into his chest. Frank gasped emptily as an arterial spray violently erupted outward. He stared in shock as his limbs turned to noodles. Frank was dead before he hit the floor.

The karkan hopped to her feet, barely worse for wear. "It is as I said, shadow witch." She recovered her knife from the dead man. The chain released my ankle and she darted from the room.

I jumped up, sword flaring from my fist again, and set my boot to chase, but Landon coughed.

"Wait."

I watched helplessly as the karkan descended the steps before turning to kneel at the man's side. "Landon?" I pulled his shirt up to profuse bleeding. "You shouldn't talk."

"Can they... Can we be saved?" he asked coarsely.

I gritted my teeth. "I don't know."

He scoffed. "We really are our worst enemy, aren't we?" His eyes went leaden.

I pulled away from him. On the monitors that still worked, black-clad federal agents gained ground on the dwindling militia forces. Infantry vehicles were posted at each doorway, and tactical troops rushed forward with crowd-control rifles.

I stepped outside the tower as scattered paramilitary forces regrouped in the mess hall. Scout, just emerging from a hole in the wall, locked eyes with me. "Retreat," I commanded, and he bolted.

I waited as a ragtag crew passed before starting down the steps. A large battering ram attached to a vehicle bashed through the barricaded front door and I skidded to a stop. Canisters of tear gas followed. I rushed back to the second floor and checked the windows. The front yard was a war zone.

I went down. With gunfire in the mess hall, I turned the opposite direction, finding a small wing leading to the back of the compound. Halfway down the dark hall, a door bashed open. A militiaman fired at breaching agents but was quickly cut down.

I spun back to the main room. An ATF agent with a gas mask rounded the corner in my path. I broke into a sprint. He fired. I ducked down, scooped up a dead militiaman's rifle, and found shelter in shadow. When I emerged several feet away, I pulled the trigger and blasted a double-paned window apart. The agent reacquired my position and opened fire again as I dissolved outside.

The compound exterior was dark while on backup power, which worked in my favor. I stayed low and hustled along the wall, dropping down as Vanguard soldiers rushed by carrying one of their wounded.

I rushed away from them and two ATF agents skirted the building in pursuit. A wave of my hand and the black sent them tumbling. I raced past.

Desperately I scurried through the yard as a hundred tiny shootouts erupted all over the property. I avoided the muzzle flashes, ducked into darkness, and winced each time another person fell to oncoming fire.

I wasn't exactly unseen, but it was quick work to distract any opposition long enough to get away. I didn't stop moving and made for a portion of fence a Bradley had driven through. Once out, I escaped to the wilderness.

Helicopters kept their distance from the battle, but their spotlights swept overhead. I trudged through thick grass as what seemed like a hundred triggers pierced the night, pressing on until the drum beat faded, in volume but not frequency, until I finally slipped into my truck some ways off the main road.

I panted hard and stared at myself in the rearview mirror. Victor and his Obsidian March plotters may be dead now, but in the end they achieved exactly what they'd wanted. The Vanguard Against Parahumans was eviscerated by monsters on all sides, and I was a naive fool for believing there would be any other outcome.

Scout hopped through the open window of the truck, obsidian mirror in his jaws. I took it from him and gave him a pat, examining the damage on his side.

It was nothing that wouldn't buff out.

I threw the old truck into drive and got as far away from this hellhole as I could.

Chapter 58

The day after was a nondescript Tuesday, with rolling clouds giving way to a burgeoning sun. I'd opted for a cheap motel to get off the road and the grid, and was currently polishing off the Blue-Collar breakfast in LaBelle's roadside diner. The hash browns were crispy and the eggs, runny.

It was all so mundane, being surrounded by honest working folk. I wondered if their lives would be affected by the intrigue of the day before, if all the scheming and political plays that rolled through this town left a stain in it or washed away in the rain. I was betting on the latter. LaBelle wasn't what I'd call charming, but it was as welcome as a weekend getaway all the same.

Continuing my good spirits, I returned across the state at a leisurely speed with the windows down. Scout popped his head out of the truck and let his tongue hang free. Zombie or no, dogs dig the wind in their face. Maybe there's something to learn from that.

Street parking in Brickell was easy to come by, and I

strolled into my coffee shop to find Mabel wiping tables and Clarence restocking the counter. The morning rush was over, the vibe was sterile, and I couldn't help looking at the shop in a new light. It lacked the warmth of the roadside diner, but then Miami was a very different place than LaBelle.

"Any word on Darcy?" asked Clarence.

I offered a glum smile. "Yes, actually. She's doing well, but she's firm on not coming back."

"That's too bad. I liked her." He had an introspective moment. "But you know what? This is easier than I thought, running the place. You can count on me, Cisco."

"I know I can. You're doing great."

Mabel wandered over with a mischievous smile. "Thanks for donating your condo last night. Kaspy's still sleeping it off, if you know what I mean."

Clarence rolled his eyes. "*Everyone* knows what you mean, Mabel." He strode off with a glower.

"Oh, Clarence loves seeing me happy," she confided. "I was always the cool party aunt."

"I know what you mean," I said.

"Oh." She leaned in with a whisper. "And speaking of partying, don't worry about the massage chair. Kaspy promised to clean it."

Ugh. Now I needed to burn that thing.

I kept my remarks neutral and decided to personally examine the damage before making any judgments. As we chatted, a car pulled up to the curb, and a huge grin overtook my face.

I headed outside as a man with a tattoo of a blue moon debarked from my Firebird. The silver paint sparkled in the sun. No traces of bullet holes or dents marred the body. I had forgotten the Igbo worked out of a body shop. It looked like they were capable of much more than stripping cars for parts.

"Complements of the Night Walkers," said the stranger as he handed me my key.

"It's..."—I shook my head in awe—"lovingly restored."

"The least we could do after you gave Ozo Ebu his vengeance. His spirit is finally at rest."

I pressed my lips together. When a Nigerian shaman mentioned spirits, it probably wasn't metaphorical.

"There is another thing," he continued. "Your history is difficult, and you've brought a lot of trouble to us. My teenage years were filled with dire warnings of the Covey's hit man. After the Bone Saints supposedly killed you, the trouble in some ways grew worse. But we, in no small part through the guidance of Ozo Ebu, have decided that cooperation serves us better. You will find no more trouble from the Night Walkers when we cross paths."

I grunted. It wasn't exactly sunshine and daisies, but the sentiment worked for me. I shook his hand, and he joined his crew in a follow car as I enjoyed the sight of mine.

I parked my baby underground and kept the pickup while I met up with Milena in Midtown. We hugged and kissed. A third of her place was boxed up, the mood both optimistic and sad. I helped her with some heavy lifting and broke down some furniture, but there wasn't a whole lot that needed doing.

"You're really gonna donate all this stuff?" I asked. "Don't worry about cluttering my place if you want to keep it."

"It's just stuff, Cisco. None of it's important."

I smiled. This was a sentimental process for her. I'd stopped by offering my muscles and pickup truck to handle the logistics, but it turned out Milena needed moral support more than anything else. Her progress was slow but it was hers. As much as I wanted to help, she was methodically cataloguing her life. That wasn't something that could be solved with a whole crew of movers.

I caught her lingering on a picture of her and my sister, Seleste, from back in high school. I rubbed her neck.

"Things were simpler back then," I said.

She sighed. "We just had no idea, you know?" She snapped out of her malaise and added the frame to a box on the bed.

Another text message came through, and I replied.

"You're busy," noted Milena. "You have that thing, don't you? You should take off."

"I wanna help you."

"You did help." She hugged me like I hadn't been around for a year. "This is cathartic for me. Doing this piece by piece, I get to say goodbye to my old life. Plus, the realtor's coming by to see the place tomorrow. Can you believe she asked to swing by at 7 a.m.?"

"What an ungodly hour to do business," I sympathized.

"Tell me about it. You know I love my beauty sleep. I'm

gonna spend one last night here and get that taken care of first thing in the morning. Don't pretend like you won't be busy tonight anyway. I have a calendar."

I clenched my jaw and kissed her.

I did indeed have a couple of loose ends to see to. The first was a show of respect for a fallen friend. I met Rita at a memorial for Agent Carter. His proper funeral would be held in his hometown of Idaho Falls, but the local law enforcement community wanted to honor his memory where he died saving lives.

I hadn't known the man well, and much of our exchanges had been adversarial, so I kept my mouth shut and faded into the background. Rita gave a nice speech about Carter being a natural for the job, about his instincts being a part of his DNA, to the point that he wouldn't have second-guessed his decision to fight the good fight even if it meant his death. I thought she was spot-on. A few others spoke, including the chief of police who emphasized the sacrifice heroes like him make all over the country each and every day.

As things wrapped up, Evan and I huddled on the sidelines.

"Not gonna lie," he said. "I'm angry. The police are supposed to prevent needless death. Instead the ATF is trigger-happy and this serial killer ends up being one of our own."

I nodded sympathetically. "You really don't know with some people. Jensen seemed like good people. But he was a lone wolf. It's almost impossible to predict and prevent someone like that."

"Maybe, but that's hardly the case with the Obsidian March."

I arched an eyebrow. "Stopping a whole clan of vampires is easier?"

"It's not easier, Cisco, but it's my job nevertheless. We've been investigating the upirs for months now and have little to show for it. I'm done looking from the outside in at this thing. We've had enough time. We sat on the militia too long and look what happened."

"They were new to Miami."

"Maybe, but the Obsidian March isn't. They're a critical threat to the security of the city. The DROP team was formed to address threats like them. I don't care what connections Beaumont has, we're gonna move on the March, and we're gonna do it soon." He locked eyes with me. "And you're gonna help me seize some of that Russian ammo."

I stifled further conversation of the King of Brickell and the Bratva as Special Agent Bell approached. "Look who it is," she said in greeting, "the real good guys."

Evan snickered. "I'm glad you finally recognize that."

Instead of a snarky retort, she dipped her head. "My eyes have been opened. I can't deny that. So is this what you do, Lieutenant Cross? You and your team take on supernatural threats?"

He glanced at me. "We're about to. Excuse me." He rejoined Booker and other members of his team.

"That man's intense," she remarked.

"You have no idea."

"I have some. It takes a certain amount of grit to face things we don't understand."

What else was there to say about that? Maybe that was why it was easy to sympathize with the plight of the Vanguard. As for Rita, she'd had her grit for a while, but there was little doubt her involvement just kicked into a different gear.

"How's the FBI managing things?" I asked.

"There are no easy answers. We've got two dead heroes and no killer. I'm hoping we can flip the media narrative on Jensen, let the people have their scumbag."

"But the militia witnesses—"

"Are all dead." She snorted. "The Vanguard is the ATF's fiasco. For better or worse, we're staying out of that. Especially with Major Petty involved. He's dirty as sin. It'll never hit the newswire, but a lot of this is his fault. He made deals with Leverett Beaumont and the militia, ceding power to organizations to keep peace in the streets."

I gnawed my lip. "Maybe he's a realist."

"You don't believe that. If the Vanguard hadn't been manipulated into going after the Obsidian March, the payback wouldn't have been as brutal. We could've gotten to them in time, and a lot more people would be alive today."

She underestimated the influence the karkan had on things at the compound. The situation was a powder keg, but it was the monster that had set it afire. Still, Rita's point was worth considering.

"I just mean things aren't as black and white as they might seem to someone in the Bureau. Sometimes you have to make deals with the bad guys to get good things done."

"Oh, I agree entirely," she said with fire in her eyes. "You just need to find better bad guys."

I watched her askew. "And that means?"

Rita checked the crowd and beckoned me a few steps further to keep the conversation discreet. "Even though Jensen is officially a hero in the public eye, my team searched his house. We discovered a hidden basement with occult artifacts. Amulets, books, that sort of thing. Weird stuff, but nothing unseemly. Jensen didn't have any literal skeletons in his closet. No bodies in the crawl space either."

"Surprised he wasn't evil incarnate?"

"Not at all. What irked me was how exceedingly normal he was. There wasn't a thing in his house to indicate he was a cold-blooded killer. But, if you know anything about the FBI, you realize ninety percent of our work is combing over financials, and Jensen didn't escape our scrutiny. Guess who was the recent beneficiary of a hidden offshore fund?"

"He came into money? A dead relative or something?"

"No deaths in the family. The transaction was a way of moving money from a person of means to someone who otherwise didn't have much in the way of finances to manage. It was payment."

My neck tightened. "You're saying the karkan's unstoppable killing spree was rooted to a simple payoff?"

"Money makes the world go round. What should surprise you is his benefactor. The money was funneled through several shell accounts that made it difficult to track, but again, FBI."

"You cracked it? Was it the Russians?"

She smiled tersely. "Jensen was paid through assets managed by the Beaumont empire."

An edge overtook me. My blood stirred. My chest welled with heat.

He wouldn't.

He wouldn't dare.

"Part of me always suspected we were doing things wrong," she confessed. "Now we know."

I gazed at her.

"You're a lone man, Cisco. With a team at times, perhaps, but you're not vetting everyone you get in bed with. You need better resources at your disposal."

"Look, Rita, I appreciate the offer..."

She bulled through my objection without pause. "If we want to survive these horrors, the federal government needs to take a more active role in these matters. And fear-mongering militias won't cut it. We need someone on the inside, someone who's as much a part of the supernatural world as the monsters are. We need someone who can get things done using extrajudicial methods."

I worked my jaw. I knew where this was leading but—

"So you're gonna be an FBI asset," she said evenly.

I scoffed. "What?"

"You heard me. You're on the government payroll now. Only don't expect us to cut you checks. This will be off the books."

"This isn't about money, Rita."

"Of course not. You already have plenty at your disposal. And believe me when I say it irks me that the FBI can't find a shred of mismanagement in your portfolio. But while I can't prove it, I know the majority of your funds come from illicit sources."

I blinked defiantly. She was going too far. "You've got the wrong idea about me, Rita."

"It's Special Agent Rita Bell, and I know *exactly* what you are, Cisco. Don't forget that."

It took me a moment to compose myself. I stepped into her space and stared her dead in the eyes. "Are you threatening me?"

A light smile played off thin lips. "Let's state facts so there isn't any confusion, Cisco. I'm a federal agent, and you are a notorious outlaw. Bonnie and Clyde were community heroes. They had connections, fans, and did good by the locals, but none of that saved them from the federal government."

"I'm not doing this to be famous," I growled.

"Good, because you know the names no one remembers? Those of government informants."

I scoffed. "I have a name for you. Whitey Bulger. He informed for your outfit, didn't he? How'd that work out for him?"

Agent Bell glared.

"He went on the run for sixteen years," I said. "That was until you arrested him, stuck him in gen pop, and let the mob beat him to death."

"You're not a murderer," she equivocated.

"I'm not a snitch, either."

She laughed. "You watch way too many movies if you're concerned about your reputation, Cisco. You're already part of a criminal organization. Everybody knows you're Leverett Beaumont's lapdog. You collude with street gangs and rogues." Her outlined eyes sharpened as she went for the hard sell. "You want to be shielded from criminal exposure, you want the feds to look the other way during future indiscretions... Cooperation with the FBI is your only escape hatch."

"Get bent," I said.

She came back with a self-satisfied smirk and a light huff. "I understand this is a difficult adjustment for you. You're used to being a one-man act, but that show's over, starting now. From here on out, you're an FBI asset, and you have no choice about in the matter"—she leaned close—"*Shadow Man.*"

I glowered as her heels clacked away on the sidewalk.

My instincts had been right all along. Rita and the FBI couldn't be trusted. That much, to me, was always a danger. But just like Jensen, you never could really know a person. In Rita Bell's case, my revelation came in seeing just how cutthroat she could be.

Chapter 59

The breeze billowing through Miami that night was faltering. The branches swayed with less force, and the exotic chill finally began to surrender to the subtropics.

I couldn't get Rita's betrayal out of my mind, but eating me worse was Beaumont's. Look, I knew who I was in bed with. I was never dumb enough to fully trust the vampire. But there was something to be said for everything we'd been through together. We shared a sort of mutual camaraderie... against the March... protecting Miami. Like other things nagging me, this was a puzzle I couldn't piece together.

Agent Bell could've been lying, of course. It was in her interests to separate me from my underworld associates, to put me on an island where the only help I had was hers.

And didn't that make more sense? Jensen had no idea I was the Shadow Man. If Leverett had wanted me dead, why all the show of going through Quentin Capshaw and Ozo Ebu?

But then, Beaumont was a meticulous plotter. He

must've been aware of my chances of survival. If he had come after me directly, the suspect pool would be extremely small. Instead, he worked through a patsy, someone who didn't know anything but dollar signs. Jensen's starting point was based on something the entire population of Miami had access to: the urban legend of the Shadow Man. The assassin's trajectory was Beaumont's rock-solid alibi.

Either theory had an equal possibility of being true. The only way to get to the bottom of it was to dig.

Tonight, however, I spent my time digging a less metaphorical hole. I unearthed hundreds of pounds of cemetery dirt under the cover of a warming night, and I waited. Of all my current problems, there was only one I was sure about, and I wasn't disappointed.

A dark figure, no longer light in step, trudged across a sea of unkempt grass, each foot stamping over countless forgotten dead. The potter's field was unattended this night. No more FBI agents, no Yoruba warriors. The world had inevitably moved on, and there was one left to do so.

It was Twelfth Night, and it was time for the karkan to return from whence she came.

The revenant arrived at her grave and gasped. The runes in the dirt had long blown away, the desiccated animal corpses were removed, and a large welcoming hole was already dug.

"I've taken the liberty of getting you started," I said, resolving from the shadow and stepping forward. "I hope you don't mind, but I'm going to incinerate your body as soon as you're gone."

The karkan turned to me with resigned grace, face half covered by clinking charms. "Do as you wish, shadow charmer. I shall never see this body again regardless."

"You use a new one every time, is that it?"

A tired shoulder sagged. "It is my calling, and it is my curse."

"I thought I broke your curse."

Lips cracked as she grinned. "This time. I thank you for the freedom, even if only a few days."

"But it's not enough freedom to stay away."

She exhaled slowly and contemplated the hole in the ground. "It's Epiphany Eve. My power is on the wane. My season is over. I may return in another, or in a thousand. This is not for me to decide."

"But couldn't you have tried?" I rebuked. "You had days of freedom, and you spent them orchestrating death and despair instead of searching for a cure." I angrily stepped closer. "I could've helped you. Freed you for good."

The karkanscholl studied me for a long minute. She lifted her hand and I flinched. Though the chains at her feet dragged along like the tentacles of a dead squid, she couldn't be underestimated. Instead of attacking, she lowered her hood, clutched the charms, and dropped the headdress to the ground.

Her face was ragged, scarred, and missing an eye. Her misshapen head was mostly bald, with an odd tuft of hair protruding on one side. Even though gray skin clung to her bones, her ears had long rotted away.

"I believe you would have tried," she said softly. "But

unlike you, I do not fight my nature. I excel at killing. I've never met my match. I am a flower that doesn't bloom often, but when I do, it's... transcendent."

I gritted my teeth. Why did I try so hard to save things that couldn't be saved? "If you come back," I gruffly warned, "what I do to you will be transcendent. I promise you that."

I could've sworn the karkan smiled. Then her eye rolled back. She lifted her head to the sky with a great exhalation and collapsed into the grave.

I waited some time as the clock ticked past midnight, till the start of Epiphany. Twelvetide was officially over. I set the body alight with a special blend of zombie powders and watched as her remnants were immolated.

I picked up her discarded facial charms and stared at them long and hard. The dozens of dangling metal plates were inscribed with runes of holy magic, ancient power awakened anew. I considered what the artifact was worth, not in a monetary sense but in knowledge. There were still so many things about the karkan we didn't know, and I wondered if she had gifted the headdress to me on purpose.

I was afraid of the power in those runes, of the temptation the karkan offered. It must have seemed so simple a prospect to Jensen. A life-changing payoff, and all he needed to do was secure a body and apply an ancient ritual. Would he have stopped there, I wondered, or would he have revisited his murderous power every Christmas, righting imagined wrongs or simply making himself wealthier?

I thought of the Bratva boss, of Society management, of

Beaumont's latest escapade. A lot of people have tried to kill me for a lot of reasons. Maybe utilizing the karkanscholl was fair game. And then I thought of Rita Bell, of the endless cycle of coercion done in the name of the greater good.

I tossed the charms into the searing flames and watched them wilt. Then I grabbed the shovel and buried the monster for good.

Chapter 60

"Be there in a bit," I texted Milena. I had already left but still had a nagging chore to take care of. One last thing.

At the roadside *ventanita*, I ordered a box of mixed *pastelitos*, mostly guava, but some cheese and meat pies too. It was standard Cuban fare that no party went without, and, as far as I was concerned, today was a celebration.

Call it my own Epiphany feast.

The karkan was gone. The feds were picking up the pieces of the Vanguard debacle. The army was defeated and in tatters, and the citizens of Miami could breathe a sigh of relief. For now.

I had no delusions that the militia movement was done for good. The sheer enormity of the New Year's march proved there was public investment. Tremors of this Christmas season would ripple in the Atlantic for years to come. As far as my beef-and-potato stew was concerned, instead of being taken off the heat, it was more like it was set to a simmer for the foreseeable future.

I sipped my *cafecito*, paid the lady for the box, and returned to the truck. Despite what Milena had said about giving her stuff away, I was sure she'd change her mind. Either way, the bed of the pickup offered her the option.

Scout scooted up to the box of pastries as I set it on the passenger seat.

"Not on my watch," I said before sending him to the back.

Milena had met with the realtor in the morning. It was a seller's market so confidence in a quick turnaround was high.

I didn't know what it was, but the city looked different. The streets were calm but not quiet. People basked in the newly come warmth, unafraid to venture from their houses, pleased simply to enjoy the outdoors with casual smiles.

There was a lot to be concerned about these days, but just as much to spur hope. At least if you put the windows down and looked around. I parked by Milena's building and once again had Scout wait in the truck.

"I might be a while," I told him with a wink. He gave me a wounded look, so I opened the box of pastries and tossed a meat pie. He caught it and eagerly chomped away.

"Made it," I texted.

"Door's open," she messaged back.

With a literal hop in my step, I detoured to the stairwell. I blazed up half the eighteen floors before realizing my enthusiasm may have been a little misguided. Being unabashedly stubborn, I forced my way up the rest of the stairs and pushed open the apartment door to a maze of taped boxes. I held the pastries behind my back and stepped through to the bedroom, where I found a single red rose placed on a bare mattress.

"Milena?"

I craned my head around the bathroom door and set the *pastelitos* down when I didn't see her. I hoofed it back to the living area and checked the kitchen, then back out in the hall.

I slowly backtracked into her apartment, running the morning's conversation through my head. There hadn't been anything...

My phone buzzed and I yanked it from my pocket. "You there yet?" asked the message.

"Where are you?" I typed back. The response was agonizingly slow, but it came.

"I'm not there, baby, and I'm sorry. I decided to do something big, a grand gesture. This isn't goodbye because I have every intention of coming back, so don't think this is something that it isn't. I just don't want to make promises I can't keep anymore."

I gulped and reread the message two times before replying. All I could write was a single question mark.

"I've had a hard time of things," she texted back. "A lot of drama, a lot of ups and downs. AND I HATE IT. It feels like Seleste dying all over again. But I was past that. I was past everything. I had taken control of my life, I was in the driver's seat, and then this happened."

"We'll get through it," I replied.

"It isn't me."

I marched back to the bedroom and searched for signs of Milena doing anything drastic. I mean, besides the packed boxes and abandoned condo. I squeezed my temples. What a complete idiot I'd been.

I sat on the bed and sent a desperate message. "Where are you?" My hand tightened around the phone as I waited for the answer.

"You're going to hate this, but I won't lie to you. I'm going to the Nether for a while. Don't ask how or where. I haven't decided yet. I only know that it's where I need to be right now. It's like when Kasper was poisoned. He needed the sun or he'd die. I feel like that but in reverse. The Nether... it calls to me. And I need to figure out why."

I nervously worked my jaw. "Great. My business in Miami is done. Let me join you."

The delay getting back to me was excruciating.

"I can't ask you to do that," she said. "We already traveled the Nether together. The West Coast, the Riviera. You've been away from Miami for too long and everything's practically falling apart. The city needs you, Cisco. Darcy needs you, and I don't. Not the way you think."

My breathing sped up and I must've gotten something in my eye. I was stunned by the message, yet I understood every word.

"I can't be babied anymore," she explained. "I can't lie in bed by myself all day, or shut myself in for safety. It's too late to protect me. That ship has sailed. And I don't blame you. Not one little bit, okay? I love you, *mi amor*. I love you but I can't."

"Let me see you," I replied. "Let's talk about this in person."

"I can't. I tried, Cisco, but it's too hard. If I was with you, I'd never leave. I'd never build up the nerve to tell you how truly messed up I am."

"You're not messed up."

"I am. I am messed up and acting like I'm not isn't helping. I need to do something about this. Don't you see? I need to take control. I need to do it my way, or I'll never have it again."

I wiped my eyes. "Let me help," I stubbornly insisted.

"You can't. I can't ask you for more space or more time. Those aren't the problems, baby. *We* aren't the problem. But we're not the solution either, not to what I'm going through. Trust me. There's no doubt in my mind about this. I need this. I need to go and find my path, even if it means some time away. But this isn't the end. At least I don't intend it to be."

"If not for you, then do it for me," I pleaded. "Let me hold you. I need to see you."

Another delay.

"It's too late for that," she said. "I'm already gone, Cisco. I'm getting rid of this phone now. Starting from scratch. Please don't try to find me. I love you."

I blinked at the suddenness of it. "I love you too," I texted back, waiting with the phone in my face. Three times the screen timed out and I woke it up again.

I waited, wondering if I should say something else or keep waiting, wondering if there was a better way to leave things. No decision was perfect. Or maybe we'd already left things perfectly said. All I knew was, the longer I waited, the more I knew it was over.

Not our relationship, but the conversation. The decision. My plans with Milena. Maybe what had happened in the Nether was different than I'd told myself. Maybe I had never saved Milena at all. Not the Milena I knew.

I was angry for a bit. So what if I babied her? So what if I did everything humanly possible to keep her safe? But that resentment passed quickly. Milena wasn't one for stupid fights. As she'd said, she didn't have a dramatic bone in her body. This was new and different, and it scared the hell out of her.

I had been willing to ignore it, to push past it with blinders on no matter what, but Milena needed more than that.

I collapsed back on the mattress, crushing the flower she had left me. My thoughts were focused in full clarity, but that didn't make them all right. That didn't mean this was easy. Hell, truly understanding something is often far more difficult than the pleasance of ignorance.

The honest truth was that, despite Milena's kind words, this was a turning point in our future. I allowed myself hope, of course, but I was hardly naive. No matter how Milena felt now, things could change at the drop of a hat. What if her time away altered her perspective? What if she changed her mind? What if she found herself in over her head? The Nether was a dangerous place. Any one of us would be in mortal danger venturing through its innards alone.

And there was Milena. Tough, beautiful, and certainly

no pushover... but now in the position of contending with diabolical silvans and tenacious fiends.

These next few hours, days, and weeks would tear me apart. It was a battle between respecting her wishes, letting her fight her own battles, and risking her being mutilated and dying a death I wouldn't wish on my enemies.

I knew, right then and there, that I would have to run down her license plate, uncover her silvan connections, and ask after her. And as much as I wanted to punch Leverett in his smug face and get to the bottom of his machinations, I needed him for this more than ever. After my fallout with silvan royalty, like it or not, Beaumont was my best connection to the underworld. As the icing on this cake of baked crap, he had a soft spot for Milena.

I stood and somehow all my gathered determination drizzled away. Milena was right about Miami. I'd thought I was building something strong, yet somehow it was all crumbling away. But she was part of that collapse too, couldn't she see?

Darcy... the Spaniard... Milena... What was happening to us?

I knew, in my bones, that something was coming. Somehow, it was like everything was just a distraction. A ploy to break us apart.

And it was working.

I scooped up the box of pastries and hurled it across the room.

-Finn

Dedication

I'd be remiss if I failed to mention the contribution of my cat to my daily writing life. This is my twenty-fifth story, and Scout has been at my feet for every single one of them.

Alas, you didn't make it to the end of this one, little buddy, and that dimmed the process. But 20 1/2 years is a damn respectable run for a cat.

This crazy bastard came up with me on the rough streets of Miami, shared a pit stop in Orlando, and then conquered LA. Now he's charging headfirst into Valhalla, where I'm sure he'll maul anyone who looks at him sideways.

Cheers to you this day, Scouticus McGillicutty. I'll kill a bottle of Havana Club for you, and your song will carry from my lips all the way to the Great Hall.

If you're reading this, it means you demand more from your urban fantasy. Bullets and fireballs are a riot, but they're nothing without a layered cast of characters and realistic plot drivers. *Black Magic Outlaw* is my stab at a cut above the rest: non-stop action, true friends banding against impossible odds, and themes that hopefully make you put the book down and ponder, if even for only a minute.

My writing process demands quality control at every step of development. I hope you agree *Black Magic Outlaw* is the premium product I strive to make it. Unfortunately, doubling down on originality and quality in an on-demand world has drawbacks. It's simply not possible for me to get you a brand-new novel every month or two. The process takes time.

That's where you come in. If you want to be part of building a better book, consider one or all of the following shows of support. The best part? These displays of true fandom don't cost you a penny.

- Join the Outlaw Underground, our private Facebook group. (www.facebook.com/groups/dominofinnfans/)

- Leave an all-too-important review where you bought the book. Each one helps more than you know.

- Recommend this book to your friends. Link it on social media.

- Join my reader group newsletter, get a free Black Magic Outlaw story, and hear from me only when I have new releases or important news. You'll never miss another launch sale again. (dominofinn.com/newsletter/)

Simple, right? Five minutes of your time makes a world of difference to me and Cisco. Thank you for your heartfelt support. I'll keep writing as long as you keep reading.

- Domino Finn

Also by Domino Finn

BLACK MAGIC OUTLAW
Dead Man
Shadow Play
Heart Strings
Powder Trade
Fire Water
Death March
Blood Craft
Open Season

SUMMONER FOR HIRE
Tooth and Nail
Hell and High Water

<u>AFTERLIFE ONLINE</u>
Reboot
Black Hat
Trojan
Deadline

<u>Shade City</u>

<u>SYCAMORE MOON</u>
The Seventh Sons
The Blood of Brothers
The Green Children

About the Author

Domino Finn is an award-winning game industry veteran, a media rebel, and a grizzled author of urban fantasy and litRPG. His stories are equal parts spit, beer, and blood, and are notable for treating weighty issues with a supernatural veneer. If Domino has one rallying cry for the world, it's that fantasy is serious business.

Take a stand at DominoFinn.com